The score was:
convictions—60, acquittals—2, mistrials—1 . . .

As I pondered the challenge of Laflamme's string of trial successes, the door shot open. "Here you go," he said, handing me a large envelope. I hoped he hadn't noticed me gawking at his trial record. I pulled back the flap, glanced at the report. I'd have to study it later to see how much it hurt Raymond.

Laflamme leaned back in his chair, smirking again. "First I tell you I got motive," he said. "With this—the medical examiner's opinion on time of death—you know what else I got?" Laflamme knew a lot more than he was revealing; that much was obvious.

"You got nothing," I said with as much bluster as I could manage. "This thing's full of holes." I pushed the report back into the envelope and walked toward the door. I turned the handle, anxious to get out of there.

"Wrongo-bongo. What I got—and you know it—is opportunity." He turned his chair toward me, arms folded. "Yup, I got opportunity."

"And I have an innocent client," I said and walked out the door.

ALIBI

Stephen M. Murphy

JOVE BOOKS, NEW YORK

THE BERKLEY PUBLISHING GROUP
Published by the Penguin Group
Penguin Group (USA) Inc.
375 Hudson Street, New York, New York 10014, USA
Penguin Group (Canada), 10 Alcorn Avenue, Toronto, Ontario M4V 3B2, Canada
(a division of Pearson Penguin Canada Inc.)
Penguin Books Ltd., 80 Strand, London WC2R 0RL, England
Penguin Group Ireland, 25 St. Stephen's Green, Dublin 2, Ireland (a division of Penguin Books Ltd.)
Penguin Group (Australia), 250 Camberwell Road, Camberwell, Victoria 3124, Australia
(a division of Pearson Australia Group Pty. Ltd.)
Penguin Books India Pvt. Ltd., 11 Community Centre, Panchsheel Park, New Delhi—110 017, India
Penguin Group (NZ), Cnr. Airborne and Rosedale Roads, Albany, Auckland 1310, New Zealand
(a division of Pearson New Zealand Ltd.)
Penguin Books (South Africa) (Pty.) Ltd., 24 Sturdee Avenue, Rosebank, Johannesburg 2196,
South Africa

Penguin Books Ltd., Registered Offices: 80 Strand, London WC2R 0RL, England

This is a work of fiction. Names, characters, places, and incidents either are the product of the author's imagination or are used fictitiously, and any resemblances to actual persons, living or dead, business establishments, events, or locales is entirely coincidental.

ALIBI

A Jove Book / published by arrangement with the author.

PRINTING HISTORY
Jove mass-market edition / May 2005

Copyright © 2005 by Stephen M. Murphy.
Cover design by Steven Ferlauto.
Cover photo by Punchstock RF.
Book design by Kristin del Rosario.

ISBN: 0-515-13946-7

JOVE®
Jove Books are published by The Berkley Publishing Group,
a division of Penguin Group (USA) Inc.,
375 Hudson Street, New York, New York 10014.
JOVE is a registered trademark of Penguin Group (USA) Inc.
The "J" design is a trademark belonging to Penguin Group (USA) Inc.

PRINTED IN THE UNITED STATES OF AMERICA

10 9 8 7 6 5 4 3 2 1

To my parents,
Bob and Teresa Murphy,
who believed in me when others did not

Drink with me to days gone by,
To the life that used to be,
At the shrine of friendship never say die,
Let the wine of friendship never run dry.
Here's to you and here's to me.

—from *Les Miserables*

CHAPTER 1

I walked down the stairs, turned the corner, and found Hillsborough County's most experienced—and largest—deputy sheriff sitting outside the jail entrance. Hank Lerner was hunched over the desk, his elbow firmly planted on top, his multiple chins resting comfortably in his palm.

"Don't get up," I said. "I'll let myself in. No need to disturb yourself."

He leaned back in the swivel chair, stretched his feet out on the grey metal desk, and rolled a toothpick around his teeth. I stood in front of the desk waiting for Hank to say something. He seemed to enjoy chewing on that toothpick.

"Pardon fuckin' me for not laying out the welcome mat," Hank finally said. "If I remember right, last time you were here, Francis, your shitfaced client barfed all over his cell and I had to breathe in that stench for days."

Normal breathing was hard enough for Hank, more like quick panting, so I supposed I had to feel sorry for him.

"What do you expect," I said, "the guy blew a point one nine?"

"And you got him off. Some kind of justice. What a fuckin' system."

"Hey, not my fault the breathalyzer machine hadn't been serviced in years. You couldn't rely on it worth a damn." I smiled, remembering how I had destroyed the arresting officer at the prelim. I heard afterwards that he had vowed never to give a breath test again and drove all his suspects to the nearest hospital for a blood test.

"You'll be happy to know," I said, getting to the point of my visit, "that I'm not defending a drunk driver this time. I'm going big-time: murder."

He spat out the toothpick, shook his head slowly back and forth. The skin under his jaw shook like jello. "Gimme a break," he said. Swinging his feet off the desk, he ran both hands over his white hair. The pink, chubby face had a pained expression.

"The shithead who shot our local football star?" he growled. "Waste of time. The way the paper tells it he might just as well plead guilty and take what's coming to him. Even a hot-shot Boston lawyer from Hah-vaad won't be able to help him."

Having lived in Manchester only six months, I was still an outsider, and even worse, a Bostonian. From Harvard no less.

"Okay, okay," I said, holding up my hands to head off an argument. "Not like I expected you to think one of your prisoners was innocent."

Hank let out a big sigh, pushed himself up from the chair. "Innocent? I'll tell you one thing. Odds are every sonovabitch comes through here is guilty of something. I don't really give a shit what it is." Shaking his head, he led me back to the cells. His black leather belt hung below his ample love handles and his handcuffs tilted noticeably to the right.

"He's all yours," he said as he unlocked the cell. After I stepped inside, Hank shut the door behind me, then retreated to his post. My eyes took a few seconds to adjust to the dim light. I spotted my potential client sitting on a bunk bed, which was suspended by chains from the wall. He sat with his elbows on his knees and his hands on each side of his chin.

"Morning, Raymond," I said.

He sat there without moving his eyes, staring straight through me. He was wound tight, tension radiating from every part of him.

I've heard criminal defense lawyers say jurors are heavily swayed by the defendant's appearance. "That cute boy just doesn't look like a murderer," they'd say. I had the opposite reaction when I looked at Mr. Raymond Walker. His blond mustache was so faint it seemed painted on. His dirty blonde hair hung down to his shoulders, making him look like a child of the sixties instead of a hip dot-com teenager. He seemed to be close to six feet tall but his jeans were at least a size too long and bunched up around his ankles. A black hooded sweatshirt hung below his waist. His left eye was black and blue and puffy. He looked a lot like the drunken clients I was used to.

"You okay?"

He stood up and walked toward the bars, staring straight ahead, ignoring me. He mumbled something I couldn't decipher.

"Pardon me?"

He turned toward me, letting his hands fall to the side. "I'm great, just fuckin' great, considering I'm stuck in this miserable hellhole with my head pounding like a jackhammer on granite."

I expected an unhappy client, but Raymond had gone beyond unhappy; he was bitter, seething, and—I thought—dangerous. I considered walking away right then, and looking back, I probably should have. But I figured I owed my old friend Larry Conway the benefit of the doubt, so I pressed on.

"If you don't want to talk now, that's fine. I'll come back

some other time. Only reason I'm here is because Larry's worried and wanted me to help."

I leaned against the bars, waiting for him to say something. He remained still, not answering, sullen, staring. After waiting a short while, I tried again. "I can't help unless you cooperate."

He turned suddenly. "Cooperate?" he yelled. "Why the fuck should I cooperate? I didn't do nothing wrong. I just want to get outta here."

"Listen, Raymond," I said, "You need some help. McHugh was a popular guy in this state; a lot of people would just as soon skip the trial and string you up right now. Especially with witnesses saying you threatened to kill him."

He turned toward me, scowling. "You wanna know the truth," he said. "I did threaten him. But that don't mean I shot him." He spat out the words. Then he looked me up and down; it was a dirty look, as if I were a dog who'd just peed on his shoes. "How can you help? What do *you* know about murder cases?" he asked, not even pretending to be polite.

"Not much," I confessed.

"Then why do I need you? I might as well get one of those dumb shit public defenders. At least they've done this kind of thing before." I decided to look on the bright side; I had accomplished something: Raymond was talking to me.

"That's a choice you got to make," I said, glancing down the hall to make sure Hank was still there.

"Figures," he said, shaking his head. "I thought Mr. Conway could've done better."

I gritted my teeth, barely keeping my temper. "Tell you the truth, if it weren't for Larry I wouldn't waste my time even talking to you. Larry knows I've never handled a murder case, but he still wants me to defend you. Maybe you should ask him why he thinks I'm so good."

For a moment his features seemed to soften as he considered what I said. Maybe there was some hope, I thought. Maybe a jury could be persuaded that Raymond Walker was a decent kid; a bit rough around the edges but that could be explained to his advantage. Larry had told me about Raymond's mother dying when he was young and his father trying to raise him when he wasn't leaning over a barstool at the local bar.

"It's no use," he said softly. "No use." For a moment I thought he had calmed down but he began pacing back and forth in front of me, walking deliberately, his long skinny arms stretched tight at his side. After a half dozen trips the length of the cell, he stopped next to me, facing the bars. His breathing was loud and quick as he gasped for air. Suddenly he grabbed a bar in each hand, then leaned his head against the middle bar. He tightened his grip, tensing his arm and shoulder muscles. A blue vein bulged from the side of his forehead.

"God damn it," he hissed. "God damn it," he repeated and then pounded his forehead against the bars. He did it again and again, using his hands as leverage to increase the force of each blow. As his forehead struck the bar, it made a dull *clang* sound.

I was so shocked that it took me a few seconds to react. "Raymond, stop that," I yelled. He froze, still clenching the bars, then turned to me. He looked pathetic; on his forehead, as if freshly painted, was a vertical red line.

Hank Lerner hurried down the hall. "What the hell's going on here?"

Raymond turned away from Hank, hiding the damage to his forehead. "No problem, Hank," I said. "Just bumped into the bars. Nothing to worry about."

Hank grunted, doubtful. "I hear any more funny stuff down here, your visit is over," he said, pointing a fat finger at me. "That clear?"

"Crystal," I said.

Hank shook his head, then returned to his desk.

Raymond rubbed the heels of his hands into his forehead. "I can't stand this," he moaned. Even though I knew few of the facts, his emotional pain made me think he might be innocent after all. I stood in the corner, my arms crossed, waiting for him to calm down. But he kept pacing the cell, one wall to the other several times before stopping in front of the bars. Suddenly he again shouted, "God damn it," and resumed slamming his head against the bars.

I could hear Hank Lerner's keys jangling as he lifted himself from his seat. I put my hand on Raymond's shoulder. "Enough, Raymond. This won't accomplish anything." I tried to pull him away from the bars. Hank's heavy footsteps were getting closer and he was shouting my name, preceded each time by a different profanity.

Raymond stopped moving. He shook my hand from his shoulder. "Larry told me what a tough life you've had," I said, "about your father kicking you out and all. Let me help."

"I don't need your help," he screamed, violence stewing deep inside him. "And shut the fuck up about my father!" Before I could react, he turned toward me and in a sweeping overhand movement swung his right fist toward my face. I jerked my head to the left. The punch grazed my right ear and landed heavily on my shoulder. Momentarily I lost my balance and fell into the bars, striking my head.

My head ached but I was alert enough to realize that Raymond had coiled his right fist and was taking aim at my kisser. As he swung, I bounced off the bars with my hands in front of me. I pushed him to the side and his punch caught only air.

"Raymond! No more," I yelled, holding up my hands.

But he wasn't ready to quit. Suddenly he pulled himself straight and lunged toward me. I ducked under a wild counter hook and shifted my weight so I could snap a straight right fist into his belly. The punch connected with a thud. I was surprised at how hard his stomach was. Raymond straightened, holding his belly. For a moment I thought he was going to shake it off, and come after me. But he groaned loudly, and fell forward onto the floor, gasping for air.

"What the hell's going on in there?" Hank yelled while running down the hallway. He was wheezing from all the exertion. "Jesus fucking Christ," he said when he saw Raymond lying on the floor. "I thought you were going to represent the kid."

Hank opened the door and I stepped outside. I looked back at Raymond, still groaning on the floor. "Doesn't look that way now, does it?"

CHAPTER 2

BY the time I got to the office I had the mother of all headaches, thanks to my head's unscheduled meeting with Raymond Walker's jail bars. As I pushed open the door, I rubbed the back of my scalp. From behind her computer, Yvette stared at me, fluttering her long black lashes.

"Do we have a headache?" she asked in a babyish voice.

I groaned, more from embarrassment than pain. I dreaded having to explain the altercation to Yvette. With twelve years experience as a legal secretary, she thought she was smarter than most of the lawyers in town. Before hiring her, I checked her references. Her old Manchester law firm raved about her. She was a fantastic worker, they said, and knew court procedure cold. She quit because the firm had gotten too big. I laughed when they told me they now had twenty lawyers. In Boston "big" meant several hundred lawyers.

After she'd worked for me only a short time, I realized she really was smarter than most lawyers. She also had plenty more to offer than her brains. She favored tight dresses and blouses that accentuated her perfect curves.

With straight silky black hair that hung all the way to her waist, she was a genuine looker with a quick wit and sharp tongue that surprised anyone who made the mistake of thinking she was just another pretty package.

I explained what had happened with Raymond. She grimaced, shaking her head. "And all the time I thought my boss was a grown-up," she said.

"It wasn't my fault," I protested. "He swung at me first."

"So? You're not a teenager anymore, you're supposed to know how to avoid fighting."

She was right of course. I should have handled him better. There's no excuse for hitting a client, even if he did take the first swing.

"And what are you doing with a murder case, especially one as big as this?" she asked, not hiding her disgust. "I read about the arrest in today's paper." She reached behind her and grabbed the *Union Leader* from her credenza. "Here it is," she said, reading: " 'Arrest in Murder of St. Andrew College Football Star.' " She turned the front page toward me. Below the headline were photos of Raymond and Brian McHugh. Raymond looked as bad in the photo as in person. McHugh's photo was a stark contrast: big smile, upturned cheeks, hair combed neatly back. St. Andrew's publicity department did a great job; McHugh did look like an All-American.

"I thought the only criminal cases you took were DWI's," she said.

"So?"

"So how does representing drivers charged with driving while intoxicated qualify you to take on a murder case?"

I took a seat in the client chair across from Yvette's desk. I could tell she was not going to let me off easy. "Alright, let's skip the cross-examination," I said. "Normally your sharp tongue captivates me, but right now I'm in too much pain to appreciate it."

She reached in her top drawer and pulled out a bottle of aspirin. Then she got up and walked to the water cooler.

"Maybe this will help," she said, handing me two aspirin and a cup of water. I thought I detected a hint of empathy in her voice.

I swallowed the aspirin and water in one gulp. "I got a call last night from a guy I haven't seen in over twenty years." I filled her in on the phone call from Larry.

"Larry Conway?" she said, holding up a pile of pink message slips. "He's called twice already today. Wouldn't tell me what it was about."

She folded her arms and swung her chair toward me. "So what's he got to do with Raymond Walker?"

"Seems his son Evan and Raymond are friends. When Raymond's father kicked him out, Larry gave him a place to stay. Now he feels some responsibility."

"So he tracked down his old buddy after more than two decades and wants him to take on a murder case. Makes sense to me."

"What're you getting at?" I asked, my headache still pounding.

"I think reunions with old friends are great," she answered. "But why not just have a few beers with him. Isn't taking on a murder case a bit much?"

"I doubt I'll get the case anyway," I said, "especially after what happened today." I massaged my head again. "I was just trying to help out an old friend, and I agreed to talk to the kid."

"Why didn't you refer him to somebody who's actually handled a murder case? There *are* a few in New Hampshire, you know."

"Sure, but Larry insisted I talk to Raymond. He wanted only me. It was the least I could do for him." I paused. "And what the heck, it wasn't a big deal." I managed a grin. "Until Raymond took a swing at me, that is."

"That's what you get for doing a favor for an old friend."

Larry had been my best friend growing up in Boston, someone I hadn't seen since my first year of law school—some twenty-three years ago—when the Army stationed him in California. We'd exchanged Christmas cards for years, each promising to look up the other. We actually scheduled a few visits but each time something came up: his wife had the flu or I was in trial. After a while, the constant scheduling changes must have worn us both down and we gave up.

When we were kids, Larry and I thought we'd be friends forever. We did everything together. How such close friends could drift so far apart was inexplicable to me. There had been no argument, no disagreement to sour the relationship. No bridges burned, just bridges unused, and until now, forgotten.

"Doesn't matter if you haven't spoken in twenty-three years," I said. "Someone close to Larry needed a lawyer and he thought of me. He knows he can trust me."

She shook her head. "Must be a guy thing," she said, handing me a pile of message slips.

I went into my office, sat down, and thumbed through the messages. There were about a dozen; one was from Sherry, my ex-wife. Yvette had written at the bottom: "She asked me if I was sleeping with you. The nerve! When I told her I had a boyfriend, she laughed and hung up." I shook my head, half-wishing Sherry's supposition were true. I crumbled the message slip and threw it in the trash can.

Larry had called at 9:15 and 9:45. I picked up the phone and called him. What a mess I had made of this reunion, I thought. When he picked up, I sheepishly explained how I had punched out Raymond. "I didn't hit him too hard," I explained.

Larry was surprisingly calm. "That's what I always liked about you," Larry said. "You never change. Even Harvard didn't take the street kid out of you. Once a street fighter always a street fighter."

"I don't know about that," I said. Larry's calling me a street fighter reminded me of my summer job before law school. I worked on the city street cleaning crew, driving an orange three-wheeled Cushman Cart with a shovel and push broom in back. On each side of the Cushman Cart was a sign saying, "Boston Loves a Dirty Street Fighter." I was supposed to sweep up trash wherever I found it. That summer was the last time I'd seen Larry.

"Tell you what," Larry said. "Don't worry about Raymond for now. I'll get the public defender to handle the arraignment and bail hearing tomorrow morning. He'll cool down, I'm sure he's distraught about the arrest. I'll talk some sense into him."

"Good luck," I said. "If he starts whacking his forehead on the bars, then you better be careful. Get out of there as fast as you can."

He grunted. "Must've been quite a sight," he said. "Why don't we get together and catch up. Breakfast tomorrow okay?"

I said that was fine and gave him directions to my favorite café. "Maybe my headache will be gone by then," I added before hanging up.

CHAPTER 3

I met Larry at the Chimes Café, an old-fashioned diner a few blocks from my office. I arrived early, and took my usual seat in a dark green Naugahyde booth in the corner. A wooden ledge above the booth held a chaotic mixture of jugs, cups, lamps, and figurines. Hanging on the walls to each side of me were two paintings, obviously by the same artist. One showed a happy autumn scene with rolling mountains, log cabins, and gold and orange maple trees. Groups of smiling hunters held their rifles proudly as they walked toward the woods. The other painting showed the same scene in winter but with icy mountains and bare trees. The blue sky had turned dark and cloudy. The hunters and their smiling faces were noticeably absent.

At exactly eight o'clock, Larry pushed open the front door of the Chimes. He stuck his head in first, searching carefully, both hands still holding the door, almost as if he were afraid to come in. I barely recognized him. His face was thin and bony, and there were dark circles under his eyes; his hair had receded slightly and was cut just over his ears. He was wearing beige cotton pants which were wrinkled as if he'd slept in them, and a grey crew neck sweater with the sleeves rolled up.

Larry looked behind the bar. The owner, Marty Loughlin, his white t-shirt wet from rinsing glasses, was talking to the only other patron, a sleepy-looking man with a three-day growth of white beard. He sat on a barstool washing down a bran muffin with a bottle of Budweiser. Larry grimaced and turned to go back outside. Then he saw me.

The look on his face went from disgust to confusion to recognition. I stood up and waved him over.

"Good to see you, Dutch," he said stiffly, extending his hand. We shook hands, something we'd never done before. "You know, I've walked by this place hundreds of times," he said, looking around. "But I've never come in."

"Hey, you don't know what you've been missing. What 'til you try their food. Remind you of the good old days."

Larry looked doubtful as we sat down in the booth; perhaps he didn't want to be reminded of the old days. "You look different," he said, pointing to my beard. "Makes you look more mature," he added as if that were a surprise.

"This is my New Hampshire beard," I told him. I'd started growing it when I moved here, determined to start over, professionally and personally.

"I could use some extra hair myself," he said, brushing his hair back to show the creeping path of baldness.

"What do you expect?" I said. "In high school weren't you voted, 'Most Likely to Recede?' " He laughed, then we looked at each other and laughed together, the awkward, choppy kind of laugh people use to hide their nervousness. We were feeling each other out, trying to find the old rhythm, the common ground we once shared. For several seconds we were silent, each waiting for the other to begin, feeling the gap of twenty years and the problem that had brought us here to the Chimes.

"How . . ."

"We've got a lot of catching up to do," I said at the same time.

"Yeah, you're not kidding. I was just going to ask how you wound up in Manchester."

"In a word: Sherry."

"Sherry?"

"Sherry's the whole reason I left my partnership in Boston. We were married twelve long years; divorce was final six months ago."

"Sorry to hear that, Dutch. Any kids?"

I shook my head. "Nah, didn't fit into our schedule. Sherry's schedule, I should say. Too many cocktail parties and charity balls to be bothered with children." I paused, trying to imagine for the hundredth time what our offspring would have looked like. "When I first met her I melted; her smile was out of this world. Only after we'd been married a few years did it dawn on me: she smiled all the time because she had nothing to say. The last straw was when I mentioned I might want kids. She went straight to her doctor and had her tubes tied, 'just in case I got any sneaky ideas,' she said." I sipped my coffee and turned to find Charlotte, the Chimes's one and only waitress, hovering over the table, her stained, baby-blue uniform a foot from my face.

"So what'll it be, boys?" she asked. At sixty-one, Charlotte considered herself exempt from the usual social niceties of normal folk. Besides, she could interrupt conversations any time she wished; she was Marty's wife, and had been for forty-two years.

"You takin' another shot at the special, Dutch?" She pushed a strand of grey hair from her forehead and spoke without taking her eyes off the check pad.

"What is the special today?" Larry asked, thinking for a moment this was a normal café.

"The special today is the same as it is every day," she snarled at Larry.

"I'll give the special a try today, Charlotte," I said quickly to give Larry a chance to recover. "Eggs over easy.

Home fries. Sausage no bacon. And tell Marty not to burn the toast this time."

"And for you?" Charlotte asked Larry.

He shook his head, grinning. "I'm not much for health food. How about just a couple of scrambled eggs and wheat toast, dry."

As Charlotte scurried toward Marty behind the bar, Larry stared at her. Her skirt ended just above the knees, giving us an unfortunate view of her chunky purple-veined calves.

"Now I know why I never came here before," he said.

"Hey, you'll get used to it. I've had fancy, and I prefer this more."

"I was right, you haven't changed all that much."

"Well, that wasn't always the case," I said. "You wouldn't have recognized me a few years ago."

"When you were still with Sherry?"

"Right. I worked with her father, the firm's esteemed founder Rodger Dodds. Defending Fortune 500 corporations when their products maimed people, or when they laid off surplus workers, usually the oldest ones."

"What's wrong with that? Everyone needs a defense. I'll bet you charged them a bundle, right?"

"Oh, we made a ton of money, that wasn't the problem." I paused, sipped the coffee, which had turned cold. I filled him in on my marital history. Sherry and I had a nineteenth century townhouse, right on Beacon Hill, a wedding gift from Dodds. When Sherry and I argued, she wouldn't hesitate to remind me where it came from. And the social life: endless cocktail parties, socializing only with the best families. For a long time, I was into it, sliding along without a worry in the world. But eventually, it got to be too much; I just got tired of all that Boston blue-blooded bullshit.

I was going on, ignoring the reason we were here. I wanted to ask Larry about Raymond Walker and Brian McHugh, but decided to wait. It was obvious we had to get reacquainted first. So I continued explaining my marital woes.

"Sherry has called me a dozen times since I've been here, always giving me a hard time."

"About the divorce?"

"Yeah. Usually she says something like, 'Well, are you ready to return to reality after your little midlife crisis?' And she's got this Brahmin drawl she can turn on any time she wants. Sounds like William Buckley after a knee to the groin. Drove me crazy."

Larry laughed, more relaxed now, throwing his head back, and I got the feeling he understood midlife crises. As we talked, I pictured Sherry with her hair pulled straight back, held in place by a diamond broach, a streak of grey amidst dark brown. Sherry thought it looked "trendy." I thought it looked silly, especially for a woman with her well-bred facial structure.

"She always reminds me what a big mistake I made divorcing her." I dumped on Sherry some more, unloading my lingering frustration on Larry. Sherry never believed I could run a successful law practice without her daddy's money and considerable business contacts, developed over the centuries by his Brahmin relatives. For Sherry, my worst offense was abandoning the lucrative income ol' Dodds' law firm provided me. "And for a godforsaken place like Manchester, New Hampshire," she'd say, her perfectly reconstructed nose pointing skyward.

As I explained all this to Larry, I tried to hide the regret I felt for wasting away so many years. Although it took me a long time to realize it, joining Rodger's law firm and marrying Sherry had been huge mistakes, a stage of my life best forgotten. I should never have let myself be seduced by the privileged lifestyle, by the veneer of superiority that money buys, or by the powerful clients who reinforced that veneer by paying the outrageous fees Dodds' firm charged.

"What about you," I said, tiring of talking about Sherry, "happily married?"

He nodded slowly. "Oh yeah, Paula's the greatest girl in the world. The greatest. And Evan too. . . ." He paused, sipped his coffee, then creased his forehead, thinking. He started to speak but put down the coffee mug, reached inside his sweater and pulled a pack of cigarettes from his shirt pocket. I sat still, stunned, as he lit a cigarette. A talented athlete, smoking was a habit he always disdained.

"What's this?"

He shrugged. "Habit from the Army. I quit ten years ago, but the last month or so—I don't know, lots of stress at work I guess—and I started again." He took a couple of long drags on his cigarette, smudged it out in the ashtray, though not even half-smoked.

For the next few minutes, he told me about his life in the Army, mostly at bases in California, and how he had returned to Manchester after his discharge to be with Paula. He'd met her when he was a senior at St. Andrew and she was a freshman. They corresponded sporadically during his four years of duty, so he decided to return to Manchester and see if the spark was still there. They were married a year later, and recently celebrated their eighteenth wedding anniversary.

He stopped suddenly, lit another cigarette. "You know," he said, taking a drag, "this could've been a great reunion. Too bad all this shit's going on. Can't get my mind off it."

I waved at the smoke rising above the table. "We can catch up later," I said. "First things first. What're we going to do about Raymond Walker?"

He sucked on the cigarette. "I don't know. The public defender's helping him out for now, but I'd sure like to get you to patch things up with Raymond and get involved." He straightened out the paper placemat, stretching it to work out the wrinkles. "Let me give you some more background information. It might help you decide."

"Shoot," I said.

"Evan and Raymond both worked at the Cinema Manchester. Ushers, doormen, that kind of thing. Great job for watching movies. As I mentioned the other night, Raymond's been staying with us for a few months since his father kicked him out. It wasn't the first time. Kid's got no mother, his father likes the sauce a bit too much. So Evan felt sorry for him, asked if he could crash with us for a while. I said sure. We had an extra bedroom, I was glad to help the kid out. And it was no problem, until three weeks ago when Raymond got himself fired from the theater. By McHugh. Then Raymond moped around all day long, driving Paula nuts."

I listened intently, but my concentration was broken by Charlotte placing a plate in front of each of us. Took only twenty-five minutes. Good thing there was only one other patron there.

"Eat it while it's hot," she ordered.

Larry stared at the home fries, sausages, toast, and four eggs on my plate, forgot he was in the middle of a story, and gasped, "You're going to eat all that?"

"That remains to be seen, honey," Charlotte said. "He ain't never finished one yet." She grinned ear to ear, without showing any teeth, her cheeks folding into two half moons.

"That's your special?" Larry asked Charlotte.

"That's right," Charlotte snapped. As she made her way back to the kitchen, she looked over her shoulder, adding, "The 'He-Man Special.'"

The He-Man Special was a legend at the Chimes, named after a brave customer who single-handedly disarmed two punks with sawed-off shotguns. After rendering the two would-be robbers unconscious, the customer sat down at the counter and quietly ordered what came to be known as the He-Man Special.

Larry started eating, and after a couple of bites, he said, "Evan felt terrible for Raymond—we all did. No job, no home. The kid was a mess. We just hoped he'd find something, get his life together." He bowed his head, ran his fingers through his hair. In a loud, cracking voice, he said, "I still can't believe the police arrested Raymond for murdering McHugh."

Perhaps it was my imagination but it seemed the Chimes

had suddenly gone silent: no bacon sizzling in the kitchen, no dishes dropping into the sink, not even a hint of Marty's wheezing labored breaths. The old man sitting at the bar swung around in his stool and stared at us with blank blood-shot eyes. He gripped the Budweiser bottle tightly in his hand and looked directly at the back of Larry's head. Several seconds passed and he finally turned back to the comfort of his bottle. The Chimes returned to normal, Marty busying himself by the sink, the old man sipping his Budweiser.

"What evidence do they have against him?"

Larry scooped the rest of his scrambled egg onto his fork, lifted it to his mouth. When he finished chewing, he said, "Friday night Raymond was visiting his girlfriend in Dover, near Portsmouth, forty-five, fifty miles from Manchester. Came home late, I don't know what time, we were all asleep. Police say Raymond stopped at the theater and shot McHugh."

"Because McHugh fired him?"

"That's what the police say. McHugh worked as assistant manager full-time during the summer and part-time when school started. The manager, Phil Graham, is the assistant football coach at St. Andrew, and knew McHugh needed the dough. McHugh was working Friday night to help Graham with the special Halloween horror movie.

"Every Halloween the theater runs this promotion where all the patrons come in costume, imitating those ghoulish freaks from *Night of the Living Dead*. This year they took in a pile of money, plus the whole week's receipts were still there, total of fifteen grand so I've heard."

"It could've been a straight robbery then."

"The police have thrown out that angle too. Revenge or robbery, take your pick," he said. "But they haven't found the money. Or, for that matter, the murder weapon. So if Raymond's guilty, what the hell did he do with the money and the gun?"

Larry rubbed his eyes. He was exhausted, worried about

Raymond's arrest. He had taken Raymond in, given him a home, tried to help him out. Now it looked as if he had failed. And if Larry were anything like the person I used to know, he wouldn't take failure easily. We used to joke about who was more competitive. As friendly as we were, there was always some kind of competition between us.

"I assume the police searched your house?" I asked.

"Top to bottom. Every drawer, every closet." He paused and glanced toward the kitchen, as if he were deep in thought. Finally, he turned back. "And they found nothing to connect Raymond to the murder."

"Nothing?" He had sounded unsure; his tone of voice had the cadence of a question, rather than a positive statement.

He shook his head. "Not a thing."

I nodded, trying to put together the pieces. From what Larry said, the case against Raymond seemed weak. But the police must have more evidence, I was sure, to make an arrest in a high profile murder case.

I looked Larry in the eye. "So what do you think?"

"About what?"

"Did he do it?"

Larry gazed toward the ceiling, closed his eyes for a second. "I doubt it, I really do. He was just starting to snap out of his funk."

"Then who?"

"Hell, I don't know. Only thing I can think of is it was a straight robbery." He hesitated. "But . . ."

"What?"

Leaning toward me, he lowered his voice and said, "A few weeks before the murder, McHugh got some strange phone calls at the theater. Evan answered the phone. Guy with a strange accent, rude, demanding tone of voice. The first time he called, Evan handed the phone to McHugh, and when McHugh heard who it was, he turned white, nearly stopped breathing, according to Evan."

"Evan told the police all this?"

"Yeah. They took notes, but far as I know did nothing with it."

We were quiet for a few minutes, thinking over the case and savoring our own memories, regretting that we'd left our friendship behind. Finally, Larry broke the silence. "All I'm asking is you give the kid another chance, at least get a feel for the case. If you think it's out of your league or it's a loser, okay, you walk away, no hard feelings. We'll still be friends, no doubt about that. What'd you say?"

In the empty confines of the Chimes Café, surrounded by bad art, tacky tourist collectibles, and one half-in-the-bag patron at the bar, Larry's voice seemed to echo. There was a desperation in his voice that was not there initially. No longer the carefree youth I remembered, Larry had become responsible in his middle age. By taking in Raymond Walker, Larry had made a commitment beyond providing food and shelter. He couldn't just abandon the kid to the system, see him convicted and sent off to jail. Maybe Larry saw something of himself in Raymond; maybe Larry really believed in the kid's innocence.

I looked over at Larry staring at me, waiting for my answer. I avoided his eyes, stared down at my empty plate, pretending to weigh the consequences, when the plate suddenly disappeared. Before I realized what had happened, Charlotte had cleared the whole table. For a senior citizen, she sure moved fast. "Now ain't that a miracle," she said to herself. "First time he's ever finished the He-Man Special."

I smiled, turned toward Larry. "Even if I could take on the case, I'm sure Raymond wouldn't want me. Not after what happened yesterday."

Grinning, Larry shook his head. "I talked to Raymond already. He was still ticked off, but impressed. He said, 'That guy Francis hits pretty hard. Any lawyer with a punch like that I want on my side.'"

Oh, great, I thought, a new technique for bringing in clients. Punch them out and you'll get hired. I don't think the Bar Association would approve of that kind of solicitation.

"I'd be happy to give Raymond another chance," I said.

Larry smiled. "You're still a good guy, Dutch. You don't know how much this means to me." He glanced at his watch and stood up. "Shoot," he said, "I've got to run."

Larry walked to the register to pay the bill. I waved to Charlotte not to take his money. "This one's on me," I told him. You can pay next time . . . at an expensive restaurant."

He slapped me on the shoulder. "Thanks a bunch," he said.

On the sidewalk outside, Larry and I again shook hands, each of us gripping tightly as if afraid to let go. Traffic meandered along Elm Street, Manchester's main drag, which was notorious for being a dead end at both ends. Together we stared at the slowly moving line of traffic, at ten miles per hour, a major traffic jam in this city of one hundred thousand. The wind whistled past us, flapping the flags posted outside the department store across the street.

"How about dinner Friday night?" Larry asked. "That way you can meet the family and we can talk some more about the case." After so many years apart, I looked forward to renewing our friendship, and I was especially curious to meet Paula and Evan. I wondered how his family life compared with my own miserable failure.

Larry gave me directions to his house in Bedford, just west of Manchester. We waved goodbye and walked in opposite directions on Elm Street. After going half a block, I looked over my shoulder at him and realized, with some bemusement, that we were both heading toward a dead end.

CHAPTER 4

I paused in front of the Derryfield Building and checked my watch, trying to decide if I should go to the office or stop by the jail. For the second day in a row, Yvette would be wondering what had happened to me. Yvette had a way of making me feel guilty if I didn't tell her where I was at all times. No doubt she would be arranging all the work on neat piles on my desk, planning out my day. It would all have to wait, I decided. My interest right now was in Raymond Walker.

Before visiting Raymond, I stopped at the clerk's office and pulled his file. I flipped through the complaint. The complaint contained three charges: first degree murder, burglary, and robbery. It alleged that Raymond had taken cash "in the approximate sum of $15,000." The punch line of the first degree murder charge read: "That Raymond Walker did, with malice aforethought and with premeditation and deliberation, shoot and kill Brian McHugh."

If I remembered correctly my criminal law course from law school, the burglary and robbery charges were unnecessary. It was really an all or nothing case. If Raymond were guilty of robbery or burglary, he would certainly be found guilty of murder. A conviction for first degree murder meant life imprisonment, mandatory, no chance of parole. If New Hampshire hadn't outlawed the death penalty, Raymond might've been looking at the gallows at the state prison in Concord. During a tour shortly after my arrival, I saw the gallows room, where unlucky prisoners years ago met their maker. New Hampshire had never gone for the electric chair or the gas chamber. Hanging still did the trick.

The State was represented by assistant attorney general Peter Laflamme. Although I had seen him around the court-house, I knew little about him. I searched the file for more information, but my concentration was disturbed by a shadow falling over the papers.

"What's this, a murder?" asked Carter Butterworth, a clerk I often lunched with. He reached over the counter and flicked the papers in the file. Like all the courtroom clerks in New Hampshire, Carter was a law school graduate. Even though he had graduated in the top half of his class at Boston College, after three tries he still couldn't master the New Hampshire bar exam, so when a position opened up in the court, he jumped on it.

"Don't tell me you're going criminal," he said, glancing at the complaint. "And a high-profile case at that."

"I'm just checking things out right now. I'm not sure I'll get involved. Helping out an old friend, sort of a surrogate father to this kid Walker."

"You'll have your work cut out for you. McHugh is— I mean was—a popular guy around here. It's not that often New Hampshire produces a football player with All-American potential."

"So I've heard," I said, then pointed to the complaint. "What do you know about this AG, Laflamme? Any good?"

"Pierre Laaa—flamme!" He rolled the "La" as if announcing a hat trick at a Bruins' game. "The fiery one. The hottest prosecutor in the state. You've got your hands full with him."

"Great, just what I need. Maybe I should give Monsieur Laflamme a call, see what evidence he's got."

"Whatever you do, don't tell him this's your first murder case," he said as he walked behind the counter toward his office. "He'll make you try it for sure."

"Thanks for the tip," I said, waving goodbye as Carter disappeared into his office. I returned my attention to the file and learned what had happened at this morning's arraignment and bail hearing. The judge had generously granted bail in the amount of two and a half million dollars. At that amount Raymond would be stewing in jail until trial was over; that is, if everything went perfectly. Usually, defendants awaiting trial were held at the county jail a short distance from the courthouse, but because of a recent increase in arrests (mostly tourists from Massachusetts, the locals said) the county jail was overcrowded, and Raymond got to stay in the basement jail of the Hillsborough County courthouse. Not a bad break actually; at least now he had a private cell, and could rest at night without covering his rear end, figuratively and literally.

I walked to the other end of the counter and returned the file to Cindy, a curly-haired blonde with a killer smile, who was shuffling through a tray of index cards. Two months after I had opened my office, Butterworth told me I was a hit with the "girls" in the clerk's office. He insisted on calling them "girls" because, he claimed, that's how they wanted it. In a drawl passed down through two centuries of New Hampshire Butterworths, he explained, "You satisfy their only requirement. You're single." He paused. "And I suppose you're not bad-looking. At least I'm told the girls think your beard is sexy." He rubbed his smooth chin. "Personally I don't understand it."

I had stored this information away for future use, but had not yet had the inclination to act on it. Too soon after the divorce, I rationalized. Even now, with Cindy smiling attentively at me, I thought only of Raymond Walker. I responded to her smile with a quick wink, then walked downstairs to the jail.

Hank Lerner was sitting at his desk writing in a green notebook. He had a tight grip on the pencil and wrote with slow deliberate strokes, pressing the pencil heavily into the paper. Smoke swirled from a cigar balanced on the edge of his desk. There were ashes on the floor below the cigar and about an inch more barely hanging onto the end, about to fall. Hank didn't move a muscle as I approached. My footsteps pounded on the cement floor, but his face stayed in the notebook. The only movement I noticed was his eyes rising up to watch me, two beady eyeballs rolling in a stationary head.

"Back for Round Two?" he snarled. "Gonna finish him off this time?"

"Very funny. As a matter of fact I actually may represent the kid. We'll probably kiss and make up."

"I couldn't be happier," he said.

Hank led me back to the cell where Raymond was lying on the cot with his hands behind his head. As Hank unlocked the gate, Raymond swung his feet to the floor.

"So you want to take another shot at me?"

"You got what you deserved," I told him. "Let's hope you got it out of your system."

He grunted while scratching his head. "Yeah, right." He stared at me, trying out the tough guy routine again. I said nothing, stared back at him. It was his call, I had other things I could be doing. He looked down at the floor, thinking, and when he raised his head the tough guy look was gone. "I got to admit," he said, his voice softening, "Mr. Conway's done a lot for me. And he says you're pretty smart. So I guess that counts for something." Then he paused, and in a quiet voice said, "You really think I got a chance?"

"Don't know 'til I learn more about this case. So do you want my help, or maybe I should give the public defender a call?"

"Not that joker again!" he protested. "Probably get the

bail raised another million." Raymond walked to the end of the cell, then stopped and looked at me. "Ah, what the hell. Not like I got a lot of choices. I'll take whatever help I can get." He held out his hand and we shook.

We sat down on the bench against the wall. The bruise on his eye had faded a little since yesterday. He never did tell me how he got it, so I asked him again.

He grimaced. "The asshole cops. One of them—guy with a moustache, goatee—not even in uniform, looks at me and says get out of the car. I didn't know what was going on so I go: 'No. I know my rights.' "

"Wrong thing to say, Raymond," I said.

"You're telling me! Next thing I know the guy pops me a right in the eye and says, 'I'll show you your rights.' "

I laughed; got to love the cop sense of humor.

Raymond told me what he'd been doing before the arrest; the more he talked the more excited he got. He spent Halloween night with his girlfriend, Cathy Sayewich, at her house in Dover. They helped her mom hand out bags of M&Ms to the neighborhood kids, then hung around the house watching TV. He fell asleep on the couch with Cathy and didn't wake up until the cuckoo clock went off at two o'clock.

"You sure it was two?" If he left after two, he'd be in the clear. The coroner had set the time of death before two. Even if the coroner were off by a few minutes, the drive from Dover would've taken at least forty five minutes, or 2:45 at the earliest. I was starting to feel better about Raymond's chances.

"Yeah. Ask Cathy. She'll remember." I decided to do just that. She had better be an impressive witness if the jury were going to believe her. Of all the alibi witnesses I could have hoped for, a girlfriend was near the bottom of the list. The prosecution wouldn't have to dig far to find bias. I kept my concerns to myself, not wanting to alarm Raymond, at least for the time being.

"Let's hope so," I said. "Where'd you go after you left?"

"Straight to the Conways' house."

"Go by the Cinema?"

"No way. Not even close. There'd be no reason to do that. I came straight home. The lights were out and everyone was asleep. I was wiped out so I just crashed."

"Anyone see you?" I asked, hoping for another alibi witness. Raymond quickly dashed my hopes.

"Not 'til morning when Evan woke me up."

"So Evan was the first person to see you after you left Cathy's?"

"Yeah. I guess so."

"What time was that?"

"Oh, I don't know, five-thirty, six maybe. Too damn early I'll tell you that."

Raymond said Evan woke him up to go fishing, which seemed to me a strange thing to do on a frigid fall morning. "You guys usually go fishing in November?" I asked.

"Well, not really, but Evan said he heard there were some big perch biting, so I figured why not."

That was it, short and sweet. Already the trial was starting to unfold in my mind. The prosecution's theory was obvious: Raymond had stopped at the theater after saying goodnight to Cathy, snuck in without being seen, shot McHugh, and took the money. There was no one but Raymond to rebut that theory. But if McHugh had died at two as the coroner claimed and Raymond had left Cathy's at two, then obviously there was no way he could have done it.

Raymond was arrested Sunday afternoon while driving away from the Conways' house. "Where were you going on Sunday when the police showed up?" I asked.

He rolled his eyes toward the ceiling, as if the answer embarrassed him. "To Cathy's. She'd called and said she wasn't feeling so hot."

Before I finished with Raymond, I needed to cover one more aspect of the prosecution case—motive. "Tell me about McHugh. Why'd you hate the guy so much?" Raymond's hatred of McHugh was the only real information I had at that point.

"He was a jerk, a real douchebag," he said without hesitation. "Thought he was better than the rest of us just because he played football. Big fuckin' deal; it's a stupid game anyway. He considered me dirt, 'cause I used to work at the rug factory."

I looked at him. "And you got fired from there too?"

"Yeah. Showed up late all the time and they canned me. My father thought he was a hot shit because he'd worked there twenty-six years. Like that was such a great thing." I let Raymond rant for a few minutes. "So my old man threw me out of the house," he said, his voice cracking, as if the memory still hurt. I asked him for his father's address, thinking he'd be worth talking to. I wrote the address on my legal pad, then continued questioning Raymond.

"How'd Evan get along with McHugh?"

"A hell of a lot better than me, that's for sure. McHugh had it in for me, but he treated Evan fine. He knew Mr. Conway gave a lot of money to St. Andrew's. One of those alumni football boosters."

Raymond stood up and walked over to the bars, then quickly turned around and came back to the bench. "I get pissed off just thinking about McHugh. He was a tough mother, mean, nothing like the papers make him out. There was something else about that guy, I can't put my finger on it. I don't know, an edge, always seemed like he was ready to explode. Like those steroid rages you read about. Maybe that's what it was, steroids. Wouldn't put it past him. Comes here out of nowhere and all of a sudden he's like this superstar football player. You figure it out!"

He hesitated, thinking. "Nope, I ain't sorry he's dead. But I wasn't the one did it."

I had only one lead so I went with it. "I hear McHugh got some strange phone calls," I said.

"I don't know about that," he said.

"No?"

He shook his head. "Uh, uh. Who told you that?"

"Evan, through Larry."

"Hmmm, he never mentioned it to me."

Before I could ask more questions, the steel door crashed open. The sound echoed throughout the jail. In walked Hank, carrying a tray of food, a trail of steam floating toward the ceiling. He seemed pleased that Raymond was still on his feet.

"Lunchtime, gentlemen," Hank announced, sneering when he said "gentlemen." He placed the tray on the small table next to the wall. I looked down at a scattered pile of brown meat covered with yellow gravy, two slices of white bread, a scoop of mashed potato, also swimming in gravy, and—I could count them—three green beans. Without another word, Hank slammed the steel door shut and marched back to his post.

Raymond immediately picked up a knife and fork and started shoveling food into his mouth. When he dipped a slice of bread into the yellow gravy, I decided it was time to go.

"Raymond, I'm going to talk to Cathy, see if she can back up your alibi."

"She will, for sure. But she's pretty upset 'bout this whole thing. Came out yesterday and they wouldn't let her see me. That bastard Lerner, afraid she'd slip me a file or something. Maybe he'd've been nicer if he knew she was pregnant."

"Your girlfriend's pregnant?" Great, I thought, Raymond's only alibi witness, who was biased enough anyway, now has even more reason to lie. No doubt Cathy knew the difficulty collecting child support from a convict.

"Yeah, couple months. That's why she was sick the day the cops picked me up. Morning sickness. Ain't that great, and here I am behind bars." He looked around the cell, shook his head. "I might never see the kid."

Raymond Walker, a father. Even if he were innocent, the thought made me shudder. Still, I tried to cheer him up.

"Don't give up yet. Let me check out a few of these leads. I'll be back in a few days, and let you know what I find. You think of anything else, you can tell me then."

"Okay," he mumbled as he scooped some meat and potato onto a slice of bread, making some kind of sandwich. I hurried down the hall, anxious to escape the stench of the county's gourmet cooking.

CHAPTER 5

I approached the Queen City Bridge and began to question the impulse that had led me to go to my apartment and throw on my old red New England Patriots sweatshirt, complete with pants so shrunken they barely reached my ankles, and jog the moist streets of Manchester. I had spent the afternoon at the office, brushing up on criminal law while Yvette buried herself in the library looking for articles on Brian McHugh.

I had planned on running only a few miles, so I could get in shape for the Walker case. A murder trial would be physically exhausting, I knew, and if I defended Walker I had to be ready, physically and mentally. I also needed to start the investigation and interview some witnesses. I decided to combine the workout and investigation. My first interview candidate lived only a few miles away, within reasonable jogging distance: Raymond's father.

I stopped halfway over the bridge, stripped off my gloves and began to rub my aching calves. The sweat was flowing from my forehead at the edge of my blue stocking cap. I wiped it away with my sleeve.

Below, the Merrimack River was swirling in response to the heavy wind. I leaned on the iron railing and stared at the dark choppy water, still huffing while spitting breaths over the rail. The river flowed around a bend, past small white cottages covered with brown leaves from the bare trees along the shore. The sun was setting, a faint light still falling on the river.

The stern of a small boat appeared from under the bridge. I recognized it as a scull, like ones I used to watch on the Charles. It moved swiftly, unaffected by the swirling water. The sculler was a young man, college age. He stroked the oars through the dirty water, his rhythm smooth and steady. Despite the freezing temperature and impending darkness, he wore only short pants and a tee shirt with no gloves or hat. As he glided away from the bridge, I strained to read the words printed on his tee shirt: *St. Andrew College.*

Pushing myself from the railing, I ran over the bridge. I picked up the pace and turned down Goffstown Road. For ten minutes I ran along one residential street after another, past two- and three-story homes, staying by the left curb so I could see approaching cars. As I ran I kicked up dry dead leaves, creating a yellow and red cloud in my wake.

In time I found my second wind and headed back to Goffstown Road. I took my first right, thinking it would connect with Goffstown, but reached a dead end. Retracing my steps, I took the next right, the one I was looking for, Seabrook Way. I slowed my pace, glancing at the houses on each side. This was a working class neighborhood, small single-family homes amongst double and triple deckers. The cars were old and dirty, two or three Chevy coups, a rusted Volkswagen van. The shrieks of small children came from back yards, loud and carefree.

I stopped at 41 Seabrook, a triple decker decorated in grey paint with white-chipped trim. A street light shone on the house, enabling me to make out the names on the mailboxes; the one on the right read: WALKER. There was no gate so I climbed the stairs. Between the two doors were three doorbells; under each was a name printed in tape. The top tape read: John E. Walker.

I looked at my watch: 4:45. Remembering Raymond telling me his father's shift ended at 4:00, I pressed the door-bell. After waiting a while with no response, I pressed again, held it for a few seconds. Again, no response. I retreated to the bottom step, looked up at the third story windows. The shades were drawn, but one window was slightly open. I walked around back, ducking under a wire clothesline held up by a green metal frame, stretching out like football goal-posts. The line was bare and the posts leaned to one side. Narrow wooden stairs led from the back porch to the top floor. The sun was setting and the developing darkness made it difficult to see the stairs. Holding onto the rail, I climbed carefully to the top and banged on the storm door.

A window creaked open from the apartment below and a porch light came on. "He ain't home," said a woman's voice. "Can't you tell that when there's no answer?" I walked down to the landing below. The voice belonged to a woman with hair as grey and mottled as the paint on the building. She leaned her head out the window, holding up the bottom with both hands, firmly as if she were afraid it would fall on her head like a guillotine. "And who might you be?" she asked gruffly.

"I'm looking for John Walker," I explained. I lifted up the bottom of my sweatshirt, wiped the sweat off my forehead.

Her cheeks puffed as she snorted, "Walker, huh, that's a good one. You got about as good a chance of finding Walker here as you would in St. Teresa's Church over there on the corner. Walker's almost never home."

"Any idea where I might find him?"

She squinted at me and stuck out her jaw. "Maybe, maybe not." She stared straight ahead as if expecting me to do something.

For a moment I couldn't figure out what she wanted, then

it hit me. I unzipped the back pocket of my sweatpants and pulled a crisp twenty from my wallet. "Will this do it?" I asked.

"Put that away," she snarled. "What do you think I am, I need a handout from the likes of you." Her brogue got thicker. She put both hands on the window sill, leaned closer to me, propping the window up with her neck.

"I'm terribly sorry," I said, putting the twenty back in my wallet. "I didn't mean to insult you."

"If you'd just tell me who you might be, seeing's you never answered me before, I might remember where ol' Walker is."

When I told her my name and that I was a lawyer, she raised an eyebrow. "You don't dress like a lawyer."

"No, I guess not," I said, looking down at my sweats. "I was running in the neighborhood and thought I'd introduce myself to Mr. Walker. He's my client's father."

"That so? Then your client must be his boy Raymond." She nodded slowly. "I've been reading about him . . . sad. He was always a wild one, that boy." She stepped back, sending the window crashing into the space where her head had been. Opening the door, she said, "My son's promised to fix that thing some day. Don't know if I'll live that long." She waved me in.

She led me into the kitchen, motioned for me to sit at the table, and asked if I'd like something to drink. I said sure. She reached in the refrigerator and pulled out a quart bottle of Budweiser. She untwisted the top and poured two glasses.

She placed the glass in front of me, and sat down in the opposite chair. She had poured too much beer into her glass and foam poured over the rim. She wiped it away with a paper napkin. Lifting her glass, she said, "Cheers." We tapped glasses and took a drink. She drank a bit longer than me and when she pulled the glass away, a line of white foam stayed above her lip. With the back of her hand she wiped away the foam mustache. For the first time I noticed thin white hair above her lip; she had a real mustache.

My hostess's name was Mabel Considine and she had lived in this small second floor apartment for thirty-five years, the last fifteen alone since her husband Ed had died. When the Walkers had moved in some twenty years ago, Mrs. Walker was pregnant with Raymond. "A lovely girl, that Mary," she said. "A shame what happened: cancer, the big 'C'. And so young too."

"I understand John didn't take it too well."

"Nobody takes that kind of thing well. There's no reason you should." With a napkin she continued to dab at the spilled foam on the table. "A little piece of you dies at the same time. Trick is to keep that piece small. Let it grow and it'll eat away at you until there's nothing left. And that's what happened to John. Every year more and more of him died. Got so he wouldn't even say hello to me. Just walk by on the stairway as if I wasn't there, staring at his feet."

She paused to sip her beer. "And the way he treated that poor boy, it was terrible. Yelling and screaming like he was some kind of dog. I tried to talk to him about it but he'd just wave me off, wouldn't listen."

I asked her what Raymond was like.

"I remember when he lost his first tooth. He was about six and he came running down the stairs yelling, 'Yook, Mrs. Considine, I yost a toof.' And he held it out for me to see, blood and all. Even though there was still some blood in his mouth, he was grinning ear to ear, so happy to be growing up." She paused. "But the cuteness ended, I don't know, when he was eleven or twelve. The sad thing is it was so predictable; he became just like his father."

"How so?"

"Always sad, depressed. Wouldn't talk to me anymore, afraid his friends would think he was a sissy for talking to an old woman. Then it got even worse." She took a deep breath. "He became a thief. I saw all the things he brought onto this property. Electronic stuff, Raleigh bicycles, you name it. He stored them upstairs or in the garage. I talked to John about it. He told me to mind my own business. Pretty soon it became my business. I started noticing things missing, rings, quarters from my change cup. But then I couldn't find my watch necklace that Ed had given me; it was fourteen carat gold, shaped like a heart, my first anniversary gift. That was it. I told John what Raymond was up to, that it better be returned or I'd call the police. And John brought it back, that night.

"That's when the beatings started. I could hear John screaming and Raymond cry, 'No, don't.' Then the slap of the belt." She shuddered. Tears formed in her eyes. "I know I'm not to blame, but sometimes I wonder: if I hadn't complained . . ."

I put my hands over hers, which were shaking involuntarily. I assured her she was not to blame, Raymond was just unlucky to have a violent father. She nodded, finished her beer. When I had done the same, she picked up both glasses, placed them in the sink and threw the bottle in a bucket underneath. "You wanted to know where Walker was, and here I am wasting your time."

"No, really . . ."

"Don't try to make me feel good. You've done enough just to listen to me. Anyway, try the IV, two blocks down and one over. Walker'll probably be leaning on a barstool talking to a shot glass."

"IV?" I asked.

"Sure. You know, the Irish Village."

I'VE spent a fair amount of time in bars, but I still wasn't prepared for the stench of stale beer that hit me when I opened the door to the IV. Mrs. Considine's prediction had proven accurate. A man wearing wrinkled blue work pants sat at the bar staring into a shot of whiskey. He was stocky, about two-twenty. His white hair was cut in a whiffle, a Boston crewcut, bare except for an inch sticking up at the front. He looked vaguely familiar. I took a seat two stools away. We had the bar to ourselves.

The bartender walked over, slapped a Miller coaster in

front of me. "What can I getcha?" he asked, scratching his head, probably wondering why a jogger would be in his bar.

"Tonic water, twist of lime," I said. My companion grunted, muttered something under his breath. "Excuse me," I said, turning toward him. "You wouldn't happen to be John Walker?"

He chugged the rest of his whiskey, slapped the glass on the bar, stared at it for a few seconds. "Who wants to know?" he glared at me with the same steely-eyed expression I'd seen in Raymond. When I saw his red eyes, I thought I recognized him. He reminded me of the old patron at the Chimes Café, sipping on a Budweiser at eight o'clock in the morning. But Walker was younger, I realized, and his hair was not more white than grey.

I pulled a wrinkled business card from my wallet and slid it over to him. "I represent your son Raymond."

He lifted the card to the light, then flipped it back to me. "Yeah, no kiddin'. My son, the murderer. Always knew he'd make me proud." His voice was thick, slurred.

The bartender brought over my tonic water, picked up the five I had left on the bar. I took a sip and looked at John Walker. "Mind if I ask you a few questions?"

He lifted his glass, saw that it was empty and turned it upside down. I motioned to the bartender to bring another. From the top shelf, he pulled down a bottle of Johnny Walker Red—what else?—and filled the glass.

After drinking half the glass, Walker said, "I don't know nothing about that murder, if that's what ya want to know. Only what I read in the paper. How much was it they say he took? What, fifteen grand? More'n I make in six months. You'd think the boy would've shared some of the loot with his dear ol' dad."

"Raymond's in jail and he doesn't have any loot," I said. "Actually, I was hoping you could give me some information about your son's upbringing, his successes, failures, that kind of thing. Something to make the jury sympathetic."

"Forget it. Kid was always a pain in the ass. The only

smart thing he ever did was stay away from his old man, and he still managed to fuck up." He shook his head and grinned, thinking back. "I kinda figured he'd do something stupid like this. He never did like makin' an honest livin', always on the lookout for the quick buck. I told him there's no such thing as a quick buck. Maybe I don't make a whole lot, but there's one thing you can be sure of. Every cent, every last penny, I earned. And honestly. Hard work, no fucking hand-outs."

I sat quietly, sipping my tonic. Walker started chuckling. "And look at me," he said, still laughing. "Look at me. See what honest work gets you."

I shifted in my seat uncomfortably. I couldn't let it rest. "Mr. Walker, I don't think your son's guilty."

He turned his head and stared at me. His eyes were a deeper red than the old Chimes patron's, reminding me of an old blues song: they looked like two cherries in a glass of buttermilk.

"You're his lawyer," he said. "That's what you're supposed to think."

I sat up straight, looked him in the eye. "And you're his father," I snapped. "What are you supposed to think?"

"Humph," he grunted, picking up his whiskey. "You're forgettin' one thing, Mr. Lawyer."

"Oh, what's that?"

He gulped the rest of his drink, stood up, walked to the door. Turning to the side, he looked back at me and pushed open the door. Before staggering outside, he said, "I know Raymond better'n you."

CHAPTER 6

THE next morning I couldn't get my mind off Raymond Walker. I was anxious to give Yvette a report on my progress, but she was gone. Taped to her computer monitor was a note written in her barely decipherable scrawl: "Had to do more research at library. Be back around 11. Answering machine is on."

I sat at my desk and flipped through a two-inch-high stack of medical records in a medical malpractice case that was coming up for trial. I stared at nurses' notes without reading them, thinking about the raw deal life had dealt Raymond Walker. Mother dies when he's still a child; father drops out of life and gives up on his son. Hard to believe Raymond's father would assume Raymond was guilty. I thought of my old friend Larry with renewed respect: he wasn't related to Raymond, owed him nothing, in fact had no reason to help him. But Larry wasn't willing to give up on Raymond. I admired that, and vowed that I wouldn't give up on Raymond either. For Larry's sake, as much as for Raymond's.

I threw the medical records across my desk, put my feet up and stopped pretending to work on something else. I needed to think, to analyze the pieces of the puzzle I had so far. I knew a fair amount about Raymond, his family, childhood, failures, especially his firing from the theater. But I knew little about McHugh. He was a football star with a recognizable name, worked part-time at the movie theater, and perhaps was receiving some threatening phone calls. I had no details about McHugh's life off the football field. Perhaps that would be a good place to start, I decided, and picked up the phone.

I dialed the number to St. Andrew College and asked the operator to connect me to the varsity football coach. I was shuffled around a bunch of people before the coach came on the line. "This is Coach Walsh," he said sternly, "how may I help you?"

I identified myself, told him I was representing the kid accused of killing McHugh, and had some questions about McHugh's background. The line went quiet and I thought I'd been disconnected. After several seconds, Coach Walsh said, "You represent the sonovabitch who murdered my star running back, ruined a perfect season, and probably cost me my job." His volume seemed to increase with each word. "And you expect me to help you."

"All I'm doing, Coach, is trying to figure out who really killed him," I said softly. "I'm on your side and all I need is some background on McHugh."

"Huh, that's a good one," he growled. "On my side, are you? If you were on my side, you'd know that I took this raw kid no other college team wanted when he graduated from Pine Creek-fucking-High School, and turned him into an All-American candidate." He paused. "All-American can-di-date," he repeated slowly, as if I'd somehow missed it the first time.

"Pine Creek High School? Where is that exactly?"

"What? Don't you know nothing? It's in goddamn Cali-

fornia, you dumb shit." And with that pleasant comment, he
slammed down the phone.

I stood up, a bit unsettled at the coach's hostility. Walking toward the window, I thought of how naive I'd been to
assume McHugh's coach would cooperate. In people's
minds, once Raymond had been arrested he was presumed
guilty, no matter what the Constitution had to say. If I were
going to change that presumption, especially in the minds of
a jury, I had to find the real murderer.

In the midst of my musing, Yvette returned from the library. "Standing around doing nothing, are you?" she said
when she saw me staring out the window. "Am I the only
one working around here?"

I laughed. "Thinking can be work too, you know."

"A lawyer thinking? Now I've heard everything. And
here I was assuming you lawyers acted first, then thought
later about how to justify your actions." She tossed a packet
on my desk. "These'll give you something else to think
about."

I walked over to the desk and picked up the packet.
Yvette had managed to secure a dozen *Union Leader* articles.

Yvette returned without her coat, wearing a one-piece
black outfit that clung to her body like saran wrap. When my
eyes lingered a moment longer than was polite, Yvette tilted
her head and said, "Keep reading, Clarence Darrow." She
came around the desk and stood behind me, reading over my
shoulder. "The stories from the Sports Pages are on top," she
said, slowly flipping through the stack. I got a quick impression of McHugh's talents: three touchdowns in a big
win over Holy Cross, an eighty-yard run against Dartmouth.
In the Army game, he played both ways and intercepted two
passes from the safety position. The guy was amazing, I
thought.

I scanned more articles, looking for details about
McHugh's high school football career. One article mentioned that he had grown up in a small town in California.

But that was it; nothing about his accomplishments, why he went to college in New Hampshire. Reading the articles, I got the impression the reporters consciously avoided McHugh's past, wanting to portray him as one of their own.

I asked Yvette what she thought about it.

"What do you expect?" she said sharply. "This is New Hampshire, you think these reporters care what happened in someone else's neighborhood? Especially California. That could be another planet for all they care."

"Seems to me people would be interested in how McHugh became such a great player," I said. "At the very least, it's worth a phone call."

She picked up my phone and handed it to me while dialing 411. "Ask for the area code for Pine Creek," she said, leaving me to my own devices.

After getting the area code, I called information in California and wrote down the number to Pine Creek High School. I dialed the school and asked for the football coach. I was put on hold for over a minute before a woman answered, "Athletic department."

"I'm trying to reach the varsity football coach," I said, feeling like I'd done this already.

"That would be Chubby Carlucci. He's in the weight room. Can I have him call you back?"

"Sure, my name's Dutch Francis. I'm calling about a former player of his named Brian McHugh."

"Oh," she said, gulping. "Oh, I see." She breathed heavily, several deep breaths one right after the other. "Well, I don't know if he can help you. That busi . . . ," she took another deep breath, ". . . business was some time ago. And now that poor Brian's dead," she paused and huffed, almost whimpering, "Coach would just as soon forget it."

"I'm sorry, what business are you talking about?"

She was silent for a few seconds. "Noth . . . nothing, I've said too much already." Her voice trembled. "I'll t-tell him you called."

"Wait . . ." Click. And I never gave her my phone num-

ber. Whatever this "business" was, it had certainly flustered
the athletic department secretary. Could it have something to
do with McHugh's activities in high school? Did it have
something to do with the strange phone calls McHugh had
been receiving at the theater? I thought it over and decided
to take off tomorrow and pay a visit to Coach Chubby Carlucci. I could catch a nine o'clock flight to San Francisco
and with the time change be in Pine Creek before school let
out. And if I were delayed, I bet I could still find the coach
in the weight room.

PINE Creek was about thirty miles east of San Francisco
in Contra Costa County. I took the Bay Bridge to Highway
24 and drove through the Caldecott Tunnel before finding
the Pine Creek exit. I stopped at a gas station for directions
and made my way to the high school. As I passed through
the quaint town square with green lawns, I wondered how
the residents had reacted to having one of their own brutally
murdered. The high school grounds spread out over several
acres, and the building itself was long and short like a ranch-
style home. I parked near the front door, and walked around
the building, listening for the sound of a bouncing basketball, the telltale signs of the gym.

I found a door to the gym ajar and walked past a half-
court game toward the sounds of grunting and clanging
metal in the weight room. It was packed with teenage boys
in various stages of preening, pumping, and posing. There
was so much testosterone in the air I was tempted to slide
under the 300 pound bench press and toss it through the ceiling. Fortunately, before I could embarrass myself, I spotted
an older man at the end of the room whose physique told me
he had to be Chubby Carlucci.

I maneuvered through the benches, barbells, and sweaty
bodies toward Carlucci. He was shorter than most of the
players but had enormous shoulders and a perfectly round
belly, like a medicine ball, wrapped in a grey Pine Creek
High School Football tee-shirt.

"Excuse me, Coach," I said. "Could I have a word with you?"

He glanced at me, then turned back to the student he had been speaking to.

"Ah, excuse me, Coach," I tried again. "I have a quick question on a former player of yours: Brian McHugh."

He turned on his heels and took a step toward me.

"Who the hell are you?"

I explained I was a lawyer involved in McHugh's murder case, and that's all I said. No need to get anybody else mad at me.

"How'd you get in here?" He said. "This is for students and staff only. I oughta call security right now."

By now there was a circle of hulking male adolescents staring down at us. At slightly taller than six feet, I was still dwarfed by the Pine Creek offensive line, who glared at me as if I were mugging their coach. One of them, a dark-haired monster with long straight sideburns, tapped Carlucci on the shoulder. "You wan' us to move this guy outahere, Coach?"

Carlucci stuck out his lower lip, turned to the kid. "Get away from me, you pissants. Whadyathink, I can't handle this situation on my own?" He held up his thumb. "Finish your sets . . . NOW!"

When the team had dispersed, he returned his attention to me. "You, in my office."

I followed the waddling coach down a dark hallway. The ceiling was so low I had to duck under the heating ducts and water pipes. The coach removed a large circular key ring from his belt and unlocked his office door. I stepped inside. After the coach settled into his seat behind the desk, I sat across from him. Carlucci played with some papers on his desk, keeping me waiting.

Finally he looked up. "Let's see some ID," he ordered.

I showed him my driver's license and bar association card. He nodded, handed them back. "You're the guy Betty talked to yesterday, aren't you?" he asked, though it really

wasn't a question. "You're a long way from home, counselor. What's your interest in McHugh?"

I had no choice but to come clean. "I represent the kid
who's accused of killing him," I said.

He straightened up. "That so? And what makes you think
I'd want to help you?"

"You probably won't be surprised to know I think the police arrested the wrong guy. I'm trying to gather information
about McHugh to see if anyone else had an interest in seeing him dead." I gazed at the photos covering the wall behind him: a dozen black and whites of football players, all
wearing the Pine Creek High uniform. "I've seen a few
newspaper articles about McHugh's football heroics," I said,
nodding at the photos. "Impressive player."

"He could always run with the ball."

"Only one thing puzzles me, though," I said.

"If there's only one thing, then you're way ahead of me."

"More I learn the more puzzled I get," I said. "What I
don't get is why McHugh went to St. Andrew in the first
place. Small liberal arts school stuck up in New Hampshire
with a small-time football program. The paper said he was a
walk-on. How does a walk-on to a mediocre team become
an All-American candidate?"

"You're making some assumptions, sir, that may not be
true." He folded his arms and leaned back. I waited for him
to elaborate but he just stared at me.

"Are you going to share those with me?" I asked. "Or
should I track down Betty—she's the athletic department
secretary, right?—and ask her what she meant about this
'business' with McHugh?"

That got his attention. He shot forward, pointing his finger at me. "You keep away from Betty, you got no right
bothering her. I find out you been pushing her around,
I'll . . ." He decided not to finish the threat and put down his
finger.

"Don't you worry, Coach," I assured him. "I'm not the

type of lawyer to go bullying witnesses. I'd just like to know a few details about this business Betty mentioned."

He leaned forward, rested his forehead in his palms. After a short while he scratched his head, looked over at me and nodded. "I don't know why I shouldn't tell you, not like it'd make any difference now that Brian's dead." He slid out a desk drawer, thumbed through some files, and pulled one out. With a wide sweep of his hand, he slammed the file on the desk, then slid it over to me.

I opened the file. It was about an inch thick, full of newspaper articles from the local paper. They were all about Brian McHugh but had nothing to do with football. The subject was far more shocking. I took a few minutes to read them, then looked up at the coach, whose face had softened considerably since we'd come into the office.

"Did anyone at St. Andrew's know about this?" I asked.

"Nope, no one," he said emphatically. "Not the coach, the admissions department, no one."

"How could a college admit a student without knowing he had spent the previous year in prison?" I asked, talking more to myself than Carlucci. "And for manslaughter? I don't get it."

"Simple," he said. "Brian lied on the application. On the question about what he'd done in the year since high school, he wrote down that he'd worked odd jobs to earn college tuition. No one checked up."

I shook my head in wonder as I leafed through the file again. Stuck amidst the articles was a letter on Pine Creek High School stationary from Carlucci to Frank Walsh, the friendly St. Andrew coach I talked to yesterday. It was a glowing letter, recounting McHugh's all-league honors, serious demeanor, hard-working family. But what was omitted from the letter is what interested me. "You never mentioned the manslaughter conviction," I said. "There's nothing here about McHugh's talents with a knife, prison, anything. How could you mislead St. Andrew like that?"

"What're you talking about, mislead?" he said, gritting

his teeth. "That's pure bullshit, counselor. Everything in that letter is God's truth. Not one lie."

"You don't think St. Andrew had a right to know the whole story, how McHugh stuck a knife in some young guy fifteen times?"

"It ain't the way the papers made it out," Carlucci said quickly. "Not like this punk Vicens was an angel. It was his knife, for Christ's sake, and he tried to stick up Brian and his girlfriend while they were on their way to the senior prom. I'm not saying I approve of killing anyone, even a low-life like him, but seemed to me from the get-go this was a case of self-defense. And if he'd had a decent lawyer, one with some balls is what I'm saying, then he never would've plead guilty and who knows what might've happened."

"Yeah," I said, "he could've gotten eight years instead of one."

He frowned. "As it turned out, though, prison was good for Brian." He reached back and pulled a photo off the wall. "Look at this kid," he showed me the photo. "Middle of senior year and skinny as a bean pole." The photo showed McHugh diving for a pass along the sideline. His arms were outstretched and his shirt had lifted up, showing his thin belly. "In prison," Carlucci continued, replacing the photo, "he did nothing but lift weights, bulked himself up. When he finished, he was a solid mass of muscle. I knew he'd be a great player."

I looked at the letter of recommendation: "So that's why you wrote, 'Brian has the potential to be the premier running back in the league.'"

"Yeah, but I don't think Walsh bought that part. Probably thought I was insulting him. Wouldn't give Brian dime one for scholarship. So Brian had to take that honky-tonk job at the movie theater and make the team as a walk-on."

Perhaps McHugh would still be alive today, I thought, if he hadn't been working at the theater. Then I remembered the threatening phone calls that Raymond had overheard. "You said no one knew about McHugh's past," I said.

"Yeah, so?"

"Was Brian trying hard to keep it secret?"

"You kidding? He didn't want anyone to know. Especially when he had those big games and the press was over him. He was scared to death the press would find out and blow his chances for All-American. A few reporters from that Manchester paper—what's it called?"

"The *Union Leader*," I answered.

"Yeah, that's it. These reporters called me up a few times for some background on Brian and I sweet-talked them like you wouldn't believe. They had no clue about Brian's conviction."

I looked down at the newspaper articles. "But everyone in Pine Creek knew. Wasn't he worried someone here would blow the whistle on him?"

He laughed. "People from Pine Creek don't ever leave, least of all to go to Manchester, New Hampshire. And don't forget, just because the Manchester *Union Leader* claimed Brian was an All-American candidate doesn't mean anyone else did. I think the *Pine Creek Ledger* ran one small article saying that Brian was the starting halfback for St. Andrew."

"What about since his murder, anyone else call you?"

He looked down and shuffled some papers on his desk. From beneath a pile he pulled out a small torn sheet of paper. "Here it is," he said. "You didn't think you were the only one to check into Brian's past, did you? Your opponent beat you to it. Peter Laflamme, Assistant Attorney General. I've got his phone number if you want it."

"No, thanks," I said, "I have it. I assume you told him what you've told me?"

"You think maybe I'd help you and not him? Guess again. You're a nice guy but I have to admit I'd rather be helping the prosecution convict the murderer."

I smiled and stood up to leave. I handed Carlucci the file and asked him if I could have a copy. He shrugged and said that Betty was off now, but he'd have her mail me a copy.

"Since I'm in the area," I said, "I'd like to stop by McHugh's parents' house. Any idea where I can find them?"

Carlucci frowned. "Yeah, I know exactly where. Try the cemetery in Colma."

"Both his parents are dead?"

He folded his arms and leaned on the desk. "Right after Brian's conviction, his parents left town. People said they were ashamed their son was a convict. They just gave up on life."

"How's that?"

"Why else would they move to Los Angeles?"

I suppressed a smile, remembering the intense rivalry between San Francisco and Los Angeles.

"But," he continued, "not long after the move they got into a high-speed collision on the freeway. Some moron sideswiped them, knocking their car down a gully. Newspapers said they died instantly."

"What happened to the car that hit them?"

"Took off," he said, gritting his teeth. "Coward left them there to die. What a goddamn world."

Carlucci moved off the desk toward the door. The interview, I guessed, was over.

"One last thing," I said, stopping him before he opened the door. "You ever hear of anyone threatening to expose Brian?"

"Nah," he shook his head. "You think Brian's past might have something to do with his murder?"

I thought about all the pieces, quickly tried to see if they fit. "Yeah," I said finally. "It just might."

CHAPTER 7

ON the flight back east I tried to sleep but my mind kept racing. I was uneasy about what I had learned about McHugh. What had Laflamme done with the information from Coach Carlucci? Why hadn't he leaked it to the press? Perhaps Laflamme was so convinced of Raymond Walker's guilt that he brushed aside McHugh's troubled past. I had a sneaking suspicion that he'd left some stones unturned, stones that might uncover the key to proving Raymond's innocence.

At the same time I thought about renewing my friendship with Larry after all these years and meeting his family tomorrow night. After our breakfast at the Chimes Café, it felt almost like old times, but with a gap of over two decades. I was looking forward, with some uneasiness, to filling that gap. We were both obviously different people. Could we still be good friends? And what would happen to our friendship if Raymond were convicted?

By the time my plane had landed at Logan Airport, the only conclusion I'd reached about the Walker case was that

I needed to hire a private investigator. The stakes in this case were too high for me to keep fumbling around. Thinking how anxious my civil clients became when their money was at stake, I had to laugh. Money was nothing compared to liberty.

THE Conway house was set back about fifty yards from the road, behind a row of tall pine trees, far from the gazing eyes of neighbors. Lights on each side of the driveway illuminated my trail to the garage. I parked my Honda compact behind a long white Cadillac, shining in the moonlight.

I took three steps on the porch and as I reached for the bell, the door opened.

"You must be Dutch Francis. I'm Paula Conway." She had heard my car, she said, and couldn't wait to meet me after all these years. Then she hugged me as if she, and not Larry, were my childhood friend. There was something calm and reassuring about the way she greeted me. Immediately I felt relaxed and welcomed by my friend's wife.

I couldn't help thinking how different Paula was from my ex-wife Sherry. She was dressed simply in a green flowery dress. She wore little makeup, her fresh clean New Hampshire features in plain view. No pretensions, no conscious effort to impress. Sherry would've been appalled.

Even without makeup—or perhaps because she wore none—Paula's face lit up when she smiled, a genuine, sincere smile, unlike Sherry's beauty pageant of upper teeth, the result of ten minutes practice in front of the mirror before every social engagement. I used to be impressed by Sherry's social skills, her ability to keep a conversation going and then gracefully flit to the next group, all the while maintaining an air of superiority. After all, she was the daughter of Rodger Dodds: a genuine, blue-blooded BAP, or British American Princess.

Paula's blood was definitely red, not blue. She put her arm through mine, a gesture that would have looked calculated if Sherry had tried it, but with Paula seemed warm and friendly. She led me through the dining room to the kitchen, where Larry was busy sliding a pan into the oven.

Larry said he'd been preparing dinner for hours and described the marinade he concocted for the roast, the cream sauce he'd whipped together for the onions. As he described the food, he made clucking noises with his tongue, already tasting how delicious the meal would be. This was a side of Larry I'd never seen: the chef. In high school I had to teach him how to boil hot dogs.

Paula and I went into the parlor so Larry could finish cooking. The parlor was huge, about the size of my entire one-bedroom apartment, and jammed full of mahogany furniture—an oval coffee table, two end tables, matching curio cabinets at each end. I glanced quickly around the room as Paula poured two glasses of red wine. My eyes drifted around the huge room and focused on Larry and Paula's wedding portrait above the fireplace, a color photo touched up to look like an oil painting. Larry's hair was thick and spilling over his ears, the way I remembered him. Paula stood beside him, staring lovingly into his eyes. I couldn't remember Sherry ever looking at me that way.

As Paula handed me my glass, she asked how I liked living in Manchester. "I'm still getting used to it," I told her. "It's a lot different than Boston, that's for sure."

"We like it that way," she said. "You know I'm a native. My great-grandparents settled here nearly a century ago when the mills were just getting started. My whole family still lives in Manchester."

"Larry never tried to get you to move to Boston?"

"Not once," she said, sitting on the couch as she motioned me to sit in the wing chair across from her. "I wouldn't have gone, if he had. I've only been there a half dozen times, and I've no great desire to go back, even if it is only fifty miles away." She paused and sipped her wine. "Larry's the same way, happy to stay home." I got the feeling she was apologizing for her husband not looking me up sooner, going through the same regrets Larry and I had shared at the Chimes Café.

"I can understand why Larry wants to stay," I said. "You've got a beautiful home."

"Oh, that's sweet of you. We've tried to keep it looking nice, but it's not been easy with an active boy."

Larry walked in from the kitchen. "Evan always was an active boy," he said, untying his apron.

"I'd like to meet him if he's around," I said, my thoughts returning to Raymond Walker. I found myself thinking of questions to ask Evan about Raymond's case.

"Follow me," Larry said, motioning as he walked upstairs. At Evan's room, he knocked on the door. The door was opened by a younger duplicate of Larry with the same shiny cheeks and thick brown hair. He looked about my height, six feet, a couple of inches shorter than his father. He flashed a perfect smile, surely helped by his parents' heavy investment in orthodontics.

"Evan, I want you to meet my old friend, Dutch Francis," Larry said, draping his arm around Evan's shoulder.

Evan shook my hand. He seemed polished and confident. "Glad to meet you, Mr. Francis."

"Evan's an 'A' student," Larry said. "Vice president of the eleventh grade, and a pretty damn good fastball hitter too."

Evan shook his head. "He's exaggerating."

Larry took a few steps into Evan's room. "You're right, you're not perfect. Look at this place; it's a mess," he said, sweeping his arm around the room. I walked in to get a better look, interested in checking out the possessions of a teenager. The computer was turned on, the screen flashing with bursts of light, laser weapons on rapid-fire, exploding a squadron of fighter jets. On the floor beneath the computer was a baseball bat and glove, a leather football, pair of hockey skates. The walls were covered with photos of what looked like the entire Red Sox lineup. I was glad to see that not all things with the new generation had changed.

On top of an oak bookcase was a framed color photo of Evan in a baseball uniform. Larry stood beside him, grinning into the camera with his arm around his son, the same scene I had witnessed moments ago. Beneath the photo were a dozen or so paperback books, the gruesome titles providing a stark contrast to the happy family scene in the photo. They were all true crime stories: sons who killed their parents, wives who killed their husbands, and every other grisly combination imaginable.

Larry gave Evan a playful slap on the back of his head, told him to pick up his room before dinner, then led me down the hall to Raymond's bedroom. "This is just the way he left it," he said, lowering his voice. "The cops looked through every square inch and didn't find a thing."

The room had a twin bed, dresser, and night table. Otherwise, it was bare. No photos, personal items, nothing.

"Anything removed?" I asked.

"Not that I know of." Larry noticed me staring at the bare walls. "Raymond wasn't much for decorating," he explained. "Evan offered to hang a few posters in here, but Raymond told him not to bother."

Evan and Raymond made a strange pair, I thought; it was hard to picture them together. Unlike Larry and I, who had grown up with basically the same working class background, struggling for everything we got, Evan had all the advantages. A huge house in the suburbs, all the paraphernalia a teenager could want, and doting parents. Evan's confident and cheerful manner was a sharp contrast to Raymond's mumbling sullenness. No mother, an abusive father, and not even a place to call home. The only thing they seemed to have in common was their size, though Evan was a bit huskier.

Dinner was a good old fashioned meal—tender roast, mashed potatoes, creamed onions and squash. No one mentioned Raymond during dinner. It was as if my presence were unrelated to his legal problems. The Conways were so hospitable, and such a close and loving family, that I got caught up in the conversation and pushed thoughts of Raymond and McHugh to the back of my mind. Larry talked about how he had started his own real estate business, cashing in on the exodus of Massachusetts residents eager to leave urban sprawl and crime behind them. I was impressed, though not surprised, with his success, which from the looks of this big house with its huge rooms and plush rugs had been considerable.

Paula steered the conversation toward me. With her gentle prodding, I spilled out my personal history, why Sherry and I never had children (no time), why we split up (incompatibility). Nodding in sympathy to my undoubtedly biased version of Sherry's inadequacies, Paula became the marriage counselor I never had. During this conversation, Evan stared past me toward the parlor, either lost in thought or bored with the subject.

"Things might've turned out differently if only you'd had children," she said. "Evan is such a big part of our lives I don't know what we'd do without him."

Evan groaned, "Ma, like enough, okay?"

Paula reached over and patted Evan on the head. "You'll always be my little boy, and don't you forget it," she said.

Larry said, "Evan's been a big help to me. Especially managing my properties." He tussled Evan's hair.

"Really?" I said, turning toward Evan. "Aren't you a bit young to be managing property?"

"Dad calls it managing, but all's I do is collect the rent and mow the grass. Doesn't take a whole lot of talent."

"You do that at all your dad's buildings?"

"At a few," Evan said.

"I've got a surprise," Paula announced. She jumped from her seat and hurried to the kitchen. She returned carrying dessert. "A special treat for the Bostonians," she said as she placed the dessert in front of me. "Boston Cream Pie. I thought this would be nostalgic."

She cut a piece for me and Larry and what looked like a quarter of the pie for Evan. Forgetting the manners he had shown earlier, Evan dug into his pie, shoveling the brown custard and white cream in his mouth as if he were afraid it would melt. A couple of times he came up for air, looked over at me, and opened his mouth as if to speak.

"So, Mr. Francis," he said finally, wiping white cream from the corners of his mouth, "I was wondering, how'd you get the name 'Dutch'?"

Larry laughed.

"Evan!" Paula said, adding a few extra 'n's to the name.

"Don't worry, Paula," I said, glad to be changing the subject. "I get that question all the time." Then I pointed a thumb at Larry. "Maybe your father will tell you that story, Evan. After all, he gave me the name."

Paula untied the apron and pulled up a chair. "Well, Lawrence?"

Larry needed no prodding. It had been over twenty years since I had heard him tell the story, but he had plenty of practice before then, having told it dozens of times to anyone who would listen. "You sure you want to hear this?" he asked, looking at Evan. Evan nodded.

"Okay," he grinned, rubbing his hands together. "We were sophomores in high school, just beginning to date, so we were still a bit shy around girls." He sipped his coffee, stuck his fork in the pie. "I met this girl Margie at a school dance—a real looker. Son, you wouldn't believe . . ." Without finishing he looked at Paula. "But of course, honey, nothing like you."

"Go on. You're so full of it," Paula said.

Larry told how he had set me up with Margie's twin sister, Mary, for a double date. They were the kinds of blondes you dream about, long straight hair, deep blue eyes, and both built like Marilyn Monroe, at least in our teenage eyes. After going to an outdoor rock concert, we drove to a diner in Watertown for greasy hamburgers. A couple of real romantics. If we didn't kill the girls with our charm, we'd kill them with the food.

"Then the check comes," Larry said, flashing a broad

grin, letting everyone know the punch line was coming. "And Dutch looks at it, starts writing something on the back. I had no idea what he was doing. All I could think of is maybe he's going to slip Mary a love note." Larry shrugged, really getting into the story. I sat back and folded my arms, knowing what was next. After all these years I found myself still annoyed at the way Larry told this story, his demeanor a tad too enthusiastic for my taste.

Larry continued. "But that wasn't it. What he was doing was making calculations. So all of a sudden, out of nowhere, he tells everyone how much they owe. To the penny. I could've died. So I said, 'Hey, what're you doing?' And he looks at me with a puzzled expression—I'll never forget this—and says, 'This is Dutch treat, isn't it?'"

Larry and Evan both chuckled, but Paula stared at them, eyes wide, as if reprimanding them. "I think that's so sweet," she said.

"Then every date afterwards," Larry added, "he insisted it be Dutch Treat. And can you believe it, Mary kept going out with him."

"That is so sweet," Paula repeated, more slowly this time.

When Larry first gave me the nickname, I hated it. It was a mark of my family's poverty, a condition that had always embarrassed my parents. Even though my father worked at least two jobs, they were usually the unskilled blue collar type. When people started calling me "Dutch," I imagined they were making fun of me, thinking I was too poor to pay for a date.

But gradually the name grew on me, especially when I heard some of the alternatives. We had kids called Monk, Turd, Rat, and even Shitfor, short for "Shit for Brains." With all those nicknames, "Dutch" really didn't sound so bad. Hell, it was no shame to be poor! My parents had worked hard for what little they had. I appreciated the value of a dollar and I was damned if I was going to spend every cent I had on a girl. I figured people should pay their own way.

The name "Dutch" stuck, and gradually I became proud to hear people say it.

I resisted the urge to explain all this to Paula and Evan, anticipating that perhaps Larry would fill them in later. Besides, we had more important things to discuss.

I stood up to help Paula with the dishes. She waved at me to sit back down. "No you don't, you're our guest. Lawrence'll help me. You go relax in the parlor, chat with Evan a little bit. Who knows, maybe you could talk him into going to law school."

In the parlor, Evan plopped down on the couch and stretched his arms along the seatback. I sat in the chair across from him. He smiled, then became quiet, staring toward the kitchen where his parents were busily loading the dishwasher.

"Evan, I know it's difficult but do you feel like talking about Raymond? If you don't, that's fine; I understand."

"It's okay," he said. "I feel bad about what's happened, that's all."

"Of course. That's understandable. Raymond was your friend, and you knew McHugh from work."

I thought I detected a frown but Evan said nothing. I continued. "I've learned some things about McHugh that may help find his killer. You know anything about his background? I mean before he came to St. Andrew."

He shook his head. "He never talked about it. I think I knew he was from California somewhere, but that's it. Not like he ever opened up to me."

I told him about McHugh's manslaughter conviction, his time in prison. From the startled look on his face, I could tell he'd never heard any of this.

"Have you told my dad?"

"Not yet, there hasn't been time."

"Hey, Dad!" he yelled toward the kitchen.

From inside the kitchen, Larry yelled back. "I'll be there in a sec."

Evan returned his attention to me. "You think that has

anything to do with McHugh's murder?" He got a hopeful look in his eyes; perhaps his friend had a chance after all.

"Maybe," I said. "But I need to explore it, ask you some more questions. For example, about the phone calls McHugh got at the theater. Your dad mentioned something about them."

"Yeah, I told the police all about that. They didn't seem to care. All's I know is McHugh sure acted funny after those calls. Like he was scared of something."

"He ever tell you who was on the phone?"

"Uh, uh," he said, "though if I was to guess the accent, I'd say Eastern European, Polish, maybe even Russian."

"McHugh ever mention anybody like that?" I asked.

Evan shook his head.

Could this caller have anything to do with McHugh's past? The guy McHugh killed was Hispanic, I remembered, not Polish or Russian. Something didn't click.

"But McHugh did act strange," Evan added. "After one of the games, he came into work, and acted real down about the football game even though St. Andrew had won."

"He say what was bothering him?"

"He was upset about not getting a touchdown in the fourth quarter. He had an open field but stopped suddenly, claimed he pulled a hamstring. But I didn't buy it. At work that night he wasn't limping at all."

I didn't know what to make of this information but decided I'd follow up on it. At this point, I had no other leads; except of course the ones that pointed right at my client.

Evan asked if I really thought there was a chance Raymond could win the case. He seemed surprised, as if the idea of Raymond beating the charges had never occurred to him.

"There's a chance, but I need a lot more evidence than what I have so far."

Paula came in from the kitchen. "Sorry, you two, we'll be right in."

Evan lifted his hand to check his watch. "Take your time, Ma. It's only been like ten minutes already."

I decided to switch subjects. "What I don't understand is you and Raymond being friends. From what I can tell, you two aren't exactly cut from the same mold. What's the deal?"

Evan threw his head back on the seat, looked at the ceiling. Still staring straight up, he said, "Met him out at Hampton Beach. Bunch of us hang out at the casino, mostly my buddies from school, shootin' the bull, playing video games and all. One time I ran into a couple of townies acting tough. I got separated from my friends and was playing this simulated racing game. The townies decided to take over the game and pushed me out of the way. There were two of them so there was nothing I could do. Just as one of them takes hold of the steering wheel, this guy comes up behind them and grabs both of them by the collar and pulls them away from the game. It was Raymond. He wasn't much bigger than them, but he talked so tough that they just gave up. By the time he finished with them, they were happy all he made them do was give me money to cover two games."

He finally lifted his head, brought his arms down to his lap. "We just hit it off after that. For some reason he liked me. Maybe I was the younger brother he never had, I don't know, though I'm only like two years younger. But what an intense guy! Always had big plans, thought he could do anything." Thinking of something else, Evan shook his head back and forth. "He'd say, 'I'm gonna be a millionaire some day, you wait.' I guess I felt like a big shot with him. He had a temper, sure, but he could also be the nicest guy in the world."

"That why you invited him to live here?"

"He got a bum deal. I'm lucky, I've got the greatest dad in the world, but Raymond got screwed. Royally. His old man just dumped on him all the time. So I figured 'why not?', what can it hurt, let him stay here a little while. At first my dad didn't want to, but after he met Raymond and learned about his tough life he went along with it. It was cool having the guy around, we had a good time last summer."

Evan paused, thinking of what he was about to say. "Until he got fired, that is. Then he really went off the deep end. All pissed off, you know, sulking like you wouldn't believe. Losing that job got to him."

"Why? Couldn't he find another job?"

"Guess not. He's not the kind of guy companies are dying to hire. Hates being told what to do. But the theater, that was the first job he ever had he actually liked. Easy work, and you got plenty of time to watch the shows."

I detected a hint of regret in Evan's voice, perhaps regret that his friend had messed up.

"What happened between Raymond and McHugh?" I asked, trying to get Evan back on track.

"They never hit it off. McHugh was a football star, and he let everyone know it. He thought he was better'n Raymond, is what it came down to. Treated him like dirt, said things like 'Your turn to clean the toilets, scumbag.' Always put him down. Hey, the guy wasn't very nice about it, but what can you do, he was huge and he was the boss, at least when Mr. Graham wasn't there.

"During the off-season, Mr. Graham took off two nights a week, let McHugh run the place. Then McHugh would come in when he felt like it during the season. Always seemed to be the same nights Raymond worked."

After a while I realized I was interrogating Evan the way I would any witness. My curiosity got the best of me; I wanted to know what brought young Raymond Walker to the courthouse jail, where he felt compelled to pound his head into the bars. "So what did Raymond do," I asked, "just sit back and take all the crap McHugh gave him?"

"He took it for a while because he didn't want to lose his job. Then one night, beginning of October, we were hanging around the lobby. Some stupid French movie's playing so we were all pretty bored. McHugh was standing behind the concession stand. He shoveled some popcorn into a cup, then walked around the counter. Pretended he was eating it, but dropped it all over the floor. Made like the cup just slipped. He turns to Raymond, says 'Walker, you're in charge of the lobby. Clean up this mess.' Raymond just looks at him, says 'Fuck you, Mr. po-tential All-American, pick it up yourself.' That did it. McHugh went ballistic. Told Raymond he better clean the shit up or he was out the door. Raymond gave him the finger. So McHugh fired him. Just like that."

My lawyer's mind was churning. The prosecution had a motive: you read every day of a fired worker killing his boss, especially when the firing was so unjust. We even have a phrase for it now: "Going Postal." So Raymond went off the deep end, the prosecutor will argue, walked into the theater, shot his ex-boss while he was sitting at his desk. Possible, I had to admit, but something about it just didn't fit. I would expect the police to have a lot more evidence before making an arrest.

Then I remembered something Larry had mentioned at the Chimes. "What did Raymond say then?" I asked.

"Well . . ." Evan paused, looked into the kitchen at his father who was walking toward us.

"What're you two talking about so much? Lot of chatter coming out of here." Larry sat down on the couch beside Evan.

"Evan was filling me in on Raymond, how he got fired and all that."

"Oh, yeah, Raymond's big mouth," Larry said, shaking his head.

Evan turned toward me. "McHugh fires him, then Raymond stares at him, saying nothing. There's dead silence. I thought for sure he was going to sucker him, and McHugh was twitching like he expected it. But all Raymond did was take off his uniform jacket, drop it on the floor in front of him, and say, 'You're a dead man.' Then he walked out without saying anything else."

So the police had more than motive to pin the crime on

Raymond. Couldn't have been a clearer threat. "You tell the police all this?" I asked Evan.

"Had to. Last Saturday, after Raymond had dragged me off to Lake Masabesic to go fishing."

I stiffened. "You mean Raymond asked you to go fishing?"

"Sure, he practically dragged me out of bed. It was so cold I would've been happy staying home."

I tried to make sense of what Evan was saying. I was sure Raymond had told me Evan was the one who had wanted to go fishing.

Evan continued. "And after we got back home, a police car came by the house. The police wanted all the employees to come down to the station to figure out who might've had a grudge against McHugh. They already knew Raymond had been fired and that he didn't get along with McHugh. I had no other choice, so I told them just what I told you." He looked at his father, shrugged his shoulders as if to apologize.

"You did the right thing, son," Larry said. "No question about it. Always tell the truth."

"But he didn't really mean it," Paula said, taking a seat beside Larry on the couch. She continued, "Just a typical boy's threat. Saying 'You're a dead man' didn't mean 'I'm going to kill you.' It's just that macho thing. He'd never do such a thing."

Now I knew Larry and Paula's opinion, but I still didn't know what Evan thought. "What d'you think, Evan? Could Raymond have done it?"

To my surprise, Evan hesitated, grimacing, deep in thought. "I don't know, he was a crazy guy sometimes. Who knows what he'd do?"

Paula interrupted, "Evan, are you saying you think Raymond could actually have killed this man?"

"I don't . . .no, ma, I guess not. Not really. It's just . . . who knows?" He hesitated. "From what Mr. Francis said, it could've involved those strange phone calls."

"What?" Paula said.

After Evan filled them in on what I'd told him about McHugh's manslaughter conviction, Larry said, "This could be the break Raymond's waited for. You think you can prove this in court, Dutch?"

"Whoa, whoa!" I held out my hands. "Who said anything about proof? All I got right now is speculation; unless they change the rules of evidence, that will get me nowhere in court."

"At least there's hope," Paula said quietly.

We talked some more about Raymond. The morning after the police questioned Evan, they came by the house with one warrant for Raymond's arrest, and another to search the house. Evan was awakened by the sirens but did not get out of bed until he saw the flashing blue lights reflecting off the walls of his room. When he looked out his bedroom window he saw Raymond leaning over the hood of Larry's pickup truck, his hands cuffed behind his back.

Evan talked about the police searching the house, how disappointed they were not to find anything. "They kept saying, 'Where's the money?' and 'Where's the gun?' I told them I had no idea what they were talking about." As if reliving the fear he felt during the search, he shivered, hugging his arms to his chest.

"This has been so upsetting for all of us," Paula said. "You know, Dutch," Paula leaned forward, looked me in the eye. "I wondered why Larry wanted to hire a civil lawyer to help Raymond. You know what he said?" She answered herself. "Even though he hadn't seen you for over twenty years, he felt like he still knew you, that you were the same guy he trusted and admired way back when; and if anyone could help Raymond, it would be you. After meeting you, I think he's right."

Larry nodded his agreement and assured me he'd take care of my fee. Just send him the bill. I was happy to hear that, especially with cash flow on the slow side. I told him I had a lot to do: a meeting Monday with prosecutor Laflamme, then Tuesday with Raymond's girlfriend, Cathy Sayewich, in

Dover. Larry said he'd met Cathy a few times, and would be happy to go with me, help break the ice, get her talking.

Feeling nostalgic, I took a disposable Kodak camera from my jacket pocket and turned it on. "Smile," I said, pointing it at all three. They all smiled as the flash went off. I took photos of all three together, then each individually, then Paula took a few of me and Larry. Pretty soon all twenty-four frames had been used up.

As close as this family was, they hadn't hesitated to take in Raymond, an unfortunate youth who seemed—at first glance at least—to have little in common with them. It was touching the way this family had adopted Raymond. There was a lot more to ask them, but everyone was worn out from discussing the case. At Paula's urging the conversation switched to more of our boyhood stories. Paula brought out another bottle of wine, poured a glass for each of us, even Evan, and we drank a toast.

"To days gone by," Larry said.

Maybe it was the wine, or the sight of these three caring people staring at me, hope and trust in their eyes. Or maybe I was susceptible to flattery, especially from an old friend. But I was feeling very good right then, glad about reuniting with my old friend and meeting his family. I raised my glass and looked at Larry. "And to days ahead," I answered, tapping my glass against his.

CHAPTER 8

CONCORD was twenty miles north on I-93, an easy drive past the state liquor store snuggled amidst tall pine trees. As I tossed a token into the toll basket, I yawned, still feeling the effect of recent sleepless nights. I rolled down the window and felt the crisp air hit my face. I had to be alert for my first meeting with Deputy Attorney General Peter Laflamme.

I thought of the information I'd gathered so far: the strange phone calls, McHugh's manslaughter conviction, his prison time. Could the calls have something to do with that case? Perhaps the victim's family sought revenge. Or maybe someone he met in prison was paying him a visit. Or could the calls have something to do with the theater? The robbery? Could McHugh have been involved in a robbery gone haywire? But why would someone murder him? Did McHugh know too much?

I couldn't fit these pieces together. The main thing I lacked was evidence. And without evidence, I thought it best to keep my theories to myself, and not tip off Laflamme. On the other hand, I hoped somehow to get Laflamme to educate me about his case against Raymond.

Anxious to meet my adversary, the prosecutor, I stepped on the gas, pushing the speedometer past sixty-five. Then I turned up the volume on the radio, tuned to one of New Hampshire's many country and western stations. Waylon Jennings's twang filled my ears: "Mama don't let your babies grow up to be cowboys. Let them be doctors and lawyers and such."

The attorney general's office was located near the supreme court building, about a half mile from the Merrimack County courthouse where I had made a few appearances. When Laflamme walked out to the lobby, he greeted me like an old friend. "Dutch Francis. Good to meet you," he said, extending his hand. Although he was thin and wiry, his handshake was hard and tight, a pretty decent effort at intimidation. I suppose I should have expected as much from a prosecutor whose name, loosely translated, meant "The Fiery One." But there was nothing fiery about his appearance. With short dirty-blond hair and a faint mustache, he looked meek, almost boyish. There were wrinkles in his white button-down shirt, and his obviously polyester polka dot blue tie was loose and hung two inches above his belt.

He led me down an uncarpeted corridor past an ancient copy machine. Taped to the top was a piece of yellow legal paper on which was scribbled "Out of Order" in bold black print. Laflamme's office was long and narrow with a wide window nearly the length of the wall looking over a row of maple trees. There was a desk at one end and a round glass table at the other. He sat down at the table and nodded to me to do likewise. As I pulled out a chair, I looked through the table to the rug, and noticed that Laflamme's brown shoes were badly scuffed around the toes. His pant cuffs were at flood level, three inches above the shoes. A New Hampshire native, I thought, feeling a little like my stuck-up ex-wife. Still, I was starting to doubt what I'd heard of Laflamme's reputation.

"What in the world made you get involved in a murder case?" he said, opening a manila file. "You usually work the civil side, don't you?"

"I like a little variety. Keeps me on my toes." I paused as he shuffled through some papers, then pulled out a thick document.

"Hmmm," he said, looking up. "So how'd you pick up this one?" As if we were just old colleagues shooting the breeze.

"I like to take cases where I have justice on my side," I said with a straight face.

"Justice?" he said frowning. "You kidding? You got yourself a loser here." His frown turned into a smug, cocky expression. I had an urge to smack the smirk off his face, but the memory of my recent indiscretion with my own client still lingered in my mind. More battles were won with smarts than fists, I knew, so I decided to play a little chess to bait Laflamme into giving me information.

"There're a few things you probably don't know about Raymond Walker." I said.

"Oh?"

"Yeah, you may change your tune."

"I doubt it, but I'm all ears."

"He's not just some punk like most of the defendants you deal with. His mother died when he was a boy. Father couldn't take it, started drinking too much, and abused his son. Raymond basically raised himself. Other than a few minor scrapes with the law, none involving violence, he's got a clean record." I then gave him a preview of my opening statement, the sad story of the hard life of Raymond Walker, as least as much as I had learned at that point.

During my whole speech, Laflamme kept quiet, leaning back in his chair, rolling his eyes toward the ceiling as if to say, "You've got to be kidding me." When I finished, he leaned forward, both hands on the table. "Come off it. We've all had conflicts with our fathers. I hear that bleeding heart crap all the time. 'He had a tough life, nobody ever loved him. So let's not *punish* him for his crimes, let's *understand* why he commits them.'"

"But Raymond didn't commit any crimes, and I think you know it."

"He's just a poor misunderstood boy, that the kind of bullshit you want me to believe?" He was getting excited, his voice high-pitched.

"Come on. You . . ."

"Well, bullshit. Your nice boy Raymond Walker pulled the trigger and shot Brian McHugh. That's all there is to it." Laflamme was riled now; he had fallen right into my trap and was itching to tell me how strong his case was.

"The kid made no secret of the fact he hated McHugh," he continued. "And he threatened to kill him—in front of witnesses, no less."

"Give me a break. You're going to prosecute my client for making the kind of threat angry people make every day of the week. Sounds flimsy to me. I'd heard you were a smarter prosecutor than that."

Before I finished, Laflamme was on his feet, pointing a finger straight at me, his mouth open, the words building up inside. When he did speak, his voice quivered. "You don't know shit about this case, do you? Well, let me help you out. Your boy Raymond ain't too smart. Not only did he threaten McHugh in public, he blabbed about his plans to rob the theater. That enough probable cause for you?"

Laflamme's eyes were bulging. As he pointed, his arm shook. But my satisfaction at forcing Laflamme into revealing his case was tempered by what he had said. My grip on the chair arm tightened, and as his sarcasm increased, I thought I would pull the arm right off.

"So who's the hot witness, one of your usual police informers?" I asked calmly.

Laflamme hesitated, then sat down, shaking his head. "Uh, uh. No way. I've said too much already. You'll find out in a few weeks anyway when the judge grants discovery.

And when you hear the tape of the witness's statement, you can cry in your sleeve."

I felt like crying in my sleeve right then. As it was I had a terrific headache, worse than after my fight with Raymond, both sides of my head throbbing. With my index fingers I rubbed my temples so Laflamme wouldn't see them pulsating.

"But I'll tell you what I can do," he continued. He turned on the speaker phone. "Dawn, can you bring in the medical examiner's report in the Walker case? Dawn?" He pushed the office button. "State employees! See what I have to put up with? I'll be right back."

Laflamme left me sitting at the table, looking through the glass at my own shoes, which seemed to shine less brightly than when I had arrived. To relieve the tension I stood up and walked around the office, reading the wall hangings. Behind Laflamme's desk there were framed diplomas on the wall, carefully arranged in a circle. He had never left New Hampshire: law degree at Franklin Pierce, bachelor's degree at Dartmouth, and high school diploma from St. Paul's. Though Franklin Pierce and St. Paul's were both in Concord, they were miles apart academically. St. Paul's was a nationally known prep school, a worthy competitor to the other bastions of New England's wealthy families—Exeter and Andover. Laflamme's family must have had some bucks to send him to St. Paul's. Yet he had attended Franklin Pierce, a mid-level law school at best, and certainly not one St. Paul's (or even Dartmouth) graduates normally attend, preferring the more prestigious Ivy League schools.

Laflamme's schooling was a marked contrast to my own; indeed, we seemed to have taken opposite routes. I graduated from public school in Boston; and through hard work such as my summer street sweeping job, generous scholarships, and a lot of luck, I managed to scrape through Harvard and Harvard Law School. As one of the few poor city kids in my class, I was always somewhat of an oddity to my Harvard classmates, most of whom had never met someone who had actually got a job by filling out an application instead of having a prominent relative push his weight around. Until my move to New Hampshire I continued along the same track as my fellow classmates—big corporate law firm, rich clients, high pay—and left behind my roots.

In a sense, Laflamme seemed to have done the same, only in reverse. He went into public service, as did many Franklin Pierce graduates. I was sure there weren't too many St. Paul's graduates collecting a paycheck from the government.

In the center of the circle of diplomas, like a bull's-eye on a dartboard, was a green rectangular chalkboard with three lined columns. Atop the left column was written: "Convictions," the middle: "Acquittals," and the right: "Mistrials." So the rumors were true; Laflamme kept his own won-loss records. If accurate, the numbers in chalk in each column certainly gave Laflamme reason to be proud. The score was: convictions—60, acquittals—2, mistrials—1.

As I pondered the challenge of Laflamme's string of trial successes, the door shot open. "Here you go," he said, handing me a large envelope. I hoped he hadn't noticed me gawking at his trial record. I pulled back the flap, glanced at the report. I'd have to study it later to see how much it hurt Raymond.

Laflamme leaned back in his chair, smirking again. "First I tell you I got motive," he said. "With this, the medical examiner's opinion on time of death—you know what else I got?" Laflamme knew a lot more than he was revealing; that much was obvious.

"You got nothing," I said with as much bluster as I could manage. "This thing's full of holes." I pushed the report back into the envelope and walked toward the door. I turned the handle, anxious to get out of there.

"Wrongo-bongo. What I got—and you know it—is opportunity." He turned his chair toward me, arms folded. "Yup, I got opportunity."

"And I have an innocent client," I said and walked out the door.

A few miles outside of Concord, still annoyed at Laflamme's attitude, I decided to take some action. I flipped open my cell phone, called the office. "Yvette, I need some help."

She sighed. "Nice of you to check in."

"You're welcome," I said. "I missed you too. You have any luck finding that investigator Carter Butterworth told me about?"

"Hold on, boss, I've got it somewhere." She put the phone down, kept me waiting a bit longer than seemed reasonable. "You still there?"

"Keep me waiting any longer and I'll be in Manchester already. Then I won't need your help."

"Yeah, right, we've been through that before. You want the name or not?"

"Yes, please."

"Okay, that's better. Name's Glenn Hedges. His office is just across the street."

I told her to call Hedges, see if he could come right over. No point in wasting any time. "By the way, any messages for me?"

"Yeah, there's a bunch here. Two interesting ones. Someone named Tim Murray, said there's a rugby match a week from Saturday and he needs you. Who the heck is he?"

"A lawyer I met at court a few weeks ago. We hit it off once we discovered we both played rugby. We've jogged together a few times since then."

"Rugby?" Yvette said, disgusted. "Don't you have enough to do here?"

I ignored her tone of voice and explained that I didn't play any more. When I reached forty not so long ago, I decided to stop playing, primarily because of the pain on Sunday mornings after a game. All my muscles ached, and the scrapes and raspberries along my legs and knees stung so much, I felt as though I were under continual attack from a nest of angry hornets. Sundays meant spending the whole day recuperating on the couch. I'd read the *Sunday Globe* cover to cover and listen to Sherry nag me about playing such a barbaric sport.

"But Murray still plays—he's only thirty-five and captains the Concord Area Touring Side."

"The what?"

I repeated the name. "But they like to be called CATS."

"CATS? These are grown men?"

"Come on. It's good fun. Murray tried to recruit me before. I told him I was too busy but would help out if the team were ever shorthanded."

"Now I've heard everything. You're actually going to play this game?"

The brake lights on the car ahead of me came on and I slammed on my brakes. "You jerk!" I yelled.

"Excuse me?" Yvette asked.

I switched lanes and passed the car, a black BMW. The driver was a woman who was frantically searching for something on her seat. I hoped it was a lit cigarette. "Not you, Yvette." I told her what had happened. She grunted, dubious. I asked her about the other interesting message.

"From your dear ex-wife. She called twice, an hour apart. The second time she said to tell you that you can't ignore her forever. And then she said she hopes you're having fun up there in Vermont."

"Vermont?"

"That's what she said. I told her this was New Hampshire. She said put down Vermont anyway. What a lovely person!"

I tried to picture Yvette and Sherry meeting, but the image just didn't click. I shuddered at the thought.

She started saying something, but her voice faded out and the phone went dead. I was on a flat part of the highway, far from mountains, tunnels or anything else that would disrupt phone service. I couldn't help wondering if Yvette had disconnected on purpose.

I thought about Tim Murray's call. With the stress of preparing Raymond's defense, strenuous physical activity would do me some good. I punched in Murray's number and his secretary said he was on a call. "I'll wait," I told her.

After a short period, Murray came on the line. "You can't do it, right? Too busy or too old, what'll be your excuse this time?"

"Surprise," I said. "No excuses this time, I'll play."

"Alright! You're going to have a great time. We're playing Portsmouth. Bunch of big, strong guys. They all played high school football together—Portsmouth High I think—so they know each other's moves. It'll be a tough match."

"Don't expect much," I warned him. "I'm not in the best of shape."

He laughed, no doubt remembering how he'd outsprinted me the last time we ran together. Guiding the steering wheel with my knees, I wrote down directions to the field in Concord, not far from the office of Monsieur Peter Laflamme.

CHAPTER 9

THE sky over Manchester was covered with black clouds, and as I entered the city limits, solid white balls of hail starting bouncing off my windshield. The black clouds darkened the streets, appropriately reflecting my mood. Turning on Elm Street, I flipped on the headlights. My thoughts turned to Laflamme. If he really had a witness, then it could be all over—conviction number 61. Clarence Darrow himself would have a tough time winning a case with these facts and I knew I wasn't any Clarence Darrow.

Yvette was frantically working on the word processor, and barely looked up when I came in. "Hello, rugger," she said. "Been in any good scrums lately?"

I laughed. Sometimes her smart-aleck comments helped relieve my black mood. "Not yet," I said. "But I will on Saturday. Want to come watch?"

She looked up. "Please!"

"You're really cruising on that keyboard," I said, changing the subject. "Why the big hurry?"

"I want to finish this motion to continue before Russell

arrives so you can review it," she said, glancing at her watch. "He should be here any minute to take me to lunch. And believe you me, that's a big deal."

Before Yvette finished speaking, the door opened. It was Russell.

"Hiya Dutch," he said. A camera hung from his neck, swinging from side to side. "What's cookin'?"

I pointed to Yvette, pounding away at the keyboard. "Right now, I'd say your girlfriend."

Russell smiled. "Look at those fingers work. She does have the magic touch."

"At least someone does," Yvette shot back with a smile. "Let me finish this, you two."

Russell sat in the client chair across from Yvette. He came by the office at least once a week, usually to drive Yvette home, sometimes to chit-chat. A freelance photographer with regular assignments from the *Union Leader* and other local newspapers, he also taught photographic composition part-time at Manchester Technical College. The first time I met him he showed me his portfolio, a combination of color foliage scenes and black and white portraits, including a few stunning ones of Yvette. If she ever realized her potential as a model, I'd be out of luck.

Like many artists, Russell was sloppy with finances and depended on Yvette to keep the household in order. Occasionally I could hear her yelling on the phone: "What do you mean you forgot to pay the bill? I left you a note on the counter."

Russell was thin, about six foot two, with a new scraggly beard. The tufts of black whiskers were too thin to cover the bald spots on his cheeks. Yvette had told me he decided to grow the beard because he admired mine so much. "It looks terrible," she complained. "I wish he'd shave it off."

Yvette looked over at Russell slouched in the chair, his legs stretched straight in front of him. "Russell," she said sternly. "Sit up. This is a law office, not a photography studio. Can't you act respectably for five minutes while I finish?"

Russell shook his head back and forth. "Always on me.

Do this, don't do that! Dutch, how do you put up with this woman all day long?" I grinned without answering and walked toward my office. Russell had always seemed a bit immature to me; what Yvette saw in him I never understood.

Yvette answered for me. "Because he recognizes quality," she said. "That's how." She printed out the motion and handed it to me. "We need to file this before four," she said. "Oh, and that investigator Hedges will be here at 12:30," she said as she ushered Russell out the door. "Good luck, he sounds like a character."

HEDGES knocked on the door at precisely 12:30. I don't know what I was expecting, but when I let him in I couldn't hide my disappointment. "You were expecting Sherlock Holmes, maybe?" he said, reading my mind. Hedges would never be mistaken for Sherlock Holmes—a hippie version of Columbo maybe, but definitely not Holmes. He had long silver hair tied in a ponytail and was dressed in baggy pants and a cardigan sweater, making me wonder exactly what Carter meant when he had said that looks can be deceiving.

Out of habit I offered him a cup of coffee. He declined and took a seat across from my desk. "No thanks, I don't do caffeine. You called me to do a job, so let's get to it." My initial impression was changing; I liked his no-nonsense attitude.

I explained Raymond's case and showed him the newspaper articles about McHugh. "What's not here," I said, "is that McHugh was a convicted felon." I told him about McHugh's manslaughter conviction.

He shook his head. "Hey, that's great investigative work. You sure you really need me?"

"Yeah, I think I do. I'd like to concentrate on the legal work, leave the investigating to a professional." I gathered more documents on the case and filled him in on all the facts I'd accumulated so far.

He leaned over my desk, writing notes on a legal pad. I waited for him to finish. "So how do you know Carter?"

"Butterworth? He's seen me testify a few times when he was the courtroom clerk; I guess he liked what he saw. I give the jury the straight scoop, no bullshit."

I asked him what he charged, thinking how scarce cash would be over the next few months.

"Fifty bucks an hour, best deal in town," he said grinning.

I had my doubts about that, but I said, "Okay, that's fine." On a yellow legal pad I made a list of things I wanted him to do. The first was to track down Laflamme's witness, the one Laflamme claimed heard of Raymond's supposed plan to rob the theater. Although I would get discovery from the prosecution in a few weeks, I didn't want to wait. I also told him about McHugh's phone calls at the theater. "Call the phone company," I said, "try to weasel some records out of them, then go over to St. Andrew, maybe someone'll want to talk about McHugh." I finished the list and handed it to him.

I heard the door to the outer office open. Yvette marched in to find both of us staring at her, "Dutch, I have to . . . Oh, I'm sorry. I forgot . . ." She took a few steps backward.

I stood up and pointed to Hedges. "Yvette, this is Glenn Hedges." I turned to Hedges. "Yvette is my trusted assistant."

"Honored to make your acquaintance," Hedges said, standing up. He walked to Yvette, clasped her right hand in both of his, his eyes tracking Yvette's body. "You are as lovely as you sounded on the phone," he added. His gaze paused at Yvette's breasts, prominently displayed in a V-neck blouse. So much for Columbo. I interrupted Hedges before he drooled on the floor. "Call Yvette if you need anything else."

"I most certainly will," Hedges said. As he followed Yvette out the door, he turned and gave me a wink. I did not wink back; in fact, it took all the restraint I could muster not to give him the finger.

CHAPTER 10

MY elbow slammed against the car door as we rounded a sharp curve on Route 101 just past Lake Masabesic, where Raymond and Evan had been fishing the day before Raymond's arrest. Larry braced himself against the dashboard and yelled at me to slow down. I straightened the wheels just before hitting the soft shoulder. A cloud of fallen leaves fluttered into the air.

"I can see your driving hasn't improved," Larry said. "Who do you think you are—a teenager?"

"Sorry, everything's under control now," I said, keeping both hands on the wheel.

I slowed down. Larry cautiously leaned back into his seat, his arms folded. He was tense, quiet, as if my driving—or perhaps Raymond's case—were more than he could handle. We drove in silence for awhile, gazing at the maple trees, some nearly bare, others with bunches of red and orange leaves still clinging to the branches. I was thinking about all the drives Larry and I had taken as teenagers, usually in his Grandpa's old car, a beauty—bald tires, burning oil, and a wire coathanger for an antenna.

I glanced over at him. "What're you thinking about?"

He sat up, reached in his shirt pocket and pulled out a pack of cigarettes. "Oh, just about Cathy, poor kid. Baby on the way and the father locked up, for God knows how long." He shook out a cigarette and pushed in the lighter.

"Don't give up on Raymond yet," I said. "We've got a long way to go."

Larry lit the cigarette and took a thoughtful drag. "You know, when Raymond first moved in, I had my doubts. Since his father had kicked him out, I figured he had to be a troublemaker. But after Evan filled me in on Raymond's family life, I understood him better."

"Yeah, no question he's had it rough."

He grimaced. "You ever see his legs?"

"No. Why?"

"Ask him to show you sometime. Father used the belt on him. Buckle left a few dozen scars."

I told him about Raymond's old neighbor, Mabel Considine, and the beatings she'd heard John Walker administer to his son.

"No wonder," he said, shaking his head, "Raymond acted as though he'd died and gone to heaven when we took him in. Christ, even when Evan was giving me all kinds of trouble," Larry continued, "I never hit him. But God, there were times when I sure wanted to."

"Evan? I find that hard to believe. He seems like such a well-behaved kid."

"True enough these days, but it wasn't always that way." He folded his arms, looked out the side window. "We gave Evan everything he wanted. New baseball glove? He got it. Color TV and DVD player for his bedroom? No problem. We spoiled him rotten. Paula warned me it would happen but I didn't listen."

I wasn't surprised at Larry's indulging Evan. Even while growing up, Larry was obsessed with possessions. He al-

ways got jealous when someone had something he didn't—
a record album, the latest hockey skates. He just had to have
the same. It made sense that he couldn't bear to have his son
lack anything. Still struggling to keep up with every kid in
the neighborhood.

In a soft voice filled with regret, Larry explained how his
problems with Evan came about. When the real estate market boomed, he started to work longer hours, develop more
properties, and take bigger risks for bigger payoffs. And to
keep politicians from imposing any more controls on real
estate developments, he had to attend political fundraisers
throughout the state. Of course he spent less and less time
with his son.

"One day—Evan was about twelve—I came home and
saw him beating up a Chinese kid who had just moved into
the neighborhood. Tall skinny kid with glasses. And Evan
was just punching the crap out of him. Had him down on the
ground, whaling on him, yelling 'Fuckin' geek, Viet Cong
asshole.' I couldn't believe it. The other kid was yelling,
'I'm not Vietnamese' over and over, but Evan ignored him."

Larry took a deep breath, ground out his cigarette in the
ashtray. "I pulled Evan off and brought him home. It was
then I found out that this wasn't the first time. I talked to him
and he let it all out, told me he could beat up anyone he
wanted to. He bragged to me that he did it all the time. Then
I talked to his friends too; at first they clammed up but I kept
at them. Finally, I found out what my son had been doing.
Evan had become the neighborhood bully, beating up any
kid who looked at him sideways. Twelve years old, can you
believe it? And not just the smaller ones, he took on bigger
kids too and licked most of them."

At Paula's urging Larry took Evan to a psychologist.
After three sessions alone with Evan, the shrink asked to
meet with Paula and Larry. Evan was angry at Larry for
never being around, the shrink told them. As Larry told me
this, his eyes became teary. Somehow Evan's adolescent

mind had come to the conclusion that Larry stayed away from home because he didn't like him anymore.

"So Evan was taking out his aggressions on other kids, when inside he really wanted to beat on me. Threw me for a loop, I'm telling you," Larry said softly.

"But now he seems like such a well-adjusted kid," I said, having a hard time picturing the All-American boy I'd met acting this way.

"He is. But it wasn't easy. I made a real effort to spend more time with him. Got home every night for dinner. Talked to him every chance I got. Lot of talking. That sure helped." He nodded his head up and down, smiled. "And you wouldn't believe what I talked to him about."

"What?"

"Oh, some stories about Boston, mostly about you and me."

"No kidding? This I got to hear." I had no idea what stories about Larry and me could possibly help Evan. Perhaps Larry had been telling some tall tales, hoping to impress his son.

"You know, things like selling newspapers to sick people at the hospital for a nickel over the cover price, begging tickets from priests at BC football games, scalping them, and then climbing the fence to watch the game."

I looked at him, surprised. "I thought you wanted to straighten the kid out, not show him what a delinquent his dad was."

"The point was to show him how to be creative and not just follow everyone else. You have to admit, we found a lot of ways to have fun. And we didn't really harm anybody," he said. Suddenly he turned toward me, loosening the seat belt so he could shift his knees. "You should've seen his eyes light up when I told him about collecting Coke caps."

"Coke caps!" I laughed out loud, slapping the steering wheel. "I had forgotten all about that." Coke caps were an enjoyable part of my childhood, especially when I was eleven and twelve.

Coca Cola had a contest where they put photos of pro football players on the inside of bottle caps. The idea was to collect caps with all the players' photos, then glue them on a special sheet over their names. Naturally Larry and I were fans of the Boston Patriots. Even now football stars pale in comparison to my memories of Gino Capelletti kicking field goals or diving for Babe Parilli's bullet passes, or Jim Nance carrying three defensive linemen on his back while stampeding for a first down. When you filled a sheet with about fifty Coke caps you turned it in at the Coke plant and got a prize, usually a team pennant or a miniature helmet. But you needed five sheets—over 200 bottle caps—for the big prize—a leather football.

Larry and I wanted a football in the worst way, so we scouted the neighborhood for every business with a Coke machine. We drew up a map showing where each machine was located, and even noted which businesses had friendly employees who would open the machine to get us the caps. We covered all kinds of businesses—gas stations, coffee shops, factories, even barrooms. It was surprising how many businesses sold Coca-Cola. Even the fire station had a Coke machine. The best times were when we arrived just as the Coke deliveryman was emptying the machine. He'd just pour the bucket of caps into our paper bags, and we'd shake the bag all the way home, listening to the clicking sound of bottle caps crashing into each other, in our minds as exciting as the sound of gold nuggets rattling around a miner's pan.

Even with this elaborate scheme, we had a tough time filling five sheets. We got about half way there, then things slowed down. Things sure looked hopeless. It seemed like we would never get that football. Then Larry came up with a brilliant idea, using a yard of string and a small magnet.

After tying the magnet to one end of the string, we would drop it down the cap receptacle, clamping the other end tightly between our fingers. Since the walls of the receptacle were metal, and attracted the magnet, our aim had to be accurate or we'd never reach the caps. So, with all the deliberation of a fly fisherman recoiling his rod, we carefully placed the magnet in the center of the receptacle, letting out enough string to avoid pulling up short. If our aim were off a fraction of an inch, the magnet would slam against the wall with a loud, distressing "thud." We would try again and again, sometimes having to endure four or five "thuds," each time like a knife piercing our hearts, before hitting the bullseye. There was no mistaking the sound: "click," a soft, gentle sound, the sound of success.

But the battle was not yet over. The toughest task still remained: pulling the caps up the receptacle without losing them. Since the magnet would stick to one of the walls, you had to slide it gently up the wall, being careful not to make any sudden movements that would shake the magnet from the wall and send it—with your cluster of caps—bouncing against the opposite wall, where the caps would invariably get knocked off and crash back down the chute.

With practice Larry and I became expert at tossing the magnet straight down the receptacle, then tugging on the string, delicately, like a fisherman uncertain how securely he has hooked the fish. A cluster of caps would appear at the opening; the one not holding the string would reach in, pull out as many caps as his short juvenile fingers could reach, then the other would tug the string again, lift the magnet all the way out, and with it the rest of our bounty. We tossed the caps, sticky and sweet-smelling from Coke spillage, into our paper bags, which were soon shopping-bag size.

That year we collected thousands of Coke caps and turned them in for dozens of leather footballs, each stamped "NFL-AFL official size," and enclosed in a clear plastic bag.

I didn't know what to do with all those footballs and gave a lot away as birthday gifts. Larry proved, even way back then, to be a shrewder businessman than I was. Instead of giving his footballs away, he sold them. He became so caught up in selling them he forgot to save one for himself. He put signs on telephone poles all over the neighborhood, offering the footballs at $15 apiece. Pretty soon parents of kids we hardly knew were calling him to buy a football for their kid's birthday.

Smiling from these memories, I braked hard as an Irish setter, wearing a muzzle, ran in the front of the car. I reached over instinctively to hold Larry back, just as my father used to do to me. He lurched forward but his shoulder belt caught him before my arm could do much good. "Hey, thanks," he said, "but maybe you should pay attention to what's in front of you, not worry about me."

I nodded, still thinking of the Coke caps and Larry's talent for making money. "So," I asked, "how much did you make selling those footballs?" When we were kids he had never given me a straight answer.

He shrugged, "Oh, probably four, five hundred bucks. Bought a new bike, some hockey skates, things like that. Not bad for a few thousand bottle caps."

Not bad indeed, especially for doing something we really enjoyed. But I still wondered how all this helped Evan. "What you're telling me," I said, "is Evan all of a sudden started saving bottle caps and turned into a nice kid."

"Hardly," he smiled. "Wasn't quite that easy. All's I know is he started opening up to me, talking about things he liked, things that bothered him." He took a long drag from the cigarette before crushing it in the ashtray. More serious now, he said, "Maybe he just needed me to talk to him, listen a little more. Before then we really hadn't talked much. Can't put my finger on it, but for the first time it was almost like we had become . . . I don't know, like I was his older brother."

The car moved smoothly now, even around the curves. For the first time since Larry had called me, I felt confident in our friendship, confident that despite the years apart we did have something genuine. As I took the exit for Route 108 and headed north toward Durham, home of the University of New Hampshire, my thoughts turned to Raymond Walker. I was sure his father had never shared his past, confided in him, treated him as if his opinion meant something.

Unlike Evan, Raymond never had a chance to work out his adolescent resentments and get rid of his mean streak.

Both of us were silent during the remainder of the drive into Durham. Larry again pushed in the cigarette lighter, opened his window a crack and lit another cigarette. I thought again of our childhood. The Vietnam War protests, the race riots, hippie movement, none of them meant a thing to us; we were too young. Our concerns were simple; we worried about acquiring bottle caps and winning footballs, and gave no thought to the problems of the world around us. I wondered if Larry, sitting beside me puffing on his cigarette, was having similar thoughts.

As we silently passed by an old red brick building in downtown Durham, our gaze was drawn to a red and white sign on the window of a coffee shop. The sign read: "Drink Coca Cola." I shuddered a little bit when the radio began playing Bob Dylan's "My Back Pages"—"I was so much older then, I'm younger than that now."

CHAPTER 11

WE passed quickly through Durham with Larry deciphering the chickenscratch directions he'd taken from Cathy, and finally made our way to Dover. Cathy's house was located a few blocks off Back Road in a rundown neighborhood near the junction of the Cocheco and Piscataqua Rivers. I pulled up next to a dirt path that passed for a sidewalk, sending a cloud of dust toward Cathy's weatherbeaten house. At one time the house had been painted white, but only streaks of faded white were now visible among patches of brown shingle. We pushed open a wooden gate hanging by its top hinge, and walked gingerly on the stone trail leading to the house. When Larry pulled open the screen door, chips of black paint fell at our feet. He looked at me and shrugged.

Larry's knock on the front door produced a muffled sound as if the door were hollow. A few seconds later we heard a high pitched voice ask, "Who is it?"

"Cathy, it's me, Larry Conway."

"Oh, okay, just a sec," Cathy said as she pushed open the bolt, turned the lock on the doorknob, then opened the door a crack. The face of a teary-eyed, red-faced girl appeared in the opening, the door still secured by a chain lock. Satisfied it really was Larry, she quickly said, "Sorry," then added, sniffling, "can't be too careful nowadays, even out here in the sticks."

"Hi Cathy," Larry said when the door finally opened.

Cathy leaned toward him, awkwardly put her arms around his shoulders, sobbing, "Isn't it just awful? Poor Raymond."

Larry said, "It's okay, Cathy," and patted her back. When her sobbing slowed, he said, "I want you to meet Mr. Francis, the lawyer I mentioned. He's an old friend of mine and has agreed to help Raymond."

As Cathy extricated herself from Larry, I reached out to shake her hand. "Oh, thank you so much, Mr. Francis," she said, taking my hand. "I sure hope you can help." She squeezed harder. I was starting to think she'd never let go.

She finally did and led us through the porch and into the parlor. Dressed in corduroy pants and a bulky white sweater that was partially covered by a flowered apron, she hid her pregnancy well. With all the crying, her eyes were dull and glazed, the skin around the eyes puffy and red. She looked very plain but her looks certainly weren't helped by all the crying she'd obviously been doing. Her hair was pulled up loosely on top of her head, and as she walked she kept pushing back a stray strand that hung over her face.

"I'm, uh, finishing up bakin' some cookies," she said, nervously rolling her hands in the apron. "I like to bake when I'm upset. Why don'tcha make yourselves comfortable, an' I'll be right back."

The parlor floor was covered by a light grey rug, so worn in parts, especially around the legs of the furniture, that you could see the white matting underneath. The room had a musty odor as if spilled water had been left to dry in the rug. It smelled old and dreary. The couch was so beat up that when Larry and I sat down, the springs gave way and we sank down so our knees were level with our chests.

"She's had a tough life, as you can tell," Larry said quietly, looking toward the kitchen to make sure Cathy couldn't hear. "Father ran out years ago and her mother's been raising her alone. Raymond says they can barely pay the rent." I looked around the room at the beat-up furniture and frayed carpet, then feeling the couch spring getting a bit too familiar with me, pushed myself up.

Larry shook his head. "Tough life," he repeated.

I walked to the fireplace. On the mantle was a photo of Raymond standing in a pile of leaves with a long rake in his hands. In the background was the rear of a house; the white splotches of paint leaving no doubt it was Cathy's house. I picked up the photo for a closer look. Raymond had a forced crooked grin but still looked happy and content, a different person than the one I had recently met.

"That was just before everything happened," Cathy said as she walked in, noticing me staring at the photograph. She was balancing a tray of chocolate chip cookies on the fingertips of one hand. "He promised my mom he was gonna clean up the place, paint the house and everything. That's gonna have to wait, I guess."

She turned away from the photo and held out the cookies, insisting Larry and I take one. The cookies were flat, like someone had pressed them with an iron, chocolate oozing from both sides. Cathy handed us each a paper napkin. I put my cookie on it and when I lifted it off, the chocolate stuck to the napkin. When I took a bite, the cookie stuck to my teeth. Not the way I preferred interviewing a key witness.

Cathy turned to place the cookie tray on the coffee table. As she bent over, the cookies spilled off the tray, landing on the table and sliding to the floor. The cookies shattered into small pieces and crumbs, all over the frayed rug and coffee table. Holding the empty tray and staring at the broken cookies, Cathy started crying, the tears streaming slowly down her face. Then she lifted the tray over her head and threw it on the floor.

"Oh, shit!" she screamed. I looked at Larry. He had stopped chewing and was holding half a cookie in his hand, the other half still in his mouth. "Shit!" Cathy screamed again.

"Cathy," Larry said softly.

"I can't stand this. I just can't stand it."

Larry stood up and put an arm around Cathy's shoulder. "It's okay, we'll clean this up. No problem."

"It's not the cookies," she sobbed. "I just can't stand what's happening to Raymond. We were just gettin' our lives together. Why, why, why?"

She turned to Larry and buried her head in his chest. While Larry gently stroked her hair, she continued sobbing and moaning, why, why, why. I felt useless standing around so I decided to finish my cookies. When Cathy had regained control of herself and separated from Larry, all three of us bent down and picked up the pieces. We put them back on the tray where they made a small mound of crumbs.

After Cathy returned from bringing the tray to the kitchen, Larry told her that I had some questions for her. "Okay, s-sure," she said. She untied her apron and sat on the couch beside Larry. I remained standing, not wanting to take any more chances with the couch spring. Instinctively Cathy kept pushing her straying hair off her forehead, though each effort was fruitless.

"I already told the police everything I know," she said. "They came by a few days ago with that asshole, Laflamme. Acted like he didn't believe a word I said."

"That's his job, Cathy," I said. "Don't take it personally."

"Well, he didn't have to be so mean." She was pouting, her lips quivering.

"You're right, and I promise not to be mean, but I may ask you some of the same questions. Okay?"

She looked at Larry, then back to me and nodded.

"Good," I said.

Some lawyers like to lead the witness on, suggest the answer they want to hear. An unsophisticated witness, even an honest one, will often adopt that answer. Sometimes it's not even a conscious thing. There's a human tendency to believe someone who's supposed to be smarter and more knowledgeable, so the lawyer's suggestion gets planted in the witness's mind. Eventually the witness becomes convinced that what the lawyer says is the way it really happened. But I avoided that technique, for both ethical and practical reasons. A competent cross-examiner would destroy that kind of witness and expose holes in the witness's memory, thereby making all of the testimony suspect. No, I wanted the real truth, Cathy's truth.

I quizzed her gently, not wanting to let on how important her testimony would be. She could make or break the case. If she backed up Raymond at least we'd have a chance. Since the prosecution would attack her credibility, I listened for any hint of exaggeration, any shading of the truth. At this early stage, it was important for me to evaluate her credibility myself so I could advise Raymond on whether to proceed to trial or cop a plea.

"Cathy, how long've you and Raymond been going together?" I asked.

She put her finger to her lips, thinking. "Long time," she said finally. "Like five, six months maybe. It was that holiday—you know—the one where all the old men dress up in soldier costumes." I glanced at Larry who was rolling his eyes. After a few seconds, Cathy snapped her fingers. "Memorial Day, that's it. We was hanging at Hampton Beach. All the kids chill there. Kids from Concord, Manchester, you know, all over." She got a dreamy look in her eyes, thinking about what was probably the most romantic moment of her young life. I wondered if she really were as dumb as she seemed. If so, Raymond was in even more trouble than I'd thought.

"I seen Raymond hanging around, but never really said 'boo' to him. Then he walks up to me and my girlfriend Kerry, asks if he can bum a smoke. Kerry goes to hand him one, and he looks at me, says, 'I want one of hers.' I coulda died. He was so cute."

I rested my elbow on the mantle. Cathy looked down at her belly, which was barely showing even without the apron, and began stroking it again, like Aladdin with the lamp. "And we been goin' out ever since," she said, looking up. "And now we're goin' to have a baby," she added, again looking at her belly. A tear streamed down her cheek. Everything about her told me she was in love with Raymond and would do anything for him. Unfortunately, the jury would get the same message.

I steered the conversation toward Halloween night. "Cathy, I need to know everything you and Raymond did Halloween night." I paused while she wiped the tear with the back of her hand. "You feel like talking about that?" I pulled a tissue from the box on the coffee table and handed it to her.

She wiped her eyes with the tissue. "That's okay. I can talk about it, no problem." In a monotone, without any more tears, she told me Raymond was with her the whole night, handing out candy to the trick-or-treaters, then watching television. Every few minutes I interrupted and asked her to go over the details to see if she would contradict herself. I wanted to find out if she would make up something if I pretended it was important. Her answers reassured me. At least, I concluded, she would not lie.

"What time did you fall asleep on the couch?" I asked.

She shook her head. "I don't remember, but it was late. Probably after midnight. I know we watched one of those talk shows, okay? So it was like after eleven."

I looked at Larry who was sitting with his arms folded, not saying anything. "And we didn't even do nothing," Cathy added coyly, as if that were an important bit of information, especially in view of her current condition.

Now came the delicate subject. "Cathy, I want you to think real hard about this. What time did you and Raymond wake up?"

This was one of those moments that gives lawyers ulcers. When a witness tells you the key bit of evidence, the case-breaker, all you can do is hope. You're helpless.

Cathy paused, stared at me, then at Larry, as if looking for us to help her. "I don't know exact times, okay?" she hesitated. "But it was late, I know that. Real late."

"Well, what was on TV? You remember?"

She shook her head. "Some talk show. And it was on regular TV; we don't get cable 'cuz Mom can't afford it. But I don't think it was Leno or Letterman or any of them. I remember it was that goofy guy."

"You mean Conan?" Larry asked.

"I think," she said. "Yeah, that could've been it."

Larry turned to me. "Conan gets off about what? One thirty? Two?"

I shook my head. "No idea, I don't watch those shows."

"If it helps any," Cathy joined in, "I seem to remember the credits coming on, you know, like at the end of the show. And the late news was starting."

That was something anyway. Not quite what I was looking for, but a start. I pressed on. "Did you look at your watch?"

"Mmmmm . . . no, I really didn't," she said. Sensing my disappointment, she rubbed her eyes. "I'm sorry," she said.

"That's okay," Larry interrupted, trying to calm her down. "All anyone can ask for is what you remember. Just do the best you can. Is there anything else that might give us some idea of the time?"

As if on cue, there came a grinding of gears, metal on metal, a sharp click sound, then "coo, coo." The cuckoo clock was going off. I waited for her to mention it, but she sat silently, waiting for my next answer. I had no choice but to ask her directly.

"What about the cuckoo clock?" I asked hopefully. "Did you hear that?"

She took her hands away from her eyes, looked at me wide-eyed. "That's right. Yeah, I did. That's what woke us up. Now I remember, Raymond made some crack about breaking that damn thing. He hated the noise." She shook her head. "I forgot about that when the police were here."

At least now I was getting somewhere. "Did Raymond leave right after the clock went off?"

"Yeah, right away. He put on his jacket, gave me a kiss and left." Her lips and cheeks puffed out as if the memory would again make her cry. "That's the last time I saw him, before all this happened," she said, her lips again quivering. Alright, I thought. Raymond may have an alibi after all.

"How often does that thing go off?"

"Every hour," she said.

"Tell me something, Cathy. Did you look at the clock when Raymond left?"

She stared at me as if I had switched to a foreign language. I would have to spend a lot of time preparing her before putting her on the stand. "Yeah," she tilted her head. "But what difference would that make? I know it only goes off when the big hand hits twelve, no other time."

For some reason she just didn't get it. Exasperated, I looked at Larry for help, but then something struck me as odd. "Larry, did you hear that?"

"What?" he said, puzzled. "I didn't hear anything."

"The cuckoo clock, it stopped." Larry looked at me as if to say, so what? I turned to Cathy. "Can we take a look at the clock?"

"Sure, it's over here," she said as she got up from the couch and led us to the hallway leading to the kitchen. On the wall was a bright green cuckoo clock with a water wheel on the side. Cathy opened the small doors in front, revealing a yellow bird. "He pokes his head in and out when it cuckoos," she said. I stared at the bird, the shingled house, the pine cones hanging from chains, and the clock face. That explained why the cuckooing had stopped.

"For Christ's sake," Larry said, understanding. "It's eleven o'clock, that thing's off by three hours."

"How long's the clock been broken?" I asked Cathy.

"As long as I can remember," Cathy said. "The hour hand was always stuck on two."

That was why I heard only two chimes instead of eleven. A chill ran up my spine. Larry raised his eyebrows but said nothing. Both of us knew the significance of what Cathy had just said. My first avenue of defense was just destroyed, convincingly. Without the clock, there would be no evidence corroborating Raymond's time of departure. Goodbye alibi defense.

Sensing our disappointment, Cathy said, "I could get it fixed."

"Good idea," I answered, trying not to sound irritated. She was clueless.

"Does Raymond have any chance at all?" With both hands clutching her belly, she appeared to be giving extra support to her unborn child.

Larry put his arm around her. "Of course he does, Cathy," he said soothingly. "It's okay. This was just one line of defense. There're others. Don't worry, Mr. Francis'll take care of things."

Before leaving, I told Cathy I would be in touch with her to prepare her to testify at the trial. As we walked toward the car, Cathy waved at us tentatively, a worried expression on her face. Larry turned toward me, looking less hopeful than his words had indicated.

CHAPTER 12

OUTSIDE of Durham, Larry started puffing on a cigarette, filling the car with smoke. I rolled my window all the way down. I considered lecturing him on the risk of lung cancer, but knowing Larry, decided against it.

"Looks bad, doesn't it?" he asked, as I pulled into a line of traffic.

"Yeah," I said quietly. "But who knows . . ."

Without speaking, Larry rolled down the window, then tossed his cigarette out, the first time he hadn't used the ashtray on the trip. I slowed down to turn onto the highway and looked over at Larry leaning out the window, the wind blowing his hair wildly, or at least what was left of his hair. Rolling the window back up, he turned to me. "What I don't understand is what happened to the gun?"

"Good question," I agreed. "And where would Raymond get his hands on a gun anyway? Manchester's not like Boston, where you can pick up handguns on most downtown street corners."

"I've been wondering that too," Larry said. "Unless . . ."

He froze. He stared straight ahead, but I could tell he was concentrating on me.

"What?"

"Nothing," he said quietly.

I wondered what he was thinking about, but decided to be polite and not press him. Forty-five minutes later, after a mostly silent drive with Larry napping every few minutes, we pulled into Manchester. As we approached Mammoth Road, Larry woke up.

"Slow down," he said. "At the light, turn left."

"Why?"

"We're real close to the theater. Let's stop by and check out the scene."

We turned south on Mammoth Road and passed a row of triple decker homes, a common sight in this working class city. Next to the triple deckers, on every other corner, it seemed, was a mom and pop business: a variety store, an Italian deli, even a Greek sub shop with signs in both English and Greek. At a fork in the road we curved left and the scenery changed. On both sides of the road were fast-food franchises: Burger King, McDonald's, Kentucky Fried Chicken, Dunkin Donuts, the entire panoply of America's culinary pop culture. Separating the greasy food joints, appropriately enough, were gas stations and quick-change oil shops.

After passing through three sets of flashing yellow lights, we came upon the Cinema Manchester. I signaled to turn into the parking lot when Larry said, "Oh, oh. We may be out of luck." He pointed to the marquee, which announced that the theater was still closed, over a week after the murder. Below the "Closed" sign, in black block letters the sign added, "In memory of Brian McHugh, St. Andrew's star halfback and our beloved assistant manager and friend." Larry frowned and shook his head slowly as I pulled into a parking space.

"Hey, we're here," he said. "Let's check it out, see if anyone's around. You never know, the cleaners might be working and'll let us in."

Above the box office was a small marquee announcing a special Halloween party featuring *Night of the Living Dead*, the gory film of corpses rising from the dead and turning everyone else into ghouls just like them. I shook my head, realizing that this black-and-white tale of death and gruesome rebirth was the last flick Brian McHugh had ever watched.

There was no one in front. The glass doors were locked. We peered through the doors, holding our hands to our eyes to shield the reflection from the afternoon sun. There was a light on toward the back of the lobby. Larry shook the glass door loud enough to bring someone out. A short, thin man with grey sideburns bounded across the lobby and pushed open the door.

"Sorry, we're all closed up," he said. "We had a . . ." He hesitated, looked more closely at Larry. "Oh, Larry, it's you. Didn't recognize you for a minute there. Good to see you."

"Hi, Phil," Larry said, shaking his hand. "Sorry to bug you like this. I know how awful you must feel with all this going on; we all do. But I wanted to take a look around with my friend, Dutch Francis."

"Phil Graham," Larry said to me as I reached over and shook Graham's hand. "Phil's the manager," Larry explained. "He was working the night of the murder, probably the last one to see McHugh alive." I remembered the newspaper article: Graham was also the assistant football coach at St. Andrew.

"That's right," Graham agreed, bowing his head. "If I'd only stayed fifteen more minutes, Brian'd probably still be alive."

Or you'd be dead too, I thought.

"Hey, Phil," Larry said softly. "Nothing you could've done."

"I don't know, maybe you're right," Graham said slowly, staring at his feet. Suddenly he looked up, more cheerful, "What's the matter with me, making you guys stand around outside? Come on in, I can put on some coffee, show you around."

He led us to the box office, just inside the door. He poured coffee grounds into a filter and switched on the coffee machine. "So how's that fine boy of yours?" he asked. "I haven't seen him since this happened."

"All right, I guess," Larry said, hesitating. "Still upset, of course. We're all having a hard time believing Raymond could've done it."

"I don't know what to think anymore. Never would've figured Walker for a murderer but he always was an ornery sonovabitch," he said. "I'm sure you know, him living with you and all. Never liked anyone telling him what to do. I can remember how pissed off he used to make Brian." He shook his head. "Cops seemed to think that was a big deal. I'll tell you this: if he did it, I hope they string him up by the balls."

I was starting to think this visit was a waste of time. Graham obviously cared a great deal about McHugh so why would he want to help Raymond's lawyer?

The coffee was ready and Graham poured some for each of us in a Styrofoam cup. I added sugar and powdered creamer in mine. The coffee was hot so I had to sip slowly; still I nearly burned my tongue. I leaned against the doorway with my back to the lobby while Graham continued, "So how's Walker doing? I understand he claims to be innocent."

"Yeah, he sure does," Larry said. Hesitating, he looked at me, obviously struggling with telling Graham I was Raymond's lawyer.

"So what can I do for you gentlemen?" Graham asked.

"We were just driving by," Larry said, stretching the truth, "and I thought it might be interesting to see things myself, get a better picture of what happened. You see, I have a hard time believing Raymond would do this. I know I can't solve anything by looking around but at least it might give me some peace of mind."

I waited for Larry to tell Graham that I was defending Raymond, but he said nothing. I struggled with telling him myself while Larry continued. "I've been in the theater a lot, but never in the office where the shooting took place."

Graham rubbed his hand over his bald head and in one gulp drank the rest of his coffee. "I coached Brian at St. Andrew, you know. Got him the job here. Best goddamn running back we've ever had. Absolute best." He looked right past us at the wall, as if he were talking to himself, thinking out loud. "I told him to take the weekend off but he refused. He'd been under a lot of pressure lately. Tough game against Army. Had that breakaway, sure touchdown, and damn if he didn't fall down at the twenty. No one touched him. Damn hamstring pull. Some fans kept calling him and giving him a hard time, cursing him out."

"Fans?" I asked.

"That's what he said, though I got my doubts whether they had any love for St. Andrew."

I was feeling pretty awkward standing there, with no apparent reason for my presence other than being a friend of Larry and being with him when he "happened" to drive by the theater. I didn't want to cause any friction between Graham and Larry by revealing my status, but I did want to get some information. So I decided to take a casual approach.

"Ever learn the names of any of these fans?" I asked.

"Naw, Brian never told us. He just kept calling them 'crazy fans.'" Then he hesitated, deep in thought. "You think maybe those fans had something to do with the murder?"

I shrugged. "What do I know? Seems odd that he was getting these calls right before he got murdered. Did you tell the cops about them?"

"Only what I told you," he answered somewhat defensively, as if to ask "just what kind of idiot do you think I am?"

"Sorry," I said. "Didn't mean anything. I was wondering if there's a way to track down these fans."

"I wouldn't know how to do that. Brian never gave us their names, phone numbers, nothing."

Something Graham said gave me an idea. "What about

your phone bills? Maybe Brian had to call them back, return a call maybe. The bills might have the phone number on it."

"You think?" He turned toward Larry. He obviously didn't want to trust anything I said. I didn't blame him either because he had no idea who the hell I was. "You really think there's a chance Walker could be innocent, Larry? Last thing I want to do is help the sonovabitch if he's guilty."

"No question," Larry answered. "I got to know Raymond pretty well and I don't see him doing this. I really don't."

"Well, then, I suppose it's worth taking a look at the bills. If I remember right, even local phone numbers are on the bills these days. I usually toss them in a desk drawer. Be right back."

He got up and walked out of the box office to the rear of the refreshment stand. He unlocked a door and disappeared behind it, leaving Larry and me to tour the lobby.

"You're not going to tell him?" I asked.

"What?"

"That I'm Raymond's lawyer, perhaps?"

"Why tell him more than he needs to know?"

I shrugged, still uncomfortable with deceiving Graham. I glanced around the lobby which looked like it had been designed by a drug-crazed hippie on a bad trip. The walls were covered with mirrored paper, shiny silver speckled with bold purple strokes. I blinked my eyes from the reflection of the blood-red carpet on the walls. The wall also reflected a distorted image of Larry, his reddish face broken by purple patches.

The refreshment stand was filled with row after row of candy. On top was the popcorn maker, "Hot Buttered Popcorn," the sign announced, and beside that the soda machine, three piles of cups reaching to the top. The wall behind the stand was decorated with cardboard cutouts of skeletons and witches. Behind a glass frame was an old black and white movie poster for *Dr. Jekyll and Mr. Hyde*.

Graham emerged from behind the stand and handed Larry a manila envelope. "Here's September and October. I hope this helps." Graham continued walking through the lobby, motioning for us to follow. "Come on, I'll give you a tour."

Inside the theater, the lights were turned low. The front curtains were partially open, leaving a two-foot gap where the two curtains met, revealing a patch of the white screen. "Just a sec," Graham said. He walked to the front of the theater, pushed aside the curtain against the right side wall, and reached in. Soon a motor cranked on and the curtains came together, eliminating the white screen.

"Up there's the projectionist's room," Graham said, pointing behind us to a glass-enclosed room above the seats. "Kind of an odd fellow, that Nathan Goode. On his off days he works in the Combat Zone in Boston, one of those porno joints, the Pink Pussycat, something like that." He shook his head.

"And these here're the film canisters," he said, pointing to two circular metal canisters on the floor by the stairs. Each canister had a tag tied to the handle identifying *The Night of the Living Dead.* "I haven't had the energy to return them to the distributor yet," Graham explained.

We walked back to the lobby. Larry stopped and pointed to the door beside the refreshment stand. "That where Brian was shot?" he asked. Graham nodded silently. After a couple of seconds, the three of us standing there quietly, Larry asked, "Mind if we go on up?"

Squinting his eyes, Graham said, "Why not." He opened the door and led us up a flight of stairs. Halfway up the stairs was a window overlooking the landing. The window was a weighted wood frame. Outside the window was an alley leading to the parking lot. Right below was a green dumpster. Graham noticed me studying it. "Police say the bastard stood on the dumpster, pulled himself up to the window."

"How'd he get the window open?" I asked, noticing the latch was now securely locked. There was also a safety lock near the middle, an inch-long knob that snapped back and forth so you could stop the window from being raised any higher than the knob.

"Police think it wasn't locked. I told them I usually check

all the windows right after the last show starts. Maybe that night I screwed up and forgot." His voice cracked. He paused, staring at the window. With a thin cracked knuckle he rubbed his eye. After a few seconds, he recovered and continued, "You know, I would've bet this thing was locked when I left, but shoot, I can't say for sure."

"What's with this?" Larry asked, pointing to the knob.

Graham moved in front of him. "Safety lock," he said. "Adds extra security. If the window's unlocked, someone couldn't get in because the knob would stop the window from being lifted more than a few inches. No way anyone could crawl in."

With a hefty tug, he pulled the window open. It moved only six inches before being stopped by the safety knob. "I can't say if the window was locked that night, but I'm sure the knob was turned. It always was."

I pushed the knob back and forth. It moved easily, without much effort. "Any way someone could maneuver this knob from the outside?" I asked.

"Funny you should ask," Graham said. "One time, must've been a couple months ago, I forgot my keys. Everyone was standing around, waiting to get in. We were all staring at the window, trying to figure out a way to climb in. We got the window up the six inches but that was it. Then somebody tried to push the safety knob with a stick but couldn't get it to move. Then one of the ushers—Evan I think it was—asked me if I had a magnet in my car toolbox. I have every damn thing in the world in there so I went and looked and sure enough there was a magnet there. Evan tied the magnet to the stick, reached in the window, attached the magnet to the knob, then turned it open. A brilliant move, I thought."

I looked at Larry, who wore a strange expression, a mix between bewilderment and admiration that Evan had paid attention to his Coke caps story. "Anyone see him do that?"

"Yeah, Goode was there, all the workers . . . I guess," he said. "And there were a few patrons hanging around. I'm sure they saw the whole thing." Nothing like teaching people how to break into your building. Then, realizing what I was getting at, Graham said, "You think one of . . . ?" he paused. "My God, I bet that's it."

It was worth considering. If the murderer were present at Graham's "break-in," that would narrow the suspects to a few unknown patrons and the workers. "Was Raymond there that time?" I asked, hoping to eliminate that possibility.

Graham hesitated, scratched his head. "Don't remember. I can't say. Maybe Evan would remember." I decided I'd check with Evan later.

There was another problem with that break-in, and I pointed it out to Graham. "So the window was unlocked that time too, you mean?" I asked.

Embarrassed at his lack of security, Graham frowned. "I guess so," he said.

We walked to the top of the stairs and Graham opened the office door. There were piles of fingerprint dust on the carpet and furniture. It looked like the police had covered nearly every area of the room. Graham pointed to a large mahogany desk, the top covered with stacks of papers. "That's where Brian was sitting, counting the money, getting ready to make the bank deposit in the night drop next door. Because of the midnight show, we made a ton of money that day. Plus there was the rest of the week's revenues." His voice became soft. "I suppose I got a bit lax about making the deposits every night, but hell, we never had any problem before." He paused and stared at the floor. "I was going to make the deposit that night but . . . Brian insisted. He could see I was tired, told me to go home early, get some sleep." He let out a heavy breath. "So I left him here—alone."

We stood in front of the desk and Graham picked up a stack of papers. "Jesus Christ!" Larry groaned. Graham turned away and walked to the other side of the office. I bent over to get a closer look. The desk was covered with a huge burgundy stain, unmistakably a blood stain, shaped like a child's map of the United States. There was a row of letter compartments above the desktop lined with green felt, and splattered with burgundy drops. From the concentration of stains in the center of the desk, I guessed that McHugh had fallen forward onto the desktop, his head coming to rest as if he had been sleeping. The murderer must've snuck up behind him, stuck the gun in the back of his head, then shot him at close range. There were some small, darker stains on the letter compartments and on the wall above them. If I was right about the angle of the shots, then these stains were probably from the splattering of McHugh's brain fragments. It was cold-blooded alright, McHugh never had a chance.

I was unprepared for the wave of emotion, a strange fear combined with a sickening feeling in my stomach, that came over me. In my many years of corporate practice I never had occasion to visit a murder scene. It was eerie to stand within a few feet of where someone had been killed. Although the blood was dry and the brain fragments removed, the scene still had a powerful effect on me. Larry had been right about my getting some ideas by looking at the theater. The first idea it gave me was that civil practice wasn't so bad. Criminal defense was a scary business.

Graham walked across the room, averting his eyes from the desk. He had turned pale and I guessed he was having an emotional reaction of his own. He stared at a map of a large lake, extending from the floor to the ceiling. "Lake Winnepesaukee," he explained. "Where my cabin is. Brian was going to spend Thanksgiving up there with me and the family. Take it easy, do a little hunting and fishing. Now . . ." He turned around and stared at the blood-stained desk, his eyes moist. "Oh, who the fuck cares anymore?"

CHAPTER 13

THE image of McHugh's blood-stained desk haunted me all that night. The next morning I decided to take a break and work on my civil cases. I had to dispel that terrible image from my mind so I asked Yvette to bring me a half dozen personal injury files. Even my clients' gruesome auto accident injuries didn't bother me as much as Brian McHugh's violent death.

After school had let out later that afternoon, I called Evan at home. Larry had already told him about our visit to the theater and to expect my call. I mentioned Graham's story about Evan climbing in the window.

"Oh, yeah," he said, "It was the craziest thing. Everyone was standing around watching. Good thing Graham always forgets to lock the window or I would've had to break it."

I stiffened. "You mean Graham didn't lock it every night?"

"No way. He was supposed to, but he always forgot. He didn't worry much because of the safety knob."

"Graham told me how you used a magnet to get the latch

open. I'll bet you got the idea from your father's story about Coke caps."

He laughed. "Yeah, he told that story enough times. I couldn't forget it if I tried."

"Any idea who was there when you climbed in?"

"Hard to say. I worked with different ushers, could be any of them. Nathan Goode, the projectionist, he was probably there. And there were a few patrons there too. You think the murderer might've seen me climb in?"

"Don't know, but it's worth checking out. You remember if Raymond was there?"

He exhaled into the phone, thinking. After a few seconds, he said, "You know, I think he was, but I can't be positive. We worked a lot of the same shifts so it's a good bet." He paused as if he had more to say.

"You want to tell me something else?"

"Well, you probably should know. Raymond and I used to joke about how Graham often left that window unlocked, how easy it was to get in. And I did talk to him about the magnet trick; he thought I was a genius."

That keeps my client on the list of suspects, I thought. Since Raymond knew about the magnet trick, it didn't matter whether he had seen Evan open the window. But there were other names on the suspect list: Nathan Goode, for example.

"What can you tell me about Goode?"

"A goofball. He was usually the first one at the theater, to set up the film and all. I think his mind went batty from being cooped up in that little room all the time. Guy sat up there reading *Hustler* and *Penthouse* magazines, had a stack three feet high. I don't even want to think about what he did up there once the lights went out and the film came on."

"Graham told us about his job at the Pink Pussycat. How'd he and McHugh get along?"

"Well, not buddy buddy, but okay, I guess." He paused. "You know, I remember one time McHugh saying he'd heard something about Nate getting arrested in Boston. He wouldn't tell me any details, except it was during a raid at the Pink Pussycat. But Nate never talked about it."

"That might be worth looking into," I said. "Anything else you remember about him?"

"It kind of pissed me off that Nate didn't come to McHugh's funeral, the only employee not there. That's all I can think of."

Before hanging up, I told Evan to give me a call if he thought of anyone else who saw him climb in the window. So far I had only four people who definitely knew how to open the window: Graham, Evan, Raymond and Goode. Graham was definitely not a suspect and Evan had no reason to kill McHugh as far as I could tell. That left Raymond and Nathan Goode. It was strange that he hadn't attended McHugh's funeral. But did he have a motive to kill McHugh? I wondered if there might be something to Goode's porn fascination and his arrest in Boston.

I decided to call Hedges. It looked like there would be a lot of work for my new investigator. His answering machine came on. I left a message for him to call right away. I mentioned that I had some phone numbers for him to research and that I wanted him to track down Nathan Goode at the Pink Pussycat. Mr. Glenn Hedges seemed like the kind of guy who would enjoy a trip to Boston, particularly to the Pink Pussycat. Probably even cut his fee.

An hour later, Hedges called back, sounding pleased as punch to be talking to me.

"Hedges," I said, ignoring his cheerful "hello," "I've got some more work for you."

I told him about my visit to the theater and how Graham had given us the bills. "See if you can track down the guy McHugh spoke to," I said, promising to fax the bills to him. "Oh, one other thing: what about Goode, can you check him out?"

"I'm ahead of you on that one, chief. Soon as I got your message I put in a call to the Pink Pussycat in Boston. Your

Goode man works Thursdays and Fridays, the afternoon shift."

"Might be worth taking a drive down there, see what he knows."

"You bet," he said. "I'll go down Thursday afternoon." Then he laughed, a high-pitched cackle. "Just in time for the 3:00 p.m. show."

I stayed in the office until five, studying the six-inch pile of mail that had accumulated in the last week. Two sets of interrogatories, three document demands, five deposition notices: all of them would have to be continued. It was time to call in the markers, get the payback on breaks I had given opposing counsel. Of course, I was asking a lot; some lawyers might not want to delay their cases for my convenience. Then I would be stuck spending needless hours filing continuance motions and throwing my calendaring fate on the mercy of the court. All for poor Raymond Walker, who was turning into a full-time pro bono case. I made a note to put together a bill to send to Larry.

After grinding through about half of the paperwork, I decided to take a walk to clear out the cobwebs. I crossed Elm Street and walked half a mile down one side before crossing over. I was staring at the display of new mysteries in the bookstore window and dreaming of the old days when I actually had time to read novels, when I saw Larry's wife Paula walking out of the post office. In knee-high leather boots, checkered skirt, black leather jacket to her waist, she looked like a college student. Her hair was pulled back in a bun, similar to the way Sherry used to wear hers, but without the severe, serious look Sherry always affected.

"Dutch Francis, how are you?" She smiled.

"I'm doing fine," I said, "though Raymond's case has been keeping me way too busy." We sat down at a wooden bench on the sidewalk, warmed by the late afternoon sun.

She shook her head. "I know you've been working so hard. Lawrence told me about your visit to Cathy's and to the theater. I don't know how you can be a lawyer and remain sane."

"I'm not sure I have," I said, laughing.

"I mean the stress must be incredible. You have to know all that law and make sense of confusing facts. You don't know who's lying or who's telling the truth. It would drive me crazy, that's for sure."

"Well, I'm making some progress," I said. "But there's still some bad stuff Raymond's got to explain." I told her about my meeting with Laflamme. "I've got some leads my investigator is checking out. With any luck we'll find the real murderer."

"I sure hope so," she said quickly. "This has been incredibly hard on Lawrence. I've never seen him so preoccupied; the case is always on his mind. And he's been in the foulest mood." She looked toward the sky, rolling her eyes. "Snapping at Evan like you wouldn't believe. You'd think it was Larry's friend who was in jail. Everything's so different now. Larry has trouble concentrating at work; he's distant at home. And Evan sits in his room, the door closed, reading those awful crime books he likes so much. Sometimes I think we're all going crazy, that this is some terrible nightmare we'll never wake up from."

I put my hand on her shoulder. "I'm doing everything I can think of to help Raymond," I said. "If there's a way to get him off, I'll do my best to find it. For you and Larry as well as for Raymond."

"Oh, Dutch, I really appreciate everything you're doing. And I know Larry does too. Seeing you again was so important to him. Too bad it had to involve all this. But when everything's over, we can all get on with living our lives, can't we?" She put her hand over mine, still on her shoulder, and squeezed my fingers.

I smiled and stared at her a bit longer than I had a right to. Since moving to New Hampshire I had been so immersed in my practice that I had made no effort to date. On weekends I would take long drives on New Hampshire's back

roads. I took up fishing again, bought a map of the state's
lakes and streams, which seemed to be everywhere, and
learned how to catch perch, catfish, trout, and fish I'd never
heard of. At first I liked the solitude, alone in the country by
a beautiful sunny lake, trying to hook a big one; it was a far
cry from the bustle of Boston. After a few months, though,
I began thinking of finding female companionship. Nothing
serious, just someone to take to dinner, share laughs with. I
had been working up the nerve to ask out a female attorney
I had met at a deposition when Larry called with Raymond's
case. Since then, dating had been out of the question. Even
if I had the time, my stress level had been so high that I
would be miserable company. But sitting there with Paula
Conway, staring at her wholesome face and slim figure, her
hand squeezing mine, my thoughts took a dangerous turn.
Luckily common sense took over and I resisted my adulter-
ous urges, saving my friendship with Larry. The lucky
sonovabitch, I thought, feeling incredibly jealous as I pulled
my hand away.

I brought the discussion back to Raymond. "I have to be
straight with you, Paula; unless I find a more likely suspect,
Raymond's in big trouble. The deck's stacked against him."

She nodded. We sat quietly for a moment, each lost in our
own thoughts. Paula moved first, slipping her purse over her
shoulder and standing up. "I'd better be going," she said.

"Of course," I said, also standing. I reached out to shake
her hand but she grabbed my shoulders, pulled me toward
her and kissed me on the cheek.

"Thank you for everything," she said before walking off
and leaving me to melt into the sidewalk.

CHAPTER 14

ON Friday morning, I stopped at the office before going to court. Hedges was waiting for me. He hadn't bothered calling for an appointment.

"I got eight minutes," I told him. "Then I'm out the door and on my way to court."

"Okay, I'll make it fast." Hedges sounded like an excited child on Christmas morning who'd gotten everything he asked for. "You gotta see this projectionist." He grimaced. "Hair so greasy it stains his collar. Dark, baggy eyes, bright green pants with four-inch cuffs, so long they dragged on the floor." Hedges shook his head in disgust. Just what I need, I thought, a fashion critic. I urged Hedges to get to the point.

"Well, the guy's upstairs in this smelly room, smoking a cigarette and watching this disgusting movie. Two women, bare-ass naked doing some things to each other you wouldn't believe." He whistled, then grinned. "You've never seen anything like this in Manchester, that's for sure."

Hedges' abrupt rambling made me impatient. "Hey, Hedges, I thought you were a no-nonsense guy. But I'm having some doubts. First you're a fashion critic, then a movie critic. You've been here nearly three minutes, and I still know nothing about Nathan Goode. What the hell am I paying you for anyway?"

"Calm down, I'm just warming up." He put his hands out. "You might want to lay off the caffeine for a while. You're getting awful worked up." I smiled and forced myself to lean back in my chair.

"Anyway, this Goode guy ain't really a good guy." Hedges chuckled at his own humor. "Kind've a creep actually. One arrest in Boston: attempted arson."

"No kidding," I said.

"Seems he was working at another sleazy joint in the Zone—the Naked Eye or something—and dropped a lit cigarette on some trash on the floor. It started burning and before you know it the smoke alarm's going off. Goode claimed he fell asleep and it was an accident. But the arson investigator didn't believe him, thought Goode wanted to get even with his boss for not paying him overtime. Charges were dropped though. Not enough evidence."

I paused, wondering what relevance arson had to a robbery or murder. Once again, Hedges anticipated my thoughts.

"I know you've got to run," he said, "so I'll fill you in later about the phone bill."

He was playing with me. I looked at my watch. If I didn't leave now, I'd be late for my appearance. "I've got a few minutes," I said, trying to act casual. "What do you got?"

His speech suddenly slowed from 45 to 33 1/3 RPM's. "No perp yet," he said ever so slowly, "but I do got an address. Over on Cheshire Village Road. Remember that fire a few weeks back where that old man died? *Union Leader* played it up big."

I told him I'd read about it in the paper. An elderly man had died because the firemen were late responding to the alarm. Seems they were across town enjoying a lobster dinner at another station when the alarm came in. The *Union Leader* was clamoring for the fire chief's resignation.

"Anyway, half a dozen calls came from there. I should have the exact apartment in a day or so."

"So what do you make of that?" I asked, getting up to leave.

"Don't know yet," he said, rising with me. "All's I know is that the fire department strongly suspects arson. Maybe it's a coincidence, what with Goode having an arrest for arson."

"You think Goode had anything to do with the Cheshire Village Road fire?" We walked together down the hall to the stairway.

"Your guess is as good as mine. But one thing I do know: Goode couldn't have called the theater from Cheshire Village Road when he was working upstairs from McHugh."

"Makes you think, though, doesn't it." My original confidence in Hedges was returning. He really did know what he was doing. "Keep digging, Glenn. You want my guess, I'd say you're onto something."

AS I pushed open the swinging doors to Judge Winston Taylor's courtroom and gazed at the blue and gold New Hampshire state flag above the raised judge's bench, I felt a deep satisfaction to be practicing law. In my last years in Boston I had lost that feeling and, like many lawyers, became disillusioned with my career choice. Moving to New Hampshire had changed all that; since I now represented individuals who truly needed help—as opposed to corporations that used my skills to protect their purses—my sense of purpose had returned. As a lawyer I found once again that I could make a difference. For the first time I viewed the courtroom as a place where people could find justice, rather than a tilted playing field where lawyers earned huge fees and justice was something to be manipulated.

Several lawyers stood around the clerk's desk with Laflamme in the middle, leaning against the desk, chatting up a storm. As I walked by, I overheard one of the lawyers ask him how many murder cases he'd tried. Laflamme answered, saying twenty to twenty-five. Then he was asked how many he had lost. Just then he noticed me and looked directly at me while answering, "None, never lost a one."

He smiled as he broke from the group and walked toward me, offering his hand. I laid my briefcase on the counsel table and shook his hand—opponents, yet for the time being, still gentlemen. He wasted no time trying to establish an upper hand. "You read through the medical examiner's report?" he asked. No doubt he thought the report was helpful to his case.

I said that I had. "I appreciate your handing it over," I said. The medical examiner's report had placed the time of death around two o'clock. Actually, if not for the busted cuckoo clock, the report would have been great for the defense. But I thought I could still use it, perhaps, to raise a reasonable doubt about whether Raymond had time to kill McHugh.

I wanted to test Laflamme's goodwill so I asked him, "Didn't you forget something?"

He looked at me, puzzled. "What's that?"

"The witness tape," I said, "if there is one."

His head jerked up and he cracked a smile. "There is one alright! My smoking gun, if you'll pardon the expression. And you'll be getting it in due time, I'm sure, after we talk to Judge Taylor."

He obviously didn't want me to get a head start on investigating his witness. So much for goodwill.

He started to turn away, but stopped suddenly. "After you listen to the tape, you might want to reconsider a plea. My informants tell me Judge Taylor wants to handle this one himself. You might not know that he's one of St. Andrew's biggest boosters, president of the alumni association a few years ago. And he's not happy that the star halfback won't be back ever again."

I leaned down to unlock my briefcase. "Maybe I'll have to exercise a challenge, get him disqualified for bias."

"Good luck," he said, chuckling. "If that's the only basis you'd have to challenge half the bench. You'll find that many members of the local judiciary were educated at St. Andrew."

I didn't like the way Laflamme pretended Judge Taylor would automatically be on his side. But I let it go. It was another of Laflamme's mind games, I figured. He was from the school of trial lawyers who try to intimidate their opponents by constantly telling them what a lousy case they had. Some lawyers, lacking confidence in their trial skills, would soon believe all the talk, conclude their case was weak and accept a bad settlement. Despite my inexperience in murder cases, I knew that wouldn't happen to me.

Besides, I didn't buy Laflamme's line about Judge Taylor being on his side simply because he was an alumnus of St. Andrew. I had always found Judge Taylor to be fair-minded. He had been my trial judge on a few minor civil cases, though I'd never had him for a criminal case. He was a no-nonsense judge, who controlled his courtroom with an iron fist.

Carter had told me that before taking the bench, Taylor had dabbled in politics, and on a whim had run for Congress. As a result he became somewhat of a legend around the state. He had little name recognition but campaigned tirelessly, driving up and down the state to shake hands with every small town politician he could find. It was before anyone ever heard of spin doctors or sound bites. Taylor campaigned the old-fashioned way: town meetings, VFW halls, the Knights of Columbus. Because of his unusual positions on key issues—he was an independent who favored abortion and opposed the death penalty—he got the voters' and the media's attention. To critics who argued that his positions on these issues were contradictory, he responded that the death penalty was wrong because only God had the right to take a man's life, but abortion was not murder since life begins at birth not conception.

His views led to some lively debates. Soon the *Union Leader*, an ardent supporter of his opponent, started publishing a regular column called "The Taylor Watch," containing quotes from his daily appearances. It was a rare day during the months before the election that Taylor's name was not mentioned at least once—usually in a snide manner—on the front page of New Hampshire's largest newspaper.

The day after the election, Taylor again made the headlines: "CLOSEST RACE IN HISTORY." To the shock of the incumbent—"an old-school political hack," Carter called him—as well as the *Union Leader*, the voting was so close that no winner was declared. A recount was ordered and after several weeks of intense debate, cries of election fraud, and disqualification of votes, the results were announced. Taylor came out the loser—by six votes. He never again ran for public office.

All in all, I thought I would take my chances with Judge Taylor. Just as I had made up my mind, I heard a door slam against the side wall. The courtroom suddenly became silent; heads turned toward the dock where a bailiff was holding open the door leading to the cells where the prisoners were detained while awaiting court. Like an usher at a movie theater, the bailiff directed the prisoners to their seats in the dock. The first three through the door were dressed in orange jumpsuits, standard dress for prisoners at the state prison. For appearances before a judge only, prisoners wore their jumpsuits, but for juries, they could wear their Sunday best and avoid the appearance, at least, of being a convict.

The last prisoner to enter the dock—and the only one in street clothes—was Raymond. Because he was detained at the courthouse jail instead of the county jail, Raymond was spared the indignity of having to dress like a marked man. Instead of the black sweatshirt I had become accustomed to, Raymond was wearing a simple white T-shirt. His eyes darted around the courtroom; he seemed scared and nervous.

Through the plexiglass surrounding the dock, I caught Raymond's eye and nodded reassuringly. He nodded back, but still seemed ill at ease. After the last prisoner was seated, the bailiff secured the door, took his position in the corner of the dock and kept watch on his charges. This spectacle over, and the courtroom again quiet, the attorneys resumed talking. A crowd gathered near the bar, Laflamme again in the middle. I sat back in the chair, alone, pretending to read my file. I was in no mood to be sociable; all I wanted was to get started. My wish was granted when a second bailiff, a red-faced Irishman named Andy O'Connor, entered the courtroom from a door behind the bench. O'Connor was known for his quick wit and a rare ability to keep attorneys in check without alienating them. True to character, he shouted: "Everyone please take a seat." Then he smiled broadly, displaying a wide gap in his yellowed teeth. "That way when the judge comes in, I can say, 'All rise!' "

Obediently, the attorneys quickly took seats near the bar. After O'Connor shouted, "All rise!" with a glint in his eyes, Judge Taylor shot out of chambers and bounded up the stairs to the bench. He dropped down into the thick leather chair with the quick movement of a man in a hurry. Immediately upon hitting the seat he slammed the mahogany gavel down three times, for no apparent reason since there was not a sound in the courtroom.

"Clerk, call the first case," he ordered.

I had to sit through three mundane status conferences—two burglaries and one drunk driving. Judge Taylor barely took his eyes off the files as he discussed each case with the attorneys. Instead of setting trial dates, the judge set new status conferences. I was worried that Raymond's case also would be continued.

When we were finally called, Laflamme jumped up and said, "Good morning, your honor."

The judge said, "Good morning, Mr. Laflamme," sounding friendlier than I'd have liked. "And who's appearing for the defense?"

"Dutch Francis, your honor," I announced forcefully.

"I'm sorry," Judge Taylor said as he flipped open his file, "I thought this was a murder case."

"It is, your honor," Laflamme answered. "Murder one."

"Yes, here it is." Taylor held up a pleading. "The complaint says the defendant Raymond Walker shot and killed one Brian McHugh during commission of a felony." He took off his glasses and glared down at me. "Counsel, please approach." I had no idea what was going on. Though there were still a half dozen lawyers in the courtroom and a few prisoners in the dock, I couldn't think of any reason to have a private bench conference.

When Laflamme and I arrived on the side of the bench, Judge Taylor leaned over so no one else would hear and said, "I was a bit confused when I learned you were on this case, Mr. Francis. I don't remember seeing you defending murder cases before."

"That's right, your honor. This is the first." I gritted my teeth, upset at Taylor for disclosing my inexperience to Laflamme.

"The first? Hmmm, I see. And your client knows that, does he?" Taylor turned to the dock and with upturned eyebrows stared at Raymond.

"Yes, he does," I answered.

"Very well. Mr. Laflamme, you have tried dozens of these cases." He looked over to Raymond again. "What are you going to do with this one?"

"We have made a very generous offer to settle for murder two, but Mr. Francis turned us down flat," Laflamme answered, shrugging his shoulders and turning his hands in a what-can-I-do gesture.

"Is that true, Mr. Francis?"

"Yes, your honor. My client insists on his innocence."

"Your client could get life in prison. Does he understand what he is risking by going to trial?" This time he turned all the way around so he was facing the dock. He looked directly at Raymond, who was bent over, staring at the floor. "It sounds like Mr. Laflamme has made a generous offer."

"My client is not interested, your honor."

"Well, then, why don't we set a trial date. You may return to counsel table."

Laflamme and I retreated amidst whispering from the other attorneys, no doubt speculating about the reasons for the bench conference. "Gentlemen, if you really are interested in trying this case, I may be able to accommodate you very quickly. I just had a trial go over. Now what date was that?" he said to himself, flipping through his notes. "Oh, here it is. What do you say about December 22?"

"Well . . ." I sputtered. That was a month away. My investigation had just begun and I needed to give Hedges some time.

To my surprise Laflamme spoke up. "That would be inconvenient, your honor," he said. I was surprised we actually agreed on something. "I start a trial the first week of December, then I planned on taking a couple of weeks off for the holidays."

"That's very well and good but what does the defendant want?" Judge Taylor asked, ignoring Laflamme. "After all, he has a constitutional right to a speedy trial. Mr. Francis, why don't you confer with your client, then let me know what he'd like to do."

I walked over to the dock and motioned to Raymond to stand in the corner so we could talk privately. We whispered while standing on tip toes, lifting our heads over the glass. "The sooner I get this over with the happier I'd be," Raymond said.

I shook my head. "I understand, but we need time to gather evidence. A month won't be enough. It's awfully risky. We haven't even found the person who was calling McHugh at the theater. It'd be crazy to go to trial now."

"Yeah . . . but . . ." He looked over at Laflamme.

"What is it?"

"I was just thinking I'd like nothing better than to fuck up that asshole's vacation."

"You can't go to . . ." I started to say when I realized he

wasn't serious. Somehow in the midst of his miserable experience in jail Raymond had found a sense of humor.

But his comment made me think. If Laflamme had back-to-back trials he'd have no time at all to prepare for this one. That would definitely be to our advantage. And he was such an egomaniac I doubted he would reassign the case.

"So what do we do?" Raymond asked.

Although it was tempting to make the trial inconvenient for Laflamme and make him unprepared, the risk was too great. "Waive a speedy trial," I said finally. "I wouldn't mind a few extra weeks of preparation either. We just can't risk going to trial right now."

"You're the boss, do it your way." Raymond frowned, looking disappointed.

"I'll tell the judge."

"Well, Mr. Francis, are we going to select a trial date or not?" I had worn out Judge Taylor's patience.

"Your honor, December 22 is just too soon and too close to Christmas; may we set trial a month later, say January 20 or so?"

Judge Taylor looked away, letting out a heavy breath. He turned a page on his calendar, then took off his glasses. "Mr. Francis, I am set to try a three-month serial rapist case January 14. I'm sure your client will not be happy stewing in our jail that long a time." He turned toward Raymond, looking for his agreement. Raymond turned toward me, trying to avoid the judge's eyes.

"Perhaps another judge could . . ."

"Don't even suggest it, Mr. Francis," Judge Taylor interrupted. "I will try this case myself." I started to get a sinking feeling in my stomach. Had Judge Taylor already made up his mind about Raymond's guilt? I decided I'd better find out just how far the judge's loyalties to St. Andrew had extended.

"Here's what I'll do," Taylor continued. "We'll have another status conference in two weeks, November 30 at 9:00 a.m."

Laflamme stood up. "But your honor, I have . . ."

"Enough, Mr. Laflamme. At that time we'll see if things have loosened up enough to allow you to try this case on December 22. And to make sure you are prepared, Mr. Francis, I am hereby ordering the prosecution to turn over all its evidence to you promptly, which means within twenty-four hours. That clear, Mr. Laflamme?"

Laflamme nodded. Judge Taylor pounded his gavel. "Next case."

CHAPTER 15

ON the walk back to my office, I was distracted, wondering how I would ever put together a defense in just over one month, especially in a first degree murder case. It was bad enough, I thought, that I had no experience in such a case, worse that at this point I had nothing to develop my defense, let alone prepare one.

Yvette rolled her eyes as soon as I walked in. "Don't tell me," she said. "You've got a trial date?"

I nodded, grimacing. "Tentative one anyway. There's another status conference on November 30; trial maybe December 22."

"You got a trial date. In a murder case!" She threw her hands in the air. "This is just great. How are you going to try a murder case?"

"Haven't we had this conversation before?"

With an exaggerated shake of her head, Yvette said, "And I can see you learned nothing from our little talk. You did say you were just looking into the case, didn't you?"

"Okay, I admit it. That's what I said."

"So now that you've worked on a murder case for all of—what, two weeks?—you're ready to go to trial. I feel sorry for poor Raymond Walker."

"Thanks for the vote of confidence," I said, knowing that Yvette spoke the truth.

"What I still can't understand is if your friend Larry needed a criminal lawyer, why would he even think of you? Especially after more than two decades?"

I thought for a moment. I had wondered that myself, ever since Larry explained how he had tracked me down by calling information in Boston, getting the number for my old firm where someone told him I'd moved to Manchester. He could have done that at any time in the past twenty-three years. Why now? I remembered what he had said on the phone: because I was a street fighter. Maybe that was the reason, I thought, or maybe there was more to it.

"Because of the books I read in high school," I answered finally, only half kidding.

"Oh?"

"Yeah, I read every book I could find about criminal lawyers. *To Kill a Mockingbird* was my favorite; Clarence Darrow's biography, *The Defense Never Rests* by F. Lee Bailey. I dreamed of being just like them, saving the lives of innocent people. Larry remembered that, so he naturally assumed I'd gone into criminal law."

Yvette had become quiet, listening intently to my story. "I've known you only a few months, Dutch," she said in a rare serious tone, "but from what I've seen you're not a lawyer who takes crazy risks. You put a lot of thought and research into your cases; you don't run off half-cocked like some lawyers I know who are always on a crusade. But with this case you're completely different; you're defending serious criminal charges, you've never handled a murder case before, you're going out on a limb for an old friend you haven't seen for over two decades. I don't get it." She paused, then looked into my eyes. "I'm sorry, I just don't."

I stood up and walked to the doorway, thinking. How

could I explain this strange feeling of loyalty I felt for Larry? How to explain that a childhood friendship stays with you your whole life? Maybe Yvette had been right when I first told her about Larry; maybe it was a guy thing. My rational lawyerly mind could not come up with a good response to Yvette's comments; there was no way to make logic out of emotion. Perhaps it was nothing more than nostalgia, trying to recapture the glory of youth. I know I regretted not trying harder to contact Larry while I was slaving away at Harvard, then at Dodds' firm.

I sat back down. "Let me tell you a story; it probably doesn't answer your concerns but it's the best explanation I can come up with. You see, if it weren't for Larry I probably would never have gone to Harvard. In my senior year of high school, I got pretty good grades and my teachers encouraged me to apply to the Ivy League. I didn't think I'd fit in with all those rich kids, but since Harvard was close by I picked up an application. It was about a dozen pages with all these essays you were supposed to type. No one I knew owned a typewriter so I used a ballpoint pen. My handwriting wasn't that great and the pen leaked all over the paper.

"I took the application to Larry's house to show him. As we read it together, the ink spots seemed to magnify, an obvious defect. Maybe at some level I thought my defects, my shortcomings would be just as obvious. When Larry finished reading the application, I crumpled it up and threw it into his trash can. I decided a state school would be easier anyway.

"I didn't know it until much later, but after I went home Larry retrieved the application from the trash. He borrowed his mother's car and drove to Harvard to pick up a new one. Then somehow he found a typewriter and typed the application himself, using the answers on my handwritten one. I had no idea he'd mailed it in until I got the acceptance letter plus an offer of a full scholarship."

"And the rest is history," Yvette said.

"Yup," I said, standing up. "Four years Harvard undergrad, three years Harvard Law School, and a lawyer is born."

Yvette stood up with me. "I think I understand now."

"You do?"

"Yeah," she said, smiling in that smartass way of hers. "This guy gets you into Harvard and what do you do? After you graduate you blow him off. Go on your merry way to law school, your best buddy be damned."

"You're brutal."

"I guess, but you're feeling guilty. I think that's why you're taking all these risks for Larry. Guilt, not friendship."

"Come on, that's not true. You're mixing up loyalty with guilt. Sure, I owe Larry, but we were good friends before he got me into Harvard you know."

"Uh, huh," she said, turning toward her computer. She was finished with this discussion. Sometimes Yvette exasperated me so much I felt like firing her. I had that same feeling now, but I didn't know if it was because of her attitude or because she was right.

AFTER a weekend of worrying, researching, and studying criminal procedure, I arrived at the office around nine thirty on Monday morning, tired but anxious to prepare for Raymond's trial.

"Guess who's here?" Yvette asked. "Says his name is Sherlock Holmes. But I didn't know Holmes wore a baseball cap."

I laughed, pushed open the door to my inner office and found Hedges sitting in the client chair, holding the baseball cap in his lap. I was glad to see him, especially with the possibility of trial only a few weeks away. I needed all the help I could get.

"I got some info for you," he said, turning around. "Grab a seat, you're gonna like this."

"Be the first thing in a long while I've liked," I said, sitting at my desk. "I need some good news."

"I checked out the apartment building on Cheshire Village Road. Pretty badly burned. Most of the tenants were re-located to empty apartments in the same complex, run by some outfit called PEVCON. I went over to the manager's office and managed to get some info out of the young lass working the phones."

"I don't want to know how," I said.

"Nothing but old-fashioned charm, my friend," Hedges said, though his smile told me there was more than charm involved. "Anyway," he continued, "I got the name of the person at the phone number in question, one Igor Rubenstein."

"Who the hell is Igor Rubenstein?" I asked, remembering Evan had said the caller had an accent; Czech, Polish, maybe even Russian he had said.

"Beats me," he said. "Lisa—that's the lass's name in case you're wondering—was kind enough to give me the new address where this Igor was living. And when I turned up the charm a wee bit more, she finally agreed to give me names and addresses of Igor's old neighbors."

"His neighbors?"

"Oh, yes. You see, if Igor's the one making these calls I figure his neighbors may know his business. Who knows, maybe they can connect him to McHugh. So first thing I do is knock on Igor's door and no one answers. Then I start knocking on the doors of his old neighbors. Most of them don't answer, though I can hear a TV from the back bedroom in a couple. Finally, an old woman opens her door, a Mrs. Irene Luhovey."

"Russian?"

"Lithuanian. Her husband Boris was a doctor. They immigrated together over thirty years ago."

"And settled in Manchester?"

"Hey, you're not the only one drawn by the charms of the Queen City. Our fame goes far and wide. From Mrs. Luhovey's description, they had a good life. And I heard all about it for nearly an hour over a cup of rancid tea. I should bill you double for that one."

"Don't push it," I said.

"Then maybe you could give me a cut of the case I landed for you."

"What case?" Between Yvette and Hedges my head was spinning.

"Seems poor ol' Boris was the old man killed in the fire. I saw an opportunity to do some marketing for you so I suggested she may have a case against the fire department. Way I figure, they could've saved the guy if they hadn't been stuffing themselves with lobster across town. I didn't know your schedule so I told her to come in this afternoon at three."

"You gave her an appointment? Today?" My jaw dropped in disbelief.

"I didn't want her to get away. You don't hook them early one of those TV lawyers will get her. Could be a big case for you. And God knows you're not going to get rich off this Walker case."

"Thanks a bunch," I said. "Just what I need, a grieving widow to cry on my shoulder. I should bill you for the time I spend with her."

"You might want to reserve judgment until you talk to her. She could help you out on Walker's case too; she saw a lot of people coming and going from Rubenstein's apartment. The way she described one of them, easily could be our man McHugh. So I figured you get her in here, show her McHugh's photo from the newspaper, then you got yourself a witness. The wrongful death case would be a bonus."

Why, I wondered, did Hedges make me wait so long before he gave me the really important news? If there was some connection between Rubenstein and McHugh, then maybe there's a motive for murder. Mrs. Luhovey could turn out to be an important witness indeed.

AT exactly three o'clock Yvette buzzed me on the intercom. "Irene Luhovey, your new client, is here. She's in the ladies' room now, cute Russian accent."

Two minutes later she ushered in a grey-haired lady with bright, rosy cheeks that matched the red lines in her eyes. She was no more than five feet tall, but her round body made her seem even shorter. Her long flowered dress clearly outlined her body; there were no bumps or bulges, just a long, even arc from top to bottom like a half moon.

"Please, you could put the cup right here, dear?" she asked Yvette, her accent thicker than I'd imagined.

Yvette placed the tea cup on the edge of my desk. With a sideways grin at me, she said, "Dutch Francis, Mrs. Irene Luhovey." Before returning to the outer office, she turned her head sharply, tossing her long black mane across her back onto the opposite shoulder.

"I am so much sorry to bother you, Mr. Francis," Mrs. Luhovey said quickly. Without taking a breath, she continued. "I was wanting to forget this whole thing, but your nice Mr. Hedges, he told me I must talk to you. My poor Boris, he don't like to sue people ever. He say it the only bad thing about America, people they always sue each other, no matter the reason. Nobody want to be responsible for themselves." She repeated, "Nobody," and shook her head quickly back and forth. "But it seemed so wrong, you see?"

"Yes, I know what you mean."

"Those firemen, the way they let my poor Boris die. They eat lobster while people burn to death a few blocks from their firehouse? Mr. Hedges is right; I cannot just walk away. Even Boris, I think he would agree with me. God rest his soul. I should know my Boris, we'd been together fifty years. Healthy like an ox, as you say. Could have been another fifty, I no kidding. You married, Mr. Francis?"

"No, I'm not."

"Not so good, you need a woman to take care of you. Like I took care of Boris. Nobody take care of their men like the Lithuanian women. That's the truth, Mr. Francis."

She sipped her tea; I thought I had an opening. "What . . ."

"Except for that afternoon," she sniffled, wiping her nose

with her index finger. "We need milk and I was wanting a cup of tea is all; tea . . . stupid tea. The men next door they were yelling and carrying on, so I had to get away. I left Boris by himself, it was only five or ten minutes, not a minute more I swear. That was ten days ago, Mr. Francis. Just a few weeks since my Boris has been gone and I've been thinking, what am I to do?"

After taking another sip of tea, she continued. "I am wanting to sue those firemen for killing my Boris. If they do their job, my Boris he still be here. I not be in Manchester with nowhere to go." She sobbed quietly, pulled a piece of tissue from her purse, and dabbed at her eyes.

I waited a few seconds. Finally, she blew her nose and put the tissue back in her purse. "There, over now, no more. Hits me once in a while. And when I get started, Mr. Francis, I cannot make it stop. Fifty years is long time to be with someone, no?"

"Of course," I said as I buzzed Yvette to bring in another cup of tea, figuring Mrs. Luhovey couldn't cry if she were drinking tea. A few minutes later Yvette brought in a fresh cup. As she handed tearful Mrs. Luhovey the cup, she glared at me as if I'd been beating the woman.

Revived, Mrs. Luhovey looked at me over her tea cup. "So what you think, I should be good American, maybe, sue these firemen?"

I really didn't know just yet and needed to ask her some questions first. For the next ten minutes, with my gentle prodding, Mrs. Luhovey explained the circumstances of her husband's death. She had lived in Cheshire Village for over twenty years with her seventy-four-year-old husband. On October 24th, a Friday afternoon, the building caught fire, no one knew how, while Boris was napping in front of the TV. The next door neighbor, Igor Rubenstein, whom she called mean and unfriendly, was in a heated argument with another man. Mrs. Luhovey had walked to the convenience store at the end of the street. When she returned, she saw a crowd of people standing outside and flames shooting out of the building. The firemen were nowhere in sight even though the fire station was only three blocks away. It turned out the firemen were all at another fire station across town, enjoying a lobster dinner together. All the tenants got out of the building except her husband. He never woke up.

"You read about it, no?" she said. "It was in papers, head-lines, my Boris's picture right there on the front page." She reached into her purse, handed me a wrinkled piece of newspaper.

I smoothed out the wrinkles and glanced at the headline: "MAN DIES IN FIRE, FIREMEN EATING LOBSTER!" There was a photo of a younger Boris Luhovey, perhaps at fifty years of age. Below was another photo showing the firemen carrying him from the smokey building in the midst of a crowd of gawking onlookers.

"Was terrible, terrible," she said. "I stood outside scream-ing for my Boris to come out. Some neighbors they tried to go back for him, but the fire was too big. I not want to think about it. Oh, Mr. Francis, I cry again."

To my dismay, she placed the tea cup on my desk, and the tears again flowed. After several minutes, I said, "Let me look into it, Mrs. Luhovey, see if there's anything I can do." In the back of my mind, though, I didn't have much hope for the case. I vaguely remembered that the law often gave fire-men immunity in cases like this. Cities would soon go broke if they could be sued every time a fireman messes up at a fire.

Before I could dismiss Mrs. Luhovey, however, I wanted to show her some photos. I pulled out the file of newspaper articles Yvette had put together.

"Mrs. Luhovey, I'm sure Mr. Hedges told you about the murder case I'm defending."

"Oh, yes," she said. "So sad, sad."

"We have reason to believe your neighbor, Mr. Ruben-stein, knew the victim."

"You no think he . . ." she paused. "Not murderer. He not nice man, but I can no believe he murderer."

"We don't know yet, but we think he may have been making threatening phone calls to the victim." I pushed the articles over to her. "Here, take a look at these photos. Tell me if you recognize anyone. Maybe someone who visited Mr. Rubenstein."

She lifted each article within inches of her eyes, studying each one. She paid particular attention to the articles about McHugh's football exploits.

Quietly, she closed the folder. "Mr. Francis, I never notice this before. I guess I not pay much attention when I read the paper. I don't know, so upsetting. That football player, he handsome young man, so handsome. I remember him, he come to Mr. Rubenstein's apartment many times. I hear him knocking on door so I look through my—how you say— peephole. He not look happy."

"Do you have any idea why Brian McHugh would be visiting your neighbor?"

She shook her head slowly. "Lots of people go there," she said. "Not look so nice to me. I no like to talk bad of people, but that Igor Rubenstein, I no like. He bad man."

"Do you remember the last time McHugh visited?"

"I not sure, only it was not long before fire. I know that."

And not long before he was murdered, I thought. I could see that Mrs. Luhovey was tired so I buzzed Yvette to show her out. I promised to get back in touch with her after looking into her case.

When Yvette returned, she said, "I hope you can help her. She's a nice lady."

"I'll give it a shot," I assured her. "Why don't you order the fire department report, and check with the secretary of state for information on the owner, PEVCON Corporation. Who knows, maybe the managers were negligent in causing the fire and there'll be a case against them. Worth checking out."

I asked Yvette to call Glenn Hedges and have him pick me up downstairs. I wanted to waste no time in having a chat with Mr. Igor Rubenstein.

AS soon as the door opened I knew I was staring at Igor Rubenstein. His high forehead glistened with sweat; dark fleshy circles hung loosely below reddish eyelids. His lower lip hung out like a boxer's after catching a solid left hook. But Rubenstein's lip was unblemished, no blood or bruising; he had a natural fat lip. He stared at me and Hedges as if we were two Jehovah's Witnesses wanting to convert him to a life of goodness and spirituality.

"Ya?" he said. He held his arms stiffly at his side as if he were ready to defend himself.

Hedges shifted his feet. For a moment I thought he would go for his gun, the gun he had told me about on the drive over. I hadn't realized I had hired an armed investigator until Hedges pulled on the neck of his sweater to show his shoulder holster and the shiny .38 he kept there. "You've got a license for that, I hope," I told him. When he didn't answer, I didn't press.

Hoping to avoid a confrontation, I put my arm across Hedges' chest, holding him back. "I-gor?" I said, emphasizing the "I."

He shook his head. "Nyet," he said. "EE-gore, that's how it is said. And you, what is it you want?"

"I'm an attorney; name's Dutch Francis." I handed him my business card. "This is my investigator, Glenn Hedges. We'd like to ask you some questions."

He handed the card back to me—seems like no one wants my card these days—and turned his back. He was wearing a white polyester dress shirt decorated with blue teardrops. He took a few steps into the apartment and grabbed a solid blue polyester tie from the top of the couch. He returned to the doorway, wrapping the tie around his neck. "Sorry," he said. "No time. I have appointment."

"That's too bad, I-gor," Hedges said, deliberately mispronouncing the name as "I" not "E." "We won't need more than a minute or two." Then he pushed Rubenstein back into the apartment where he stumbled a few feet before landing on the couch. I sat down beside him as Hedges slammed the door shut. Hedges leaned against the door with his arms folded.

Rubenstein froze, his tie half-finished. He stared at Hedges, then at me. "How do I know you are who you say?"

Hedges shrugged, pulled out his wallet and showed Rubenstein his PI license. I handed him back my card. This time he studied it carefully. "Am I under arrest?"

Hedges laughed. "No, no, I-gee, you got it all wrong. We're not the KGB, you know. We just need to get some info. We understand that one of your acquaintances met an unfortunate end recently."

Rubenstein finished with his tie and pulled it tight against the droopy skin of his neck. The red color had drained from his eyelids. He leaned back. "I am knowing nothing about what you are saying," he said, shaking his head. "Nothing."

"Not so fast there, Mr. Rubenstein," I said. "What we want to know is whether you had a visitor by the name of Brian McHugh. A star football player, now unfortunately deceased."

At the mention of McHugh, Rubenstein froze. He averted his eyes and played with his tie. "I sorry," he said, mumbling into his chest. "I don't know this person."

Hedges moved toward Rubenstein. "I'm disappointed in you, I-gee. We thought you wanted to cooperate." He leaned over Rubenstein, glaring. "In fact, we know quite a bit about you. For instance, we know you received a visit from McHugh not long before he was murdered."

Rubenstein's eyes widened and he jumped to his feet. "Fuck you," he screamed. "You got no fucking right to come into my house and be threatening me. Who the fuck you thinking you are?" He took a step toward Hedges, but only one step. Before he could take another, Hedges quickly slammed his open hands into his chest, sending Rubenstein flying back toward the couch, his head whipping back.

"Threats?" Hedges said. "I didn't hear any threats. Dutch, did you hear any threats?" I shrugged, playing along. "I'm offended by that, I-gee," Hedges continued. "Truly offended. You do recognize the name Brian McHugh, don't you?"

"Ya, I read the papers, so what?" He rubbed the back of his neck, sat up straight.

I stood back, marveling at Hedges. For a guy with a mellow disposition, he didn't hesitate to get rough. After the embarrassment of my first meeting with Raymond, I was happy to leave the rough stuff to Hedges. He leaned over Rubenstein, his hands resting on the couch back, trapping Rubenstein's head. "I'll tell you so what, I-gee," Hedges snapped. He reached in his back pocket and pulled out the Cinema Manchester phone bill. He showed the bill to Rubenstein and rested it on the couch back while reading off Rubenstein's phone number. "Sound familiar?"

"Okay, okay," Rubenstein said, gently pushing at Hedges' arms to free himself. Obliging, Hedges stepped back. "That my number, sure, but understand . . ." He glanced at me. I crossed my arms and stared back. "I talk to McHugh. We do some business together, that is all. I know nothing about why he was killed. I tell you, nothing."

Hedges moved closer to Rubenstein, reached over and tightened his tie so that the skin in his neck folded, nearly covering the tie. "Of course not," he said. Rubenstein swallowed, tugging at his collar for air. "But what we want to know, I-gie, is just what kind of business you had with the recently deceased."

"Is nothing, really," Rubenstein said through choked breaths. "You see, we Russians, we love the games of chance. This Brian McHugh, he was helping me to win some money, that is all. He was very important football player, score lot of touchdowns. He want to help." Rubenstein held his hands out as if he were making all the sense in the world.

Hedges got a glazed look in his eyes and sat down in the chair across from Rubenstein. "Looks like we're going to be here a while," he said, looking at me.

"That's okay, stay, relax," Rubenstein said. "No problem.

You want drink maybe?" He pointed to the kitchen. "In freezer. Nice bottle of Stolichnaya. I get for you." He started to get up but Hedges held out his hand.

"Not so fast, I-gee. Though I like the sound of a shot of Stoli, I think you'd better stay put. What do you say, Dutch?"

I hesitated, wondering why Hedges would want to drink vodka at such an important time. Then I realized his strategy. "Why not?" I said and walked to the kitchen. I pulled the bottle from the freezer, searched a few cabinets before finding three shot glasses. I poured a half shot in two of the glasses and a double in the third. Boxes were strewn about the kitchen, some half-empty, others taped shut, evidencing Rubenstein's recent move. I could hear Hedges making small talk with Rubenstein, chatting about the neighborhood. I put the bottle of Stoli on the counter and sifted through a couple of boxes, full of utensils, Star Market glassware, until I found a pile of notebooks. I flipped open the top one. There were a half dozen columns with names, dates, amounts, and games. There were bets on football, basketball, even soccer, college and pro. It seemed there was no game Rubenstein wouldn't take a bet on. Most of the bets were small change: $50 to $100. But there were a handful of big ones, thousands of dollars. I turned the pages toward the end of the book, where last month's games were listed. The bets got progressively higher as the month of October wore on. There was a $1,000 bet the first week, then each week the amounts went up, all the way to $28,000. At first I was so enthralled with the dollars I didn't notice a striking similarity to the big bets. They were all for St. Andrew football games.

The bettors' names were hard to decipher, though most seemed to be Russian. Four or five bettors bet regularly on St. Andrew.

"What is taking so long?" Rubenstein yelled at me.

I closed the book and stuffed it into my pants, covering the bulge with my jacket. "Be right there," I said. "Had to find some glasses." I returned the Stoli to the freezer and picked up the three glasses.

"Here we go," I said, handing half a shot to Hedges. I gave the double to Rubenstein, keeping the other half shot for myself. Rubenstein held his glass out and we tapped our glasses together just like old friends. "Salud," he said and downed the glass in one gulp. Hedges and I did the same. It was the smoothest vodka I'd ever had and I regretted taking only half a shot.

"I-gee was just telling me about his business," Hedges said. "With all the Russian immigrants here, he's managed to become quite a successful bookie."

Rubenstein shook his head, wiping his lips with the back of his hand. "I no like that word 'bookie.' It sound like the Mafia, like that movie *The Godfather.* I love that movie, such wonderful violence, but no, I am Russian, not Italian. I prefer the term 'Luck Facilitator.'"

"What?" Hedges nearly choked.

"Luck Facilitator," Rubenstein repeated. "Here." He removed his wallet from his pants pocket and pulled out a business card. He handed it to Hedges.

"Jesus H. Christ," Hedges said. "'I-gor Rubenstein,'" he read. "'Luck Facilitator.' Who would've believed it?"

"Is true," Rubenstein said. "I specialize in the games of luck. Say you bet money on a football game. If you win, you had good luck. Lose, you had bad luck. Okay? My job, it is to make sure your luck is the good kind."

"You're the middleman," Hedges said, shaking his head. "Your luck is always good." He handed me Rubenstein's business card. I looked at it and put it in my coat pocket.

"Let's forget this 'Luck Facilitator' bullshit, I-gee," Hedges snapped. He was losing patience with Rubenstein.

I didn't want Hedges to fly off the handle again so I gave him a look to let me take over. "If I was to guess, I-gor," I said, "I'd say a better word is 'fixer?' We know you bet heavily on St. Andrew football games. Was it just a coincidence that you had this regular contact with St. Andrew's star halfback?"

"I no understand what you mean?"

I remembered what Evan had said about McHugh complaining about a hamstring pull after one of his games even though he wasn't limping. Of course, I realized, McHugh needed an excuse for why he hadn't scored with a clear field ahead of him. I decided to put some cards on the table. "What I mean is that you and Brian McHugh were working together, maybe shaving points?"

Rubenstein reached for his shot glass, brought it to his lips before realizing it was empty. He wiped a bead of perspiration from his upper lip. "No lie, he did do that. Nobody was hurt; his team still won the game. And they were only small bets."

"Small bets?" I said.

"Sure, twenty-five, sometimes a hundred dollars. No big deal."

"Don't bullshit us, Mr. Rubenstein," I yelled, getting to my feet. "We don't have time for that crap. Is $10,000 a small bet? How about $28,000?"

Hedges looked startled. I nodded and winked, patting my jacket so he would know where I had hidden the evidence. Rubenstein took advantage of Hedges' momentary inattention and stood up. "I must go to bathroom."

"Sit the fuck down," Hedges said. "If you're innocent, I-gee, why you bullshitting us?"

Rubenstein flopped back down. "Okay, so there were some big bets, one, two, maybe more, who knows."

"What I want to know," I said, "is why Brian McHugh would shave points for you."

Without hesitating, he said, "He like the money too. I give him a cut of my winnings."

I suspected this was a lie, and so apparently did Hedges, though what happened next took me totally by surprise. The one thing I had learned about Glenn Hedges was to expect the unexpected. But he soon outdid himself. From the corner of my eye, I could detect only a blur as Hedges shot out his arm and swept a glass table lamp across the room. He had hit it so hard that the side was smashed in before hitting the floor, simply from the force of his arm. The lamp hit the far wall with a loud crash, shattering into a dozen pieces. A look of terror came into Rubenstein's eyes as he sat as far back on the couch as he could.

"You ever been to California, I-gee?" Hedges asked through clenched teeth.

Rubenstein shook his head, first sideways then up and down. He hesitated. "My s-sister, Lena, she live in San Francisco. I visit once in while, that is it." His voice was starting to slur after only one shot. Perhaps Rubenstein had a drinking problem.

"What did Lena tell you about Brian McHugh?" I asked him, guessing where this was going.

It was either fear or the effects of the vodka or perhaps both that got Rubenstein talking. He finally came clean, telling us he had visited his sister in late September and read an article about local high school football teams in the Bay Area section of the San Francisco Chronicle. The article mentioned that Pine Creek High's new halfback would challenge some of the rushing records set by Brian McHugh. He recognized the name and asked his sister about McHugh. She said there was some scandal involving McHugh. It was in all the papers but she couldn't remember the details. Rubenstein did his own investigation and soon learned that St. Andrew's All-American candidate was one and the same: an ex-convict who had done time for manslaughter.

Being a resourceful type, Rubenstein then concocted a plan to use this information to his advantage. As I had guessed, he had blackmailed McHugh to shave points, threatening to expose his background. By the end of October, McHugh had rebelled, telling Rubenstein he had had enough. The guilt of shaving points had gotten to him.

"So that's why he visited you shortly before he was killed?"

"Ya, he very angry, yelling at me, threatening to go to the police if I didn't leave him alone."

"And you decided to show him who was boss, right? Teach him a lesson. So you went to the theater and shot him through the head. Isn't that right?" I was yelling now, in my best cross-examination mode.

"Never, never," he yelled back. "I not do that. When he was leaving that day, I am telling him—I no lie—I not bother him again this season. What I want is to see if he winning this All-American award. Ya, is true. Then maybe the next season I make some real dollars. That is truth, understand?"

"You're bullshitting us again, I-gee," Hedges said.

"No, I swear. I not kill him."

He sounded almost sincere. But he had lied to us so often in a short period of time, I didn't believe him. I had to put him at the top of our list of suspects; he was a blackmailer and a liar, for sure, but was he also a murderer? Why would he kill McHugh, the goose that had laid his golden eggs? If McHugh had gone to the police, Rubenstein would've been looking at some prison time. But would McHugh have risked his chance at All-American just to get rid of Rubenstein? Maybe, I thought, Rubenstein killed him out of anger, lost his cool at McHugh's change of heart and took his revenge.

I knew I would need solid evidence to pin this murder on Rubenstein. With what I had now—suspicions—Laflamme would brush me off. We had to buy some time, collect enough evidence against Rubenstein to give the jury a reasonable doubt about whether Raymond were guilty. I had the notebook, but I needed more. Like the murder weapon, or the money.

"If you're so innocent, EE-gor," I asked, "you won't mind if we look around your apartment, right?"

"There is nothing here," he said. "Anyone can see that. But if you want to look, you go ahead. You find nothing." He said it with such assurance that I knew we would find nothing. To be safe, Hedges scoured every room. He came

up with nothing. Short of beating a confession out of Rubenstein, there wasn't much else for us to do, at least for now.

I wanted Rubenstein to know he wasn't off the hook yet,
so I put some pressure on him. "The only way I'm going to
believe you're innocent," I said, "is if you deliver the real
murderer to me."

"How can I do that? What do I know about murder?" He
wiped his forehead with the sleeve of his polyester shirt,
succeeding only in pushing the sweat from one side to the
other.

"You're a bookie, right? Excuse me, 'Luck Facilitator.'
You must know a lot of people. The kind of people who hear
things, like if someone's bragging about getting away with
murder. Or maybe about killing a star football player. Ask
around, keep your ears open, then let us know what you
hear."

He was still shaking when he said, "I will love to do that
for you, absolutely. I will help you. You will see, I am no
murderer."

I handed him a fresh business card. "Call me within a
week. That's all the time I can spare." I pulled the notebook
from my jacket and waved it at him. "You come through I'll
give this back to you. But if not, then . . ." I let the sentence
hang.

"Then what?" he asked, pulling off his tie.

Hedges opened the front door and I followed him out. I
stopped in the doorway and stared at Rubenstein, giving him
my tough guy look. "Then," I said, "I'm sure you'll have fun
explaining this book to the police."

CHAPTER 16

HEDGES stopped his car in front of my office, blocking traffic on Elm Street. An Asian guy driving a blue Isuzu Trooper and wearing a Michigan Wolverines baseball cap had been riding Hedges' bumper. He leaned on his horn and yelled something I couldn't hear. I hurried out the passenger door, not wanting to inflict Hedges' wrath on this unsuspecting motorist. I told Hedges I would call him after I'd gone through Laflamme's evidence box. As I waved goodbye, he gave me the thumbs-up sign, then turned around and gave the Michigan fan the finger.

I was starting to feel optimistic about the case. On the drive from Rubenstein's apartment, I told Hedges that for the first time I thought Raymond had a chance to win. I believed I could convince a jury that Rubenstein had become enraged at McHugh's refusal to continue shaving points and worried that McHugh would turn him in. His clients had bet a lot of money on St. Andrew and would be sure to seek revenge if Rubenstein let them down. He simply could not let that happen, I guessed, so he had confronted McHugh at the theater and tried to scare him by placing a gun to his head. Perhaps McHugh had reached for the gun and Rubenstein shot him accidently, or maybe McHugh had refused to back down and Rubenstein shot him in a senseless rage. It didn't matter to me. Either way, Raymond would be in the clear.

THE next morning, I told Yvette about the meeting with Rubenstein. While she nodded in apparent agreement, she showed none of the enthusiasm or optimism that Hedges and I had shared earlier. Frowning, I asked her what was wrong.

"Sorry to rain on your parade, Bucko," she said. "But I got news and it ain't so good." Waggling her index finger, she beckoned me to follow her to the inner office. She pointed to Laflamme's box which was on top of my desk. My enthusiasm over Rubenstein instantly dissipated.

She pulled a pile of papers from the box. "These are the State's investigative reports," she said. "Nothing surprising here. They questioned all the employees of the theater, who went on and on with how much Raymond hated McHugh."

I thumbed through the reports. The State had done a thorough job. They had documented every cross word McHugh and Raymond ever had with each other. And they had witnesses to each one. They had talked to Evan and Larry in great detail about every aspect of Raymond's life. There were typed notes of Laflamme's conversation with Coach Carlucci, newspaper articles about McHugh's arrest and conviction, most of which I had already received from Carlucci, and correspondence from the California Department of Corrections about McHugh's prison sentence. They had even talked to the family of McHugh's stabbing victim, trying to determine if any of them wanted to avenge the death. But they came up with nothing.

What was surprising was the omission of any mention of Rubenstein. Perhaps the State's investigator had neglected to ask Evan about the phone calls. Or maybe Evan had neglected to mention them. But why wouldn't he mention them?

The biggest surprise, though, was at the bottom of the box: a transcribed and signed statement from someone named Frank Killian. "You're not going to like that," Yvette said. I glanced at the statement. She was right. Killian was Laflamme's surprise witness and from my quick read of his statement, it appeared he confirmed Laflamme's claim that Raymond had confessed to the robbery. I had a big problem.

Beneath the statement was a cassette tape, marked "Killian statement." "I didn't have a chance to listen to that yet," Yvette said.

"I'm not sure I want to," I answered.

Yvette walked to the outer office and returned carrying the portable cassette player she kept on her desk. "I'll leave you alone to wallow in your latest misery," she said. "But don't get discouraged yet."

"Why not?"

"This statement was taken by the State's investigator," she said. "But Killian may not be so sure of himself once you sick Sherlock Holmes on him."

I laughed, the seriousness of the situation momentarily forgotten. I watched Yvette walk back to her desk, her black wool pants revealing all of her fine curves, before snapping the tape into the recorder and pressing the "Play" button.

The tape lasted less than forty-five minutes, though the key part took only about five minutes.

I listened to the tape with a lump in my throat and acid forming in my stomach. At the end of the interview, I pushed the "Stop" button and immediately picked up the phone.

"Larry," I said when he answered. "We've got to meet soon. Tomorrow if possible."

He asked if something was wrong. I told him we'd obtained new evidence, some of it helpful to Raymond's defense, some not. I wanted to discuss it with him in Raymond's presence, I said, so I wouldn't have to go through it twice. He agreed to cancel his first few appointments and meet me at the jail at nine o'clock tomorrow morning.

LARRY stood just inside the back entrance to the court-house, blowing on his hands. "Damn, it's cold," he said as I opened the door. He reached out and I removed my glove to shake skin to skin, my warm hand grasping his icy one. "So, Dutch," he said, "what's going on? You were pretty vague on the phone. You got some news from the AG, Laflamme?"

"Yeah, I learned some things." I took a step toward the stairs and said, "Let's go see Raymond so I can fill you both in."

Larry grabbed my arm, stopping me on the second step. "You sounded down on the phone. Is it that bad?"

"I'm not sure yet."

He let go of my arm and stood there on the landing, his eyes closed. I looked up at him, waiting. Larry opened his eyes and looked directly at me. Then he took a step down, and the two of us walked side by side to the jail entrance.

Hank Lerner was not on duty. Sitting behind the grey desk was a deputy sheriff who looked barely old enough to shave. He had rosy cheeks and the fresh, well-scrubbed look that made me think he would have a hard time tolerating the stench of Hank's cigar. After the introductions, he nodded, picked up the phone and asked for Hank. When Hank picked up, a confused look appeared on the deputy's face. He hung up and said, "Hank gave you the okay, but he said something I don't quite get." He shrugged his shoulders. "Hank said to be sure to serve you two full helpings of lunch."

I laughed, picturing the disgusting brown sauce on Raymond's mashed potatoes the last time I visited during lunch. "Nice of Hank to think of me," I said. Larry looked at me, puzzled. "I'll explain later," I told him as we followed the deputy down the corridor to Raymond's cell.

As the deputy unlocked the cell, Raymond slowly lifted his torso from the cot, then sat on the edge. He shook his head back and forth, shaking off the cobwebs. "Oh, hi," he said, rubbing his eyes. "Must've overslept. Forgot to order a wake-up call, I guess." A newfound sense of humor. Too bad it wouldn't last long.

"What's going on?" he asked.

"Mr. Francis has some information on your case," Larry said. "I'm interested in hearing it myself." Larry stood by the side wall, his arms crossed behind his back, looking at Raymond sitting on his right. I stood to his left, leaning against the bars. For ten minutes I gave them a full account of my meeting with Rubenstein: McHugh's conviction for manslaughter, Rubenstein's blackmail, McHugh's point-shaving, and my theory about Rubenstein shooting McHugh.

"That sounds pretty good to me," Larry said. "Why the long face then?"

"There's more," I said. I pulled the tape player from my briefcase and pushed the play button.

When Killian's name was mentioned, Raymond leaned forward and Larry turned toward him, raising an eyebrow.

The tape began with the investigator reciting the name and number of the case.

Q: This is Gerry Walsh, investigator for the New Hampshire Attorney's General's office. State and spell your name for the tape.
A: Name's Frank Killian. That's K-i-l-l-i-a-n.

Q: And Mr. Killian, how old are you?
A: Gonna be nineteen next February 14. That's Valentine's Day.

Q: I know. Please tell us how you know the defendant Raymond Walker.
A: We hung out together. You know, like at the beach. We'd shoot the bull, play some video games at the arcade I worked at, fun stuff like that.

Q: Would you characterize yourself as a friend of Mr. Walker?

A: Charac . . . what?

Q: Were you ever friends?

A: Oh, yeah. For about three years. Up until last month.

Q: Did something happen last month that affected your friendship?

A: Well, I guess you could say that. He showed me something. He come into the arcade one night while I was workin'. He was carryin' this gym bag, a long red thing with a blue handle. He points to the bag and says, "Take a look at this." I had no idea what he was talkin' about, you know. So he reaches in and pulls out this rubber Halloween mask, the kind goes on right over your head. It had these huge wart-like things sticking out all over, long white hair and a really disgusting face.

Q: Did Mr. Walker say anything about the mask at that time?

A: Yeah. He says he was gonna wear the mask on Halloween night. There was some kinda special midnight show at the theater he used to work at, and they were gonna make a ton of money. So he was gonna sneak in afterwards with this mask on so no one would recognize him, then rip them off.

Q: Did he say how he was going to rip off the theater?

A: All he says is he would just rob them when they're counting up all the money.

The tape continued on with the investigator going over this same ground several times. At the end he asked questions about Killian's family, schooling, and work history. By the time I shut off the tape, Raymond was ready to explode.

"That sonuvabitch!" he yelled. "I get my hands on him, I'll break . . ."

"Enough, Raymond," Larry interrupted. "That won't get us anywhere. We've got a serious problem here."

I folded my arms and leaned back, waiting for Raymond's explanation.

"You don't believe that asshole, do you?" Raymond confronted Larry. "He's a lying piece of shit, is what he is."

"He'd better be," I said. "Or your goose is cooked."

Raymond stomped his feet. "Come on, don't tell me you believe this bullshit story."

"I don't have to believe it," I said. "The question is whether the jury'll believe it. And from what I've heard so far, I can't think why they wouldn't." I paused. "Unless you know something that would enlighten me on that point."

"I got a lot of information, that's for damn sure. Killian's setting me up and I can tell you exactly why."

For the next fifteen minutes, Raymond told us all about Frank Killian, who had dated Cathy before Raymond got into the picture and stole her heart. I didn't know if the jury would believe Killian or not, but after hearing Raymond's side of the story, I started to believe again that—at the very least—there was a reasonable doubt whether Killian was lying.

I told Raymond I would have Hedges interview Killian, see what other impeachment he could dig up. "Then we can focus on Rubenstein," I added. "Gather more evidence of his dealings with McHugh."

Larry pulled a white handkerchief from his back pocket and rubbed his nose. "But what if the jury doesn't believe Rubenstein killed McHugh? After all, he needed McHugh to shave points. By killing him, Rubenstein lost his cash cow. Like you said, he could've shot him by accident, but I guess it still worries me."

"It worries me too," I said, "especially if we can't destroy Killian's credibility."

"What the hell's going on here?" Raymond shouted, pounding his fist into the palm of his other hand. "Are you two giving up on me now? Just because of this lying sack of shit, Killian?"

He was nearly hysterical, the same tormented young man I had first met a few weeks ago. But now I understood him better. I looked around the cell: at the toilet in the corner, unseated, open, yellowed; the chipped and cracked porcelain sink beside it, a dark mustard color; and the tiny cot hanging on the wall covered by a paper thin blanket. This is what a guilty verdict would mean: living in squalor for life, which for Raymond meant nearly sixty years. And this was nothing compared to the conditions at the New Hampshire State Prison in Concord, where the cells were crowded with two or three inmates, where every day brought the threat of being raped by older, stronger inmates, until he became as hardened and depraved as they were.

"Raymond," I said softly, "we believe in your innocence but we have to give it to you straight. Larry's right: if the jury doesn't think Rubenstein is guilty, we have no one else to point to. And of course he swears he's innocent."

"What else you expect him to say?" He paced the cell, his head down, not looking at either me or Larry.

I ignored his question. "There's one other possibility," I said. "But I wouldn't hold out much hope for it. Rubenstein had been giving us so much bullshit, I threw some back at him and challenged him to find the real murderer. Just to shake him up a bit. But I don't really expect he'll come up with anything, especially since I think he's guilty."

"But if Mr. Conway's right and the jury doesn't agree, then I'm dead meat, right?"

"Probably," I admitted.

Raymond stopped pacing and seemed to calm down. He glanced at Larry, then looked directly at me. "Then let's hope Rubenstein comes up with something," he said quietly.

CHAPTER 17

AT 10:15 Saturday morning, the Derryfield Building was deserted. I switched on the lights to my office and put on a pot of coffee. I found a paper plate for the crumb donut I had picked up on the way over and put my cup under the coffee as it dripped. As I munched on the donut and sipped on the dark, extra strong coffee, I tried to devise a strategy to deal with Raymond's ex-friend Killian and my prime suspect Rubenstein.

In less than three hours I would be in Concord playing rugby, and I was already exhausted. Last night I awoke from a disturbing dream. Ever since Tim Murray had asked me to play, I worried about being fit enough. In my dream those worries were magnified. I pictured myself pulling up short after running fifty yards, my chest heaving as I gasped for air, the opposing ball carrier skipping past me on the right side. He laughed as he ran by, easily evading my out-stretched hands. I got a quick glance at his face. The blood-shot eyes and pointed nose could be only one person: Rubenstein. Then the scenario replayed, only on my left side. Another ball carrier ran by, younger and quicker than the previous one. I missed him by several yards and one of his teammates yelled, "Way to go, Killian." The next ball carrier ran straight at me, head down so all I could see was a mass of grey hair. I stood my ground and made the tackle.

I woke up in a sweat. I tried to take my mind off the rugby match, but still couldn't sleep. My worries about the match were replaced by worries about the Walker case.

After yesterday's meeting with Raymond and Larry, I had walked over to the bar association office to try out their computerized legal research—Lexis and Westlaw. For nearly twenty years I had practiced the old-fashioned way so I was slow to embrace the new technology. Stubbornly I insisted that the old way had worked so why change, and I ignored computers. Besides, I decided, I liked the weight of the case books, the musty odor in the older ones.

With books the words were always there, right in front of you where you could run your fingers over them, read them once, then read them again if you so desired. Even if you lost your place, the book remained, timeless and accessible. If you didn't like what you read, you could toss the book across the room. Try that with a computer.

But after arriving in New Hampshire, I had decided to take a fresh look at all aspects of my life, including how I practiced law, so I signed up for a computer seminar put on by the bar association. I spent nearly an hour searching for cases comparable to Raymond's, hoping to find some tips on trial strategy, pitfalls to avoid. I found some that were close, but nothing was really on point. I was getting frustrated searching through case after case, using key words that turned out not to be so key, clicking on hypertext that led nowhere, then getting lost trying to find my way back to the case.

Finally, having found nothing useful, I gave up. Then this morning, after ten minutes, I found everything I could want right in my own office. Searching the one bookcase that passed as my scant law library, I cracked open my new and still stiff copy of McNamara's *Criminal Procedure*, the bible for New Hampshire's criminal lawyers.

Scanning the index to McNamara's treatise, I cursed myself for wasting time yesterday in the library. Everything was right here, neatly set out in black and white. I just had to look at the table of contents and turn to any subject. McNamara had concisely set out every pitfall imaginable, and made suggestions on how to avoid them. I had violated the cardinal rule of trial lawyers—KISS: for "Keep it simple, stupid."

The phone rang and I closed the book. I glanced at the clock: quarter to twelve. Saturday phone calls were rare. My first inclination was to ignore the phone and let the answering machine pick up. But my instinct said it might be important, so I lifted the headset. "Dutch Francis here."

"Mr. Francis, I am so glad you are there. I have some news for you, very good news I am sure."

"Who is this?" I asked, though from the accent I had a pretty good idea.

"Igor Rubenstein," he said. "We, um, met on Thursday. You remember, you took with you my book. And since I very much want it back, I have been asking everybody I know for information about that murder. This morning I get a call from someone . . . I think, maybe, will be helpful to you."

Suddenly I felt wide awake. "Of course, continue." I found a legal pad and readied my pen.

"This man call me, he say his name is Jack. That is all, he not say his last name. He had heard that I was asking for information about Brian McHugh. He tell me he want to be placing some bets on football games a few weeks ago and someone give him my name." He hesitated and coughed. "You not tape recording this, are you?"

"No, of course not." Though, I thought, it wouldn't be such a bad idea, even if illegal.

"So I was saying to you," he continued. "This Jack he go to my apartment but he never come inside."

"Wait," I said, finishing my note. "What day did he go to your apartment?"

"Yes, very good, that is important. He say it was day of fire. When he got there, he saw Brian McHugh; he recognize him from newspaper. He say something happened, maybe help to find murderer."

"What happened?"

He paused. I could hear him breathe into the phone, a long hissing sound. "I am sorry, he would not say."

"What! He told you all that but he wouldn't say more? What's he trying to pull?"

"Pull? What you mean?"

I pounded my fist on the desk. "Goddamn it!" I yelled.

"Jack ask me who wants this information and I say, a lawyer, but I not give him your name." He was breathing more heavily now, probably afraid he'd messed the whole thing up. "But," he added, "he give me his phone number. He say, 'Tell this lawyer to call me if he wants to know more.' So I got his phone number."

"Good for you, Igor, good for you." He read the number to me and I copied it down.

"So now I get my book back, okay?" I could picture him wiping his sweaty forehead.

"Not so fast, I-gee. First I got to talk to this Jack fellow, then let's see what he has to say. Could be a pile of bullshit, you know."

"No, I no think is bullshit. He sound like telling truth. I think he help you solve case, you talk to him, okay?"

"Sure, sure."

"Then you give me back my book, right?"

"Goodbye, Igor," I said and hung up.

I immediately dialed Jack's number. It rang half a dozen times before the answering machine came on. There was no message, just loud music, a loud rap song that pounded on for ten seconds before the inevitable beep.

I paused, trying to decide whether to leave a message. I decided I wanted to hear Jack's reaction first-hand so I hung up without saying anything. Then I dialed Hedges, thinking he could run a reverse search of Jack's phone number. He didn't answer either, but I left a message along with Jack's number.

On impulse I dialed Larry at home. Paula answered. "Sorry to bother you, Paula, but I got some information today that I wanted to talk to Larry about."

"Of course, I'd be happy to let him know. You sound worried. Is there bad news?"

"Nothing like that," I said, sensing her concern. "Just a lead we'd talked about. Who knows where it'll take us."

"Oh, Dutch, don't forget—Thanksgiving dinner. You're going to make it, aren't you?"

"Pardon?" I didn't remember anyone mentioning Thanksgiving dinner.

"Lawrence was supposed to invite you yesterday. He did, didn't he?"

"Well . . ."

"That's just like him, always preoccupied. I'm sure all he talked to you about was this case. As I told you the other day, it's the only thing on his mind. Anyway, Lawrence and I would love to have you as our guest on Thanksgiving."

"Um," I stammered. "That would be great. I'd love to sample some of your fine cooking again."

"Right. I'm sure you'd love any home-cooked meal." She paused. "And you can bring along a date, you know," she said. "If you want to, that is."

Nope, I thought, not a good time for double dating, or even single dating. "I don't think so," I said, trying to sound cheerful, "but if I do I'll warn you beforehand."

"Well, alright." She sounded disappointed. "I'll see you then. Five o'clock sharp."

ON my way out of the office, I stopped by the mailroom and picked up the mail. On Saturdays the mail was typically light and there were only a handful of letters there. I noticed one was from the New Hampshire Secretary of State. Antic-

ipating the response to Yvette's request for information on
PEVCON Corp., the owners of Igor Rubenstein and Mrs.
Luhovey's building, I ripped open the envelope as I walked
toward my car. Attached to the enclosure letter were PEV-
CON's Articles of Incorporation, listing the company's officers. As I read the names, my eyes blurred. I stopped in the
middle of the parking lot, refocused and looked again. I realized I was unconsciously pulling at my beard and blocking
a car trying to enter the lot. The paper fell from my hands. I
picked it up, waved a hurried apology to the driver, and got
in my car.

Inside, I rested the Articles in my lap and stared at the officers' names. I rubbed my palm over the folds in the paper,
trying to smooth them out. No matter how many times I
rubbed, the folds remained. I continued staring at the name
of the president and treasurer—Lawrence Conway—and
the vice president and secretary—Paula Conway. Of course,
P-Ev-Con. Paula and Evan Conway. Larry had named the
company after his wife and son.

CHAPTER 18

I didn't know what to make of this information. So Larry owned an apartment building, so what? I knew he was a real estate developer so no surprise there. Was it only a coincidence that he owned the same building that McHugh had visited shortly before his death? Or where a man had died in a suspicious fire? Of course it was, I told myself. Larry was a successful businessman and Manchester was a small city. The odds were pretty high, I guessed, that Larry would have some interest in any randomly chosen rental property in the city. He probably owned dozens of apartment buildings.

My mind was preoccupied when I stopped by my apartment and changed into the CATS rugby uniform that Tim Murray had dropped off last week. I decided I'd call Larry as soon as I returned from the game, see what he had to say about PEVCON.

In the meantime, I still had some leads to follow. As soon as I got on I-89 I flipped open my cell phone and tried Jack again. When the noisy rap music came on, I hung up immediately, not wanting to suffer through even ten seconds again. I turned on the radio and scanned a few stations before finding the news. The northbound traffic was light. New Hampshire was between the foliage and ski seasons so tourism was slow. Most of the foliage had died and the trees were nearly bare, only a few dying leaves clinging on. The sky was clear and blue. The tourists were missing out, I thought. Even the dead leaves looked beautiful framed by the blue cloudless sky.

The rugby field was north of downtown Concord, midway between the State Prison and the State House. Tim Murray said I couldn't miss it: "There are convicts on one side, criminals on the other."

Wearing a maroon jersey with a neatly starched white collar, Tim stood in the middle of a circle of other maroon jerseys, leading the CATS in stretching exercises. Across the field I saw the Portsmouth side, a sea of blue jerseys with a single white stripe, all well wrinkled, running wind sprints. Even from a distance, they looked huge; this could turn out to be a long day.

Tim broke from the circle when he saw me approaching. "Ah, Dutch," he said, shaking my hand. "Good of you to come. That makes a full fifteen. Where shall we put you?"

"I'm not in the best of shape," I said sheepishly, realizing I was crazy to be doing this. "But I think I can handle fullback." I swallowed, hoping Tim would agree. At fullback, I could stay behind the rest of the team and wait for the ball to come to me. Most of the time, the fullback takes it easy, fielding kicks then kicking the ball back down the field. Unless the other side has some superstar kickers, I should be able to relax.

"Excellent," Tim said to my relief. "That would work out just fine. Come on. I'll introduce you to the lads." Rugby players, I remembered, had a habit of pretending they were British.

The "lads" weren't much younger than I was, and they had the unkempt look of experienced ruggers. Long sideburns, curly locks hanging over their ears and down their necks. My neat haircut and trim beard looked out of place. Even Tim looked two weeks overdue for a haircut.

Tim started with the forwards. The number eight, Big Ben, stood at least six seven. He growled "cheers" in an accent that may have been British—I couldn't be sure—while he was jumping for passes on a lineout. The passes were thrown by the hooker, Sammy, whose bushy sideburns covered his cheeks. Except for a patch of bare chin, he had a full beard. Next Tim introduced the props, the front line of the scrum who were suitably stocky with matching stripes shaved down the top of their heads. Each had a porcine name: Hog and Swine. When Tim announced their names, Hog sang: "And that's all folks." I was glad those two were on my side.

We quickly went through the rest of the forwards, and then approached the backs. They were standing in a circle, passing the ball, underhand, in a counterclockwise direction. We joined the circle, side by side. Each time a back caught the ball, Tim yelled his name. "That's Neil, scrumhalf," he said. When Neil passed it along, Tim announced, "Dicky, wing and a mighty fast one at that." And then, "Our center, Boozer. You'll see why at the party." Tim went all around the circle, shouting each player's name as he caught the ball. The ball then came to Tim, who tossed it to me and yelled, "Our new—or should I say old—fullback and a helluva trial lawyer, Dutch Francis."

The referee blew the whistle and the circle broke up. We lined up in our positions, ready for the kickoff. At the other end, the Portsmouth team began screaming "yee-hah," "who-ooh," and other indecipherable sounds. One of them, a huge monster with a long black beard and dark eyes, sauntered to our side and yelled, "You're not CATS; you're pussies!" His teammates laughed heartily. It was going to be an interesting match.

As Neil dug a hole with his heel, preparing for kickoff, I stared across the field at the Portsmouth players. One of them looked familiar; he was thin with curly brown hair. I was sure I had met him recently. Who was it?

Neil raised his right hand, waiting for the referee's whistle signalling kickoff. Oh my God, I said to myself; it's Laflamme. When I first met him at his office, he had seemed uncomfortable in a suit and tie. Here, on a dirty rugby field on a damp and cold November day, wearing rugby shorts and a long-sleeved shirt as he swung his arms getting ready for the kickoff, he seemed at home.

As I waited for Neil's hand to drop, I glanced from Neil to Laflamme. Butterflies swarmed in my stomach. I had enough worries without having Laflamme there to remind me of my difficult murder case, namely whether my forty-two-year old body could handle eighty minutes of rugby. It had been a long time since I'd played.

Finally, the referee blew his whistle and Neil dropped his arm to the side, and stutter-stepped forward. He snapped his foot and the ball sailed to the Portsmouth goal, where the fullback easily fielded it. The Portsmouth fullback raced up-field, joining his teammates, then passed the ball quickly along the line. I followed the CATS toward the ball, careful to stay far enough behind in case of a quick kick. I was impressed with how efficiently the Portsmouth backs, including Laflamme, shuffled the ball outside to the wing, a tall and wiry kid with a baby face. They had the look of a confident and disciplined team.

I felt my heart race when Babyface made a deft head fake to leave our wing grasping at air. Someone yelled, "Get outside." Babyface flew toward the sideline, outsprinting our pursuing centers. I was frozen with uncertainty. If I blocked his path down the sideline, I would leave our goal defenseless, vulnerable to a short kick over my head. Not sure whether to charge or retreat toward our goal, I did neither. I made sort of a half run, half jog toward the sideline, a useless defense either to a run or kick. Sure enough, Babyface got by me easily.

Just as Babyface appeared on his way down the sideline

for a score, Boozer sprinted diagonally in front of me from the opposite side. I was the most relieved person on the field when Boozer's head collided with Babyface's side, easily knocking the ball into touch. Just then Laflamme ran up to me, brushing my shoulder with his. "Nice tackle, Francis," he sneered in the same tone of voice I had heard in his office.

Always ready with a quick witty comeback, I answered, "Up yours, Laflamme." So much for civility among lawyers, I thought, as Laflamme ran back to his teammates, chuckling all the way.

I felt like calling it quits right then. Tim ran over and put his hand on my shoulder. "Loosen up, ol' man. You're as tight as a drum."

As Laflamme assumed his position at inside center, I mumbled under my breath, "Wait 'till I get you in court." But I knew the criticism was justified: if I were that slow defending Raymond in court, Laflamme would eat me alive.

Five minutes later I got a chance to redeem myself. On a lineout Big Ben snatched the inbound pass from Sammy and turned toward our side. But before he could hand off the ball, Blackbeard grabbed his shoulders and spun him completely around. Ben looked helpless in the madman's huge hands. With Ben now facing them, the Portsmouth forwards stripped the ball, and sent it on its way down the line of backs.

I was determined not to make any more mistakes. As the ball was passed down the line, I clenched my fists and pumped my feet up and down. The last thing I wanted was to be caught flatfooted. When the Portsmouth outside center, a burly redhead with a handlebar moustache, broke a tackle, I took two steps forward. He charged full-speed at me. I wasted no time and ran right at him. I wanted to act decisively and win the confidence of my new teammates and show up Laflamme.

As I lowered my shoulder for the hit, I momentarily lost sight of the ball. My shoulder connected solidly with the redhead's stomach. He groaned, "ugh," and hit the ground like a fallen tree. I scrambled to my feet and pulled at his arms to release the ball. He was still groaning, gasping for air, and gave no resistance. The only problem was he didn't have the ball. I looked on the ground where he had fallen, then to both sides. No ball. I knew the worst had happened when cheers erupted from the Portsmouth side. I looked back to see Babyface touching the ball down in front of the posts. Not a CATS player near him.

I kicked the dirt, sending a divot ten yards downfield. When I realized what had happened, I felt like kicking myself. Red must have passed the ball to Babyface just as I lowered my shoulder. I was so intent on making a solid hit I didn't even notice Babyface in the area. He probably couldn't believe his luck.

Laflamme was the first to say something. "Great tackle, Francis. Next time get the guy with the ball."

Boozer got in Laflamme's face. "Shut the fuck up, Laflamme," he screamed. Somehow Boozer also knew Laflamme, who grinned and walked away. Turning to me, Boozer said, "That was a helluva stick. Look at that sonovabitch still groaning on the ground."

The Portsmouth trainer had run onto the field to tend to Red. He carried a bucket of water and applied a wet sponge, known as the magic sponge to ruggers, to Red's head and stomach. The magic sponge was used for all injuries, from knee sprains to concussions. It contained no medicine, but its water was known to relieve the most agonizing pain. Once you had seen the sponge produce its magic, you dared not question how it worked. Anyone who made that mistake would be cursed, and most likely injured himself within a short time.

I walked over to check on Red. "You okay?" I asked.

He looked up at me, still clutching his stomach. "Yeah, I'm okay," he said through labored breaths. "But, I'll tell you something, mate. That won't happen again."

The Portsmouth fullback's perfect kick-after made the

score seven nothing. For the rest of the half, we had several scoring opportunities but just couldn't cash in. Neil proved to be a master at scrumhalf, continually keeping Portsmouth off balance. Almost instinctively he knew when to pass to the standoff, or ground kick past the Portsmouth backs, where he would pick up the ball and run for a long gain.

For a time the game turned into a kicking match. Whenever we put the ball into the Portsmouth end, their fullback sent it sailing right back to us. His squat fireplug build gave his short legs leverage to make long high kicks. I was relieved to catch the first one, a sixty-yard spiral. My return kick didn't match his for distance, but still sailed forty yards before bouncing out of bounds.

As the end of the half approached, sweat was pouring off my face and neck, drenching my collar. The flow increased when Fireplug boomed a kick toward our goal. I turned and ran to the spot where I thought the ball would land. If I dropped the ball in front of me, it would be a knock-on and Portsmouth would get a scrum right outside the goal. Another Portsmouth try could put the game out of reach. Since I felt responsible for the first one, I didn't want to give them another opportunity. As the ball came down I turned to my side, instinctively as if I had no control of my movement. I felt a surge of excitement when I realized that I was remembering my old tricks: catch the kick from the side, so if you drop the ball, you won't commit a knock-on. Just pick it up and run.

Fortunately I held onto the ball. Neil was screaming at me: "Touch. Kick to touch." But before I could make the kick, two Portsmouth forwards slammed into me. They were making shrill grunting sounds, the kind I last heard during a visit to the zoo. I twisted around so my back was against the two gorillas. Then I dug my cleats in the ground, desperately trying to stay on my feet. The gorillas pulled on my arms. I knew it would be disastrous to drop the ball or be knocked to the ground. Soon I heard the unmistakable snorts of Hog and Swine joining the maul to battle the gorillas. Now I was being tugged from all sides. Aside from the animal sounds, all I could hear were CATS encouraging me to "hold on" or "stay up." I cradled the ball to my chest as the surging mob lifted me in the air. I had no control over where my body went. I felt like driftwood in the ocean, thrust toward shore by the tide, then sucked back out by the undertow. As I bounced up and down I caught a glimpse of the now overcast sky, swarms of dark clouds framed by flailing arms and sweaty heads. In the background, somewhere between the clouds, in sharp contrast to the overwhelming greyness, I saw a patch of blue.

Someone yelled, "Get his fuckin' fingers." Grimy hands tried to pry my fingers off the ball. It was an old trick, bend the fingers back as far as possible, even break them, to make you release the ball. I tightened my grip, frustrating their efforts. Just when I thought I had won the battle, I felt a sharp pain in my right hand. "Bastard," I screamed. I looked at my attacker; it was Laflamme. He had bitten off a piece of skin over my knuckle and was grinning as he watched me struggle and moan.

Mercifully, the referee blew his whistle. "Time," he announced. "End of half."

I laid on the ground, still clutching the ball against my chest, gasping to catch my breath and cursing Laflamme. My hand was bleeding. There were teeth marks, an upper and lower set, beneath the blood. Tim and Neil lifted me to my feet. "You're a pretty tough guy," Neil said. "For a lawyer."

They guided me to the sideline where I stretched out flat on my back. Every muscle ached and I felt old and tired, a has-been on the rugby field. I wondered how I'd ever make it through the second half. There were easier ways to spend a Saturday—sitting safely in the law library for one. Tim offered me some orange slices. "These'll give you a burst of energy," he reassured me. At least he didn't offer Geritol. "This'll be our half," he continued. "You'll see, we'll come back."

When I regained what little sense I had left, I glanced around the field. Laflamme was on the opposite sideline, talking to two men in suits. I got up and started toward him. I was pissed. "Hey Laflamme," I yelled from the middle of the field. "You dirty sonovabitch." He didn't even glance at me; his attention was focused on the suits, who seemed excited about something. They were walking backwards, waving their arms, beckoning Laflamme to follow. Laflamme picked up his sweats from the ground and ran toward them.

"Hey, where you going?" I yelled.

Laflamme kept running but turned his head back to me. "Sorry I can't stay and watch you make an ass of yourself," he yelled. "But looks like there's some new evidence that will sink your boy."

"What're you talking about?"

He ignored me and kept running with the suits to the parking lot. They jumped into a white sedan and, with one of the suits driving, sped out of the lot toward the highway.

I stared after them, wondering what the hell was going on. I knew I'd find out sooner or later what new evidence Laflamme thought he had, but what really annoyed me was that I wouldn't have a chance to slam him to the ground with a hard shoulder tackle.

The referee blew his whistle to start the second half. The kickoff came to Sammy who fielded it cleanly. The CATS came back strong, keeping the ball in the Portsmouth end for most of the half. With a few minutes to play, Ben came off a lineout and spun his way across the end line, slapping the ball down for a try. We were still down 7 to 5; for a tie, Neil had to make the conversion kick from a tough angle near the sideline. His kick sailed far enough but struck the upright squarely, bouncing back onto the field. Portsmouth led by two with only a couple of minutes to play. To take the lead we needed either another try or a dropkick through the uprights, a difficult maneuver, rarely tried, but good for three points.

Portsmouth came on strong, controlling the ball dangerously close to our goal. Sammy won a scrum and Neil sent a kick past midfield. "Three minutes," the ref yelled.

"Bullshit," Hog muttered under his breath. "We've played nowhere near forty minutes." The referee was probably just anxious to get home.

While we were distracted by the referee, Portsmouth fielded Neil's kick and mounted an attack. Quickly they passed the ball to Red, their outside center. Somehow he broke through the line and ran straight at me. I had a sudden sense of déjà vu all over again, as Yogi Berra might have said. I knew that if I made a mistake the game would be over.

I was sure Red wasn't up to getting slammed to the ground again, so I ran directly at him, conscious this time of Babyface following on the wing. I lowered my head as if readying for the same hard hit as before. Instead of following through, though, I veered toward the wing. As I expected, Red passed off when he saw my head lowered. I stretched out my left arm and tipped the ball in the air with my fingertips. My momentum carried me right under the ball. I pulled it in and looked toward the Portsmouth goal, at least thirty-five yards away.

I was vaguely conscious of a sea of white and blue jerseys in front of me. They were charging toward me, framed by the goalpost in the background. I heard voices from all directions, a jumble of indecipherable noise. There was no way I could run through that crowd. But if I didn't score quickly, the whistle would blow and the game would end with a CATS' loss. Without thinking, I dropped the ball to the ground. Just as the tip of the ball grazed the grass, I kicked it with all my might. As soon as I hit the ball, I was shocked I'd done it. I had never tried a dropkick in a game. The "thud" sound as my foot hit the ball told me I had hit it solidly.

The ball sailed high in the air and seemed to hesitate over the crossbar, then dropped behind it, right in the middle of the posts. CATS were jumping up and down all around me, slapping me on the back and pulling at my jersey. I was still in shock that I had tried such a risky play. Amidst the jubilation of my teammates, I heard a high-pitched whistle. "Time," the referee yelled. "CATS win eight to seven. Good match, lads."

CHAPTER 19

STILL feeling shocked by my dropkick, and grinning at the result, I followed Tim's baby blue BMW down Main Street. I was feeling giddy, completely swept up in the backslapping of my teammates. For a few minutes I had pushed to the back of my mind the serious problems of Raymond Walker, and was looking forward to the rugby party. But my cell phone on the floor by the passenger seat reminded me of some unfinished business. I reached down, grabbed the phone, then punched in Jack's number. To my surprise, the obnoxious music did not come on.

"Yes," said a male voice.

"Is this Jack?" I asked.

There was no answer.

Finally he said, "Is this where I'm supposed to say, 'Who wants to know?'"

"Sorry, name's Dutch Francis. I was told you had some information I might be interested in."

"Hold on." He put his hand over the receiver; I could hear only muffled voices. He came back on. "Yeah, you the lawyer for the guy accused of killing that football player, what's his name?"

"Right, Brian McHugh from St. Andrew."

"I think I know who really killed him."

I slammed on the brakes and pulled to the side. Tim's BMW disappeared around a corner. "I'd like to hear more."

"Not so fast, mouthpiece, I got a way I want to play this. Rubenstein said he'd take care of me if I cooperated. I need some security; I can't just give away my information, know what I mean?"

"What're you looking for?" I asked, wondering what Rubenstein had promised him.

"Tell you what, why don't you and me get together, work on something that's—let's say—mutually beneficial. Where you located right now?"

"About two blocks from the State Capitol, heading toward O'Dowd's Pub. You want to meet me there?"

"Yeah, I know the place. I want to call Rubenstein first, then I'll be there in twenty, thirty minutes. We'll talk."

"Wait. What's your last name? How will I know you?"

"Name's Gibbs. And don't worry about knowing me. You're a lawyer, right?"

"Yeah, so?"

"I'll find you. You guys stick out like a sore thumb."

Same to you, I thought as I hung up. I pulled away from the curb, wondering how I'd ever find O'Dowd's Pub without Tim leading the way. I turned the corner and noticed his car two blocks ahead, waiting at the curb with his caution lights flashing. I honked to get his attention and he pulled out ahead of me.

I reviewed in my mind the conversation with Gibbs. He sounded so sure he knew the real killer. Could this be the break Raymond had been waiting for? Or was this guy Gibbs playing some kind of game for kicks or money? I was hopeful, but cautious. He could be the key witness in the case, and here I was meeting him at a pub while boozing it up at a rugby party. What would my law school professors say? Tim honked as he passed a space right in front of O'Dowd's, pointing for me to take it. I waited at the entrance while Tim parked a short way down the street. A sign above the door contained a green shamrock and the discomforting message, "We cheat tourists and drunks."

Inside, a handful of players from both teams milled around the bar, still in their dirty uniforms, chatting together while they sipped on cups of beer. Ben had his arm around Blackbeard as he recounted how he had outjumped Blackbeard on the lineout before scoring in the first half.

Rugby parties were curious affairs. After beating on each other for eighty minutes, both teams gathered at a local pub to drink gallons of watered-down draft beer and sing lewd songs, unleashing the immature, sexist, ridiculous youths that lurked inside. All inhibitions were discarded, no matter the occupation: lawyers, carpenters, truck drivers, even accountants. An outsider wandering into the midst of a rugby party would think both teams were lifelong friends, and he the only stranger.

Tim led me through the crowd to a keg strategically placed on a table beside the bar. He poured beer into two paper cups. He handed me one, tipped his cup to mine and said, "Son of a gun. That was beautiful, beautiful. What a play. A drop kick. Whoever heard of such a thing?"

I smiled. "Not me. I'd fooled around with it in practice a few times, but never in a game."

We both laughed as we sipped the beer. Tim kidded me about saying I was out of shape. "You ought to be playing every week," he said.

I shook my head. "Uh, uh, too busy." And even if I weren't, one look at the damage inflicted on my body would have discouraged me from becoming a regular player. Both my legs were encrusted in mud and the bloody abrasions on my knees had started to sting. There were so many bruises on my shins and calves that I gave up trying to count them. I remembered how helpless I felt in the middle of the maul, with both sides tugging me in different directions like a

wishbone. At least Laflamme's teeth marks on my hand had
stopped bleeding. The wound had dried to a hard scab in the
shape of two semicircles but fortunately there was no sign of
rabies—yet.

We sat on stools against the side wall and soon were
joined by five or six CATS, each anxious to tell his version
of the final play.

Boozer said, "I could tell right away you were going to
kick. You had that look in your eye." I didn't bother inform-
ing him that look was one of utter bewilderment.

A few more Portsmouth players arrived, and immediately
lined up along the bar awaiting their turn at the keg. Half a
dozen of their fans were with them. Behind the bar was a
huge mirror, ten feet high and stretching the full length of
the bar. On the wall across from the bar, where a few CATS
sat, were dozens of framed mirrors, each two feet by three
feet and imprinted with the name of a European beer. They
were arranged in groups by country. Above our heads was
the Irish section, by far the largest, with mirrors reading
"Guinness is good for you" and "Make friends with Murphy." As I sipped the tasteless American draft in my paper
cup, I longed for the dark, strong flavor of an Irish stout.

After we had exhausted the retelling of the game, Tim did
what lawyers invariably do when they get together—talk
about work. I told him about Raymond's case. "In fact, I saw
my opponent today," I said, adding, "and it seems Boozer
knows him too: Assistant Attorney General Peter Laflamme.
The sonovabitch took a piece out of my hand." I showed
them the wound.

"The dirty piece of shit," Boozer said. "I know him, but
I wish to hell I'd never met him. He doesn't look like much
but he's a tough sonovabitch."

Tim added, "On the rugby field and in the courtroom."

"You've met him in the courtroom?" I asked.

"We both have," Tim answered, nodding toward Boozer.
"Years ago," he explained, "Laflamme wanted to play for
the CATS. I told him we had no openings. I could've fit him

in if I'd wanted, and he wasn't a bad player, but there was something about him I didn't like. So he joined the Portsmouth side, even though he lives and works here in Concord."

"And he never forgave you, did he?" Boozer said.

"But he shouldn't have tried to take it out on you," Tim answered.

"A few months later Boozer had a little problem with the booze," Tim continued. "After a rugby party he tried to drive himself home. Weaving all over the road. Concord cop pulls him over, gives him a bunch of field sobriety tests. No problem—Boozer aces nearly all of them but the cop still wants to do the blood test. Boozer refuses—hey, he had a few brain cells left. So he loses his license for a while but, what the hell, he knew he was plastered. Laflamme prosecuted the DWI."

"Why Laflamme?" I asked. "Don't the county counsels prosecute drunk driving cases?"

"Usually," Boozer said, "but my wife works in the clerk's office here in Concord. Filing papers and that kind of shit. Someone figured ol' Thompson, the county counsel, would have a conflict of interest so they give it to Laflamme."

Tim continued. "So before trial I make a motion to suppress Boozer's refusal to take the blood test. Usually I wouldn't have a chance but our trial judge was Vinnie D'Angelo, head of the local chapter of Alcoholics Anonymous. Vinnie D. believes in giving alcoholics a second chance. Only problem is his beliefs sometimes conflict with the law. He sees that this is Boozer's first offense, that he passed most of the FSTs, so he grants our motion. Suppresses any evidence of Boozer's refusal to take the test. Laflamme goes through the roof. Without the refusal in evidence, he knows it'll be tough to win."

"I don't blame him for being upset. D'Angelo's ruling sounds shaky," I said.

"But it gets better. Laflamme gets so pissed off he becomes irrational. He withdraws all offers to plea bargain. Decides to try it anyway."

"I would have taken probation. I started going to AA anyway," Boozer said.

Tim continued. "Laflamme's first witness is the arresting officer, an Irish cop wouldn't you know. Ruddy face, big grin, the whole bit. Laflamme asks, 'After you administered the field sobriety tests, Officer, did you have any conversation with the defendant?' Paddy says, 'Yeah, I sure did,' then he adds, 'I offered him a blood test and he refused.'"

"You shoulda seen the look on D'Angelo's face," Boozer laughed.

"The cop disobeyed the judge's order? Why'd he do that?" I asked.

"Seems Laflamme forgot to tell him," Tim answered. "But D'Angelo thought Laflamme was being sneaky, trying to pull a fast one."

Tim paused and sipped his beer before continuing. "D'Angelo screams 'Sidebar' and, steam coming from his ears, looks down at Laflamme. 'You don't ever pull that crap in my courtroom.' Laflamme is stammering, 'But, your honor, I didn't know . . .' 'Shut up,' D'Angelo snaps. 'You're lucky I don't throw you in jail for contempt. As it is you've wasted the county a lot of money. I'm declaring a mistrial.'"

Tim raised his hand, palm out, and Boozer slapped him five, both shouting, "Yeah."

"Laflamme was so embarrassed," Tim added, "that he dismissed the case."

"So that was Laflamme's only mistrial," I observed, remembering the scoreboard in Laflamme's office. I immediately wondered how I could use this information to my best advantage.

"Any idea why he took off at halftime?" I asked.

"He knew we were gonna whip his team's butts," Boozer said, "that's why."

"He said something about new evidence in my murder case."

"Oh yeah?" Tim said. "The two guys in suits did look like cops." He paused. "Wait a sec . . ." His eyes wide, Tim put down his beer and pointed to the TV above the bar. Brian McHugh's face was on the screen above the words, NEWS FLASH! The camera panned to a male announcer looking serious, then to a shot of a lake. "Hey, turn the TV up," Tim yelled to the bartender.

I caught the end of the announcer's statement.

". . . today from Lake Masabesic. Ballistic tests have proven the gun was used to kill Brian 'Bruiser' McHugh, St. Andrew's star halfback. Police have not said whether the gun is connected to Raymond Walker, the nineteen-year-old charged with McHugh's murder. We will bring you updates as soon as new information comes in. Now we return to our regular . . ."

I swallowed, worried.

Boozer smiled. "Hey, could be a big break for your case," he said.

"Or break it," I said, my stomach sinking. Lake Masabesic: where Raymond went fishing the day after the shooting. I did not like the implication. If the gun were traced to Raymond, he wouldn't stand a chance at trial. I'd have to recommend a plea, if Laflamme would even offer one.

My thoughts were interrupted by shouting from the end of the bar. It was Blackbeard, repeating the challenge he had issued after the match. Right after my dropkick had sailed through the goalpost, Blackbeard had pointed to the CATS, jumping all over each other, and screamed, "You pussies may've won the match, but we're sure as hell gonna kick your ass at the party." True to his word, he now stood on a chair holding a beer cup high over his head, his black beard spotted with foam. He sang in a voice so bad it would be a compliment to say it was off-key:

"We call on the CATS to sing us a song. So sing you bastards, sing."

The start of the singing meant enough beer had been consumed to anesthetize aching joints and limbs and make the competitive juices once again begin to flow. As Tim had predicted, Boozer emerged as the CATS' leader, accepting Blackbeard's challenge without hesitation. He imitated Blackbeard by standing on a chair, holding a beer cup over his head. With the action starting, I scanned the room, trying to find anyone out of uniform. There were a few guys chatting with Portsmouth players, so I figured Gibbs wasn't among them. I had hoped he'd arrive before the singing got out of hand.

Too late. The first song was a rowdy Australian tune about vomiting into the Pacific Ocean, featuring several different synonyms for "vomit":

"If you want to throw your voice then you've got no other choice but to chundah in the ol' Pacific sea."

No one ever accused rugby players of being profound.

As Boozer began the final verse—something about a "technicolor yawn"—a Portsmouth player jumped on a chair, following the ritual of holding a beer cup over his head. It was my nemesis, Red, his glazed eyes indicating he had forgotten the day's embarrassments. He sang in a loud, unduly confident voice:

> *"I used to work in Chicago*
> *in a department store.*
> *I used to work in Chicago.*
> *I don't work there anymore."*

That set cups rising throughout the bar, each player jockeying to be next to sing a verse. Someone sang:

> *"A lady came in for some lobsters,*

some lobsters from the store.
Lobsters she wanted, crabs she got.
And I don't work there anymore."

The mention of "lobsters" brought to mind Mrs. Luhovey's case. I looked around the bar, thinking of Mrs. Luhovey while searching for Gibbs. The bar was almost completely packed with sweaty players, singing intently. A couple of young men, perhaps twenty years old, stood apart from the crowd intent on their own conversation. They were in street clothes. One was tall and lanky with a thin black moustache that made him look a little like Clark Gable. His friend was huskier, a few inches shorter, with a haircut that made me think of Curley from the Three Stooges. They were an odd-looking pair. While talking to his friend, the Clark Gable clone glanced around the room as if searching for someone. When he saw me also looking around, he turned to say something to Curley. Was he Gibbs?

Slowly I made my way through the crowd. The pub was disintegrating into complete chaos. Both teams alternated leading the singing, the competition continuing from the rugby field, each trying to be cruder than the other. When the singing reached a feverish pitch, players swung their cups to and fro, splashing beer on the floor and on each other. I splashed through small puddles of beer as I came up to Clark and Curley.

"Jack Gibbs?" I asked.

Clark turned around. "Francis? The lawyer?"

"The same."

"You don't look like a lawyer," he said, looking me up and down.

In a dirty rugby shirt, shorts, mud-caked knees, blood-encrusted hands, and beer-soaked socks, I had to admit he was right. "Let's find a quieter place to talk," I suggested.

He turned to Curley. "What d'ya think, Mick? Wanna join us?"

Mick smiled and said, "Nah, it's just getting interesting."

He nodded toward the entrance where two women were standing, looking bewildered. All eyes were now upon them. The crowd became silent. No doubt the two women, dressed casually in dungarees and sweaters, had expected to have a nice chat over a cold beer, unaware of the ongoing debauchery. They took a few tentative steps toward the bar. The crowd buzzed with anticipation, and before the duo reached the bar, someone yelled, "Rugby Princess!"

Immediately Boozer pulled a table across the entrance, blocking their exit. Gesturing to his teammates, he jumped on top. Swine and Hog grabbed the arms of the youngest-looking woman, who was mousey-looking with frizzy brown hair touching her shoulders. They tried to coax her onto the table with Boozer. She resisted, put her hands over her face, and halfheartedly said, "Stop."

Her friend saw the gap-toothed smiles of the Pork Patrol and, laughing, pushed her friend toward the table. She shouted, "Go on, Christy, don't be chicken."

Christy rolled her eyes, pointed at Hog and Swine, saying, "Watch the hands," and held out her elbows so they could lift her onto the table. The entire pub crowded closer for a better view. Everyone was standing shoulder to shoulder, beer cup to beer cup. I tapped Gibbs on the shoulder and with my eyes indicated we should go to the other end of the bar. He shrugged and followed me through the crowd. Mick stayed behind where he had a better view of the rugby princess.

The noise level was only slightly lower in the back. By the time we got to an open space, I turned around and saw Boozer grinning insanely. He winked at Christy and sang:

"Alouette, gentille Alouette, Alouette, je te plumerai."

Then he grabbed a strand of Christy's hair in one hand. While pointing with the other, he sang:

"Does she not have scraggly hair?"

The entire pub joined in a resounding chorus:

"Scraggly hair, yes, scraggly hair. Oh, Alouette, gentille Alouette . . ."

People pushed from all sides. Neil got jolted from behind and spilled his beer on Tim's back. CATS and Portsmouth players were intermingled, everyone joining in the singing.

Jack Gibbs stood a few feet behind me, leaning on the bar. He stared at the singers, waiting for me to start.

"Does she not have furrowed brow?" Boozer sang.

The chorus: *"Furrowed brow!"*

Boozer: *"Furrowed brow, scraggly hair."*

"Oh Alouette, gentille Alouette . . ."

"So what do you have?" I asked Jack.

"First things first," he said. "I couldn't reach Rubenstein, but I left him a message to call me here. Soon as I get a solid commitment from him, I'll tell you what I got."

I didn't like what I was hearing. If Gibbs took money from Rubenstein, his testimony would be worthless, especially if Laflamme learned that Rubenstein had reason to divert suspicion from himself. "So what did Rubenstein promise you?"

"A little inside information to get me through the college basketball season. Should make me a pretty penny."

Great, I thought. Either way, with money or a tip on a bet, Gibbs would be tainted. But at least a tip would be harder to trace than cash. "He's good for it," I said. "You can tell me now." I wanted to push him before he completed the transaction with Rubenstein. Maybe I could dissuade Rubenstein from following through and perhaps salvage Gibbs' credibility.

He hesitated as if he were turning over in his mind everything I had said. He held up his hand. "No hurry, I'm not going anywhere." Then he looked toward the front of the bar where his friend Mick was enthusiastically chugging beer and singing along.

I folded my arms and waited. I felt like grabbing him by the neck and squeezing the information out of him. I had a client who was looking at life in prison and this clown was negotiating with me for a hot tip on a bet. I had no choice but to wait. If I pushed him too hard, he might clam up and I'd never learn what he had.

The singing was getting louder.

"Does she not have shifty eyes?"

"Shifty eyes!"

"Shifty eyes, furrowed brow, scraggly hair. Oh . . ."

Suddenly Mick broke from the crowd and waved at Jack to come to him. I waited in the back as Mick directed Jack to the phone hanging off the hook by the side of the bar. Jack went over and picked up the phone.

"Does she not have crooked nose?"

"Crooked nose!"

"Crooked nose, shifty eyes, furrowed . . ."

After a few minutes, Jack waved at me to come to the phone. "It's Rubenstein," he said. "He won't tell me anything until you assure him I've come through."

I picked up the phone. "I-gor?" I said, unable to resist mispronouncing his name again.

"Ya, it is I," he said. "This Jack he supposed to tell you the name of the real murderer. All I say is I make it worth his while to tell truth, that is all, truth. Has he told you anything?"

"Not yet, but I'm sure he'd tell the truth even if you weren't helping him out."

"Ya, of course, but you know the gamblers. How you say: always looking out for number one."

I mulled over which would look worse: Gibbs providing information before he received a hot tip or after. Either way, there were risks. If Gibbs were going to bullshit me, he'd do it no matter what. I decided to give in to Gibbs.

"Igor," I said, "do me a favor and give Gibbs your hot tip." I looked at Gibbs, made sure he could hear me. "Now that I've met Mr. Gibbs, I can tell he's an honorable man. I believe he would've come forward anyway, even if you hadn't made him any promises. So I'll put him back on and you tell him whatever you want, okay?"

"If you say so, okay, I'll do it."

I handed Gibbs the phone. He nodded, took a small note-book and a pen from his pocket. "January 6, okay, Boston College—Georgetown. Got it. Thank you very much, Mr. Rubenstein. This could be a very enjoyable winter." He hung up and turned toward me.

From behind me I could hear his friend Mick approaching, shouting something that got drowned in the singing.

"What's going on?" Mick asked.

"Does she not have luscious lips?"

"Luscious lips!"

"Luscious lips, crooked nose . . ."

Gibbs ignored him and turned toward me. "You're right," he said. "I am an honorable man, giving you this information. I could still keep it to myself, you know."

I agreed with him. "You're doing the right thing."

Jack began the story that would turn my defense of Raymond Walker—and my whole life—upside down. "I got a tip that Rubenstein was a good guy to place bets with, so I went by his place in Manchester. Must've been a week or so before the McHugh murder. First time I was there so I was kind of wandering around trying to find the entrance. I see this guy mowing the lawn; teenager, maybe seventeen or eighteen. One of those preppy types, nice neat haircut, sweater with patches on the elbows. He doesn't see me 'cause I'm walking on the sidewalk behind some bushes. He shuts off the mower and picks up this red plastic gas can and then he takes them both down to the basement."

". . . furrowed brow."

"By now I'm sure this is Rubenstein's building so I stop and just watch. There was something about the way this guy was acting: you know, suspicious-like. So after a minute or so, the guy comes running out of the basement. When he opens the door, smoke comes pouring out."

My attention was focused entirely on Gibbs. His friend Mick stood beside him, half listening to Gibbs while turning every few seconds to check out the action at the front of the bar. Even though the singing was as loud as ever and I was getting bumped constantly by passing bodies, I listened intently to every word. It was the same sense of focus I'd had when making the game-winning dropkick. Now I had one goal in mind: winning Raymond's case.

"Does she not have great big tits?"

"The guy walks fast, looking around. I step back so he doesn't notice me and I can tell he's nervous. He goes about thirty feet when the front door, which is just up the stairs from the basement door, flies open and this big guy comes running out, screaming for the kid to stop."

"You hear what he was saying?" I asked.

"Nah, just a lot of yelling."

". . . slender neck!"

Mick took a swig of beer and now listened as intently as me, acting like this was the first time he'd heard Gibbs' story.

"So this arguing's gone on—seem's like one or two minutes—but couldn't have been that long. All the time the smoke's getting thicker. And these two are getting hotter, right? The one from the building is pointing toward the basement and the smoke. Then the kid pushes him away, turns and starts running."

". . . luscious lips, crooked nose . . ."

I held up my hand to stop Gibbs. Although I knew the answer, I had to ask. "Okay, who were these two?"

Before he could answer, someone slapped me on the back. "Dutch, what're you doing back here? There's a party going on." It was Tim Murray. He wanted to drag me back with the team. I explained that I'd be right with him, I had a little business to conduct. He looked suspiciously at Jack and Mick, tried coaxing me a little more, then made me promise to join him in five minutes.

". . . scraggly hair . . ."

After he left, Gibbs continued. "The one came running from the building, I didn't recognize him 'til I saw his picture in the paper. That was your man, no question, Bruiser McHugh."

"And the other one," I asked, "the one with the lawn-mower?" I thought about Larry owning PEVCON and remembered something Evan had said during my dinner at the Conways' house: he often helped out his dad by doing some groundskeeping.

Gibbs looked at his friend Mick and shrugged. "Never saw him before in my life," he said.

"Wait a second, you said you had information on the identity of the murderer. What gives?"

Gibbs turned toward Mick and shrugged. "I've told you everything I know. Seems to me a good lawyer could do a lot with that particular evidence."

"Bullshit! You've given me nothing." I was disappointed in Gibbs' story. I thought he had something more concrete, something I could sell to a jury. He seemed to be suggesting that Evan—or whoever this groundskeeper was—had lit the fire, which was hard for me to swallow, and that Evan and McHugh had argued over something. Did McHugh see Evan light the fire? Gibbs couldn't hear what they were saying. I couldn't believe that person was Evan Conway.

"So that's it?" I asked, my voice getting testy.

Gibbs must've sensed my rising anger. He nudged Mick to head toward the exit. "That's all I got," he said, walking away. He turned around for one more comment. "But if you ask me, you find out who was mowing that lawn, you got yourself a murderer."

CHAPTER 20

THE drive to Manchester was a blur. I turned up the volume on the radio and kept punching the station buttons after a song had been playing no more than five seconds, searching for news of the gun. I had driven ten miles on Route 93 before realizing the transmission was revving loudly in third gear.

Jack Gibbs' comments echoed over and over in my head. After he and Mick had left, I started feeling lightheaded. I held onto the bar rail so I wouldn't fall, but as I stared straight ahead at the far wall, I got even dizzier from all the mirrors. The small ones advertising foreign beers bounced reflections back and forth from the big mirror behind the bar, so that I could see the "Guinness is good for you" sign reflecting itself endlessly. Gibbs and Mick slipped out of the bar before I could get their addresses. Maybe Hedges had been successful, I hoped, in doing a reverse search of Gibbs' phone number.

The last thing I remembered was saying hurried good-byes to Tim and the other CATS while Boozer finished singing "Alouette." As I opened the door, I stopped momentarily to watch Christy get revenge on Boozer by pouring a full cup of draft beer over his head.

In twenty minutes I passed the sign announcing the Manchester city limits. "Dammit!" I yelled, slamming my fist on the steering wheel. My anger was part disappointment that Gibbs didn't have more evidence and part worry about Evan. The pieces of the puzzle remained jumbled in my mind.

What had Gibbs said? Find the kid who was mowing the lawn and you'll find the murderer. He was definitely stretching but what worried me was the gun being found at Lake Masabesic. My initial thought was that Raymond might have thrown it there, but of course Raymond was not alone when he fished the lake. He was with Evan Conway.

These jumbled thoughts filled my mind as I turned onto the Amoskeag Bridge exit, then left on Elm Street. I had no idea where I was going. I just wanted to drive. The streets were nearly empty, surprising for a Saturday night. Street lights illuminated the back of the courthouse where Raymond was quietly killing time. A block away the siren of a fire engine sounded, and before I could slow down, the engine shot past me and turned toward the old mills by the river. Even though I was alone in the car, I shook my head back and forth, doubts still clouding my mind.

I drove the full length of Elm Street and, forgetting the street was a dead end, at the end had to slam on my brakes. I left the car in neutral, pulled the emergency brake, and leaned my head back against the headrest. I needed to think, to try to absorb all the evidence, and see if I could make any sense of it. I sat for a long time, failing to reach any great revelations. I tried the radio again but could find no more news on the gun.

I sat straight up, staring into the darkness of Elm Street's dead end. There was movement from the house on my left. A porch light came on. I shifted the car into gear, made a U-turn, and drove toward the other end of Elm. I had already passed the Green Radish from the other direction, but now the bright light on the corner seemed more inviting. I pulled over and parked. Usually I wasn't the type to drink my troubles away, but at this point sitting in a noisy barroom seemed far more bearable than looking at the four walls of my apartment.

Just inside the front door was a horseshoe-shaped bar. Four men in their early twenties slouched on barstools, their elbows leaning on the bar. They were staring at the TV, watching the Bruins get their usual beating from the Canadiens. One of them, wearing a black and blue Pendleton shirt, jumped up when the Bruin's center touched the puck in front of the net. He screamed, "Yeah, shoot, shoot you stupid shit." His enthusiasm was contagious and his buddies jumped up and screamed along with him.

To the right, a few feet from the bar, were padded benches with small tables, each separated by a partition of beads hanging from the ceiling to the floor. I sat on a bench in the corner, leaned my head against the red velvet wallpaper. I stared at the TV, thinking of the hockey games Larry and I used to play. Neither of us could skate worth a damn but we loved street hockey. Larry loved it because he could act out his aggressions, especially when he got an open shot at the goalie. He'd stand in front of the goal daring the goalie to make the first move, then smack the hard orange ball at the goalie's face.

Back then, a goalie was considered a sissy if he wore a mask, so most went bare. After a few bloody noses and chipped teeth from Larry's hard shots, the goalie would be very careful to keep his glove close to his face. And if he were really in pain, he'd start flinching as soon as Larry touched the ball, moving his arms just a little bit to protect his face.

That was just what Larry had wanted. The next time he got the ball he would stare right at the goalie's face, searching for a spot to place the next shot. Then, expressionless, he would slide the ball along the pavement, past the goalie's

immobile stick and into the net. Goalies never figured out
how to defend him.

I was halfway through my second bottle of Molson
Golden Ale when the guys at the bar turned around to check
out three women who had walked in. Even in the faint light,
I could tell they were well worth looking at. They took a
table near the end of the bar. The one facing me was blonde
with shoulder-length hair combed to the side so it hung over
her shoulder and rested above her breast. Across from her
was a redhead with her hair in a bun and her breasts in nothing. As she slid into the booth, they swayed noticeably, un-
encumbered beneath a tight, long-sleeved cotton shirt.

The third one had her back to me. The only feature I
could make out was her hair, which was dark and so long it
covered the back of her chair. She turned around to check
out the group at the bar and I smiled at her. She stared at me
for a moment, then stood up. After saying something to her
friends, she walked toward me flashing a broad smile. I remembered how taken I was when she first had dropped by
my office. Even though she was now dressed in jeans and a
tight V-neck sweater instead of a knit dress, her slim figure
was well accented. Long rectangular earrings hung from her
ears, sparkling like aqua-colored fishing lures.

"Why, Dutch Francis, what in the world are you doing in
a seedy place like this?"

"I was going to ask you the same thing. Where's Russell
tonight?"

"In Boston, for the Bruins—Canadiens game. He's staying there for the night—with a friend. At least that's what he
says." Yvette laughed quietly. When I didn't respond, she
said, "Hey, Dutch, what's the matter? You don't look so
well."

"It's nothing really."

"Come on. What happened, you lose that rugby game or
something?"

"Actually we won. That's not it." I looked down, picked
up my glass, swirled the beer around. "This isn't the time to

talk about it. Why don't you join your friends, enjoy girls' night out?"

She nodded at me. "Just wait here," she said, then walked back to her friends. As she talked, she turned and pointed at me. The blonde looked over and nodded. The explanations over, Yvette pushed the beads aside and sat down in the bench across from me. "It's all taken care of. I'm going to talk to you about what's ailing you."

"What about your friends?"

"Don't worry about them. I'll join them later at Gladstone's. They want to go dancing."

She flagged the waitress, ordered a gin and tonic. I stared at her, resting my head against my fist, needing all the support I could get. When the drink arrived, Yvette stared back at me, slowly pushing the lime up and down with the small stir straw. "Something must really be bothering you. I've never seen you so down." She sipped the drink. "It's Raymond Walker, isn't it?"

I repeated Gibbs' story. "I had my doubts about Gibbs," I said, "but . . ."

I was distracted by the TV. Another news flash came on, interrupting the hockey game. The camera zoomed to a shot of Lake Masabesic. I stood up and walked to the bar to hear better.

Yvette looked puzzled. "What . . ."

"Come here," I said. "Listen."

She joined me at the bar. The hockey fans stared at her while we focused on the announcer, the same one as before:

New Hampshire State Police have announced a break in the Bruiser McHugh murder case. Earlier today the police recovered a gun from Lake Masabesic. Sources have told this station that ballistic tests confirmed the gun was the one used to murder McHugh. Police have learned that the gun was owned by Lawrence Conway, a Manchester real estate developer with close ties to accused killer Raymond Walker. At the time of the

murder, Walker was living with Mr. Conway's family.
Police do not consider Conway a suspect, but believe
Walker took the gun without Conway's knowledge or
consent.

I stood back, stunned. My jaw dropped and I stared at the
TV, not seeing anything. The bar seemed suddenly silent and
still. I was vaguely conscious of Yvette staring at me, moving her lips as if speaking, but I heard nothing. After a moment she grabbed my arm and guided me back to the table.
Like a robot, I sat in my seat, took a long swig of beer.

"Dutch . . . Dutch!" Yvette shook me.

"I can't believe it," I said. "I can't believe it."

Yvette gazed at the ceiling. "I don't know what to say."

"Larry . . ." I started to say but I was too stunned to
speak. I waited a moment to regain control. "Larry never
mentioned he owned a gun. I can't believe this."

Was Larry mixed up in McHugh's murder? Could he
have solicited Evan to burn his own building? First Gibbs,
now the gun. I felt sick. Part of me just wanted the whole
thing to go away so I wouldn't have to consider the implications of what I'd heard. Could my old friend have changed
that much? I couldn't believe it, there had to be some other
explanation.

In my college psychology courses, which I took in the
ivy towers off Harvard Yard, the professors taught a theory
that said a person's character was fixed early in life. If someone were a bully as a kid, he'd always be a bully. And if a
kid stole bicycles or lied to his parents, he could never be
trusted. He may stop stealing or telling lies when he grew
up, but if he needed to steal or lie he wouldn't hesitate to do
so. His behavior may change but his values, instilled at an
early age, would last a lifetime.

I had some doubts about all those psychological theories—the idealist in me said that people could change—but
my own life seemed to support them. I tried to live the high
society life—attending catered cocktail parties in designer

clothes where privileged people congratulated each other on how rich, smart, or successful they were, never appreciating that their success was more a function of birth than achievement. For many years I pretended to fit in, pretended that my wife and I really were compatible, pretended that her friends were my friends. Gradually the deception ate at me until the veneer I had acquired began to tear away, exposing my core—just another city kid from Boston. And that's how I viewed Larry—a fellow city kid from Boston.

Larry was not the violent type. As a kid, he believed in fighting only as a last resort. If he got in a fight he would always feel guilty afterwards, even when he won, because fighting meant the failure of persuasion. He was a born salesman; persuasion was his most cherished attribute.

"One thing is clear," I said. "The gun narrows the list of suspects. The murderer had to be someone with access to Larry's gun."

"Yeah, I have to agree with you there. The obvious ones: Raymond, Evan, Larry. What about Paula?"

"I think we can safely rule her out."

"And Rubenstein? Could he have gotten ahold of the gun?"

"I don't see how, but who knows." I paused, remembering something Hedges had said. "There's one more possibility: Nathan Goode."

"Who?"

"The projectionist at the Cinema Manchester. Hedges said Evan and Raymond would hassle Goode by pretending to shoot him. I wonder if they told him about the gun."

"Goode knew how much the theater was bringing in," Yvette said. "And he was one of the last ones to leave after the show."

"Right," I said, thinking of the angles. "He could've shot McHugh too."

"Fifteen grand would be a lot of money to someone like him," Yvette said. "And he hated McHugh, so he had a motive."

"But what about Larry? I had always wondered about his business. I hate to think it, but maybe he needed a lot of money, and the only way he could get some fast cash was through insurance. So he sent Evan to torch his building."

Yvette sipped her drink and looked at me over the tilted glass.

"How could he endanger all those people?" I asked, not expecting Yvette to answer, but she answered anyway.

"Maybe he tried to help. Didn't the fire report say that the alarm on the corner was pulled?"

"Yeah, so?"

"Larry could've told Evan to pull it as he was leaving the scene, try to save everybody. And it would've worked, except Mr. Luhovey had fallen asleep and the firemen decided to feast on a lobster dinner."

I tugged at my beard, thinking Yvette may be right. "Or maybe Evan did this on his own," I said, "wanting to help out his father, show him what a clever kid he was."

"Yeah, clever. The kid's a genius. Only McHugh caught him lighting the fire, maybe threatened to turn him in. You ask me, that's why McHugh got shot."

The waitress swooped up my empty bottle, quickly replacing it with a full one. "But even if I assume Larry had something to do with this arson," I said, "I can't believe he would kill someone."

Then I remembered a piece of evidence Laflamme had produced when he delivered the Killian tape: a boot print found on the window sill outside McHugh's office. The police believed it was made by the murderer. I reminded Yvette of the print.

"The cops claim it was size nine and a half," I said. "If I were to guess, I'd say Larry was around a size eleven."

"And Evan? What size is he?"

"Raymond says he and Evan wore the same size, nine and a half. In fact, the boots Raymond was wearing when he was arrested belonged to Evan."

Yvette sipped her drink.

"What a fucking mess!" I said. My instinct said it couldn't be Evan Conway. He had a few quirks, sure, like being a bully when he was younger and his fascination with true crime books. But the few times I had talked to him, he had not exhibited any violent tendencies and had seemed like a normal, well-adjusted kid. And children of loving, attentive parents don't become killers. Do they?

"You know," I said, rubbing my eyes, which had become itchy and sore. "I'm thinking of what Raymond told me. Day after McHugh's murder, Evan asked him to go fishing at Lake Masabesic. But Evan claimed it was Raymond who wanted to go fishing. At first I shrugged off the discrepancy, thinking it wasn't important. But now . . . now I'm thinking maybe Evan was lying, trying to throw some suspicion at Raymond. There was a period of time, Evan had said, when he separated from Raymond. They fished different areas of the lake. I wonder: is that when Evan got rid of the gun?"

"Makes sense," Yvette agreed.

I started drawing comparisons between Evan and Raymond, seeing the similarities. "Don't forget," I said, thinking out loud. "Both knew how to manipulate the window to sneak into the theater. Both knew the theater layout."

"Makes you wonder about Larry, doesn't it? Why didn't he tell you his gun was missing?"

I shifted in my chair. Her question was making me queasy; my stomach churned and made gurgling noises. This was not the Larry Conway I had known and it was hard to think he could've done these things. His love of money had always bothered me, but his good qualities had overshadowed this bad one.

"I don't know," I said finally. "I don't know."

"The way I figure it is McHugh knows Evan lit the fire, he's got to talk to him about it."

"And Evan gets worried, decides he has no choice; he's got to get McHugh out of the way," I said, finishing her theory. Evan Conway, the kid with the mean streak who enjoyed beating other boys silly, with his library of gruesome true crime books, just might have it in him. I flashed on my dinner at the Conways, how Larry put his arm around Evan and hugged him, the proud papa. Evan—polite, respect-ful—would do anything for his dad, but would he commit murder? I shuddered.

"This is terrible for you, isn't it?" Yvette asked softly, placing her hand over mine. She rubbed the back of my hand, turned it over, then squeezed tightly. "I'm so sorry," she whispered.

I gritted my teeth, grasped her hand in both of mine, and looked into her eyes, framed by the lures hanging from her ears. "The worst thing is I can't understand how Larry could let Raymond take the blame. Somehow, that seems worse than all the rest."

Yvette opened her mouth, hesitated. She sat back, looked up at the TV. The hockey game was over. "But, Dutch," she said, turning back toward me, "Larry didn't let Raymond take the blame, he hired you."

I pulled my hands back and stared into Yvette's eyes. "What're you saying?"

She bit her lower lip and blinked. "I hate to say it but he went out of his way to hire you. Why?—after more than twenty years."

The answer was obvious and so painful, thinking it pierced me like a knife. "He knew I'd never suspect him—or his son," I answered.

She looked down, averting my eyes. "He was your friend and he deceived you. Brilliant, absolutely brilliant."

In the two and a half hours since I had left O'Dowd's, it had never occurred to me that Larry had used me. I had gone back and forth on whether to believe Gibbs' story, even thought of my old friend as an arsonist. But this was differ-ent. Larry had manipulated our friendship to cover up a crime. He had deceived me and in the process made me an accessory to this horrible act. And he had sacrificed Ray-mond's freedom, maybe even his life. The thought sickened me.

I gazed up at the green and yellow light hanging by a chain from the ceiling. The colors all blended together, almost dripping off the bulb. "Dammit!" I slammed my fist on the table. "I wish I were wrong, but it fits. It just fits. I don't know what else to think."

I felt moisture on the end of my mustache. When I touched it with the tip of my finger, I realized it was a tear. Yvette reached over the table, picked up my hands, and locked her fingers in mine. She squeezed tightly. I could see moisture also forming in her eyes. I bowed my head and gritted my teeth. My breathing quickened and the pain pounded inside my head, as I continued to cling to Yvette's warm soothing hands.

TEN minutes later I pulled into Yvette's driveway, parked behind Russell's white Dodge pickup. Her friends had snuck out of the Green Radish without saying goodbye, leaving Yvette to comfort her distraught boss. When she realized they had gone, she ran her fingers through her hair and said, "I didn't really want to go dancing anyway." We had left the Green Radish hand in hand and I drove her home the same way. My left hand did double duty, holding the steering wheel, then with a quick cross-body move, awkwardly shifting gears, my right firmly grasping Yvette's hand.

After I cut the headlights, the moon behind the clouds provided the only light. I stared straight ahead, fixated on the blackness of her house. Even in the darkness, I could make out the storm shutters on the upstairs window, probably Yvette's bedroom. I couldn't tell if they were false shutters, for show only, like many found in New England homes. Yvette squeezed my hand, brushed the hair from her eyes, and broke the silence. "Dutch?"

A chill ran down my spine. I returned the squeeze. "Yes, I know," I said softly, lifting her hand to my lips. Still with my left hand on the steering wheel, I kissed her hand lightly. For whatever reason—all the beer, the flood of emotions since the rugby party—my mind was no longer working logically. I gave no thought to consequences, to the future as I kissed her hand harder, then placed her fingers—first the little one, then progressively to the index finger—in my mouth, rolled my tongue around them, and sucked each one. Yvette moaned softly, braced her back against the seat, tightening her muscles. As I sucked I pushed her finger back and forth between my partially clenched teeth, scraping the skin. Yvette shivered. When I finished with the index finger, she leaned over and put her right hand behind my head. She pulled me toward her and kissed me on the lips, hard. If I had any inhibitions at first, they were gone now. I returned the kiss, only harder. It had been a long time since I had kissed a woman so hard. And with such desire. I didn't want to stop. Before long our tongues found each other. As I ran my fingers through her hair, Yvette whispered, "Come with me," and pushed open her door.

When the door opened the interior light came on and, because the key was still in the ignition, the warning buzzer sounded. I fumbled with the key, trying to pull it from the ignition and stop the buzzing. The sound jarred my senses. Yvette walked around to my door, waiting for me to join her. The moon appeared from behind the clouds and shone on the house. I glanced at the windows and saw that the shutters were genuine. I gazed at Yvette's face, at her earrings reflecting the moonlight, like stars in a dark and unknown universe. Something made me stay in my seat; I don't know if it was the alcohol wearing off or a sudden sense of caution activated by the buzzing of the door. As blue as I felt, I knew that this wasn't the right time. In the long run, there could be serious consequences, for Yvette and me, and of course, for Yvette and Russell. There would be too high a price to pay—for both of us.

I stayed in my seat and unrolled the window. Yvette frowned. I held out my left hand, reaching for her. She took my hand between both of hers and rubbed the back of my hand along her cheek, then around her neck and down to her breasts. I shivered at the touch of Yvette's firm full flesh, the twin objects of my adolescent fantasies since the day she first walked into my office. I was torn between giving in to my base urges or taking the high road. An office affair could spell disaster for my business, especially since the whole office consisted of Yvette and me. As hard as I tried to put him out of my mind, I still kept thinking of Russell. How would I feel in his shoes? Out of town for one night and his girl takes her boss home to sleep in his bed.

I released Yvette's hand and opened the door. When I stepped out of the car, I still hadn't made up my mind. But standing up straight made my stomach turn, all that bad draft beer from the rugby party swishing around. Yvette put her arms around me, pressing her breasts against my chest, and against my gurgling stomach. Her breathing quickened and I could feel her breaths in my ear, bursts of hot air taking the chill out of a cool autumn night.

A slight wave of nausea suddenly came over me. In my mind I tried to imagine where this was going: the key romantic moment with Yvette, our clothes shorn in a pile on the floor, our naked bodies pressed together, and just as we begin the ultimate act, me throwing up all over her sheets.

I pulled away and shook my head. "I'm sorry, I can't," I said. When I saw the disappointed look in her eyes, I said, "It's not that I don't want to. Right now I want you more than anything. But now's not the time. My stomach's doing flips. I'm afraid I'd disappoint you."

"You wouldn't," she protested.

"And there's . . . Russell. I don't know if I can do this to him."

Yvette sucked in a deep breath and blinked. For a moment I thought she was going to cry, but she surprised me. She smiled, then leaned down and kissed me lightly on the forehead. "That's what I like about you," she whispered in a cracked voice. "You always do the right thing." I watched, somewhat regretfully, as she hurried up the steps and through the front door of her home, the home she shared with Russell Bruant, her boyfriend.

CHAPTER 21

AT ten o'clock on a Sunday morning traffic was light on Route 101, the same road I had driven with Larry last week. Instead of turning at the Dover exit, the way to Cathy Sayewich's house, I continued east and made my way to Hampton Beach. I don't know what impulse led me there, perhaps I just needed to inhale the salt air and stare at the Atlantic. A quart of cold water and four aspirins had only slightly reduced the throbbing in my head. It had been at least ten years since I had drunk so much, and for so long—four hours of nearly continuous drinking. Even though I had downed four or five Molson Golden Ales at the Green Radish, I preferred to blame the buckets of cheap keg beer at the rugby party for my hangover. I knew for sure it was to blame for the sour taste in my mouth. As my stomach churned, I thought of Yvette and Larry and wondered what I would say to each of them on Monday. I rolled down the windows and sucked in the cold air as it slapped me in the face.

I was disappointed to find the arcade boarded up, although I should have known Hampton Beach would close down after Labor Day. As a child, I spent many summers hanging around the arcade, playing the pinball machines, table bowling and skiball. Larry used to tag along with my family.

One time we spent hours playing skiball, trying to get enough tickets to trade for fancy baseball gloves. We needed two hundred tickets and after an hour and a half we had only fifty, and no more dimes. We stuck the tickets in our pockets, thinking we'd try again next time, and started walking out, dejected and defeated. At the end of a row of skiball machines, near the front door, Larry stopped suddenly. "Wait a second," he'd said. "Do you see what I see?" I shook my head. He looked around nervously, bent over and pulled something from the coinbox.

"What is it?" I asked.

With his hands clenched tightly against his belly, he moved closer to me. "Look," he said, opening his hands to show a metal stick, flat and wide at the end, about six inches long. "This is the magic wand that will get us those gloves. Watch."

He walked to an uncrowded area, bent down and stuck the metal stick in the coinbox. Then he pulled back the lever, and the scoreboard rattled, sending the numbers to zeros. The magic wand was a pass key carelessly left in the machine by an attendant. We could play all the skiball we wanted at no charge.

We took turns, and became experts at rolling the ball in the middle ring, racking up 100 points each time. Half an hour passed and we had accumulated enough tickets for four baseball gloves. "Let's get out of here," I urged Larry, "before we get nabbed." I wanted that glove but Larry insisted on playing a few more games. "We can get some extra gloves, and sell them just like the footballs," he said. Our pockets soon became stuffed with tickets as both of us got caught up in winning game after game. It was an exhilarating feeling, but it didn't last long. While Larry was taking his turn, I felt a tight grip on my arm, and turned to see a uniformed security guard behind me. Another guard grabbed Larry's arm, and said, "Give me the pass key, son. The fun's over."

As I drove by the boarded-up arcade, I remembered how terrified I felt when the guards escorted us to a back room. They made us empty all the tickets from our pockets. "Looks like a clear case of petty theft, wouldn't you say, Paulie?" the fat one said, a stern expression on his face. "Sure," Paulie agreed, wiping moisture from his upper lip and nodding knowingly, "minimum of 30 days in juvenile hall. Just like those kids last month."

Larry sat there stonefaced, unfazed, but the guards' threats frightened me. My teeth chattered and sweat poured down my face. Larry sat still, his arms folded across his chest, a disgusted look on his face. But when he bit his lower lip, I realized he wasn't as cool as he pretended. After staring at us in silence for thirty seconds, Paulie finally said, "Maybe you kids have learned your lesson. You get no prizes, boys. Don't do it again. If we see you in here the rest of the summer, you'll be in big trouble." They let us go, but we didn't dare go back for a whole year.

I parked across the street from the arcade, in front of the bandshell, where the sounds of French horns and trumpets, sometimes in the same key, filled many a warm summer evening. Without the summer crowds, the benches and stage were vacant, creating an eerie stillness. As I began walking along the empty sidewalk, I half-expected a tumbleweed to roll past me.

I dragged myself through the sand to the shore. The wind howled off the ocean and into my eyes, making them water profusely. The moisture nearly froze on my cheeks. I walked along the shore, jumping away as the waves splashed toward me. The movement helped me think more clearly. My thoughts were preoccupied with the murder weapon, Larry's explanation why he did not tell me it was missing. I also wondered whether I should tell Larry about Gibbs and his story. Part of me wanted to confront Larry directly, rather than sending some gruff, potbellied policeman pounding on his front door, arrest warrant in hand. The other part, the lawyer's part, wondered how I could use this information to the best advantage of my client, Raymond Walker.

The vast empty beach stretched ahead of me. The last time I had been to Hampton was during high school. We had piled a bunch of guys into a station wagon, then stretched out on the beach all day long, drinking beer and ogling the girls. In those days the boardwalk was crowded with hippies—long dirty hair, sloppy bell bottom jeans with torn cuffs dragging along the sidewalk. Most of my friends found the beads, the flowers, and the "hip, groovy, man" talk laughable. Even as young, impressionable kids, we had a hard time understanding why guys would want to look so silly. When I was even younger, my parents used to look at some beaded hairy hippie strumming a guitar and say with disgust: "beatniks." Years later I learned that my parents were behind the times: not realizing that the jazz-loving, poetry-reading beatniks had given way to the rock-and-roll hippies.

ALTHOUGH there were no hippies on the beach now, I saw some signs of life. A handful of people were tossing a football ahead of me. There were a few joggers being chased by wet barking dogs. The sun barely peeked through the dark, thick clouds. The clouds were moving quickly, getting closer together, obliterating the sparse patches of blue sky. To my right the waves rolled rhythmically back and forth. The tide was powerful and strong, and even though I stepped back from the ocean as the waves pounded ashore, my pants still were splashed with salt water.

A jogger bounced down the concrete steps from the sidewalk and headed toward the water, forty yards ahead of me. He was wearing a grey-hooded sweatshirt with the hood up, and matching grey sweatpants, the kind we used to wear as kids. When he got to the water's edge, he turned left and ran along the shore, away from me. I stared ahead at the jogger, moving quickly, now a hundred yards away. He looked familiar. As I stared at him, I noticed he was tall and thin, the same size as Larry; like Larry, he had a receding hairline and a small bald patch on the crown of his head. And Larry used to be a jogger. Without thinking, I started running. The closer I got the more certain I was that it was Larry. I was angry now, the rage of betrayal seething through my veins. I wanted to catch him, tell him about Jack Gibbs, see the look of shock and surprise on his face, as he realized his scheme had been discovered. I wanted to scream at the top of my lungs: I know about Evan, I know you used me, I know you used Raymond, I will make you pay, old friend, I will make you pay!

I closed the gap to seventy five yards. I ran at full speed through the soggy sand, leaving my footprints beside Larry's—side by side as if we had run together as a team. I yelled, "Larry!" but he kept on jogging, and didn't even turn around. As I drew closer I yelled again. He still did not hear me. At forty yards I knew it was him. The same sharp pumping of the hands, fists clenched, elbows in, long equal strides.

Huffing and puffing, my legs still tight and sore from yesterday's game, I caught him. I yelled, "Larry!" and grabbed him by the shoulder. The jogger stopped abruptly and lifted his fists. The snarl in his face was menacing. "What the fuck?"

"I'm sorry," I gulped. "I thought you were someone else. Sorry to interrupt your run." I turned around, ran to the sidewalk, and still sprinting, hurried back to my car.

CHAPTER 22

"HE'S called three times this morning already," Yvette said as soon as I opened the office door.

It was late: 10:15. When the alarm had sounded at seven, I reached over and clumsily knocked it with the back of my hand right off the night stand. It crashed to the floor, silent. I went back to sleep. Over two hours later I rolled out of bed and staggered to my feet. I barely remembered showering, dressing, or driving to the office. Without a single cup of coffee, I was still groggy, my mind dull, totally incapable of grasping what Yvette was saying.

"Who?" was all I could manage to say.

"Who do you think?" she said, walking around her desk to get a better look at the pathetic person in front of her. She nodded, smiled. "I see you haven't improved much since I last saw you."

I rubbed my eyes. "Listen, Yvette, I'm sor . . ."

"Don't say it," she interrupted. "We're both grown-ups. We knew what we were doing. But it's a good thing you knew better than me." She put her hand on my arm, rubbed the sleeve softly. I looked into her eyes. There was a dullness, perhaps sadness, that hadn't been there before. I had an urge to pull her close and kiss her. But too much was happening now. I had to figure out what to do about Raymond and Larry before I could complicate my life any more. Yvette and I had some unfinished business, but it would have to wait.

"Here are the messages," she said, back to business, and handed me three pink phone sheets. All were from Larry; he had called every forty-five minutes or so.

"I'll take care of it," I said, not knowing what I was going to do. I poured myself a cup of coffee and sat at my desk. I sipped the coffee, stared at the messages, each marked "urgent," and shuffled them, one atop the other, several times as if waiting for some revelation. Finally, I walked to the window and stared at the drug store across Elm Street. The blue "Rexall" sign flashed every three seconds. The sign was huge, at least twelve feet high, partially blocking the words painted on the window behind it. The only letters I could see were ". . . edges" and below that ". . . gator."

"Yvette," I yelled. "Please call Glenn Hedges and ask him to come over right away."

I sat back down and stared at Larry's phone messages. The first two were from home at 8:30 and 9:15, the last five minutes ago. "Yvette, any luck on Hedges?" I yelled. She stuck her head in the doorway. "Not there. The answering machine says he'll be back at noon. I left a message for him to call ASAP."

I put down the messages and stood up. I grabbed my jacket from behind the door. I decided I'd better talk to Raymond before saying anything to Larry. "I'll be back," I said. "I've got to pay someone a visit first."

To my surprise Raymond was wide awake, a rare condition for him at ten thirty in the morning. He was standing near what passed for a window, using the light to read the newspaper.

"Can you believe this bullshit?" he asked, shaking the

paper. "This is crazy. How could Mr. Conway's gun be the murder weapon? The cops must've made some mistake."

I sat at the end of the bench, leaned my head against the wall. "I don't think so, Raymond," I said.

"What're you saying, you think I'm guilty now?"

I shook my head. "No, it's not that." I told him about Gibbs and how the evidence pointed to Evan as the murderer. It was a lot easier to talk about now than the first time with Yvette at the Green Radish. The practice must've helped since the words came out quickly.

When I finished, Raymond stared at me in disbelief, his mouth gaped. He shook his head. "That son-of-a-bitch," he said slowly. He tensed his jaw muscles, squinted his face so tight the wrinkled lines made it look like a walnut shell. He insisted I repeat everything Jack and Mick had said. "That cold-blooded asshole, letting me take the rap on this," he snapped, crumbling up the paper and tossing it against the wall. He paused, then inhaled deeply. "He thought he pulled off a big one. Kill McHugh and blame it on Walker. What a hot shit."

As unlikely as it had once seemed, I felt a strange affinity for Raymond. Each of us had put our faith in a friend, believed in his loyalty, and then was betrayed.

"What do we do now?" he asked quietly.

"I'm going to put Hedges on Gibbs' trail, make sure we get him subpoenaed for trial. Then when Gibbs points the finger at Evan, we pray the jury believes him."

Raymond got quiet and stared toward the ceiling. "Evan's mom will just die," he said, shaking his head. "She's a nice lady; I wish this didn't have to happen to her."

I tried to picture Paula Conway's face when she heard the news. Her orderly, neat world would explode. How would she deal with her son and husband being implicated in a murder? No doubt the ladies at the Bedford Country Club would be whispering behind her back. Already there had been enough victims from this whole affair: McHugh, Raymond, his pregnant girlfriend Cathy, and me, for starters. I hated to add Paula Conway to that list.

"I know, Raymond," I said, "but she's going to find out sooner or later. The question is when."

Raymond slapped his open palm against the bars. "I feel bad for Mrs. Conway," he said. "But we should wait until trial before we spring it on them, don't you think?" he asked, looking up at me. "The Conways I mean. The only way this is going to work is if we surprise them. If we tip them off, they'll come up with something to take the heat off Evan."

I considered Raymond's idea; I had already given much thought to what to tell Larry. I had gone back and forth several times, balancing my friendship with Larry and my duty to Raymond. It was a choice I hated to make. To deceive my old friend and set his son up for a murder accusation would be pretty tough. Deep inside I wanted to find a way to save everyone: Raymond, Evan, and Larry. But I knew that was impossible.

"You're probably right," I said finally. "Larry finds out what we're up to, he'll be all over us, maybe even try to prove you're guilty."

For the first time since Larry had brought me into this case, I really believed I could win. But whatever the verdict, I would pay a high price for defending Raymond. There was no way I could salvage my friendship with Larry; my ethical responsibility was to my client, not to my old friend who had promised to pay my fees. That much was clear. Larry had a price to pay too, for his son's arson and murder, and for setting me up. I could not pick up his tab; Larry would have to pay his own way. This trial definitely would be dutch treat.

HEDGES was waiting for me when I returned to the office. He was sitting in my desk chair, his hands folded behind his head and his feet on the desk, staring out the window. I let him sit there while I took a client chair. For the second time that day I told the tale of Jack and Mick.

Hedges listened attentively, like a child hearing a fairy tale for the first time. When I finished, he shook his head.

"You are in one tough spot, Dutch my man. The way I figure it, you don't have much of a choice. You got to finger the Conway kid. It's the only way. I sure am glad I'm not in your shoes."

"Thanks for the advice, but I kind've figured that out already." Hedges meant no offense, but I was in no mood for his antics. "I need you to find Gibbs and subpoena him for trial. Give a subpoena to his buddy Mick too, just to be on the safe side."

"This could be fun," he said. "Find Clark-Gable-clone Jack Gibbs and his pal Mick-the-Stooge. No problem." He started to get up.

"Not so fast," I said. "There's one more thing I need you to do." I walked over to the file cabinet and pulled the Luhovey file. "I'll have Yvette make you copies of the newspaper articles and the articles of incorporation," I said. "I want a complete asset check on Larry Conway and PEV-CON. If you can, find out how much insurance money was paid out on this fire. I need as much evidence of motive as I can get." It would take solid evidence to convince a jury that an upstanding member of the community would use his son to torch his own building to collect the insurance money. The rest would follow: McHugh's stumbling onto the arson and Evan's murdering him to protect himself—and perhaps his father.

"Oh, and one other thing: see what you can find out about Evan's criminal history. His father said he had a history of beating up the neighbor kids. I'm thinking he may have been picked up a few times. Be great if you could find some history of lighting fires."

"Sure, but you realize juvenile records are confidential. There's no way you could get them."

I rested my hand on Hedges' shoulder as I escorted him to the door. "Glenn, that's why I hired the best. I wouldn't dream of giving you a job any run-of-the-mill PI could do. This is a job for a man with talent."

If I thought my compliments would flatter Hedges, I was wrong. He fell for none of it. As he opened the door he turned and smiled at me. "I got one thing to say, boss."

"Oh?"

"Yeah . . . fuck you."

I couldn't tell if he was mad or playing with me. But one thing was certain: he was gone. I shut the door and picked up two more messages from Larry that Yvette had taken while I was at the jail. I got through to his secretary on the third ring. "Mr. Conway's on the other line," she said, "but he wanted me to interrupt him if you called. I'll buzz him now."

Larry sounded excited. "Dutch, I've been trying to get you since yesterday. Your home phone was busy all day, must've been off the hook. Didn't you get my messages today?"

"Yeah, sorry," I mumbled. "I've been tied up."

"You see the paper? About the gun?"

"Yeah, I saw it," I said slowly.

"We've got to talk. I have some information on that. What about getting together this afternoon?"

"Fine, five thirty okay?" I wanted to talk to him alone, after Yvette had gone home.

"That's fine."

"Oh, and Larry?"

"Yeah?"

My voice quivered. I started to say I might have some information for him, but caught myself just in time. "N-nothing," I said, "nothing at all."

CHAPTER 23

I paced from one end of my office to the other. Another forty-five minutes before Larry arrived, I thought, as I glanced at the grandfather clock. I hadn't been able to concentrate on any work since talking to Larry. I decided to take a walk to clear my head.

"Yvette, lock the door when you leave. I'll be back for my meeting with Larry." She was sitting at her desk licking and stamping the mail.

"Where you going?"

"Just for a walk, get some fresh air."

It must've been the distressed look on my face or the high pitch of my voice but Yvette suddenly looked worried. She knew what I was going through. She discarded the smart-aleck attitude and actually showed some empathy.

"Dutch?"

"What?" I took my hand off the doorknob. Yvette stood up and came around her desk. She was wearing a beige satin V-neck blouse. The top button was open, providing a glimpse of cleavage. As she moved, her breasts swayed back and forth, stirring my memories of last Saturday night.

"Oh, Dutch," she said, "I hate to see you in such pain. I know how important your friendship with Larry is." She put her hands on my shoulders and hesitated, fighting the same impulse I had been fighting since the night of the rugby game. I sensed she wanted to hug me so I moved closer to her, lifting my arms slightly but still holding back. She bit her lip and tentatively slid her hands around my neck. Slowly we drew together as we wrapped our arms around each other, Yvette's breasts pressing against my chest.

But something stopped me from throwing aside all caution. My first thought was to distance myself from her, from Larry, from everybody. The last thing I wanted was human companionship. I didn't want to feel better. I wanted to wallow in my own misery, as if I were the only man who'd ever had a friend stab him in the back.

But I was feeling more comfortable with Yvette's embrace and realized I had been stroking her hair. I pulled a few strands back from her eyes and caressed her head, running my fingers through the long black strands. Before long I was running my fingers all the way through her hair, across her shoulders, down her back, and to the end at her buttocks. Yvette lifted her head and kissed me. My desire to be alone was soon forgotten and I kissed her back. With my fingers pressed into the rounded flesh of her buttocks, we rubbed our bodies against each other.

Who knows where we would have wound up if the phone hadn't rung. "Don't answer it," I said.

She leaned back and shook her head. "You'd better go. From what I can feel here, Bucko, I'd say the cold air will do you some good."

Reluctantly, I realized she was right. It was already five o'clock, I had an appointment in half an hour, and she had to get home to Russell. I went outside and circled the block a few times. The walk had worked; my thoughts were no longer focused on Larry. Now I thought only of Yvette. And the cold air hadn't changed how I felt.

By the time I got back to the office, the wind had started blowing hard down Elm Street. I unlocked the front door and tried to pull it open but the wind forced it shut. It was as if some force were trying to stop me from getting inside. Tugging with both hands, I wrestled with the wind-blown door. Finally, I opened it enough to allow me to jump inside. Just as I stepped into the lobby, the wind blew the door slamming shut, almost crushing my foot.

I hurried into the elevator, hoping that Yvette had stayed late, and I'd catch her before she left. As soon as I pulled shut the heavy wire gate, I wished I'd taken the three flights of stairs. Riding the Derryfield Building's only elevator reminded me of playing the slots in Atlantic City. Sometimes you get lucky and it worked, but often not. There was no rhyme or reason to its extended vacations. Fortunately, this time it cooperated, lurching upward.

Yvette was gone. It was 5:25. I sat down at her desk waiting for Larry. As I glanced around the office, I thought of how things had changed since Boston. If Larry had come to my Boston office, he would have basked in the ambience of a corner office atop a State Street skyscraper, gazed at museum quality prints on each wall, and marveled at an eighteenth century roll-top desk, the refinished oak glistening like new. He would have ridden a special bank of reliable elevators—reserved only for the firm's employees and clients—an express ride to the top. If he wished, he'd have been served coffee by our conference room attendants, a dozen young women carefully chosen for their poise and attractiveness by the senior partners, whose only function was to cater to the whims of clients. It was easy to sweet-talk clients as they gazed at the view of Quincy Market and Boston Harbor while our leggy attendants filled their bone china coffee cups.

Larry was late and I felt like pacing again. I walked into my sparsely furnished inner office. The only remnants of my

Boston firm that Larry would see were the grandfather clock and lawyer's bookcase along the north wall, both of which I had bought from a North Shore antique shop to celebrate landing my Boston job, which—not counting my current self-employment—had been my only job.

I looked around at the bare walls, covered only by light blue paint. I had planned on buying some art at the local gallery until a new client convinced me otherwise. He was a woodcarver, scratching out a living by selling his carvings of ducks and dogs at flea markets. He looked around the office, pointed to the bare walls, and said, "I just love the spare style." Since then, I've told clients the office was professionally designed in the "spare" style.

The room was warm and stuffy, light steam rising from the radiator. I opened the window on the north wall. Stretching my arms over my head, I breathed in the cold air, and looked out across rooftops and red-brick chimneys to the old Amoskeag textile mills along the Merrimack River. Even though the view was not glamorous, I still enjoyed gazing at those silent memorials to times gone by.

At their peak the mills pumped out enough shirts, sweaters, and overcoats to clothe all of New Hampshire, bringing prosperity to the hardworking citizens of Manchester. But like many things in life, the mills and the prosperity they produced did not last. As consumer tastes changed and technology rapidly advanced, the mills sent their employees packing for other jobs or other towns, then gradually closed down. From ready-to-wear to worn-out in three generations.

I stared at the mills for a few minutes, the falling sun's light still glowing on the horizon, casting a faint light through the broken windows, thinking of the turn my own life had taken in the past six months, when I heard the door to the outer office open. It was Larry. I greeted him without shaking hands. He refused my offer of coffee, which was fortunate since Yvette had shut off the machine.

I decided to sit beside Larry in one of the client chairs in front of my five-foot oak desk, turning them so we were face to face. He was wearing a dark, pin-striped suit, maroon suspenders, and a silk Armani tie with a wild design, swirling snake-like figures in bright, eye-catching colors. He was almost too well-dressed for Manchester and looked every bit the prosperous real estate developer he claimed to be.

I placed the yellow legal pad on my lap and clenched the Cross pen so tightly my fingers cramped. There was so much to tell, so much not to tell. I had to be careful about what I said. I leaned back in my chair and looked at Larry's face. Even though he tried to act casual, the tension showed in his cheek muscles; they twitched involuntarily. For the first time I noticed the smile lines—curved, distinct lines framing his mouth, leading directly to the bulging cheek muscles. Although my stomach was churning, I was trying to stay calm. Here was one of my oldest friends and I was deceiving him, plotting to accuse his son of murder.

Larry spoke in an apologetic tone of voice. "Dutch, I'm sorry this had to happen so late in the case. I never dreamed the police would find the gun."

I stared at him in disbelief. Was he admitting guilt? "You mean you knew the gun was missing all along?" Though I felt like screaming, I spoke in a controlled, low voice, my teeth clenched tightly.

He was looking at the floor, not meeting my eyes. His Adam's apple bobbed up and down. "I'm sor . . ." he coughed. "I'm sorry, Dutch. I should've told you. It was stupid. I thought I was helping Raymond."

"So you lied to me from the very beginning?"

"No, I didn't know about the gun then, only after I'd hired you. When the police searched the house, they found nothing incriminating, which I fully expected since I believed Raymond was innocent. Later, when we were driving from Cathy's place and talking about the murder weapon not being found, it occurred to me that the police hadn't even asked about my target pistol. It was in the top drawer of my desk inside a wooden box. I hadn't used it in months. When

I got home I went upstairs and looked in the box. The gun was gone and so was the clip and the extra box of bullets."

I listened to every word, making sure to remember this story. While I listened, I watched Larry's demeanor. He shifted in his seat and stared at the floor, grasping the arm-rests with both hands.

"So why didn't you tell me?"

He shook his head. "I couldn't," he said. "I just couldn't. I was afraid you'd have to tell the prosecution, maybe have an ethical obligation or something. And I was also afraid you'd drop the case, and Raymond would have no one to help him."

"Didn't you think to check for your gun when you learned that a .22 caliber bullet had been pulled out of McHugh's brain? Didn't you wonder how Raymond could've gotten a gun?"

"You've got to understand, I believed Raymond was in-nocent. I never wondered how he got a gun because I didn't think he had a gun." I had never seen Larry like this. He was shaking, his arms folded around his chest. The slickly dressed real estate developer who'd walked into my office fifteen minutes ago had turned into a scared, nervous, vul-nerable man. I had no intention of helping him out. I glared back at him without speaking.

"It seems crazy now, looking back, but I made no con-nection between McHugh's murder and my target pistol. I hardly ever used the thing. I can't even remember the last time I'd opened that desk drawer."

I wasn't buying any of his story. I slammed my fist on the desk and the Waterford crystal paper weight I'd brought from Boston, a gift from my first satisfied client, crashed to the floor, cracking into a dozen small pieces. "You son of a bitch! You led me on even after you knew about the gun. You let me fumble with my investigation, knowing I wouldn't get anywhere. And you claim to be my friend?"

"Dutch, you've got to understand. It wasn't like that. I didn't know what to do, I was scared, I didn't even tell Paula or Evan the gun was missing. And I thought you could still pull it off. I knew you were a fighter, that you—of all people—could pull off a miracle."

I leaned back, balancing the chair precariously on its back legs. A sense of nausea came over me, followed by a surge of anger. "Bullshit!" I leaned forward and the chair legs hit the hardwood floor with a bang. "That's bullshit and you know it. That has nothing to do with why you wanted me on this case."

His voice became soft. "What do you mean? Why do you think I wanted you?"

I waved my hand, dismissing him. I had to keep quiet. I'd already come dangerously close to saying too much. I stood up and walked to the window. The sun had set over the old Amoskeag Mill. The edges of the clouds were streaked with red and yellow; rays of light filtered down to the roofs of the red-brick cottages that used to house the mill workers.

"Dutch," Larry said behind me, "I wanted you because I felt bad for Raymond. That's all."

I turned around. "That's all?" I asked. "So there wasn't a part of you that wanted to see your old friend again? Our friendship was an afterthought, is that what you're saying?"

"You know that's not true. Maybe I needed an excuse to call you, but when I thought of who could help Raymond, I immediately thought of you."

I turned toward the window. Some of the color had left the clouds and a light greyness had descended over the mill. "So what do you want me to do with Raymond now?"

"I don't see that you have a choice. You've got to plead him guilty. Maybe Laflamme will go for second degree, give Raymond some reason to live." He said this as if it really made him sad, as if his hopes and dreams to save Raymond from a conviction really had been shattered. If I hadn't suspected that he was covering up for his son Evan, or maybe even himself, I might have even believed he was sincere.

"I'll think about it," I said.

"Think about it? What do you mean?" His voice had an edge to it.

"Just what I said. I'm not ready to throw in the towel so fast. There are a few angles I've got to look at."

"But what chance do you have now? The police have the murder weapon for Christ's sake. Do you want to guarantee Raymond spends the rest of his life in prison?"

"What happened to the concerned guy who said he didn't want Raymond to have one of those plea-bargaining public defenders?"

"That was before."

"Before what? Before you knew that the truth would come out? Before you had completely set me up?"

"You're talking nonsense," he said as he stood up. "I don't think we'd better talk about this any more tonight. Neither of us is thinking straight. I'll call you later."

I said nothing while he walked out. As I listened to his footsteps along the hall, I had a strange thought. I visualized Larry getting into the elevator, pulling the gate shut, and pushing the button. But the elevator wouldn't move. And when he tried to open the gate to get out, the gate wouldn't budge. I pictured him standing there, his hands on the bars, looking out, trapped behind the wire bars, maybe for eternity.

CHAPTER 24

I spent the Thanksgiving weekend resting, thinking, and planning my trial strategy. On Wednesday I had left a message on Larry's answering machine that I was bailing out on Thanksgiving dinner. I felt bad for Paula but there was no way I could sit at Larry's dinner table, chatting with his wife and son, thinking all the while how I would nail Larry and Evan at trial. Then I pulled the plug on my telephone and on my social life. Other than a daily three-mile run in the brisk fall air, I lived like a hermit. No calls, no visits, no talking — except to shopkeepers, who invariably asked, "How was your Thanksgiving?" I responded with a grunt or a desultory "fine" and went on my way. No use ruining a lousy mood by being friendly.

When I arrived at the office on Monday morning, Yvette was on the phone, holding it a foot from her ear. She pointed at the receiver with her free hand and mouthed some words I couldn't decipher. At my puzzled look, she rolled her eyes back, put her hand over her mouth like a megaphone, and whispered, "Sherlock Holmes. He says it's urgent." She rolled her eyes. "And to ask me for a date. What should I tell him?"

For a moment, I felt a tinge of anger. How dare Hedges hit on my assistant? But of course I thought of Yvette as more than my assistant. I was feeling possessive of her. I didn't want anyone else to have her. "Tell him to take a fuckin' hike," I said finally.

Yvette sat back, surprised, and put her hand over the receiver. "I don't mean about the date, silly boy. What I mean is: do you want to talk to him now?"

Embarrassed, I grinned and told her I'd take the call in my office. As I picked up the phone I pretended I wasn't mad about Hedges hitting on Yvette. In an excited voice, he said he had some interesting information and wanted to meet right away. I told him to come right over.

Five minutes later Hedges was sitting in my client chair. I stared at the bulge in his jacket, wondering if he were carrying his .38. As he started to give his report, I interrupted. "Oh, before I forget, you should know that Yvette's spoken for."

"Really? Too bad." He paused. "For you, I mean. I've seen the way she looks at you."

"Come on, she's my employee."

"Sure."

I hesitated, surprised that I'd been discovered. "Well, is there something else you wanted to talk about?"

Hedges pulled a file from his briefcase, leaned forward, and dropped it on my desk. "Bing-go! We hit the jackpot. My old connections on the fire department came in handy." He flipped open the file. "This is a juvenile arson report from three years ago. Your instincts were right: Evan Conway is a firebug."

"Oh my God! He actually did this before?" I flipped through the report.

"Seems like when he was twelve or thirteen he had a thing about GI Joes. Used to light a firecracker under them,

see how far they'd fly. Then burn them with a cigarette
lighter."

"Why'd he do that?"

"Hey, people get their kicks in different ways. This kid,
he likes to see things burn. I came across a lot of them when
I was working in the department. Strange fuckers, but dangerous. See how Evan would burn only the faces, melt them
to nothing." He pointed to the narrative at the bottom of the
first page.

"You suppose this had something to do with his father
being in the army?"

"Transferring hate for his father to a GI Joe?" He shook
his head. "That's outta my league. Have to check with a different kind of expert for that one."

I read the end of the report. Evan had been turned over to
the custody of his parents with a warning. Another offense
would result in delinquency proceedings. The police sent a
copy of the report to the arson squad to warn them to be on
the alert if there were any fires in the neighborhood. The report contained a statement from a witness, a neighbor, who
had seen Evan playing with matches outside his home. He
had chased him off, but Evan returned an hour later and
dropped a lit pack of firecrackers through the front door
mail slot. Another neighbor reported the GI Joe burnings,
saying Evan had been doing that for months.

I thought back to my conversation with Larry during our
drive to Cathy's house. He had told me that Evan went
through a difficult period. Although he'd mentioned fighting, he hadn't said a word about starting fires. Maybe, I
thought, those true crime books in Evan's room meant that
he had more problems than poor taste in reading material.

"This will definitely come in handy," I said, closing the
file. "Got any other news for me?"

"You are one tough guy to please. Check this one out."
He handed me another file. This one was marked "KIL-
LIAN" in large black letters. "A signed statement, some
major differences from the one the police got."

I smiled, pleased with Hedges' work. In all the excitement of discovering Evan's involvement, I had forgotten about Killian. It was essential that I be able to attack his credibility. An inconsistent statement was the best ammunition I could ask for.

"And yes indeed, I did track down your star witness and his sidekick: John—aka Jack the Quack—Gibbs, and his sidekick Michael—aka Mick the Quick—Ryan." He paused. "You like those nicknames? Made them up myself, bet you never would've guessed. Anyway, both of them are from the Concord area, not the cream of the local gentry, mind you, but not the worst dudes in town either."

I didn't like what I was hearing.

"I went out to Jack's apartment. Locked, no one home, shades drawn, the whole bit. So I waited around for the landlady to get home. Unfriendly Japanese lady—she scowled and yelled at me in broken English. It took me a while to figure out what she was saying. Seems Mick lived there too. But they left on Thursday; hauled a couple of suitcases and a cooler into Jack's black Plymouth station wagon and took off. She has no idea where they went."

"Great," I said. "That's just great. What're you going to do now?"

"I got some leads. The landlady gave me the license number. She thought it might come in handy some day so she copied it down. Thank God for nosy landladies. I'll find them."

"Subpoena them for December 28. I have a feeling Judge Taylor will stick to the December 22nd trial date, so I don't want to take any chances. I've got to have Gibbs there."

I was about to tell Hedges goodbye when I remembered something. "Hey, what about Larry and PEVCON's finances? Weren't you going to check that out?"

Hedges closed his file and stood up. "You are one tough man to please," he said. "I've got some leads so don't worry. Come trial, I'll have what you need."

I was right about the trial date. At the status conference

later that week, Judge Taylor confirmed the trial would start
on December 22nd. Laflamme had changed his vacation
plans and told the judge he now had no objection to the trial
date.

"Having heard no objection," Judge Taylor announced,
"and there being no apparent desire to settle this matter"—
he raised an eyebrow in my direction—"we will begin jury
selection on December 22." Even though we were the only
attorneys remaining in the courtroom, he pounded his gavel
before leaving the bench.

THE weeks before trial passed quickly. I put all other
cases on hold.

My days were spent shuttling between the office and the
jail. Raymond and I pored over the evidence, looked at it
from different angles, plotting our rebuttal. My biggest
worry was serving the subpoenas on Jack Gibbs and Mick
Ryan. Since the status conference, Hedges had been chasing
them up and down the White Mountains. Last week he'd
called from Lake Winnepesaukee with news that they were
somewhere in the area, and he was still hot on their trail.
Hedges had better come through; without Gibbs the case
would be lost. As I thought of all the time and effort I would
invest in this trial, I began to wonder about the wisdom of
trying a case that depended on a flake like Jack Gibbs.

In all the excitement over Raymond's case, I had completely forgotten about Mrs. Luhovey. The news about Larry
owning PEVCON put me in a difficult position with her
case. Even though she consulted me about suing the fire department, I knew that Mrs. Luhovey's best chance of recov-
ery was from the owner, which meant I would have to go
after Larry and try to prove he had negligently owned or
managed the property. I was in an impossible conflict of interest. As I saw it, my ethical obligation was clear: withdraw
from the case. I hated to abandon Mrs. Luhovey but I had no
choice. I buzzed Yvette and told her to schedule an appointment so I could give Mrs. Luhovey the bad news in person.

There had to be a dozen lawyers in Manchester qualified to handle the case.

Yvette proved more efficient than ever. After lunch I arrived at the office to find Yvette standing by her desk, picking through a box of chocolates with Irene Luhovey looking over her shoulder. "Look what Mrs. Luhovey gave us," Yvette said, looking up. Pushing the box toward me, she said, "Take one."

I shook my head. "Have to stay in shape," I said.

"Now, now, Mr. Francis," Mrs. Luhovey said. "A little vice not so bad sometimes, you know. Once in a while, is okay to break the rules." She was a lot more cheerful than the first time we'd met. Knowing she was doing something about her husband's death, hiring me, must have comforted her. She chose an almond covered in white chocolate and held it out to me. "For you," she said. "Go ahead, take."

Realizing I was outnumbered, I popped it into my mouth. "Not bad," I said.

Smiling approvingly, Mrs. Luhovey said, "You see, is okay to enjoy life. In my country, me and Boris, we ate the sweets every day with our tea. So much wonderful."

I walked to my office with Mrs. Luhovey close behind. Her stockings were bunched up around her ankles, leaving eight inches of flesh-toned folds beneath the hem of her flowered dress. "I'll get the tea ready," Yvette called out after us.

Without waiting for an invitation, Mrs. Luhovey took the same seat as before. She carried a large black purse, about eighteen inches high. She held it in her lap as we talked. "The papers you wanted," she said, handing me a manila envelope. Inside were the death certificate, funeral and burial bills, and her lease agreement. The death certificate listed asphyxiation as cause of death, and mentioned tuberculosis as a contributing cause.

"So sick he was, since a young man," Mrs. Luhovey explained. "Those labor camps, you wouldn't believe the diseases. Terrible, terrible places. And when Boris got sick, they made him go to a sanitarium. A year he spent there. Lost half a lung." She paused and looked down. "But it never slowed him." Wagging her finger at me, she repeated, "Not one bit."

I tried to break the news gently. "I'm sorry, Mrs. Luhovey, I have some bad news. Something has come up . . . What I'm trying to say is that I can't represent you."

"I no understand," she said. "My case is no good?"

"No, no, nothing like that." I told her about Larry owning PEVCON. I tried to explain the rules of ethics, that I had a conflict of interest because of my friendship with Larry. The more I talked the harder her features became. She sat up straight and folded her arms.

"You tell your friend not to worry," she said. "I never want to be suing the owner anyway. The firemen were the ones, they let my poor Boris burn, while they made like pigs with lobster, the paper say. Let them pay. Am I right?"

"Well, Mrs. Luhovey, the thing is . . . your best case, legally, is probably against the owner. If Larry's company was negligent in causing the fire—and it very well may have been—then it's responsible too. In my opinion, if you don't sue PEVCON you would be giving up your best case."

Mrs. Luhovey turned as Yvette brought in the tea. There were two round chocolates in brown paper on the saucer. "Oh, wonderful. Such a dear." She smiled at Yvette, grabbed her hand and squeezed. She looked at me. "Mr. Francis, so lucky you are."

"Of course, I know. Yvette does good work."

"Indeed," she said, a glint in her eye. "Too bad she is— how you say—spoken for, no?"

Yvette and I glanced at each other and chuckled. Too bad indeed, I thought, watching Yvette leave.

Mrs. Luhovey sipped her tea then leaned forward. "Mr. Francis, how can I say? I want you to be my lawyer, that is all. If that mean I cannot sue owner, that okay with me. Do you understand me?"

I was taken aback. I hadn't realized Mrs. Luhovey was so

intent on my representing her. The implications of what she said were swirling around my mind. What would happen if I sued the fire department only? Wouldn't they bring a cross-complaint against PEVCON? Then I would be in the same pickle. The whole thing didn't feel right. I needed to give it more thought, perhaps do some research on the rules of ethics. For the moment, I decided to try a different tack to dissuade Mrs. Luhovey from retaining me.

"Mrs. Luhovey, even if ethically I could still represent you, I'm not sure you would be comfortable pursuing this case."

"What do you mean? I no understand."

"The fire department's attorney will ask a lot of questions about your relationship with your husband," I said.

"What sorts of questions?" she asked, raising her eyebrows.

"About the things you two did together," I said. "How well you got along, and um . . ." I paused. "You know, that kind of thing." She finished her tea.

"Mr. Francis, what is it you are saying to me?" she asked.

"There's one question they always ask. Always."

"Oh, and what's that?"

"When you sue for wrongful death of a spouse, the defense is entitled to know all about the marriage. And that includes your . . ." I coughed, looked down. "That includes your sex life."

I guess I expected her to slow down a bit, to lose some enthusiasm for me, if not for the case. I had seldom been so wrong. Instead of stomping out of the office, as I had contemplated, she smiled, squinting her eyes, the crow-feet lines stretching toward her hairline. "That is suiting me just fine. And I tell you what: they will be getting an earful too," she said, winking.

So much for my powers of persuasion. "Very well," I said. "As you wish."

She stood up to leave but I asked her to wait a moment, I had a few more questions about the fire.

"Mrs. Luhovey, I'm just wondering if you saw anybody mowing the lawn before you went out for your tea that day."

She straightened her back as if that would help her remember and stared at the ceiling, squinting her eyes shut, her head still upraised. After a few seconds, she shook her head back and forth. "No, sir," she said. "I no remember seeing anybody. But could be. How I remember? I so upset: the smoke, firemen, my Boris."

"Did you ever see who cut the grass?"

"A cute young man. I remember him; always say hello ma'am and smile at me."

"You don't remember seeing him that day though?"

"I sorry, Mr. Francis. I wish I could help, but I no remember. What I say? He could be there and I no see him." She turned toward the door, shuffling her feet to leave. Suddenly she turned. "Maybe," she said, pointing her finger at me. "Maybe he work on side of building. Ya, that could be. A tiny bit of grass near the parking spaces. I would not have seen him."

"Thank you, Mrs. Luhovey," I said. "You've been very helpful. I'll be in touch soon. I promise."

Yvette opened the door and guided Mrs. Luhovey out. "Let me help you to the elevator," she said.

After Mrs. Luhovey left, I stared out the window, thinking how I'd botched that meeting. On the way out she had told Yvette that everything was fixed, that I was the most wonderful lawyer anyone could ask for.

CHAPTER 25

DECEMBER 27: TRIAL

After three and one half days of jury selection and a few days break for Christmas, we were ready to start the trial. The sight of the empty jury box made the butterflies return to my stomach, the same butterflies I had experienced on the rugby field in Concord. Only this time it was worse: they were doing aerobics. The stakes now were a lot higher than winning a masochistic game imported from merry old England. Someone's freedom—for the rest of his life—was at stake. Instead of worrying about missing a tackle, I concentrated on remembering each detail of my opening statement. It was important that I maintain credibility with the jury from the very beginning, start building the foundation of Raymond's defense so that by the end of trial the jurors would be convinced the right thing to do was to acquit Raymond. Throughout the trial I had to be as sharp as possible: each question had to be framed clearly, each objection asserted aggressively. I had to be at my best, for Raymond's sake.

I walked to the defense table and nodded at Laflamme as if I didn't have a worry in the world. In a few minutes the door in the back of the dock swung open and Hank Lerner led Raymond into the courtroom. Raymond was wearing a light brown suit Yvette had picked out especially for the trial. To convey a sense of warmth and honesty Yvette chose a brown plaid wool tie. By now the black eye and bump on his forehead had disappeared, so he looked almost respectable. With his short hair and sharply creased suit, he easily could have passed for a management trainee at New Hampshire's own Indian Head Bank.

Stiffly, conscious that all eyes were on him, Raymond sat down beside me. Glancing at me, he forced a smile and folded his hands on the table. He squeezed his fingers together so tightly the tips soon turned white. The suit coat was a snug fit and I could see his chest heaving in and out. He stared straight ahead as if bad luck would befall him for looking directly at anyone.

Unlike in many states, a murder trial was still a rarity in New Hampshire and a handful of reporters occupied the seats behind the bar. Gus Decker, legal affairs reporter for the *Union Leader*, sat directly behind Laflamme. His seating choice was consistent with his newspaper's strident support of law and order.

Directly behind me were Larry, Paula, and Evan, shifting anxiously in their seats. At first Larry insisted he would attend the entire trial but then he missed most of the jury selection because of a closing on an apartment building he had sold. Last night he screamed at me when I told him Judge Taylor had excluded him and Evan from the trial, except for opening statements, until their testimonies were completed. Even though the judge had made the same order for all potential witnesses, Larry complained that I wasn't fighting hard enough.

Since the Conways were in the courtroom, I had to be very careful during opening statement. The last thing I wanted was to tip them off about Raymond's defense before I had a chance to question them on the stand.

With Raymond seated beside me, Hank brought out the jury and sat them in the jury box across the aisle from Laflamme. Although Laflamme pretended to read his file, I could tell he was stealing glances at Amanda Sharpe, a twenty-five year old jazz pianist in the front row. Her long stringy hair and loose-fitting clothes disguised what upon closer inspection was a very attractive woman. When she revealed during jury selection—or voir dire to lawyers—that she volunteered at Planned Parenthood three days a week and had walked door-to-door handing out pamphlets for the local Democratic candidates, I figured Laflamme would bounce her. But he must have seen something about her he liked. I smiled at her as I took my seat.

Unfortunately Amanda was the most liberal one in the group. There was a fair mix of the Hillsborough County populace including a self-employed house painter, a middle manager at a defense contractor in Nashua, and a mother of four-year-old twin boys who insisted her mother-in-law would watch the children so she could sit on the jury. My guess was she probably welcomed the rest.

I worried most about Marie Driscoll, an English professor at Notre Dame College a few blocks down Elm Street, and Anthony Giminsky, a sixteen-year veteran of the FBI. Mrs. Driscoll attended church every Sunday morning, cooked dinner for her husband every night, and flunked half of her students every semester. Despite her five-foot frame, she was a tough bird. She worried me, though, because she viewed the world as black or white; something was either right or it was wrong. She would have no trouble believing poor, uncouth Raymond Walker was guilty. But it would take a bit of work to convince her a nice middle class boy like Evan Conway was a murderer.

Giminsky was a mistake, a result, I realized, of my trial rustiness. I had violated the cardinal rule of jury selection: never get caught without at least one challenge left. He was the last juror seated and I was sure I could get him excused for cause. Even though he admitted he thought the courts coddled criminals and personally disagreed with the Supreme Court decisions upholding the Miranda warnings, Judge Taylor refused to excuse him. When the judge asked him if he could put his personal beliefs aside and follow the law as provided by the court, Giminsky nodded his head vigorously up and down and said "absolutely." Give me a break, I thought. But I had used up my last peremptory challenge so there was nothing I could do about it. The fair-minded FBI agent was on the jury.

The early trial date had taken its toll on Laflamme. The three and one half days of jury selection had exhausted him. There were dark circles under his eyes; his every move was slow and deliberate. Not the kind of pep I had come to expect. I knew he was tired when he didn't brag about his recent guilty verdict—win number sixty one—and instead whined, "Thanks for ruining my vacation." At least Judge Taylor gave us a few days off for Christmas, time I used to fine tune my trial strategy. Celebrating the holidays would have to wait.

We waited quietly for Taylor, the only sounds coming from Laflamme turning the pages of his trial notebook and a few jurors in the back row whispering. Finally, the door to the judge's chamber opened and the bailiff appeared with Judge Taylor right behind him. Raymond stood up, anticipating the order of "all rise." Judge Taylor was on the bench before the bailiff finished his instruction.

"Are both sides ready to proceed?" Judge Taylor asked after everyone had sat back down.

Laflamme and I simultaneously responded, "Yes, your honor."

"Very well, gentlemen. Mr. Laflamme, you may give your opening statement."

"Thank you, your honor." Closing his notebook with a flourish, Laflamme stood up and took his place behind the podium. He brought no notes with him. With his hands clutching the sides of the podium, Laflamme gazed at the jury, making eye contact with each one, left to right on the first row, up to the second row then right to left. The whole time, and it probably took ten seconds, Laflamme said not a word. By the time he eyed the last juror, the courtroom was deathly silent.

"Ladies and gentlemen of the jury," he began in a deeply resonant voice, mustering energy he kept well hidden. "You have been asked to sit here for the next few weeks because we—both myself and defense counsel Mr. Francis— thought you were the best people for the job, that you would listen to the evidence carefully and reach a fair and just verdict. You have been given an awesome responsibility: to judge whether this man . . ." He turned his head toward Raymond, wisely avoiding the tired routine of pointing his finger. ". . . is guilty of the crime of murder in the first degree. You have already told us during jury selection that you were willing to accept this responsibility, and we will hold you to that promise. To assist you in meeting your responsibility we promise to present the evidence in as clear a fashion as possible. When you finish listening to all the evidence—the prosecution's as well as the defendant's—you will be convinced, as I am, that the defendant Raymond Walker indeed is guilty of murdering Brian McHugh, the young college student, potential All-American halfback, and assistant manager of the Cinema Manchester. He is guilty beyond a shadow of a doubt."

He stepped to the side of the podium and stood two feet from juror number six, Amanda Sharpe, the object of his earlier attention. But if her beauty distracted him, he didn't show it. He was as smooth as if he had given the same speech hundreds of times before.

"The story I am about to tell you is not a pretty one. It is not the kind of story that will make you feel good inside. In fact, nothing you hear during this trial will make you feel good inside. Murder—cold, callous, calculated murder, as happened here—is never a pleasant subject. Brian McHugh was a young man with a bright future. A freshman halfback on the St. Andrew College football team, he was considered by many football experts as a serious candidate for the All-America team. Brian developed his football talent late in life and came to St. Andrew from California as a non-scholarship player. That's right: a walk-on All-American candidate. To pay his tuition he worked as assistant manager at the Cinema Manchester, which is where he met the defendant. Brian McHugh never got the chance to be on the All-America team, to play in the National Football League, to graduate from college, to fulfill any of the dreams he had worked so hard for: all because of the act of one jealous, resentful man, the defendant Raymond Walker."

Each time Laflamme mentioned Raymond's name, Raymond shifted in his seat. At the mention of "murder," his left leg began shaking up and down, seemingly out of control. The reality of the trial and the seriousness of the charges against him started to sink in. I glanced at the jury; fortunately no one had noticed Raymond's sudden shaking.

With his introduction completed, Laflamme then described the stormy relationship between Raymond and McHugh. "What motive did the defendant have to kill Brian McHugh?" Laflamme asked rhetorically. "The evidence will establish at least two motives, two of the oldest motives known to man: revenge and greed.

"The defendant intensely resented Brian McHugh because Brian was successful, popular, with a bright future, everything Raymond Walker was not. The defendant hated Brian for firing him; never mind that Brian had good cause to do so—the defendant's unsatisfactory job performance and insolence.

"Because of his employment there, the defendant knew the Cinema Manchester would take in a lot of money Halloween night. He also knew the theater made its bank deposits on Friday nights so—on top of the high receipts from the Halloween shows—there would be all of the receipts from the entire week."

I liked the greed part. It would fit in nicely with my defense. Laflamme continued to accommodate me: "There is no question that this was an inside job, that the murderer knew how the theater operated, knew there would be a lot of money that night, and knew how to get inside undetected." Keep going, I thought. Laflamme was making my opening for me: everything he said applied equally to Evan Conway.

"But the prosecution's case against the defendant does not rely only on his obvious motive and opportunity to commit this terrible crime. As you will soon see and hear, there is direct, incontrovertible evidence of the defendant's guilt. You will hear the testimony of an acquaintance of the defendant who will testify that four days before this crime was committed the defendant bragged about his plans to rob the theater."

Suddenly the table began vibrating. My pen slid across the yellow legal pad, making my notes look like the scribbling of a four-year old. I looked over at Raymond and saw the reason for this sudden interruption. His left leg was shaking much faster, and the momentum made his knee jerk against the table. Fixated on Laflamme, he was totally oblivious to what was happening. I put my hand on his shoulder and the shaking stopped, even though he continued to stare at Laflamme.

Laflamme bent over and picked up a poster-size photograph. He held it over his head. "And we will present evidence taken from the crime scene, including this photograph. The Manchester Police Department meticulously examined the theater, including the office where the murder occurred, searching for fingerprints or other evidence left behind by the killer. Not surprisingly, the only fingerprints in the office the police could identify were those of Brian McHugh and his boss, Philip Graham. The defendant obviously wore gloves to avoid leaving fingerprints. But he forgot about another kind of print, one that conclusively places him at the crime scene: a print of his boot. On the window sill a short distance from where McHugh's body was found, the police discovered a bootprint barely discernible to the naked eye. Using sophisticated photographic techniques they managed to produce this photograph."

He stretched his arms even higher and marched back and forth in front of the jury so each one could get a good look at the photo. "This is a photograph of a man's left boot, size nine and one half. The wear marks on this photograph match exactly the wear marks on the left boot, size nine and one half, taken from the defendant's foot after his arrest."

I noticed several jurors look over at Raymond. Mrs. Driscoll squinted her eyes and nodded at Laflamme. Even liberal Amanda Sharpe scratched her forehead. I had no doubt that at that moment all of them believed Raymond was guilty, but since Laflamme had given me a copy of the photo before trial I was prepared to rebut this damaging evidence when the time came.

Laflamme saved the best for last. "This evidence by itself establishes the defendant's guilt. But to make your decision easier we will present one more piece of evidence." I knew what was coming and was surprised Laflamme had waited so long. Laflamme paused and turned to look at me, a puzzled expression on his face, as if waiting for me to object. Again he bent over and from a box beside his seat pulled out Larry's pistol. An exhibit tag was attached to the trigger with a string.

"As is customary in cases of this type, the police have conducted ballistic tests of the bullet that killed Brian McHugh. They then compared the results of those tests with bullets shot from this gun. Those tests prove that Brian McHugh was killed by a bullet shot from this very gun, this gun which the police found in Lake Masabesic weeks after the murder, this gun which the defendant stole from the family that took him in after his own father had thrown him out, this gun which the defendant had fired on many occasions before October 31st; yes, this gun . . ." Now he held the gun over his head, curling his little finger around the trigger so it dangled back and forth like the pendulum of a clock. ". . .

this gun, the weapon defendant Raymond Walker used to murder Brian McHugh."

Turning abruptly, Laflamme walked back to his seat. He sat down and dropped the gun on the table in front of him, the dull thud of metal on wood filling the courtroom. The jury sat silently, completely still. It had been an impressive performance, all done without notes, without pause, without any trace of doubt of the defendant's guilt. I had my work cut out for me.

Breaking the silence, Judge Taylor asked, "Mr. Francis, do you wish to make an opening statement at this time?"

"Yes, I do, your honor."

"Proceed then," he ordered, and as if to warn me to be brief, added, "we will take our lunch recess in forty-five minutes."

Forgetting the butterflies that had afflicted me earlier, I placed my outline on the podium. I glanced toward the public seats. Larry and Paula stared at me intently, anxious, a look of hope on their faces. Evan stared straight ahead at the back of Raymond's head. Slouched in his seat, Raymond looked down at the floor, avoiding all eye contact with me.

As I positioned the outline so I could find my place at a glance, I was conscious of the contrast with Laflamme and the impression my using notes would have on the jury. But because I was insecure about trying a murder case I decided to keep the outline as a psychological crutch.

"Ladies and gentlemen of the jury, you have just heard a moving opening statement by assistant attorney general Laflamme. No doubt you are angry and upset that a good man like Brian McHugh lost his life so violently and needlessly. I share your anger; I share your outrage. Indeed this was a terrible crime.

"Nevertheless, I must insist that you remember your oath as jurors. You have promised to keep your minds open until you have heard all the evidence—not just the prosecutor's witnesses, but the defense witnesses as well. Like most things in life, there are two sides to this case. The oath that you have taken, that you have sworn under penalty of perjury to abide by, requires that you remember this. When you hear Mr. Laflamme tell you that Raymond Walker left his bootprint at the theater, that he had experience shooting the murder weapon that was found in the lake, that he bragged about robbing the theater, you must not conclude— even subconsciously—that Raymond Walker is guilty. You must remind yourself that there is another side to this story. Tell yourself: 'I must keep my mind open until I have heard both sides.' Unless you do this, you will be abdicating your responsibility, and worst of all denying my client a fair and just trial, as our great constitution guarantees him.

"It is customary at this point for the defense attorney to lecture the jury about the burden of proof, about how the prosecutor must prove the defendant's guilt beyond a reasonable doubt, to emphasize that the defendant is not required to prove his innocence, and to point out how very difficult the prosecutor's burden is. Though it is customary, I will not deliver that lecture to you. Once you have heard all the evidence—from both sides—you will have more than a reasonable doubt about Raymond Walker's guilt. I say this because I am confident the evidence will establish that Raymond Walker is innocent of the terrible crime with which he has been charged."

Now I was starting to warm up. The words were coming more easily and as I went on I forgot all about my outline. I could tell by the way the jurors sat forward on their seats that I had their attention. Only Mrs. Driscoll sat back with her arms folded; she had that you've-got-to-be-kidding-me look.

Before describing the evidence I gave them some background about Raymond, similar to the version I tried out on Laflamme at our first meeting. I admitted Raymond's disputes with McHugh, that he was mad and had made threats. But I tried to downplay it by pointing out that the threats were made in the heat of the moment and there was no evidence Raymond ever intended to follow through. "Most importantly," I told the jury, "after being fired, Raymond Walker had more reason than ever to forget his anger at McHugh. He learned something that gave his life new meaning, that made him look toward the future and not fret over the past. He learned that his girlfriend, Cathy Sayewich, was pregnant, that in a few months he would be a father. The bitterness went out of him. He did not think about Brian McHugh. He thought only of his unborn child and his love for Cathy."

I didn't feel all that hot about this part of my opening statement, but it was all I could come up with to counter Raymond's obvious motive to kill McHugh. I realized Laflamme easily could make the argument the other way—that Raymond had all the more reason to want to rob the theater to get money for his new family—but I figured I still needed to insert some kind of doubt about motive.

After describing Raymond's activities Halloween night and the two days afterwards, I laid out our defense. "I told you earlier that I abhorred this terrible crime. This was without question a vicious, cold-blooded act, committed by a person with no regard for human life. A person who wanted money so badly he was willing to kill another human being to get it. Such a person deserves the strongest punishment our laws can inflict. Such a person deserves no mercy. That person is not—I repeat NOT—Raymond Walker, the young man wrongly accused of this crime.

"The police and prosecution have made a terrible mistake, a mistake that will become apparent to you as more and more evidence is presented. And part of the evidence we will present to you will be the testimony of a witness whom the police never bothered to question, a witness who will exonerate Raymond Walker from all the charges that have been levied against him. For this witness observed the victim Brian McHugh get into a violent argument with the person who later killed him. This person had a real motive to kill Brian McHugh, for Brian witnessed him commit a crime—a crime that resulted in the death of an innocent man—and could have sent the killer to prison for the rest of his life. To prevent intimidation of this witness before he is able to give testimony, I will not reveal his identity, or that of the actual killer, at this time. Instead, please bear with me as we go through the evidence, and rest assured that at the close of the evidence you will be as convinced as I am about who murdered Brian McHugh. And that person most definitely is not Raymond Walker."

While I gathered up my outline, I looked each juror in the eye, left to right along the top row, then right to left along the bottom row. They stared at me in stunned silence. It was obvious they never anticipated such a bold defense. I picked up my outline and walked back to my seat. Before sitting down I glanced over at Larry. His mouth hung open. His eyes bulged. With a bewildered look he watched me take my seat. Beside him Evan had his head bowed, looking at the floor so I could not see his face.

"Why, thank you very much, Mr. Francis." Judge Taylor sounded pleased he would have some entertainment ahead of him. "Let's take our lunch recess. Jurors, remember my admonition. You are not to discuss this case with anyone until you retire for deliberations. We will reconvene at two o'clock."

CHAPTER 26

AFTER the jury had shuffled out of the courtroom, I leaned over to talk to Raymond. Before I could say anything, I was interrupted by a sound from behind us. "What the hell is going on? Why didn't you tell me about this?" Larry was leaning over the wooden bar, whispering so the bailiff wouldn't hear. "I thought we were working together on this thing." He turned to Raymond. "Raymond, did you know about this?"

I put my hand on Raymond's shoulder to prevent him from blurting anything out. "Larry, now's not the time to talk about this. For strategic reasons, we couldn't tell you everything. Raymond's chances depended on keeping this as quiet as possible."

"That's bullshit. You know damn well I can keep confidences." Evan and Paula joined Larry at the bar.

Paula showed none of the anger Larry obviously felt. "Hello, Dutch," she said. "That was a beautiful opening statement. You sounded so confident."

Evan stared at Raymond, silent, while Larry insisted I tell

him who the murderer was. "I can't tell you now." I tried to put him off. "You'll find out soon enough."

"That's not good enough, Dutch. That's no way to treat me."

Larry's voice got louder and Paula put her hand on his shoulder. "Lawrence, why don't you let Dutch try the case his way. After all, that's why you hired him."

Larry paid no attention to her. "I got you involved in this case," he continued. "Don't you think you could at least level with me? Are you shutting me out because I didn't tell you about the gun? Is that it? I don't understand how Raymond's defense could be harmed if I know what the hell is going on."

This animated conversation caused newspaper reporter Gus Decker to look up from his note pad. He had been busily making notes but stopped suddenly, got up and walked toward us. Holding up his pencil like a student trying to get the teacher's attention, he said, "I'd like to know that too. Who are you going to finger?"

"No comment," I said a bit too quickly. Fortunately I was spared having to say anything else when the bailiff appeared to bring Raymond back to his cell. "Sorry, I have to get back to my office," I said, picking up my briefcase.

As I walked out the door, Larry yelled after me. "We'll talk later. I want some answers, Dutch."

At two o'clock, I was back at counsel's table with Raymond. Hank Lerner, the senior and still chunky bailiff, walked out of the judge's chambers. "Afternoon, counselor," he winked at me as he passed by on his way to the hall. "Time for everyone to take a seat," he shouted, and the jurors filed in, taking their seats. After everyone was seated, Larry and Evan walked into the courtroom, ignoring the judge's order excluding witnesses. Paula was not with them.

"Remain seated and come to order," Hank commanded.

"Are you ready to proceed, Mr. Laflamme?" Judge Taylor asked.

"Yes, your honor. The prosecution calls Mr. Frank Killian to the stand. He's in the hallway. I'll get him."

I stood up. "One moment, your honor. Before this witness comes in, may we approach the bench?"

Taylor's scowl told me what he thought of that suggestion. "It's early in the trial, Mr. Francis. I don't want to get in the habit of wasting the jury's precious time for private chats."

"I agree, your honor. But this is a matter of extreme importance. And I certainly don't intend on making it a habit."

"Very well, Mr. Francis," he sighed. "Approach."

"I didn't want to say anything in front of the jury," I whispered while Judge Taylor leaned over from the bench. "But your honor ordered that witnesses be excluded from the courtroom until their testimonies are complete. There are two—albeit unwilling—prosecution witnesses in the front row."

Taylor frowned. "Is that true, Mr. Laflamme?"

"Yes, it is. But those are the Conways, the family the defendant was living with at the time of his arrest. I didn't think the defendant would object if they sat in."

"Did you bother to ask Mr. Francis if he would object?"

"Well, no. I never thought of it."

"Not good, Mr. Laflamme. My orders are to be followed to the letter unless there is a stipulation otherwise, then you come talk to me. Now, what should we do about the Conways? I don't want to prejudice the defense by making it appear to the jury that Mr. Francis does not want these witnesses hearing the testimony."

"Perhaps I could tell them myself," Laflamme offered.

"Would that be satisfactory, Mr. Francis?"

"Yes it would." I was pleased at the judge's concern to appear fair and decided to push him just a little bit more. "And perhaps they could be told to leave while the court instructs the jury about sidebar conferences so it won't look so obvious."

"Good suggestion. Let's proceed." Still seated, Taylor rolled his chair back to the bench.

As Laflamme and I stepped down, the judge said for the jury's benefit, "Mr. Laflamme, please bring in your first witness." Then he turned to the jury. "Ladies and gentlemen of the jury, sometimes during the course of the trial it will be necessary for me to confer with the attorneys outside of your hearing. Please do not be offended when we do this. The court and counsel are mindful of your time, and will make every effort to keep the trial moving along. But when matters of law are raised it is occasionally necessary for us to have these sidebar conferences. You should make no inference or conclusion from the mere fact that counsel has requested a sidebar conference or that I have granted or declined such a request."

While Judge Taylor was diverting the jury's attention, Laflamme gave the news to the Conways. I watched Larry's already tense face tighten even more. He looked at me as if blaming me for his eviction. To avoid drawing the jury's attention, I looked away and sat down, my back to him. Laflamme then directed Killian to the stand where the clerk administered the oath. I could hear Larry and Evan get up and walk out. After this day was over, I would have to talk to Larry again, a discussion I wasn't looking forward to.

Frank Killian was about Raymond's age, stocky, with wide shoulders and a thick neck. I had spent a long time listening to the tape of his statement, comparing it to the signed statement Hedges had obtained, and meeting with Raymond to plan my cross-examination. There was no question Killian was a key witness, potentially our most damaging. Laflamme obviously wanted to start strong, force the jurors to make up their minds early, hoping they would overlook any weaknesses in later prosecution witnesses.

As Killian sat back in the witness chair, he pushed a lock of dirty blond hair off his forehead. He tugged on the sleeves of his polyester suit, undoubtedly purchased at Laflamme's favorite clothing store. His wide tie seemed to strangle him;

folds of flesh bunched up around his collar. This was probably the first time he'd ever worn a tie.

"Good morning, Mr. Killian," Laflamme began. Killian looked down, not responding, and continued to tug on his sleeves. Laflamme slid the podium to the far end of the jury box.

"Mr. Killian!" Laflamme said loudly.

"Oh, sorry," Killian said as he looked up. "I'm not used to being called mister."

Amanda Sharpe giggled and even Mrs. Driscoll cracked a smile. Not a good start for the prosecution. Laflamme suddenly reddened.

"Well then, let us begin." Laflamme began by asking Killian about his background, trying to get him to relax. He grew up in Portsmouth, dropped out of high school in the eleventh grade, and ever since has been working at a Portsmouth video arcade handing out change. A real American success story.

The introduction over, Laflamme paused, glanced toward the jury, ready to ask the important questions.

"Mr. Killian, have you ever been friends with the defendant, Raymond Walker?"

Killian leaned forward, his eyes darting from Laflamme to Raymond and back. "Uh-huh, yeah. For a long time."

"When was that?"

"For about three years. Up until October of this year."

"Did something happen in October that affected your friendship?"

"Well, I guess you could say that. He showed me something."

"What was it the defendant showed you?"

Killian swallowed, causing his fleshy neck to jiggle. As if aware of the movement, he reached up, touched his tie but decided against loosening it. "He come into the arcade one night while I was workin'. He was carryin' this gym bag, a long red thing with a blue handle. He points to the bag and says . . ."

"Objection." I jumped to my feet. "The witness is going beyond the question, which I believe had something to do with what the defendant showed him."

Laflamme frowned, rolled his eyes. But Judge Taylor agreed with me. "Yes, Mr. Francis, that is correct. Mr. Killian, try to answer only the question that is put to you."

"Yes sir, sorry," Killian answered, looking like a scolded child. "I'll try."

Laflamme started over. "Mr. Killian, where did you happen to meet the defendant on this occasion?"

"Like I said, it was in the arcade. I was working and he just walked in."

"Was the defendant carrying anything?"

"Well, yeah. I told you, the gym bag. And he showed me what was inside it."

"Will you please explain to his honor and the jury what you saw in the defendant's gym bag?" Laflamme sighed, hoping Killian would get it right this time.

"Raymond unzips this bag and says, 'Take a look at this.'" Even though Killian again went beyond the question, I let it slide, not wanting to alienate the jury so early in the trial. Killian continued. "I had no idea what he was talkin' about, you know. So he reaches in and pulls out this green rubber Halloween mask, the kind goes on right over your head. It had these huge wart-like things sticking out all over, long white hair and a really disgusting face."

"Let me stop you there, Mr. Killian. Did the defendant say anything about the mask at that time?"

"Oh yeah. He says he was gonna wear the mask on Halloween night. There was some kinda special midnight show at the theater he used to work at, and they'd make a ton of money. So he was gonna sneak in afterwards with this mask on so no one would recognize him, then rip 'em off."

"Did the defendant say how he was going to rip off the theater?"

"All he says is he'd just rob them when they're counting up all the money."

Laflamme should have quit right there; instead, what Killian said next gave me more ammunition for cross-examination. The jury was riveted to Killian. Despite his unsophisticated demeanor his story sounded plausible. While he was testifying, Raymond's whole body tensed, his eyes locked on his ex-pal on the witness stand. Every time Killian glanced in Raymond's direction, he quickly turned away.

"Mr. Killian, you told us you were a friend of the defendant. What made you come forward with this information?"

"I didn't think he was serious at the time. Raymond was always kind of a bullshitter . . ." He looked up at the judge, expecting to be scolded. "Uh, sorry." He continued. "But he always talked big and stuff, always saying he was gonna be a millionaire some day, really hit the big time, that kind of sh—ah, crap. So I just shined him. Then Halloween weekend I seen the news on Channel Nine and they was saying the Cinema Manchester had been robbed and the manager killed, I just couldn't believe it."

"So what did you do?"

"I called the police and reported what had happened. I figured it was my civic duty."

"Thank you, Mr. Killian. No further questions."

As Laflamme sat down, the courtroom became hushed. By the time Taylor spoke, only a few seconds had passed, though it seemed like minutes. "Mr. Francis, do you wish to cross-examine?"

"Absolutely, your honor," I answered immediately and jumped to my feet. My aggressive demeanor already had the desired effect as Killian retreated slightly in his seat. He knew there would be a fight. I didn't want to give the jury any time to think about his direct testimony, so I went right after him.

"Mr. Killian, do you recall talking to my investigator, Glenn Hedges, last month?"

"The dude with the ponytail? Sure, he was cool, I talked to him."

"After you spoke to him, he wrote a statement for you to sign. Is that right?"

"I guess, yeah."

"You read the statement before signing it, didn't you?"

"Course, I looked it over. Seemed okay to me."

I handed the clerk the original statement and Laflamme a copy. After the clerk marked it as Defendant's Exhibit A, I handed it to Killian.

"is that your signature on the last page?"

He flipped through the pages and looked at the signature. "Sure looks like mine."

"Mr. Killian, let me direct your attention to page two, third paragraph. Do you see that?"

"Where it says about the bag?"

"That's it. Let me read: 'Raymond unzipped the bag and pulled something out. It was some kind of green rubber thing, a mask or something.'"

"Have I read that correctly, Mr. Killian?" When he hesitated, I asked, "So you really didn't get a good look at what was in the bag?"

"Hold on a sec. That's what it says, but that's not right. It was a mask, for sure."

"Are you saying you didn't read this statement before signing it under penalty of perjury?"

"I skimmed it. That's what I did. I must've missed that part. Sorry."

I scowled at him in disgust. He was stupider than I'd thought. "Mr. Killian, do you see on the statement that the word 'green' is written above another word that has been crossed out?"

"Yeah, I can see that." His voice got lower. I bet he wanted to hide because he knew I had him.

"Looks like the word crossed out says 'yellow.' Would you agree with that?"

"Okay, I'll buy that."

"And what are those letters beside the crossed-out word, 'yellow'?"

He threw the statement in front of him, then stared to the side of the courtroom, away from the jury.

"Mr. Killian?"

"I can't be sure," he said.

"Can't be sure? Isn't it true that those letters are 'FK,' your initials? Didn't you initial that change from yellow to green?"

He picked up the statement again, acted as if he were reading it for the first time. "I guess I did, yeah."

"So you did read this statement before signing it, right?"

He grimaced, thinking of a way out. But there was none. "I guess that's right."

This cross-examination was going better than I'd expected. Killian was such a dumb guy, I thought I could get a lot more out of him so I kept pushing.

"Mr. Killian, on direct exam you told Mr. Laflamme that you called the police because you thought that was your civic duty?"

"Well, sure." He lifted his head, a proud patriot.

"But you didn't decide to do your civic duty until you had heard about the robbery at the theater?"

"Like I said, when Raymond showed me the mask, I didn't think nothin' about it. He was always bullshittin' me."

"Mis-ter Killian," I said, emphasizing the "Mister." "Did my client say anything to you about killing anybody?"

"No, I would've remembered that. He definitely did not."

"He didn't say anything about wanting to get even with the assistant manager, Brian McHugh?"

"Uh-uh." He shook his head back and forth.

"So at the time of your conversation with Raymond you didn't think you had a civic duty to call the police?"

"No, I didn't. I said that already."

"And that was because you knew he wasn't serious?"

"Well, I guess not, or I probably would've called them."

It was a minor point but I felt compelled to make it. I had to make the jury question Killian's self-proclaimed status as some kind of civic hero. But I had other, more important, points to make.

"So you never believed Raymond intended to rob the theater until you saw this news program, is that what you're saying, Mr. Killian?"

"That's right, I didn't think nothin' of it until then."

I walked toward the witness stand and raised my voice. "Mr. Killian, you thought nothing of it because the conversation never took place, isn't that true?"

"No, sir. I told the truth."

It was time to stop playing with him. I had to get to him now or the case could be over, no matter how strong the later evidence was. I lowered my voice to just above a whisper.

"You've known Raymond Walker for a few years, haven't you?"

"That's right, I already said that."

"Consider yourselves good friends?"

"Most of the time, I suppose."

"You know his girlfriend Cathy too, don't you?"

His eyes widened. Slowly he nodded his head up and down. "You could say that."

"Well, that doesn't answer my question. Do you know her?"

"Yeah, I know Cathy. We used to go out together." Without moving his head, Killian glanced nervously at Raymond.

"When did you stop going out with her?"

"Sometime during the summer, May, June maybe. I don't remember exactly when."

"You didn't like it when Raymond started going out with Cathy, did you?"

"Her choice. She can do what she wants. Nothing I can say about it." Despite his bold words, there was a slight catch in his voice, as if he were on the verge of losing his cool.

"You were upset at Raymond for taking Cathy away from you, weren't you?"

"I wasn't happy about it, if that's what you mean. I liked Cathy, figured she could do better."

"And you were better than Raymond Walker, is that what you're saying?"

"No doubt about it."

"You were better because you'd be able to provide Cathy a good home, is that right?"

He hesitated, not knowing where I was going. But he liked the compliment so he agreed. "Sure," he said, getting smug.

I looked up from my notes and paused a moment before asking, "Mr. Killian, how many jobs have you had in the past two years?"

"What do you mean?" Suddenly he looked worried.

"How many different jobs have you had in the past two years?" I said slowly. "That's pretty clear, isn't it?"

He shrugged. "I dunno."

"You don't know? Isn't it true that you've had six different jobs in two years? And the longest one lasted three months?"

He looked down. "I guess that's right."

"But you thought you were better than Raymond Walker." It wasn't a question and Laflamme could've objected. But I didn't give him a chance.

"You told Cathy you were better than Raymond, didn't you?"

Killian got a pained expression on his face. He looked up at Taylor. "Judge, do I have to answer these questions? I don't see what my love life has to do with this."

Taylor looked over at me then back at Killian. "Answer the questions as best you can, Mr. Killian."

"What was the question again?" Killian sounded exasperated.

I repeated the question.

"I told Cathy I still wanted to go out with her. And she said we were finished. She was in love with Ray-mond." He emphasized the first syllable with a mocking sing-song tone.

"And you were in love with her, weren't you?"

He gritted his teeth, not answering.

I asked a different question. "You had sex with her several times, didn't you?"

He looked at the judge, then toward Laflamme. No one came to his rescue. "A few," he admitted.

"And you hoped to marry her, right?"

"I never asked."

"I didn't ask you that. Isn't it true you hoped someday to marry Cathy Sayewich?"

He rocked back and forth, biting his lip. "Yeah, you could say that."

"So would it be fair to say then that you were upset about losing Cathy to Raymond?"

"Sure, 'course."

"You were so upset at losing Cathy to Raymond that you threatened to get even with him, didn't you?" I raised my voice in as threatening a manner as I could muster without sounding like a bully.

"Are you crazy? If I wanted to get even with him I wouldn't have waited. I would have done something right away."

"You mean you wouldn't have waited until November to call the police?" I didn't bother to wait for an answer. "By the way, when was the last time you talked to Cathy?"

"I have no idea. It was a while ago."

"Wasn't it in late October?"

"I don't know, maybe. So what?"

"It was in late October that Cathy told you she was pregnant with Raymond's child, didn't she?"

"Yeah, she told me." Killian clenched his teeth. He sucked in a deep breath, so loud you could hear the "hiss" as air passed through his teeth. "I couldn't believe she'd been so stupid," he said finally, his teeth showing.

"And that's when you decided to get even with Raymond, isn't it? Right after learning Cathy was pregnant."

"No way, you got it wrong."

"But that's how you felt. You wanted to get even. You wanted to hurt Raymond because of Cathy." I walked to the side of the table and turned toward the jury. All eyes were on me. "You wanted a chance to win Cathy back, so when you heard about the robbery, you remembered Raymond used to work at the theater so you made up this story so he'd go to jail." To emphasize "story" I pounded my fist on the table and turned abruptly toward the witness stand.

Laflamme jumped up during this speech, yelling, "Objection! Objection!"

Even though Laflamme didn't state the legal basis for his objection, Judge Taylor sustained it. "This is cross-examination, Mr. Francis. You may ask all the leading questions you want, but you are not to give speeches. Is that clear?"

"Yes, sorry, your honor," I said, contrite.

Killian had been shifting to the edge of his seat, as if he were going to jump up. He was so excited he ignored Judge Taylor's ruling and answered me anyway. "No, never, I did not make up this story," he shouted. "That would be lying and I'd get in trouble."

I spread my arms out wide and again turned to the jury. "Exactly," I said slowly. "It would be perjury." I sat down, dismissing Killian, and said, "No further questions."

CHAPTER 27

AFTER court I hurried to my office to see whether Hedges had called. Yvette sat at her desk organizing stacks of papers. I froze when I saw Russell sitting in the client chair, reading a *Modern Photography* magazine. On the cover was a black-and-white photo of a busty nude lounging on a sandy beach. There were all kinds of shadows, the model in different shades of grey; supposed to be real meaningful, I guessed.

"Oh, Russell, how are ya?" I tried to sound casual.

"Okay, just waiting for my woman." At the mention of "my woman," Yvette grimaced. Russell returned to the magazine.

"Don't mind him," Yvette said. "He's engrossed in an article on the latest development in Ansel Adam's zone system. At least it keeps him quiet for a while." She smiled, nodding, reassuring me there was nothing to worry about. "So how's it going?" she asked.

"So far so good. Killian hurt a lot, but I think I got the

jury wondering about his credibility. We'll see. Any word from Hedges?"

"Yeah, he called an hour or so ago. He says he's close to finding Jack Gibbs. He'll stop by tomorrow morning with a full report."

"Let's hope he has some good news." I leaned against the wall beside her desk.

"As a matter of fact I have some good news right here," she said, smiling. "Hedges had some kind of connection at Monadnock Casualty, PEVCON's insurance company. He made a few phone calls and got them to agree to send some info on the Cheshire Village fire claim. Here you go. Came in today by messenger."

She handed me a photocopy of an insurance claim form. It was signed by Larry on behalf of PEVCON, Inc. and requested payment for the fire loss at the Luhovey building. Stapled to the claim form was a copy of the insurance check, a tidy sum. I stared at the date: December 7, over a month after McHugh was killed.

"You're right," I said. "This is interesting. I think the jury will believe this kind of money would provide enough motive for arson. . . ." I stopped and looked at Russell, who was still staring at the magazine.

"Maybe you could ask Larry about the check tonight. He wants you to join him for dinner at his club. Four times today he's called, even when I told him the first time I'd give you the message. The man sounded mighty upset."

"Not tonight. I just can't face him now. If he calls back tomorrow, tell him I had to prepare for trial, make something up if you have to."

"Sure, I'll do what I can."

She glanced at Russell, then back at me. "I left something on your desk." She stood up and walked toward the inner office. "I'll get it for you."

I followed her to my desk. She turned around, facing me, glancing over my shoulder at the open door. Russell hadn't moved. "Are you okay?" She straightened my tie, which I had already loosened anyway. "I'm worried about you."

Again I felt touched by her concern. "I'm trying not to think about it. Only thing I can do is try to win this case. Nothing else matters right now."

Yvette looked toward the open door at the sound of Russell flipping the magazine shut. "You ready, hon?" Russell yelled. "About time to get going. Dutch isn't paying you overtime, you know." Was there a hint of hostility in his voice? Maybe he suspected something, even if Yvette hadn't mentioned it. I would think a man would know if his girlfriend were attracted to someone else. Fortunately, with Sherry I never had to worry. She was too busy with social engagements, charity dinners especially, to have any time for an affair.

"Be right there," Yvette said, rubbing my cheek as she walked past. I followed her to the door.

As Yvette put on her coat, Russell turned to me. "I've been thinking, Dutch. You must need a photographer for some of your cases and I could use the extra money. What about giving me a shot?" I was surprised; Russell had never asked for work before. Was he blackmailing me now?

"You think you'd like that? Taking photos of accident scenes, scars, that kind of thing? Not very creative."

"Hey, depends how you do it. You know you'd get the highest quality photos. And from what I hear of the way the business is going . . ." He glanced at Yvette. "Your cases could use a little boost."

"Thanks for the offer, Russell. I'll keep you in mind, but it won't be until the trial is over. This thing takes up all my time."

Russell and Yvette said good night, leaving me to put the finishing touches on outlines of my cross-examinations of tomorrow's witnesses, all police officers. At ten thirty, hungry, weary, but with the adrenaline still pumping, I headed for home, worried I'd bump into Larry Conway on the way.

I got to my apartment around nine. It was dark and there was someone hanging around the front door. At first I was worried it was Larry intent on revenge. He had to be wondering how much I knew and what I would tell the jury. Since he couldn't watch the trial, he could only get basic information about the trial from the newspapers and TV. The suspense must have been driving him nuts.

In the moonlight I had a hard time making out the person's facial features. I walked to the side of the building and edged my way along the lawn, keeping to the shadows. The man—I knew it was a man—turned away from me. He folded his arms and leaned against the building. I was about twenty yards away and stopped, wondering if I should walk right by him or wait him out. My decision was made for me. Still facing away from me, the man said, "You would make a damn poor PI, Dutch. I've had my eye on you since you pulled into the parking lot."

Hedges turned around and smiled, shaking his head.

"Thanks for scaring the shit out of me," I said.

"You're getting paranoid in your old age," he said, laughing. "Lucky for you I got some good news." He blew on his hands. "You think you could invite me inside any time soon? I'm freezing my ass off standing around out here."

I got Hedges seated on the couch with a bottle of Molson Golden in one hand. He kept the other hand on the radiator, trying to thaw it out.

I also sipped on a Molson and waited for Hedges' report, hoping he really had invaded my personal space with good news.

"Here's what happened," he began. "I hand Jack-the-Quack the subpoena, and the little worm crumbles it up, throws it back at me. He starts yelling 'I don't give a shit about this. I ain't gonna testify.' That right? I says. 'Damn straight,' the worm says."

Hedges jumped to his feet, his ponytail bouncing across his shoulders. "So I got in his face," he said, getting excited. He put the bottle on the floor and reached over and grabbed my lapels. "Just like this," he demonstrated, pulling me toward him, his garlicky breath hitting me full force. "'You ignore this piece of paper,' I says as I stuffed it into his mouth, 'and I'll have the sheriff throw your ass in jail. Nolo contendere—no contest, you moron—you're dead meat.'" With a menacing sneer, Hedges released my lapels, sat back down. "I saw that on one of those cop shows on TV. I think he'll be there," he added, rubbing his hands together.

Great, just what I needed, my investigator intimidating a witness. Gibbs' testimony will be tough enough as it is; I don't need any added problems.

"Um, Mr. Hedges," I said slowly, trying to stay calm. "You think intimidating our witness will help this case?"

"Come on, Dutch, you . . ."

"This is my key witness for Christ's sake. How the hell am I going to prepare him now? After what you've done, he won't have anything to do with me."

"Gimme a break, he was no friend of yours anyway."

Hedges had me there. It wasn't like Jack Gibbs was such a willing witness in the first place. "Okay, okay. Let's hope he shows, that's all. I've got enough to worry about." Like convincing the jury that Larry had a good motive to have his building torched. "You find anything on Larry's finances?"

"The info's just coming in." He turned around, reached into the pocket of his jacket, which he'd hung on the back of the couch. "Here, check this out." He handed me a computer printout. It listed all of Larry's properties, including mortgage amounts and dates of sales. There were sixteen properties, mostly apartment buildings with three or four single family homes. In the last two years Larry had taken out second mortgages on exactly half of the properties. And three of the apartment buildings had been sold in the past year. Even without details about Larry's personal finances the conclusion was inescapable. All of this activity showed a pattern of financial distress, a motive to torch the Luhovey building and collect the insurance proceeds, another piece of the puzzle that I would present to the jury.

"I don't think you'll have a problem convincing the jury that this guy was on the skids," Hedges said. "In fact, if you want me to testify as an expert witness, I could easily say that Conway's financial situation fits the profile of arsonists I saw all the time when I was on the department. Piece of cake."

"I don't think we'll need to do that," I said, imagining Laflamme having a field day with Hedges, covering all the work he'd done for me. And tell me again, Mr. Hedges, what was the name of that X-rated movie you watched for two hours in Boston? No thanks.

"So what else you need me to do, Dutch?"

"Just make sure Gibbs shows up, that's all."

"I'll do that, Rubenstein too. I subpoenaed him last week." In my haste to subpoena Gibbs, I had forgotten how important Rubenstein would be. Of course, I would need Rubenstein to testify why McHugh was visiting him on the day of the fire. I was sure Rubenstein wouldn't be too happy about admitting on the stand that he was a 'Luck Facilitator.' But that couldn't be helped.

"Good job," I said. Then I reached into my briefcase. "Here," I said, pulling a notebook out. "Give this back to Rubenstein. I don't want Laflamme arguing that we were manipulating his testimony."

Hedges thumbed through the book. "Maybe I'll copy a few pages before giving it to him," he said.

When I gave him a sideways glance, he said, "Hey, it's not like I'm stealing or anything. Okay, tell you what. I'll make it up to him."

"How's that?"

He smiled. "I'll bring him another bottle of Stoli."

CHAPTER 28

A block from my office the cold wind whipped against my face, numbing my cheeks and bringing tears to my eyes. A December morning in Manchester was not for the faint of heart. Although the temperature was only five to ten degrees lower than Boston's, the wind made it seem much colder. A gust hit me full in the face, blowing my cap into the gutter; when I bent over to retrieve it, I noticed the newspaper rack. The *Union Leader* headline read: "WALKER ATTORNEY CLAIMS POLICE ARRESTED WRONG MAN."

I put a few coins in the machine, pulled out a newspaper. The story was by Gus Decker. As I read I forgot all about the cold: "Dutch Francis, attorney for Raymond Walker, told a Hillsborough County jury yesterday that the police had arrested the wrong man. Although Francis refused to disclose the name of the man he claims was the actual murderer, he promised that a surprise witness would tell all." The story went on to summarize my opening statement, mentioning several times that I gave no clues as to the actual murderer or the surprise witness.

I folded the paper, placed it inside my briefcase. At the courthouse, a crowd of reporters were hanging around the back stairs. They were clutching notebooks, chatting with Gus Decker. When they saw me, they left Decker and ran toward me shouting questions. There were two women and three men, none of whom looked familiar. One of the men was louder than the others. He had curly brown hair that hadn't met a comb in a few days and a goofy grin that made him look confused. I stared at his ID tag: "Dan Sweeney, *Boston Globe*." Crime must've slowed in Boston for the Globe to be interested in this case, or else this guy was a rookie, the only reporter who would accept an assignment in frigid Manchester.

"Mr. Francis, who did it? How about filling us in?" He was practically shouting in my ear. Other than drafting press releases bragging about my defense verdicts in product liability cases, I had no experience dealing with the media in Boston. But I always hated seeing lawyers on the news, brushing off questions with a terse "no comment," as, regrettably, I had done yesterday in court. It sounded arrogant and left the impression they were hiding something, even when the question seemed innocuous.

So I tried to fend this one off a bit more diplomatically. I looked around the group, pretending not to know who had asked the question. "All of you know I can't give away my case. But hang around today, you may get a few clues."

They followed me up the steps, and as I reached for the door, it burst open. A cameraman came through followed by a female TV reporter with a microphone. She smiled, stuck the microphone in my face. "Mr. Francis," she said in an ingratiating tone, as if I should recognize her. (I did. She was Virginia Turner from Channel 9, a devilish beauty, dark and seductive like Lauren Bacall.) "What's a civil lawyer like you doing with a murder case?"

I stopped and turned to look down at her. She had done her homework. So she was not just another ditzy newsreader; there were some brains behind that heavily made-up face. "My friend . . . um . . ." I stammered, hesitating. She had caught me off guard. "No comment," I mumbled as I let the door slam shut behind me.

I pushed open the swinging doors to Judge Winston Taylor's courtroom and gazed at the blue and gold New Hampshire state flag above the judge's bench. The courtroom was already packed with spectators, the jury seated in the box. The jurors were whispering among themselves while looking at the crowd of reporters following me, no doubt feeling that any case that attracted this kind of attention must be important. Laflamme huddled in the corner with two uniformed police officers, also whispering. With all the whispering the courtroom sounded like a Catholic church during confession.

As soon as Raymond was seated Judge Taylor took the bench. I leaned over to Raymond. "You okay?"

He nodded. "Yeah, except I'm still pissed off at what Killian did to me. The sonovabitch."

He had a right to be angry, but at least we'd gotten the worst out of the way. "Don't worry," I told him. "That was their best shot. It'll be easier from now on."

Taylor wasted no time with small talk. He looked tired, bags under his eyes as if he'd had a poor night's sleep, and he was in a terrible mood. "Mr. Laflamme," he grumbled, "your next witness."

Laflamme directed a police officer to the stand. As he took the oath, he shouted his name: Francis Xavier Foley. Laflamme took Officer Foley through his police career: fourteen years with the crime lab, testified hundreds of times on forensic issues, everything from matching scraps of cloth to a defendant's shirt to basic fingerprint analysis.

Foley had the demeanor of a polished witness. Before answering Laflamme's questions, he turned toward the jury, made eye contact, talked to them as if he were teaching a class. As he went through the details of his experience, the jury sat in rapt attention. The witness's expertise established, Laflamme asked, "Officer Foley, what work have you done in connection with this case?"

Foley pulled the microphone closer to his mouth, the increased volume further attracting the jury's attention. "I inspected the crime scene in detail. Then I took photographs of specific items I found interesting."

"Can you describe specifically what photographs you took?"

"Actually, I concentrated on one particular area, the window sill near the manager's office."

"In connection with the photographs that you took, did you make any notes?"

"Yes, I have them here." Foley reached down, picked up a manila envelope he had brought to the stand with him. He reached into the envelope, pulled out his notes. "These are my notes. They state the precise location in the theater where the photos were taken, the date and time of the photo, and the shutter speed and aperture settings I used."

Laflamme asked the clerk to mark a blowup of one of the photographs as the People's next in order. It was the same one he'd waved in front of the jury during opening statement. "People's Exhibit 1, marked for identification," the clerk announced, handing the photo back to Laflamme.

Laflamme handed the photo to Foley. "Officer Foley, can you identify this photograph?"

"Of course, this shows the bootprint I personally observed on the window sill of the theater, just off the stairs to the manager's office."

"Your honor, we move exhibit 1 into evidence."

"No objection," I said.

"There being no objection," Taylor said, barely lifting his head, "Exhibit 1 is admitted in evidence."

Laflamme continued with his examination. "Officer Foley, please explain to the jury why you took this photograph."

"Certainly," Foley answered. He stood up, put the blown-up photo on an easel and pulled a laser pointer from his shirt pocket. "We concluded that the murderer gained access through the hall window, right here"—he set the red laser dot on the window—"which was left unlocked. The window actually had a safety latch which the defendant was aware of. I spent a lot of time examining the area around the window, primarily for fingerprints. We found no fingerprints, but we did find this boot print on the window sill. It was barely visible with the naked eye, but I sprinkled some black powder on it. My own concoction; all it does is darken existing images, like the print made by the sole of the boot. It makes it easier to see, that's all. And after doing that, I took the photograph, exhibit . . ." He stepped in front of the easel, bent down to read the exhibit tag. "Sorry. Exhibit 1."

"Officer Foley, did you compare this photograph of the boot print found on the window sill to the defendant Raymond Walker's boot?"

"Yes, I did."

Laflamme then had the clerk mark Raymond's boot as Exhibit 2 and handed it to the witness. With the next several questions Laflamme established the chain of custody of the boot, which was found on Raymond's right foot the day he was arrested. Foley testified that he had spent several hours examining the boot and comparing it to the photograph of the boot print.

Finally, forty-five minutes after Foley had taken the stand, Laflamme got to the whole purpose of his testimony. "Officer Foley, based on your background and experience, as well as all the work you did on this case, have you reached an opinion concerning what boot made the print found at the murder scene?"

Laflamme glanced at me, anticipating an objection. Even Taylor seemed to wake up from his snooze. He raised his head, stared down at me while raising an eyebrow. Unlike fingerprints, the analysis of boot prints was not universally accepted, and Foley had not testified to any particular expertise, other than a few prior cases, to offer such an

opinion. I was well aware of these objections, but I decided
to let Foley answer.

"Yes, I have." He didn't bother waiting for the next
question. He held up the boot next to the photo. "You can
see this photo shows a right boot. The wear marks are on
the inside near the large toe and outside the heel. Right here
and here. . . ." He circled the marks with a red pen. "If you
compare the wear marks on the boot"—he pointed to the
boot—"to these ones on the photo you can see that they're
identical."

"So is it your conclusion that this boot made the print
depicted in the photo?"

"No question about it."

That was all Laflamme wanted. He sat down.

"Cross-examination, Mr. Francis?" Judge Taylor bel-
lowed, definitely awake now.

I looked down at the four-page outline of Foley's cross-
examination that I had prepared last night, pondered my
strategy and stood up. In as confident a voice as I could
muster I said, "No questions."

Judge Taylor leaned forward. "Pardon?"

"I have no questions of this witness, your honor."

"I thought that's what you said." With a barely discernible shake of his head, Judge Taylor glanced at Raymond. He had the same look of pity as at the status
conference.

Laflamme's next witness was another police forensics
expert, Lieutenant Mark Kramer. He had a red handlebar
mustache, waxed to flamboyant curls, that made him look
very much like a cop, but not much like a scientist. Kramer
had conducted the ballistics tests on Larry's gun. As expected, his testimony was consistent with the report. After
establishing Kramer's expertise—which included hundreds of trial testimonies—Laflamme handed the gun to
the witness.

"And was this gun—Exhibit 3, the gun found in Lake

Masabesic several weeks after the murder—the very same weapon used to murder Brian McHugh?"

Laflamme was rolling now, no doubt anticipating another check mark on the win column of his chalkboard. With his head down hovering over his notes, Judge Taylor raised his eyes slightly, gave me a sideways glance. I did my best to look serious, as if I were fully aware of what was happening and I had nothing to worry about.

Imitating Officer Foley, Kramer held the .22 caliber gun in front of his eyes, making sure the jury had a good view of the murder weapon. He removed the clip, inspected the trigger and the hammer as if he'd never seen the gun before. The jury sat motionless, every eye trained on the witness.

Finally, Kramer answered. "Our tests were conclusive. Without question, this gun . . ." Kramer held the gun by the handle as if preparing to fire it, "is the murder weapon."

With the jury hanging on every word, Laflamme asked Kramer about the different tests he had conducted and the details of his analysis. Kramer had blow-ups of the test bullets and the fragments extracted from McHugh's head. Explaining the similarities between the two, he pulled out a laser pointer like Foley's. Must've been standard police issue this year.

"If you look closely you'll see that these scratch marks on the side are identical, as are the slight gouges up here." His laser had a red arrow, which he placed on the tips of the bullets. "These marks are distinctive, that is, they must've been made by the same firearm." He then explained how gun barrels have characteristics that leave unique marks on the bullets that are fired through them.

Kramer went on for fifteen minutes, giving the jury a first-rate lesson in ballistics. Every few minutes, he would make a key point, pause a few seconds to let the point sink in, all the time twirling the end of his mustache. By the time he finished, the jury was looking down, avoiding all eye contact with me or Raymond. If the jury were polled right then, Raymond's fate would be certain.

When it was my turn to cross-examine, I didn't bother getting up, and again pretended this witness's testimony was of no consequence. "No questions," I said.

Judge Taylor leaned forward, stretching so far over his bench I thought he was going to lay on his belly. Casting a stern look at me, he announced, "We'll take our recess at this time." After reminding the jury of his admonition not to discuss the case, or make up their minds until all the evidence was in, he stood up quickly, his black robe fluttering from the sharp movements. As he descended the steps, he turned toward his chambers door, and shouted, "I'd like to see both counsel in my chambers."

I looked at Raymond and shrugged. Laflamme and I followed Taylor into his chambers. No one spoke. The judge was not smiling when we sat down across from his desk. In fact, the frown lines on his forehead were so sharp I was afraid he'd burst a blood vessel.

"Coffee, gentlemen?" He looked directly at me. "Or perhaps a muffin, Mr. Francis. You must be exhausted from all this strenuous work. A little nourishment will do you good."

"I don't understand, your honor."

"Quite clearly you don't." Taylor then slammed his fist down on the desk and his brass gavel paperweight teetered toward the edge. I pulled my toe back from the desk, anticipating getting it crushed. "Do you at least understand that your client's freedom is at stake?"

"Of course, what . . ."

"Then why don't you try to defend him, just a little tiny bit. I'm not asking for Clarence Darrow here, or for heaven's sake even Flea Bailey, but Jesus Christ I've never seen anyone sit down for crucial testimony the way you've been doing this morning."

"I don't think . . ."

"The prosecution's got the murder weapon practically in your client's hand, the bootprint shows he was at the theater. This is a slam dunk. And you don't even try to challenge these witnesses, not one question, not even a standard

'Can you say with 100% certainty that this gun is the murder weapon?' Not even a motion to suppress, for Christ's sake. Nothing."

"Your honor, I know what . . ."

"If you think you'll get this conviction overturned due to incompetent counsel you'd better think again. I won't let it happen in my courtroom. You'd better plead this case now." He turned to my opponent. "Mr. Laflamme, is the State's offer of second degree still open?"

"I would assume so, your honor, though I haven't checked with my superiors since trial began."

Taylor picked up his phone. "Here, make the call. I want this case dealt."

Laflamme started to punch in the number. The frown lines on Taylor's forehead were now bright red.

"Don't waste your time, Peter. My client's not pleading." I looked Taylor straight in the eye. "He's not guilty and he's not pleading."

"You going to tell me this cockamamie story about someone else did it? Someone slipped the boots on him when he wasn't looking."

"Not exactly, but . . ."

"Bullshit! I heard your opening statement. Very eloquent. They taught you that much at Harvard. But absolute bullshit. Some dude you can't even name. Forget it."

"You know the rules, judge. You tell the jury the same thing every day. You just said it five minutes ago: 'Don't make up your minds until all the evidence is in.' Maybe you better wait 'til you hear our side before you fly off the handle."

Taylor's mouth hung open. His eyes bulged. "You be careful, Francis, or I'll hit you with contempt so fast it'll make your head spin. Right now you're very close to sharing a toothbrush with your client the next several nights."

"I meant no disrespect, but I know what I'm doing. And you should know that some trials are hard to call." Then I added, remembering his close loss in the Congressional race, "just like some elections."

"Indeed." That made him pause. He stared at me, slowly nodding his head up and down, still seething. "Okay, I'll give you a chance, see what you got. But I warn you, you're skating on thin ice."

CHAPTER 29

IN the afternoon I continued my strategy of sitting back, letting the jury hear all the evidence as if I had nothing to worry about. To hell with Taylor. It wasn't his decision anyway. The only people I had to persuade were the ones sitting in the jury box. But at least Taylor had toned down his hostility, and tried—with some difficulty—to keep his sneering in check.

Laflamme called two more police officers. It turned out to be an all-cop day, blue uniform after blue uniform on the stand. That was clever of Laflamme, I thought, parading all these representatives of right, honor, and justice in front of the jury, further distancing Raymond from the good guys.

Officer Victor Dunn was the first policeman at the crime scene, so he got to describe all the gory details of the hole in McHugh's head, grayish "brain matter" clinging to the wall, pools of blood on the desk and red-spotted dollar bills strewn all over the floor. "The murderer was standing about three feet away from the victim," he looked at the jury while pointing to police photos of the theater, "and was standing behind the victim and slightly to the left when he fired."

I pushed my chair back and started to stand up. There was no foundation for this testimony since Dunn had no basis for concluding the murderer was male.

"Object . . ." I started to say.

"Mr. Francis, you have an objection, do you," Judge Taylor smiled at me, still condescending. "Well, perhaps you could enlighten me as to the legal basis."

I had no doubt the objection would be sustained. But common sense won over my lawyer's instincts. "Sorry, your honor. I'll withdraw the objection." After all, I was claiming the murderer was male, so why confuse the jury just to win an objection?

After Laflamme finished going through Dunn's reconstruction of the murder, I stood up for cross-examination. Taylor's face beamed. "By all means proceed, Mr. Francis. We are all most anxious to hear your questions." He glanced sideways at the jury.

I disappointed Taylor again by asking the witness only one question. "Officer Dunn, in your search of the murder scene did you find one piece of direct or circumstantial evidence linking my client with this murder?"

"No, I didn't but . . ."

"Thank you, Officer, you've answered the question."

Laflamme's next police witness was Sergeant Francois Cody, a barrel-chested Quebec native. His voice was deep, gruff, a resonant bass, almost as if it emanated from the end of a long tunnel. His assignment had been to time the drive from Cathy's house to the theater. I was sure his intensive police training had greatly assisted him in this most demanding task.

"Sergeant Cody," Laflamme asked upon finishing his preliminary questions, "did you draw any conclusion as a result of your test drive?"

"Yeah, sure did." Nodding, he repeated himself. "Sure did."

"What was your conclusion?" Laflamme asked.

"At one, two a.m., there's very little traffic between Dover, where the suspect claims he was that night . . ." He turned toward Raymond. ". . . and Manchester. I drove the speed limit, something most drivers don't do that time of night, and I made the trip in forty-five minutes. So, yeah, I concluded the suspect could've been at the theater in forty-five minutes, easy."

I figured this was leading to the testimonies of the medical examiner and Cathy Sayewich tomorrow, and since I wanted to play my cards then, I asked no questions. But my dummy routine was wearing thin and I had to struggle to keep from saying anything. Every part of me wanted to join the fight, mix it up with Laflamme, show the jury what I had. Discretion won out over machismo, though, and the dummy act continued.

After the jury had been dismissed for the day, Raymond tugged on my sleeve. "When do we get our chance? I feel like I'm getting the crap beat out of me!"

"You are . . . so far. But our turn will come soon, and when it does all hell will break loose."

As the deputy approached to take him back to his cell, Raymond shook his head, sad, worried. "I hope you know what you're doing," he said as the deputy led him away.

"I wondered that myself," said a voice from the back of the courtroom.

"There are ethical rules about eavesdropping on attorney-client communications," I said.

"Then tell your client to keep his voice down. I could hear him all the way back here." Laflamme's cocky demeanor had returned. At first I had him worried but my dummy act made him think I was just bluffing, that I really didn't have any solid evidence. "You know, Taylor's not far off base," he said. "You cooled him off a bit, but after today he's going to be on your ass again."

"What, you concerned I'm not competition enough?"

"Hey, I didn't say that. All I'm saying is you got a loser

on your hands and you know it. Might as well cut a deal now. Who knows, maybe I could get you thirty-five, thirty if the boss's having a good day."

"I'll pass it along. If my client wants to accept, you'll be the first to know." I picked up my briefcase and left him standing there, alone, in the empty courtroom, what I hoped would be the soon-to-be scene of Laflamme's loss number three.

I walked slowly back to my office. It was quieter than the morning; not a reporter in sight. In the dark, the air seemed chillier, more biting as the cold seeped through my clothes. But I paid no attention to the weather; my mind was still on Laflamme. It was after five so Yvette would be gone. I trudged up the stairs since the elevator had a handwritten "Out of Order" sign hanging from the gate. The landlord might just as well invest in a printed one. As I turned from the stairs to the aisle leading to my office, I hesitated. Someone was sitting on the floor by the office door, his head in his hands. The sound of my footsteps made him look up.

"Only way I can talk to you is to hang around your office," Larry said.

"Sorry, you know how it is. Trial takes up all my time." I unlocked the door and let him in.

"Why do you think I needed to talk to you? Laflamme wants me to testify day after tomorrow. Evan too."

"Oh," was all I could say. Shit, how could I have let that slide by. I hadn't planned on Laflamme calling Larry and Evan so soon. I motioned Larry to sit down by my desk.

"So are you going to give me some tips on this? Make sure I don't blow your strategy, whatever that may be." He was trying hard to hide his anger. Paula probably had something to do with that.

"I can't tell you what to say. Just tell the truth."

"You shitting me? That's all you can say, just tell the truth. That's what I'm paying you for?" He was getting agitated, clenching his teeth as he spoke. "Seems to me you might want to give me a few hints about what Laflamme might ask, so I don't look like an idiot up there. And pardon me for being pushy, but I did think you might want to ask me a question or two, or maybe that doesn't come under your job description either." The gloves were coming off.

"Look, Larry, I don't need the snide comments. I'm doing the best I can on this case."

"That's what worries me."

I stood up, walked to the window, staring into the darkness. I clenched and unclenched my fists, stretched my arms toward the floor, trying to loosen the muscles. "Laflamme's going to ask you the obvious questions: what time did Raymond get home, did he ever threaten McHugh, did he have much experience with the gun, that kind of stuff."

"That's easy enough, I can handle those questions. And you, what're you going to ask?"

I inhaled, turned away from the window. "I'll ask you about Raymond, give you a chance to tell the jury what a great kid he was. Anything else you want to know?"

Larry groaned, looking down. "No, that's okay." Then he stood up, walked to the window beside me. He stood there for a minute or so, silent and still, staring into the darkness. Finally, he pointed toward the north end of Elm Street. "My first building's down there," he said quietly. "Nineteen years ago. Wow, doesn't seem that long." He paused and turned toward me. "What's happened to us, Dutch? The last thing I expected was for this case to affect our friendship."

I thought of the Sunday night phone call, our breakfast at the Chimes Café, dinner at his house. "Yeah, yeah," I mumbled. Then I thought of the rugby party in Concord, the twenty plus years we had no contact, Yvette's advice and wisdom, and especially Larry's withholding information about his missing gun. I thought about why he had wanted to hire me. "I know," I said finally. "I know that you expected something completely different."

CHAPTER 30

"NO kidding?" I said as I leaned back against the wall of the phone booth. Through the glass door I could see lawyers conferring with clients, clerks running down the hall, manila case files in hand. Fifteen minutes before the morning session and the courthouse was bustling with activity. Lawyers were leaning against the walls outside the courtrooms, talking excitedly into cell phones. Since I had forgotten to recharge the battery on mine, I was forced to resort to old-fashioned methods. As soon as I'd arrived I searched for an open phone booth, starting in the basement and working my way up until finally finding one on the third floor.

I called Yvette to check for messages. There were over a dozen. I told her to leave the message slips on my desk, I'd deal with them later. "Oh," I said, remembering something. "What was that all about with Russell the other day, wanting work and all?"

"Don't worry, he doesn't suspect anything," she said quietly, sounding disappointed. I was sure she'd told him something, but I guessed we all had to keep our secrets. "He just needs the work. I gave him hell after we left the office."

"I might be able to throw some work his way."

"No, please, that would be too uncomfortable. For you and for me. Besides, my job is the only part of my life that doesn't involve Russell and I'd like to keep it that way."

"Okay, I understand," I said, though I really didn't. Ever since the Green Radish, my relationship with Yvette had been undefined. At times we seemed on the verge of throwing aside caution and going for it; but because of the trial and all that had happened with Larry, we were usually all business. At least she was still doing a great job.

After hanging up, I walked into the lobby and glanced at the round, grammar-school-style clock on the wall. It was already nine o'clock. Court was just starting and I didn't want to be late. Judge Taylor didn't need another reason to get angry at me. I hesitated, though, when I saw Cathy Sayewich sitting in one of the green plastic chairs outside the courtroom. "I know Mr. Laflamme said to be here at two," she said as I approached. "But I couldn't just sit at home, waiting all morning. I'm too nervous, I need to be here." Her belly heaved as she spoke, her three-month pregnancy showing slightly.

"Don't worry about it," I told her. "Just answer the questions as best you can. Remember what we talked about and you'll do fine." I had met with Cathy a couple of times since Larry and I had visited her. Last weekend we'd rehearsed her testimony for several hours. Her story hadn't changed; she swore Raymond would never kill anyone. Of course, the more her belly swelled the easier time Laflamme would have attacking her credibility.

I glanced up at the clock: 9:01. Oh shit, I thought as I pulled open the outer door. "You sure?" Cathy asked, anxious. "I just know I'm gonna screw up. Maybe you could meet me for lunch, give me some more pointers."

"I don't know, Cathy." There wasn't a whole lot more I could tell her and, besides, I had too many other things to do at lunchtime. I stepped into the anteroom and saw Judge Taylor already on the bench. "Shoot, I've got to go," I said, leaving a shaking Cathy staring at my back.

Laflamme was at counsel table and Raymond sat at the other end, an empty seat between them. The jury looked up from their paperbacks as I entered. "Nice of you to join us, Mr. Francis," Judge Taylor said.

I gave him my most apologetic look. "Sorry, your honor. I'm ready now."

I pulled a legal pad from my briefcase as Laflamme guided Philip Graham to the stand. It had been almost two months since Larry and I had visited Graham at the theater but he appeared to have aged two years. The skin under his eyes hung in looping circles, like a cartoon character from *Mad Magazine*. His speech was terse, to the point, each answer punctuated with periods, the last word spoken with a clipped finality. He described what he and McHugh did the night of the murder, his closing procedures, why he left early.

"What time did you leave?"

"It was around the time the show was ending. I'd say 1:30, 1:35."

"And you had arranged with Brian McHugh to make the bank deposit?"

"Yes, that's right. Brian could see how tired I was; he insisted I go home."

"Mr. Graham, how much money was Brian supposed to deposit?"

"The whole week's revenue, so we had quite a bit of cash. Around fifteen grand, I'd say."

"Was it typical for you to make the deposit for the whole week after the Friday night show?"

Graham rubbed his eye. "It was then," he said, pausing. "Not anymore."

"During the time the defendant worked at the theater, did you follow the same procedure with regard to depositing the week's receipts on Friday night?"

"Yes, we did, the whole staff knew that."

"Including the defendant?"

Graham glanced at Raymond. "Yes," he said, his voice cracking. "Including Raymond."

Now that he'd established a financial motive for Raymond to rob the theater, Laflamme proceeded right to the other motive. "Did you ever hear the defendant argue with the deceased, Mr. McHugh?" Laflamme asked.

"Yes, I did. They argued all the time, but I never thought anything of it." Again Graham looked at Raymond, struggling with his words. He wanted McHugh's murderer punished but he also wanted to help out Raymond.

Sensing his witness's struggle, Laflamme asked, "Mr. Graham, you liked the deceased, didn't you?"

Graham brought his fist to his nose, looked down, nodded. "Best goddamn football player I ever coached, I'll tell you that. I wanted him to make the All-American team."

"And you want to see his murderer punished, don't you?"

"Damn right I do, absolutely."

"Do you have any reason to think the defendant, Raymond Walker, killed Mr. McHugh?"

Graham paused, and for a moment I thought he was going to spring a surprise on me. I started to object—the question clearly asked for inadmissible opinion—but I had a hunch Graham's answer would be helpful so I let it go. He didn't let me down.

"Sure they argued a lot and Brian did fire Raymond. You might even say they hated each other. But like I told the police, it was nothing anyone would kill over."

"Nothing you would kill over, you mean?"

"Well, of course. Life's full of disagreements, you just learn to live with them."

"But didn't Raymond Walker see these arguments, his firing by McHugh, as more than disagreements? Didn't he dwell on McHugh, talk about how much he hated him?"

"He might've said that once or twice, but it didn't mean anything I'm sure."

"You're assuming it didn't mean anything, aren't you? You don't know if Walker was really serious?"

Laflamme was losing control of his witness, no doubt regretting he had called him to the stand. I could've objected to his leading questions, but I stayed quiet, enjoying Laflamme's struggle as he lost points.

"Course I can't read his mind, but . . ."

"Did you ever hear Walker say he'd get even with McHugh if it was the last thing he did?"

"Those exact words?"

"Anything like that?"

"Well, I can't remember the exact words, but I might've heard him say something like that."

"You 'might've'? What does that mean? Did you hear him say words to the effect that he'd get even with McHugh if it was the last thing he did, or not?"

"Yeah, I did." He hung his head, quiet. I glanced at the jury; their heads were bowed too, mulling over Graham's testimony. "But that didn't mean he was going to shoot him. He was just mad, that's all."

"Move to strike as nonresponsive, your honor," Laflamme said.

I sat back, enjoying the way Laflamme was getting aggressive with his own witness, while Graham defended Raymond.

"Yes, it was nonresponsive," Taylor ruled immediately. "The motion is granted and the jury is instructed to disregard the last statement by the witness, beginning with 'But that . . .' through 'that's all.'"

"No further questions," Laflamme announced.

I didn't bother waiting for Taylor's cue. "I have just a few questions, Mr. Graham. Did you ever hear my client say he wanted to kill McHugh?"

"I'd remember that for sure; the answer's no."

"You said you wanted McHugh to become an All-American football player. Were you involved in recruiting him?"

"We didn't recruit Brian, Mr. Francis. He was a walk-on."

"Did you ever contact his high school coach, try to get an idea of what kind of player he'd been then?"

"I kept calling Coach Carlucci at Pine Creek High School in California. For some reason I couldn't figure out, he never called me back. After a while, he sent me a letter, saying what a great kid Brian had been. It wasn't much but it was something."

I pulled out the newspaper articles from Pine Creek regarding McHugh's arrest and jail sentence and had the clerk mark them as next in order. "Mr. Graham, did you know that Brian McHugh had a criminal record?"

"What? I don't believe that."

"You were unaware he'd been convicted of the crime of manslaughter?" As Graham straightened, the jury seemed to straighten with him. I had deliberately held back this evidence until now, just so the jury would realize they couldn't make up their minds until they'd heard all the evidence.

"Manslaughter? Brian McHugh? You're mistaken, Mr. Francis."

"Let me show you a newspaper article from the *Pine Creek Citizen*. Do you recognize that photo as depicting Brian McHugh?"

He shook his head, biting his lower lip. "That's him all right. This is unbelievable." He read the article while the rest of the courtroom sat quietly. I expected Laflamme to object, but he sat back in his chair, seemingly unconcerned about this evidence.

"He never told you he killed a man who had tried to rob him?" I asked Graham.

He shook his head. The court reporter looked up at me, hoping for an audible answer but I let it slide. "And I assume he never told you he spent a year in prison?"

"No, not a word. I don't know what to say. I'm shocked."

I asked Graham specific questions about McHugh's crime. Of course he knew nothing, but I had accomplished my purpose: to show the jury that McHugh wasn't perfect. He'd made mistakes, big mistakes, and he had big secrets, secrets he'd kept from the man who'd helped him more than anyone else in New Hampshire. Perhaps McHugh himself was untrustworthy was the implication. I retrieved the article from Graham and placed it in the exhibit box.

"Mr. Graham, directing your attention to the night of the murder, was the window near your office locked or unlocked when you left?" I hated to lay this guilt trip on him but it might score me some points.

"I . . . I don't know. I've thought about that a lot. I always tried to lock it, but sometimes I . . . I forgot. I guess I'm getting old." His voice trailed off, each succeeding word quieter, trailing in the distance. Then he perked up. "But I do know the safety latch was on, that I know."

"Did the police tell you that they think the murderer got in through that window?"

"I did hear that."

"A month or so before the murder did you happen to lock your keys in the theater?"

He nodded, embarrassed. "Yeah, I did. And good thing that time the window was unlocked, we got a magnet to slide it open, then climb in."

"Specifically who did that: get the magnet and open the window, then climb in from the alley?"

"Well, it was Evan Conway." He gave me a puzzled look.

"In any event, it was not Raymond Walker?"

"Oh, no. Definitely it was Evan."

I left it there, hoping Laflamme knew nothing about the crowd that had watched Evan open the window, learning of an easy way to break into the theater.

"You mentioned on direct exam that Raymond was aware of your practice of depositing the week's receipts after the Friday night show. Is that something you told all of your staff?"

Graham nodded. "Like I said, that was common knowledge."

"So, for example, the projectionist Nathan Goode knew of that practice?"

"Well, yes."

"And the other ushers, including Evan Conway, knew of that practice?"

Graham raised his eyebrows and the flesh under his eyes shook like jello during an earthquake. He had no idea where I was going with these questions. He looked from me to Laflamme before answering. "Su . . . sure, he knew."

When Laflamme said he had no re-direct, I glanced at Raymond and together we breathed a sigh of relief.

As Laflamme called his next witness, I pulled a thick textbook from my briefcase: *Forensic Pathology*, the bible of the business, the how-to of carving up stiffs to discover how and when they'd met their maker. I was not used to questioning forensic pathologists, in this case the state medical examiner, so I needed all the help I could get.

From a recent profile in *Manchester Magazine* I learned that Dr. Marie McAulley was not a typical medical examiner. A graduate of Tufts Medical School in Boston in the early 60's, at a time when only a handful of women entered the medical profession, for several decades she had a successful practice as a general surgeon in Nashua. Then she decided late in life to make a career change. After she caught the governor's attention with some timely and generous campaign contributions, she lobbied for the position of chief medical examiner and received the appointment five years ago. She personally performed over two hundred autopsies a year, an admirable feat especially considering her $100,000 salary was considerably less than she'd made in private practice. The magazine also printed photos of the chief medical examiners of the other five New England states. All shared common features: they were male, balding, and overweight. Marie McAulley had her grey hair tied in a bun; at sixty-three years old, in a plaid knee-length skirt that revealed her trim figure, she put her Elmer Fudd colleagues to shame.

"Dr. McAulley, what are your duties as Chief Medical Examiner of the State of New Hampshire?" Laflamme asked after McAulley had been sworn.

"I perform autopsies, supervise my team of assistants who also perform autopsies, testify as to various opinions in court cases like this one, and do a few mundane things like write reports." She spoke with a slight drawl, drawing out the long "a" the same way I'd heard so much in my Harvard days. I hated it then but coming from her the sound took on an air of authority that commanded the jury's attention. Immediately I knew I had no chance to impeach this woman's testimony. Even if I caught her in a bald-faced lie, the jury would find some reason to excuse her.

"From time to time," Laflamme continued, "do you travel to crime scenes?"

"Frequently, but only murders. For a host of reasons, it's important to examine the body within twenty-four hours of death."

"In the course of your duties did you examine the victim in this case, Brian McHugh, at the Cinema Manchester?"

"Indeed. I got the call around 5:30 in the morning. I had just finished dressing for the six o'clock Mass—which I attend every day—so it didn't take me long to get there."

Even though we'd heard enough details earlier from the police officers, Laflamme still let McAulley describe how she'd found McHugh: bent over the desk, dollar bills strewn about him. Because he had fallen on the desk face-first, the blood had pooled to his forehead, and also to the backs of his thighs, bottoms of his feet. As soon as she verified he was dead, she took his temperature to determine time of death, "what we pathologists call calor mortis."

"Doctor McAulley, please describe the manner in which you took Mr. McHugh's temperature?"

"At the theater the police officers assisted me in moving the body to the floor so I could insert the rectal thermometer. Once the body was moved to the lab, an hour or so later, I started the post-mortem and took the liver temperature."

"What were those readings?"

"According to my notes which I dictated at the time, the rectal temperature at five fifty a.m. was approximately ninety-five degrees. An hour and a half later, the liver temperature was roughly ninety-three and one-half degrees."

"How did you use those readings to calculate time of death?"

"It's actually a fairly routine calculation. We know from experience that the body cools a degree and a half the first two hours after death, then an average of one degree per hour thereafter until the body reaches room temperature. Since the temperature had dropped nearly four degrees, counting backward from five fifty, the time of death had to be close to two o'clock, two fifteen at the latest. Same with the liver reading."

Two o'clock, exactly the time when Cathy Sayewich's broken cuckoo clock had sounded, on the hour every hour. Did Raymond wake up then? Or an hour earlier? If he left Cathy's at one, then Laflamme could argue that Raymond had plenty of time to make the trip from Dover to Manchester to kill McHugh by two.

"Thank you, Doctor." Laflamme bowed deferentially. Turning to me, he said, "Your witness."

I had only one point to make and I had to do it without alienating the good doctor. "Doctor, is there a more accurate method of determining time of death available to forensic pathologists such as yourself?"

She sat back, tightening her lips. "What do you mean?"

"Are you familiar with a method of determining time of death by measuring the potassium content in the eyeball?"

She squinted at me. "Of course."

"Please describe that method to the jury."

"Potassium concentrates in the eyeball at predictable levels from which you can calculate time of death, but it's not effective until twenty-four hours post mortem."

"Is the potassium method considered more accurate than the temperature methods you employed?"

"Some studies have indicated it is more accurate, but when you're dealing with a relatively known time period, as in this case, the differences would be inconsequential."

"How inconsequential?"

She brushed a strand of hair from her forehead, scratched the corner of her eye. "Perhaps a quarter of a degree, no more."

Exactly what I wanted her to say. Now I had to put on the finishing touches. "Did you bother to measure Brian McHugh's potassium level at any time?"

"No."

"Why not?" She shifted in her seat, glaring at me. I turned a page in *Manchester Magazine*, double-checking the answer.

"First of all, it would've made no difference in this case." She paused, glancing at the magazine on the table in front of me.

"And second of all?"

"Our budget does not allow for it," she said reluctantly. "We simply don't have the capacity for those tests."

"So you were forced to rely on less reliable methods in reaching your opinion on time of death?"

"Mr. Francis," she spread her hands, turning to the jury. "You must understand, the methods I used are well-accepted. Every medical examiner in the country uses them to one degree or another." The jury was nodding, accepting what she said. I was losing points.

"To one degree or another. You accept then that there is some margin of error when determining time of death using rectal and liver temperatures?"

She smiled. "Mr. Francis, medicine is not exact. I can give you only my best estimate based on all the information available to me. Could I be off by a few minutes? Yes, I believe it's safe to say I could."

"Well, isn't it true that the time of death could have been before two o'clock?"

"Before two o'clock?"

"Exactly."

"If so, not by much." I could sense the jury glaring at me, hostility simmering. No doubt they liked Dr. McAulley and didn't want me giving her a hard time. I lowered my voice so I sounded kind, gentle.

"I apologize, Doctor, for belaboring the point but just one or two more questions. You said earlier that the temperature drops one degree an hour after the second hour."

"That's right." She nodded, happy that I got it right.

"And that the rectal and liver methods could be off by as much as a quarter of a degree?"

"Well . . ."

"You do recall saying that, Doctor?"

"Of course, yes. Please go on."

"Doesn't that mean your calculations could be off by fifteen minutes?" I smiled. Dr. McAulley squinted. "A degree an hour, a quarter of a degree equals fifteen minutes," I explained.

"I understand the mathematics, Mr. Francis. What you say is correct, of course." She looked down, straightened her skirt.

"So it is possible the time of death could've been as early as one forty-five?" I decided to push her, just a little bit. If Raymond had left Cathy's at one o'clock when the cuckoo clock sounded, then he would have arrived at the theater at 1:45, if Officer Cody's testimony was to be believed. It would have been nearly impossible, I realized, for Raymond to get to the theater, climb to the window, unlock the safety latch, and confront and kill McHugh by one forty-five.

"Possible, yes," she said. I felt fortunate that I got as much as I did out of Dr. McAulley. At least she'd given me an opening to argue that there was some doubt Raymond had the opportunity to kill McHugh. That was all I wanted, a small opening, another piece of the puzzle I hoped to use to gain an acquittal for my client.

THAT night, I sat in my apartment with the TV tuned to an inane sitcom, which I ignored while thinking over the day's proceedings. Cathy's testimony had gone as expected, despite her nerves that morning. She stammered a few times, betraying her anxiousness, but came across as a truthful witness. Unsophisticated, to be sure, but on the level. She left the jury with some important impressions: when Raymond had left her in the early morning after Halloween, he was in a good mood, happy about her pregnancy, looking forward to the future. Not the state of mind Laflamme would've wanted. She remembered clearly—more clearly than she'd ever indicated to me—that when the cuckoo clock woke them up, the late-night news was on the television. She must've forgot seeing the closing credits on the talk show. It took Raymond several minutes to gather his things and use the bathroom before kissing her goodbye. The news had started at one o'clock and Raymond took about ten minutes to leave, meaning I could argue he left at 1:10 a.m.

Given Dr. McAulley's slight concession that McHugh could have died at 1:45, I could argue that it would have been impossible for Raymond to make the forty-five-minute drive to Manchester at the speed limit, park and climb through the window in time to commit the murder.

At ten to ten, what Yvette called "Lone Ranger Time" in reference to the TV show's theme song, the William Tell Overture, the phone rang. I pressed the mute button on the remote control and picked up the phone.

"Laflamme wants me there first thing in the morning," Larry said as soon as I answered. "Evan too," he added. The tension from last night's meeting still hung between us.

"Great," I said quietly. I didn't want to talk to him again. After my brush-off yesterday, why would he call?

"Are you both ready?" I asked.

He exhaled. "Who knows? I figure all I can do is answer the questions truthfully, as you advised, let the chips fall

where they may. That's the way the cookie crumbles. Too
many cooks spoil the broth. . . ." His voice cracked.

"Larry, you okay?"

"Oh, yeah. I just decided I'm going to testify in clichés.
That way the jury'll have no idea what I'm talking about."

"Sure, sure." The pressure was getting to him. I could understand why. He had kept this sham bottled up for months.
The guilt must have been eating away at him; the closer
Raymond's case got to verdict, the worse the guilt. And at
this point, I really didn't give a shit. He had brought this on
himself, dragged me into it, and I was going to drag him all
the way through, to the inevitable end.

Despite my lawyerly instincts, I had trusted Larry im-
plicitly, set aside all doubts in favor of the powerful memory
of childhood. The memory was not of events or activities,
since I well remembered that Larry could be mean and self-
ish at times; it was a memory of feeling. When I met Larry
at the Chimes Café that old feeling from childhood had returned: the sweet innocent feeling when you knew the better
part of your life was ahead of you, not behind, when life
meant exploring, learning, playing, and constantly pursuing
plain old fun. That was the feeling that caused me to believe
that Larry hadn't changed in twenty years, that our friendship could pick up as before.

"You better get some rest if you want to be sharp tomorrow," I said after a long silence.

But Larry had more to say. "Evan told me something
tonight I thought you'd want to hear." He paused. "Hey,
Evan, come here," he yelled away from the receiver. "Tell
Dutch what you told me. . . . You know, after his opening
statement."

"Uh, Mr. Francis." Evan cleared his throat. "Yeah, you
know after I saw you give your opening statement, I was
pretty floored. It was amazing."

I could hear Larry in the background: "Go on, tell him.
We don't have all night."

"Anyway, so I told Dad that I'd like to do that someday, become a lawyer, I mean."

"Good for you," I said, though I was thinking he'd never get by the moral character requirement.

"Yeah, thanks," Evan said, though he had nothing to thank me for. He said a quick "bye" and Larry took the phone.

"Can you beat that? I thought I'd raised him better."

"Right," I said. Maybe he could do real estate transactions, I thought, help you screw some more people, or cover up your arsons. "Look, Larry. I got to go. Long day tomorrow."

"Yeah, sure. I understand. Just one thing more, Dutch."

"What's that?"

"You going to ask me any questions tomorrow?"

He was feeling the heat, knowing I had something up my sleeve but afraid to let on that he knew what it was. I had quite a surprise in store for him but there was no damn way I was going to reveal my cards. "Who knows?" I said softly before hanging up. "Maybe I'll have a question or two."

CHAPTER 31

LARRY was on the witness stand. He was nervous, his high forehead glistening, confused eyes darting around the courtroom. Every few minutes he looked directly at me, then quickly turned away. For twenty minutes Laflamme led Larry through his direct examination. Larry readily admitted he owned the murder weapon and that Raymond had gone target shooting with him and Evan two or three times. And yes, Raymond was proficient with the gun, knew how to load it, shoot it straight. Even cleaned the gun afterwards. No, Larry didn't hear Raymond come home that morning. Everyone was sound asleep. He had no idea the gun was missing until much later. He was shocked when the police called and told him they had pulled the gun out of Lake Masabesic.

Beside me Raymond was fidgeting. He kept crossing one leg over the other, then reversing them while rubbing his hand constantly across his face. He leaned over, as if to whisper in my ear, hesitated, then said nothing. When Laflamme finished, Larry pulled a white handkerchief from his back pocket and wiped his forehead. He squirmed in the seat, his button-down blue shirt darkened with beads of sweat. He knew the worst was yet to come. It was my turn.

"Mr. Conway," I said formally for the jury's benefit, "let's get it out in the open right away. You and I have known each other a long time, isn't that right?"

He spoke without opening his mouth, as if he were ashamed to admit it. "Over thirty-five years."

"But up until the beginning of November we hadn't talked in over twenty years?"

He agreed.

"And you contacted me at that time—after over twenty years—because you wanted me to defend Raymond Walker in this very case?"

Laflamme rose from his seat. "Your honor, I object. The relationship between defense counsel and this witness is totally irrelevant."

Judge Taylor narrowed his eyes as he looked quizzically at me. "I am a bit curious, Mr. Francis, where you're going with this." I opened my mouth to respond but Taylor continued. "However, this is a murder case so I'll give you some leeway." I stood still, wondering if my hearing were faulty. Could the judge actually be giving me a break?

"Thank you, your honor. Now, Mr. Conway, you told me you wanted to help Raymond because you—and your family—felt close to him, considered him almost like one of the family?"

"That's right. Raymond had lived with us for several months. We felt an obligation to help him out."

I changed direction abruptly, pretending he had said something of consequence, though my only purpose was to keep him off guard. "Mr. Conway, please tell the jury what business you are in?"

He hesitated and scratched his chin. "Well, real estate development. I build apartment buildings, office buildings, that kind of thing."

"And you own a lot of property, don't you?"

"Well . . . Yeah, I guess."

"You guess?"

"What I mean is, I have title to a lot of property, sure. But the bank owns most of it." He turned to the jury and shrugged.

"Some of the property you own—or should I say 'have title to'—is residential rental property, correct?"

"That's true."

"Including an apartment complex called Cheshire Village?"

"Are you asking if I own Cheshire Village?"

"Exactly."

"The answer is no."

I stared at my notes, surprised. Larry obviously knew I had something, but he was going to make me work for it. I decided to get right to the point.

"Is it true that you are president of a corporation called PEVCON?"

Larry stiffened, clenched his fists, glanced at Taylor, who was busy taking notes. "That's one of my companies, yes."

"PEVCON stands for Paula and Evan Conway, doesn't it?"

"Now just a minute," Laflamme yelled, jumping to his feet. "This has gone too far. Mr. Francis has forgotten that this is a murder trial, not one of his usual civil . . ."

Without letting Laflamme finish, Taylor shouted back, "Mr. Laflamme, I will not allow speeches. State only the legal basis for your objection." Alright, I thought, I'm finally going to get some breaks. My feeling of relief was short-lived, however, as Taylor turned toward me, a stern expression on his face. "I've let you go pretty far with this one, counsel. That's enough. Objection sustained."

The legal pad slipped from my fingers, hitting the floor with a loud slap. I stared up at the judge, my heart racing. Larry's testimony was crucial. I had to have evidence of motive. There was no way around it. Without evidence of why

Larry and Evan would want McHugh dead, Raymond didn't have a chance.

I thought desperately about alternate strategies but my choices were limited since I couldn't show my hand with Larry sitting there. Scuffing his shoes on the hard wooden floor, Larry rolled up his sleeve and looked down at his watch. Even from fifteen feet away I could see it was a Rolex, solid gold with a glistening gold band, reflecting the light from the dull fluorescent lamps overhead. I had never seen him wearing that watch before.

"Your honor, earlier you pointed out that this is a murder case, requiring more leeway than usual. If we could meet at sidebar, I think I could convince your honor to allow this testimony."

Judge Taylor exhaled loudly, emitting an exasperated "ugh" sound at the same time. "Very well, Mr. Francis, approach."

As Judge Taylor leaned over the side of the bench, with Laflamme standing close by, I explained the relevance of the testimony. I spoke low so the jury, and especially Larry sitting only five feet away, couldn't hear me. Abruptly Judge Taylor sat back in his seat, his eyebrows shot up, his lips pressed tightly together. Behind us the jurors stirred in their seats. "Wait a minute," Laflamme whispered slowly, the tension evident in his voice. "I've never heard this before. This is a total surprise." He looked over at Larry. "The State requests a recess."

Taylor had regained his composure. "Oh, no," he said scratching his head. "I want to hear this testimony." As he said this, he nodded and a trace of a smile formed on his lips, as if all the pieces had fallen in place.

Back at counsel table, I leaned down to Raymond. "Here we go," I whispered. He nodded and recrossed both his legs and his fingers.

"Mr. Conway, do you have the question in mind?"

"Yes I do. You are correct. PEVCON does stand for Paula

and Evan Conway. My wife and son give me a lot of help in my business."

"Is it correct that PEVCON owns Cheshire Village?"

"That is true."

"Your son Evan does some landscaping and gardening work for Cheshire Village, correct?"

Larry looked bewildered. He grimaced, squinting his eyes. "What's that have to do with this? Evan's a hard-working young man so I try to give him an opportunity to earn some extra money. So?"

I ignored his question. "Is it correct that Evan worked at Cheshire Village last October?"

Larry folded his arms and looked at Judge Taylor, who was busily writing notes. Larry turned back to me. "I don't understand where you're going with these questions."

"Never mind where I'm going; answer the question, please."

I knew Larry wasn't used to being pushed around. I felt strange doing it. But he was stuck; we were in court, the lawyer's battleground, and I had the power. He answered, "I'm sure he did, he's been working there over a year."

"Including last October?" I wanted to cement that month in the jury's mind before Larry knew where I was going.

"Certainly, I'm sure."

Now I had him. "Last October an apartment building in Cheshire Village caught fire?"

I could see the surprise on his face. He nodded. "Yes, unfortunately, that was one of my buildings."

"Did you collect any insurance money from that fire?"

"What are you getting at?"

"Never mind what I'm getting at. Answer the question."

Again Larry looked to Taylor for help. "Do I have to answer that? Aren't I entitled to privacy in my financial dealings?"

"Mr. Conway, sometimes a person's right to privacy has to give way to the pursuit of justice. Please answer the question."

Larry frowned. "It was a few hundred thousand. The building had a lot of damage."

"A few hundred? Wasn't the amount closer to five hundred thousand?"

"That sounds right, yeah."

I walked back toward Raymond, then shuffled my papers as if I were looking for something. I just wanted to buy some time, create a dramatic pause in the proceedings. Larry had looked uncomfortable ever since I had started questioning him. He didn't know where I was going with my questions, but he must've known I had something up my sleeve. It was time to take it out. "Watch this," I whispered to Raymond as I leaned down.

"Mr. Conway, your son Evan is now seventeen years old?"

"Almost eighteen."

"Is it true that Evan has a history of lighting fires?"

Larry's eyes widened, nearly bulging out of his head. "How dare you?" he shouted, leaping to his feet. His face had turned bright red. "How dare you say such a thing? What's gotten into you?"

"Please sit down and answer the question, Mr. Conway," Judge Taylor said.

Slowly Larry resumed his seat. "That is absolutely not true and . . ."—he pointed his finger at me—"I consider that defamatory. How dare you?"

"Wasn't Evan arrested a few years ago for setting GI Joes on fire?"

He sat back, the defiant look diminishing. "I'd hardly call that a history."

"What about throwing lit firecrackers into a neighbor's mail slot? Would you call that a history?" Hedges had done a thorough job searching every offense in Evan's background.

Reluctantly Larry agreed. Then he glared at me. The look on his face showed a mixture of shock and disappointment. Was he disappointed that I hadn't played along with the scenario he had so carefully planned? Was he shocked that I had discovered the truth? I had to give the knife one more twist.

"After the fire at Cheshire Village in October, which was the same month your son Evan was working there, did you speak to the fire investigators?"

"Of course."

"And didn't they tell you they suspected arson?"

"They didn't know what caused the fire. That's what they said."

"I'll ask the question again: didn't they say they suspected arson?"

"They were looking into that possibility."

"Didn't they tell you that was their primary suspicion?" I pressed harder.

"Okay," he said reluctantly, "they said that was at the top of their list."

"Mr. Conway, did you ever tell the fire investigators at any time that your son Evan worked at Cheshire Village?"

"Of course not. Why would I?"

"Did you ever tell them that Evan had a history of starting fires?"

Larry slammed his fist onto the witness stand, knocking over the paper cup, which was full of water. The water flowed across the stand away from Larry and started dripping onto the floor. Clerk Rabedeau jumped from his seat, pulled a wad of paper towels from his desk drawer, and began wiping up the water.

"I can't believe this," Larry said. I looked toward Judge Taylor, who was sitting on the edge of his seat. Before the judge could admonish him, Larry said, "I had no damn reason to tell them that Evan had done some foolish things when he was barely a teenager. No goddamn reason whatsoever."

"Mr. Conway . . ." Judge Taylor began.

"I'm sorry, your honor. I'm just in shock, I can't believe these insinuations."

"This is a court of law," Judge Taylor responded. "We follow certain formalities here. One of them is that profanity will not be allowed." I was surprised at Judge Taylor's tone, especially considering how easily he had let Killian off after his swearing.

"Mr. Conway," I said, "I have just a few more questions. How was PEVCON doing last year?"

"What do you mean?"

"Making money, losing, what?"

"I don't know. You'd have to ask my accountant."

"You don't know if you made any money last year? Didn't you file quarterly tax returns just a few months ago?"

"Okay, I meant I don't have the exact numbers. Let's see, last year—I'm pretty sure we were losing money. That's right, the mortgage was variable and rates went up. So we had a negative cash flow."

"How negative?"

"Look, I don't know."

"Give us an estimate."

"Say two hundred thousand."

"You lost two hundred thousand dollars from PEVCON last year?"

"Approximately."

One of the jurors muttered under her breath. Larry turned to look at her. "Look, it's a tough market now. Real estate's not doing as well as it used to."

"And because of the negative cash flow you tried to sell Cheshire Village last year?"

"I did."

"Is it correct your listing expired in September?"

Larry hesitated. I picked up the file Yvette had obtained for me, containing the broker's listing, description of Cheshire Village and a sample of newspaper ads for the property. I scanned the first few pages and looked up at Larry, quietly, awaiting his answer.

"I think that's right," he said.

"Is it true you received no acceptable offers?"

"As I said, it was a tough market."

"So at the time of the fire in October, you had received no offers for Cheshire Village?"

Larry turned toward Judge Taylor, holding up the paper cup that had spilled earlier. "Your honor, may I have some more water?"

After the bailiff had poured another cup of water and Larry had taken a slow sip, he answered. "No, no offers."

"Mr. Conway, is it true that a man, an elderly tenant, died as a result of that fire?"

"Yes, Boris Luhovey, a good man, I understand."

"Did you know that Brian McHugh was a witness to that fire?" A hum swept through the audience, reporters whispering to each other, while writing furiously. Judge Taylor stared at Larry and suddenly stopped his note taking.

I turned to the jury. They sat ram-rod straight, attentive. Even Marie Driscoll, the school teacher, had a softer look on her face. The jury's hostility toward Raymond, so evident throughout most of the trial, was dissipating.

Larry leaned forward in his seat. As he had at the beginning of direct examination, he pulled his handkerchief from his back pocket. But instead of wiping his forehead, he wiped the insides of his hands, ringing the handkerchief around his fingers.

"Um, no. I never heard that before."

"You had a tenant in that building, a neighbor of the Luhoveys. A Russian man named Igor Rubenstein. Correct?"

His eyes were becoming glazed. "Yes, of course."

"Did Mr. Rubenstein ever tell you he had a meeting in his apartment with Brian McHugh just before the fire?"

He shrugged.

Judge Taylor leaned forward. "You must answer out loud, Mr. Conway."

"No," Larry said quietly. "I mean he never said anything like that."

"One last question, Mr. Conway. When did you discover that your target pistol was missing from your desk drawer?"

Larry crumbled up the empty paper cup. He nodded, almost to himself. "About two weeks after the murder."

I walked back to counsel table, laid the legal pad on the desk. "I apologize. I said one last question and I have to ask a few more. Did you bother telling me, the attorney you had selected to defend Raymond Walker, that your gun was missing?"

"We talked about it."

"We talked about it after the police pulled your gun from Lake Masabesic." He said nothing.

I continued. "Did you go to the police when you learned that your gun was missing?"

"No, I didn't think it had anything to do with this case."

"Please, Mr. Conway, is that really the reason?"

Laflamme came awake at last. "Objection, argumentative."

"Sustained," Judge Taylor said.

I ignored Laflamme and the judge and stared straight at Larry. "Isn't the real reason you didn't tell anybody the gun was missing because you knew your son had used the gun to kill Brian McHugh and then had thrown it into the lake?"

An uproar rose in the courtroom. Each juror seemed to turn and look at the juror sitting in the seat beside them, as if seeking confirmation that they heard the question correctly. Raymond's knee, still shaking steadily throughout Larry's testimony, slammed against the underside of the table, sending a loud thud across the courtroom. At the same time, Raymond whispered, "Yes!"

Larry jumped to his feet. He grabbed the sides of the table as if steadying himself during an earthquake. He glared at me.

Judge Taylor said softly, "Please answer the question, Mr. Conway."

But Larry still stood motionless. He looked up and again glared at me, the pieces finally falling together. "You think my son and I had something to do with this murder?" His voice was low, intimate, as if we were the only ones in the courtroom. He sounded so calm that he made me nervous. A shiver ran down my spine. "Dutch, how could you?" he continued. "We were friends. Have you lost your mind?"

I said nothing. I stood still and stared, stared at my oldest friend, the friend with whom I had shared my childhood, the friend whose son I had just publicly accused of committing arson and murder. The jury could see the shock on Larry's face. The shock was genuine, anyone could see that. Larry was shocked because I had the gall to point the finger at his own son, something he never would have guessed when he decided to look me up after twenty years. His carefully concocted plan had gone very much awry, indeed.

CHAPTER 32

SLOWLY Larry stepped from the stand. Passing in front of the clerk's desk, he held his head down. He stopped suddenly in front of counsel table and raised his head, his eyes burning holes through me. I could see the hurt and anger there, the years of friendship tossed aside, our memories of each other forever tainted by this distasteful episode. While our eyes were locked on each other's—in that brief moment—both our lips seemed to move. Mine formed the silent question, "Why?" I'm not much of a lip reader, but I was sure Larry's lips mimicked mine, also asking, "Why?"

As Larry resumed his slow walk past me, Judge Taylor asked Laflamme if he had any other witnesses. Laflamme stared at his notes, flipping the pages of his yellow legal pad as if searching for the answer. He was having second thoughts about calling Evan, I guessed. He knew I would tear Evan apart on cross-examination. And after my cross-examination of Larry, Laflamme probably wanted to distance himself from Evan. No matter how weak the evidence against Evan might be, Laflamme couldn't risk having his case tainted with the mud I was going to sling. Although Evan would testify that Raymond had threatened to kill McHugh, Laflamme didn't really need that evidence. Through Killian Laflamme had introduced evidence of Raymond's admission of the robbery and through Larry he had proved Raymond's proficiency with and access to the murder weapon. When Laflamme finished flipping through his notes and looked up at the judge, I was hoping he wasn't smart enough to dance away from his game plan and rest his case. I wanted him to call Evan and try to salvage what had just happened, but my hope was quickly dashed. For all his personal faults, Laflamme was still a good lawyer. I cursed under my breath when he said, "No further witnesses. The prosecution rests."

Taylor nodded, understanding Laflamme's strategy. "Does the defendant have any witnesses?"

I glanced at Raymond, who wore a perplexed expression, knowing we weren't prepared to present witnesses. I planned on calling Raymond as the defense's last witness, hoping to set up his testimony with witnesses who would nourish the seeds of Evan's guilt that I had planted through Larry. The main witness, of course, would be Jack Gibbs.

"Mr. Francis?" Judge Taylor asked, interrupting my thoughts. "My question was a simple one. What is your answer?"

I could have asked for a break but I had devised a strategy of my own, and had to carry it out immediately. "Yes, your honor," I announced as if breaking a spell. "The defense calls Evan Conway." Laflamme fidgeted. Like a high-stakes chess match, I had countered his risky move with one of my own, a move that, if I weren't careful, could prove suicidal. I needed to lure Evan into damaging admissions, as I had with Larry, before he realized I was trying to cast the blame at him.

"I believe he's waiting in the hall," I told the bailiff who walked outside to call Evan.

As Evan entered the courtroom, he stopped in front of his

departing father, looked at his shocked expression and said, "What happened, Dad?"

"Come on, move along," the bailiff pushed on Evan's arm.

"Unbelievable," was all Larry said as he slowly moved up the aisle, his head down, then through the swinging doors.

Before beginning my questioning, there was one technical issue I needed resolved. If Laflamme had called Evan as a prosecution witness, I could have asked him leading and suggestive questions. But that changed when Evan became my witness. Now I'd have to ask him non-leading questions, most beginning with the five "W's"—who, what, why, when and where—which would severely hinder my ability to persuade the jury to accept my version of the murder, unless the court designated Evan as an adverse or hostile witness. I decided to raise the issue right away.

"Your honor, I would like to inform the court that I am calling Evan Conway as an adverse witness pursuant to the rules of evidence."

"Objection," Laflamme shouted. "There's been no showing whatsoever that this witness has any interest adverse to the defendant. In fact, the evidence is to the contrary. He was the defendant's friend, he let the defendant live with him. If anything, this witness is adverse to the prosecution."

"Enough, Mr. Laflamme," Taylor shouted, holding up his hand. "I've warned you already about speeches. One more time and you'll be sanctioned." The jurors nodded with satisfaction at Taylor's dressing down Laflamme. Earlier they had seen him hammer me pretty hard; now he was earning the jury's respect by showing he could dish out his venom equally. And it also made me look better in the jury's eyes. Before Laflamme could defend himself, Taylor ordered, "Approach."

"Your honor, I apologize if I went on too long," Laflamme began as soon as we reached the bench, "but I was so flabbergasted that Mr. Francis would even consider this witness adverse. He was the defendant's best friend for crying out loud." The tension of the trial was starting to get to my opponent. For the first time, I heard worry in his voice, the whiny sound some people make when things aren't going their way. With his successful trial record, Laflamme probably hadn't talked that way in a long time.

"While that's true, Mr. Laflamme," Taylor said, "Mr. Francis's theory—as I understand it—is that this witness actually committed the murder." He looked at me for confirmation that that indeed was my theory. I nodded. Taylor continued. "That being the case, there's no question that the witness is adverse, is there?"

"Well, of course that's just a theory," Laflamme shot back, directly attacking the weakness in my argument. "There's been no evidence whatsoever to support it. The rules of evidence would mean nothing if an attorney could evade them simply by making up a ridiculous theory."

"But it's hardly ridiculous in view of Larry Conway's testimony," I said.

Taylor gave me a skeptical look. "However weak the evidence may be, Mr. Laflamme, I believe I have to give Mr. Francis some leeway here. And, besides, as I recall this witness was originally on the prosecution's witness list, wasn't he? I'll allow Mr. Francis to pose leading questions."

At the counsel table, I whispered to Raymond, explaining what had transpired. He put his hand on my wrist, squeezed tightly, nodding his approval. On the stand Evan seemed almost as lost as Frank Killian, looking around the room, trying to get comfortable with his surroundings. I asked him about school, how he'd become friends with Raymond, how he came to invite Raymond to live with him. All the background information the jury needed. He answered each question precisely, nodding his head up and down, the motion signifying certainty with his answer. As far as he knew I was still a friend. He had no reason to fear me. Looking at this handsome young man, his hair neatly combed, his straight white teeth flashing, I was reminded of someone else: his father at that age. And now, I was about to destroy a young man's life. In one day I would ruin the lives of two generations of Conways. That seemed a modest price to pay for the lives of Brian McHugh and Raymond Walker, not to mention Boris Luhovey. I hesitated, glanced one last time at my notes to delay the inevitable, then turned toward Evan. With an innocent expression, he looked at me expectantly.

"You and your father are very close, aren't you?" I finally asked.

"Yeah, we are. I'm an only child, so my dad and I always spend a lot of time together."

"And you've helped him out in his business, haven't you? PEVCON, that kind of thing?"

"Sure. I mean sometimes a tenant would need help lighting the stove pilot. I did that. Vacuum the hallways, a little painting. Yeah, I liked to do those kinds of things."

"Did you ever do that kind of work at the Cheshire Apartments?"

He hesitated, glanced at Raymond, then back at me. "All the time," he said. "That was PEVCON's biggest building."

"When you mowed the grass at Cheshire Village, did you use a gas lawn mower?"

"Y-yes."

"And you stored the lawn mower and the cans of gas in the basement?"

"I think so. I usually did."

"Did you mow the grass there last October?"

"October? I'm sure I did. I did all the garden stuff every few weeks."

"Evan, I want you to think carefully about my next question: In October did you ever see Brian McHugh at Cheshire Village?"

"Brian McHugh?" He scratched his head, wondering where I was going with this line of questioning. "Don't remember seeing McHugh at Cheshire Village, ever." His tone was matter-of-fact.

I had expected a denial, so I quickly switched direction. "Is it true that there was a fire at Cheshire Village in October?"

"Yeah, a bad one. An old man died."

"Did you go to Cheshire Village the day of the fire?" He shrugged, looking confused, and I added, "To mow the lawn."

"I don't think so," he said, biting his lip, "but I'm not sure." I imagined he could see the trap door swinging open below him as he finally realized my intent. Was he guessing I had a witness, someone to place him at the scene when the fire started?

I liked his uncertain, cautious demeanor; it would give the jury more reason to doubt his testimony. While he was still pondering where I was going with these questions, I hit him with the big one. "Evan, remember that you're testifying under penalty of perjury," I said sternly. "Isn't it true that you got into an argument with Brian McHugh at Cheshire Village shortly before the fire?"

Evan fidgeted, shifting in his seat, looking from me to the jury to Laflamme. I don't know why but I had convinced myself that he wouldn't commit perjury, that this young, innocent looking murderer would tell the truth.

"I'm sorry," he said. "No, that didn't happen."

I paused, letting his answer fill the courtroom. Just as well, I decided. I'll prove him a liar so the jury can reach its own conclusion. The jurors were staring at Evan, wondering. He noticed them and turned away, averting their judging eyes. Again he scratched his head: a nervous habit.

"But I don't get it," he said, his voice cracking. "Why are you asking me these things? What's the fire got to with Raymond?" He looked around the courtroom, searching desperately for some sense of normalcy. "Are you saying that I caused the fire?"

In a way I felt sorry for Evan: everyone in the courtroom except him knew why I was asking these questions. He was alone on the stand, made to feel ignorant, stupid and, most importantly, guilty. At that moment, I didn't like myself very much.

"You'd been arrested before for starting fires, hadn't you?"

Evan couldn't hide his surprise. "How'd you know about that?"

"It's true, isn't it?"

"I was just a kid and I did some stupid things. That doesn't mean I burned my dad's own building. Y-you don't think I did that, do you? I can't believe this." He was rambling and I let him go on. If Evan were anyone other than my friend's son, I would have liked nothing better than to see him—my suspect—squirming, stuttering, struggling to explain himself.

I answered him gently, not wanting to alienate the jury by being too hostile. "We'll come back to that. Right now I want to change subjects and ask you about Raymond Walker. You and Raymond spent a lot of time at the shooting range, didn't you?"

He glanced at the jury, getting suspicious. "We'd go out there couple of times a month, just playing around, nothing serious."

I walked to the clerk and reached down to the exhibit box. "Is this the gun you shot at the range?" As I asked the question, I placed the gun in front of Evan, letting it drop just hard enough for the jury to hear it.

Evan picked it up, rubbed the handle, wrapped his fingers around it. As if mesmerized, he curled his index finger around the trigger, engrossed in the gun. I waited. The jury watched intently. This was going better than I'd expected. Unlike most witnesses who shy away from a gun, even an unloaded one, Evan wasted no time picking it up. He was comfortable holding it in his hand, putting his finger around the trigger. An experienced shooter, perhaps a murderer. He agreed this was the gun.

"Who was in charge of the gun when you and Raymond went to the range?"

"It was dad's gun, so I was always in charge. Dad was very careful about that gun."

"And when you finished with the gun, were you supposed to return the gun to your father's desk?"

"Yes, that was my job. I always made sure the gun was in his desk drawer, then I locked the desk. Only Dad and I knew where the key was kept."

"Just you and your father, is that what you said?"

"That's right."

"Not even Raymond? Did Raymond know the where the desk key was kept?"

"If he did, I didn't know about it."

"You never told him?"

"No, my dad didn't want anyone else to know. Even my mom didn't know where it was."

"Did you put the gun back in your father's desk the last time you used it before Brian McHugh was murdered?"

"Absolutely," he nodded again, his head moving at a faster pace. "I'm sure I did."

"Then how did the gun wind up in the lake?"

Evan glanced at Raymond, as if expecting him to answer. "I have no idea, no idea."

I paused, letting the answer hang in the air, giving the jury a few seconds to appraise Evan's answer. I wanted to get Evan to supply two more pieces of the puzzle.

I changed subjects. "Saturday, November 1st. You went fishing, do you remember that?"

He scrunched up his face, trying to remember the date. To help him out, I added, "That was the day before Raymond was arrested."

"Yeah," he said. "I did go fishing. Raymond asked me if I wanted to go out to Masabesic Lake, see if I could get some perch."

"Raymond asked you? Isn't it true that you asked Raymond?"

He shook his head. "Uh, uh. That's not true. Raymond wanted to go fishing, not me."

I made a mental note to cover that subject when Raymond was on the stand, then moved on. "You and Raymond spent the day out at the lake, just the two of you?"

"Uh-huh, yeah," he nodded.

"You take your tackle box with you, the big green metal one?"

"I always take that with me. No sense fishing if I don't have hooks."

"Did you and Raymond split up for any period of time?"

"About forty-five minutes, an hour, something like that. He fished the northern lake."

"So you were alone for that period of time?"

"Yeah. There was no one else out there. Too cold for most people, I guess."

"And you kept your tackle box with you, is that right?"

"Sure. I gave Raymond everything he needed, weights, a few hooks, some bobbers. He didn't need the tackle box for anything."

"Thank you." Yes, thank you, Evan Conway. I wanted Evan to say he kept the tackle box because I suspected that's where he stored the gun. I glanced over at Raymond, reminding myself why I was destroying my friend's son's life: I couldn't let an innocent man take the blame.

"Just a few more questions. You look a bit taller than Raymond. Did you two ever share clothing?"

"Once in a while I would borrow a tee-shirt, but not too often. His clothes were usually too small for me."

"What size shoe do you wear?"

"Nine and a half."

"Same as Raymond?"

"Yeah, funny how I'm three inches taller and we have the same foot size."

Again I dug into the evidence box. I pulled out Raymond's boot and put it in front of Evan, right beside the gun so the jury could see them together. All three of them: the gun, the boot, and Evan Conway.

This time Evan didn't touch the evidence. He stared down at the boot, finally realizing what I was doing. He was breathing heavily, his chest moving in and out with each breath. With his shirt sleeve, he wiped his forehead and rubbed the moisture from his eyes.

"Hey, Mr. Francis, I don't know what you're driving at here."

"Well, let me make it clearer. You've worn that boot before, haven't you?"

This time he did pick it up. Turned it over to check out the sole. Put it back down with a loud clunk. Looked past me to Raymond, puzzled, uncertain how to answer. "Once in a while I did. Not that often, but once in a while."

It was time to quit tiptoeing around. The jury had to get the message now, loud and clear. "Isn't it a fact that you wore those boots the night you shot Brian McHugh?" I moved toward him, my voice getting louder.

"No," he screamed, a look of panic on his face. "What I mean . . . I didn't shoot . . ." He twisted in his seat, uncomfortable, looking for an escape. "Mr. Francis, how could you say that? You were my father's best friend." His mouth hung open, dumbfounded.

"You killed McHugh to keep him from telling the police that you torched the Cheshire apartments, isn't that right?"

"No, no, no." He shook his head back and forth with each denial.

"You were helping your father out of a tough financial spot by trying to collect the insurance money?"

"That's not true!"

"Isn't it a fact that after the murder you hid the gun in your tackle box, took it out to the lake?"

"Come on, no way!" he shouted back.

"When you separated from Raymond, you threw the gun in the lake, figuring no one would ever find it."

"That's crazy! You're making this up."

"And you thought you'd pin the murder on your friend Raymond Walker, didn't you?"

Laflamme jumped to his feet, screaming, "Objection, objection. This is totally improper." I ignored his objections and asked the question again, even louder. Taylor pounded his gavel, at first slowly, then as Laflamme and I competed to be heard, Taylor picked up the pace, pounding, pounding, before standing up and staring down at both of us. I didn't care how Evan answered, I had made my point. The jury heard what I said.

Judge Taylor gave us his sternest look. "That is quite enough, counsel. You are never to behave that way in my courtroom again." He was talking to both of us, but mostly he stared at me.

Repentant, I lowered my eyes, then glanced at the witness stand. The tears were flowing down Evan's cheeks. He clutched his stomach as if he were in pain, rocked back and forth on the stand, both hands over his belly. Ignoring Judge Taylor, he said, "I can't believe you're saying this." He looked at Raymond. "Raymond, stop this, please. You know I would never do that." Still rocking, he picked up the boot, clutched it to his chest, a security blanket. "No, I didn't. I swear I didn't."

He stared at me, hurt. I felt so bad I wanted to go to him, put my arm around him and tell him everything would be all right. There's been a big mistake, Brian McHugh is still alive, the Cheshire Village apartments are as good as new. You can go home to your mother and father, back to your idyllic suburban lifestyle.

Suddenly he stopped rocking. He lifted the boot off his chest, raised it over his head, and slammed it down on the table. The temper Larry had told me so much about was finally evident. In the still of the courtroom, the sound was amplified, crashing off the walls, a wrecking ball hitting the side of a building. In my mind I pictured walls crumbling, the roof and foundation collapsing, the imaginary structure forever destroyed just like my friendship with Evan's father.

Quietly I said, "No further questions." Evan stood up and jabbed his finger at me, shouting, "You're wrong. Wrong! Wrong!"

CHAPTER 33

RAYMOND paced from one wall of the cell to the other, then from the bars to the cot. "That was great. Great! You did a helluva job. Did you see the look on Mr. Conway's face when he finally figured it out? I won't forget this, believe me. I'll take care of you."

"Slow down," I told him. "We've got a long way to go. Things went pretty well today, but who knows what the jury thinks. And we still have Jack Gibbs on Monday. He's the key, our only evidence linking Evan to McHugh and the fire."

"Oh, we don't even need him now. I'm telling you, the jury's on our side." He was more animated than I'd ever seen him. There was a lilt in his voice and he walked with quick, deliberate steps. Somehow the anger and worry had disappeared, replaced by a cheerfulness bordering on cockiness.

"I could see that babe in the first row shaking her head at Evan," Raymond continued, "and she even smiled at me a few times. Yessiree, it's in the bag. We ought to forget Gibbs."

"Can't. I told the jury I had a surprise witness so I've got to put him on. Otherwise they'll be suspicious, wonder what we're hiding. Besides, I still think we need Gibbs if we're going to win this thing."

My calls to Jack Gibbs had not been returned. The same obnoxious music still played on his answering machine and I left the same message each time: how important it was that we talk before he took the stand, call me collect, any time etc. I was worried. Usually you don't call a witness, especially an unfriendly one, without talking to him first. It's nearly impossible to know what questions to ask without first running them by the witness. Then you prepare your questions accordingly, eliminating the subjects where the witness is uncertain or will testify unfavorably, emphasizing the helpful parts of the testimony. In the best direct examinations you build the evidence slowly, adding more significant items with each question, keeping the jury in suspense so that at the end you reach a climax. And when you finish, the jurors are preoccupied with that climactic testimony, mulling it over in their minds, analyzing how it affects their judgment, and in the process ignoring the other attorney's cross-examination. But without speaking to the witness beforehand, without this essential preparation, you could easily be surprised. And surprise could lead to disaster. It was a risk I just had to take.

"You know . . ." Raymond stopped pacing and looked me in the eye. "It's crazy but I kind of feel sorry for Evan. I wonder how he's taking all this. Imagine what it's like at the Conways' house now, a lot of screaming I bet."

I didn't want to think about it. "Before you get too sympathetic for Evan, remember you wouldn't be here if it weren't for him. He didn't have much sympathy for you today."

Raymond sat down on the cot and leaned forward, staring at the floor. With his index fingers he scratched each eye.

After a few seconds he said, in a melancholy voice, "I guess you're right."

I was surprised to find Yvette still at the office. "It's nearly five thirty," I said. "You should be off duty."

"I couldn't go home without finding out how it went with Larry today." She was standing behind her desk, organizing loose papers into a neat pile. She put an elastic around the papers, then turned her back to place them on a shelf. "And I was worried about you."

"Me? Why?"

She turned around. "What do you think? Your best friend's on the stand and you had to accuse his son of arson and murder."

I tossed my briefcase on a client chair and sat in an adjacent one. "All in a day's work," I said, stretching my legs. "Destroy a childhood friendship and get your client acquitted; the price you gotta pay."

"I just thought you'd want to talk, is all." Her voice was soft and gentle, soothing and understanding. I did want to talk, especially to Yvette. Maybe more than talk, I thought. After such a stressful day in court, I was emotionally spent. My usual defenses were down and I was ready to toss aside all caution. I may have lost a friend in Larry, but perhaps I could gain a stronger friend, maybe even a lover, in Yvette.

"Where's Russell tonight?"

She blinked and smiled. "Why do you ask?"

I loosened my tie. "I wouldn't want you to get in trouble at home now, would I?"

"This is Friday night, so where else would Russell be: at a sports event."

"Bruins again?"

"Uh, uh. Celtics. He thinks they may actually win for a change." Yvette stood up and put her coat on. For a moment I was afraid she was leaving.

"You got other plans?" I asked.

She shook her head.

"Want to get a drink, maybe a bite to eat?"

When she smiled, I nearly jumped out of my seat and wrapped my arms around her. I wanted to scream and holler and punch my fist in the air like a little kid after scoring a touchdown.

"What did you have in mind?" she asked.

"Oh, what about the Mill Club. We could listen to the jazz trio, maybe grab some food there." She buttoned her coat. I added, smiling, "Or we could go back to the Green Radish if you like."

WHEN we got to the Mill Club, I drove right past it and kept on driving until I got to my apartment. Yvette and I hadn't talked much since leaving the office but we both knew what the other wanted. We had walked down the hall bumping our shoulders together. We kept bumping shoulders all the way down the hall, keeping our hands to ourselves, neither one of us acknowledging the physical contact.

As I opened the door to the apartment and flipped on the lights, Yvette walked in tentatively, as if she were afraid to enter, knowing perhaps that she was about to turn her world upside down. She laid her coat neatly on the couch, then looked around at my sparely furnished apartment, the breakfast dish still in the sink and the *Union Leader* strewn on the living room floor.

"What a . . . um, cute place you have," she said with a mischievous smile.

"Thank you so much," I said. "I spent oodles of money on the designer. Only the best for Dutch Francis, you know." I opened the refrigerator and found a half-full bottle of Chardonnay. "Wine?"

Yvette was staring at my framed photos of Boston foliage scenes. "I didn't know you were so creative."

"Easy to be creative when nature provides those colors." I pulled the cork from the bottle, held it up and waved it at her.

"Oh, sure," she said, leaning against the kitchen entranceway. "Why not."

I knew what I wanted and I hoped I knew what she wanted, though she seemed less enthused than I. It was almost as if we had reversed roles from the time after the Green Radish. I was ready to take our relationship to the next level and deal with the consequences, but Yvette seemed to be holding back.

An electric feeling ran through my body, a feeling I hadn't had in a long time. I couldn't remember ever feeling this way about Sherry, though I'm sure I must have. Slowly I searched the cabinet for two wine glasses. I wanted to stretch this evening out, continue this great feeling. The anticipation of having sex with Yvette was a greater high than I had imagined. After seeing her and Russell together in the office, I was surer than ever they were not going to last. Russell would make some woman very happy perhaps, but I just couldn't see that woman being Yvette. I thought any man who could run off with the boys on a Friday night and leave such a gorgeous woman alone had a serious character flaw. I had convinced myself that he didn't deserve her, that I did, though I didn't focus too much on exactly why I deserved her.

I poured two glasses of wine and sat on the couch beside Yvette. "To us," I said, tipping her glass with mine.

"Yes," she said, biting her lip. "To us."

While I sipped the wine Yvette shot hers down in one gulp. She put the empty glass on the floor and turned toward me.

"Dutch, there's only one thing I ask."

I waited expectantly, not breathing.

"If this . . . if we don't work out, I want to be able to keep working for you. As much as I care for you as a person, I think you're one terrific lawyer. I don't think I could ever work for anyone else."

"Yvette . . ."

"I'm serious," she said, interrupting. "I don't want to lose you."

"You won't lose me," I said, taking her hands in mine. "And we will work out. But if we don't, you know you'll always have a job with me. You mean far too much to me. You know that, don't you?" With my hand, I lifted her chin slightly. Then I leaned forward and kissed her like I've never kissed anyone before. We kissed like teenagers, exploring and probing, content with touching only lips and tongues.

We separated for a moment, each taking in the other. I pushed her hair back, rubbing her temples. Her skin was clear and smooth, her eyebrows thick and finely trimmed. I stared into her eyes, still amazed at their brightness; they seemed to be talking to me, welcoming me, inviting me to keep going. At that moment I thought there could be no better feeling than this: being welcomed by a beautiful woman, her every gesture, look, and movement screaming that she wants me. My ego was being massaged to perfection; my thinning hair thickened, my grey whiskers turned brown, and my slight pot belly rippled with muscles. I was a king, a god, a man among men. I could do no wrong, I would win all my cases, and I would make love to the most beautiful woman imaginable.

I bent down to kiss her again, taking her lips with all of mine, not sparing anything. She held back nothing, pressing her lips tightly against mine, moaning softly, as we explored each other's mouths with our tongues. I have no idea how long we went on like that; we kissed and kissed, neither one talking. I came up for air only to pull off my tie and lift her blouse over her head, forgetting to undo the buttons. She helped me out and while she finished removing the blouse, I noticed the shade to the window overlooking the parking lot was up. "Let's go in the bedroom," I said.

I helped Yvette to her feet. With one arm draped around her, I used the other to unbutton my shirt and loosen my belt buckle and zipper as we walked to the bedroom. The only light came from the kitchen, just enough to allow me to see Yvette's incredible figure. I tried to unhook her bra from the back and she laughed, unhooking it herself from the front. As her breasts poured out, I paused and stared. "Never seen tits before?" she asked, laughing.

"Not like those," I said, as she leaned back on the bed. I reached down to suckle her. Laughing, I said, "At least not without having to pay a two-drink minimum." She slapped me playfully on the top of the head, then massaged my head while I explored her breasts with my tongue and lips. When I finally entered her, my mind was instantly at peace, tingling with excitement and the increasing tension, and my body reacted to Yvette's every movement, thrusting when she thrusted, turning when she turned, and exploding in spasms simultaneously with her own until our exhausted spent bodies collapsed onto each other, drenched in the other's sweat and love.

CHAPTER 34

AS I prepared for the last phase of the trial over the weekend, my thoughts kept returning to Yvette. I would make a note on my outline for Gibbs' direct examination, then stop and draw a doodle of Yvette's body, exaggerating the curves, reliving the intense feelings of Friday night. My work was also interrupted with less pleasant thoughts, about my ex-father-in-law Rodger Dodds. Odd, I thought, that it was Dodds, not his daughter, who intruded into my consciousness. Before Friday night, Sherry was the only woman I had made love to for nearly fifteen years. While Sherry was soon becoming a distant memory, her father, my mentor and an accomplished trial lawyer, still exerted his influence on me. "Always start the week with a bang," I could hear him say. "While the jury's still fresh, eager, and interested, hook them with a big one."

As I stared at my notes, I realized I couldn't start with Gibbs. His avoidance of a subpoena and refusal to speak to me about his testimony made him a loose cannon. What he told me at O'Dowd's Pub certainly was helpful. But I had no idea if he would testify to the same facts, and if so, whether he would come across as truthful. I was worried. I needed to have a witness who would make an impression on the jury, an impression favorable to my defense. I decided to make a phone call.

"Ya?"

"Igor, this is Dutch Francis. You were scheduled for 1:30 Monday. I want you to testify in the morning instead, 9 o'clock. Okay?"

Igor was not overjoyed at this news. He had planned on sleeping in. "I have very important date Sunday night," he said. "Stay out late, too late."

"Igor, you got your book back, right?"

"My book, of course. You are man of honor, is true."

"So I'll see you at nine?"

He paused. "Ya, nine, is okay."

As I hung up, I could hear him mumbling "son of a . . ." A sleepy witness was better than an uncertain one, I decided. I needed Igor to place McHugh at Cheshire Village during the fire. And with his knowledge of McHugh's criminal past, Igor would quickly change the jury's impression of the football hero victim and perhaps deflect some their sympathy.

On Monday morning Igor was as heavy-lidded and red eyed as when I first met him. If he were sleepy, then I couldn't tell the difference. He answered my questions quickly, on occasion too quickly, and the court reporter had to tell him to slow down and repeat his answers. I asked him how he had first met Brian McHugh and he admitted soliciting him to shave points. He told the jury how he had learned of McHugh's criminal past, about McHugh spending a year in jail, and defrauding his way into Saint Andrew.

"Did he ever shave points for you?"

"Well . . ." he paused. I worried he would get cold feet, change his story. I crossed my arms and glared at him. Damn, I thought, I should've kept his book. Now I had no leverage. But Igor kept to his word, though he answered slowly as if he were giving the information reluctantly. "Ya," he said, "three times. His team they still won game, but Brian kept score down." I felt a twinge of guilt for not telling Igor he had the right not to testify and assert his fifth amendment rights. All he had cared about was that I didn't turn over his book to the prosecutor. Without the book, he said, nothing they can do, right? They cannot prove nothing. What I didn't point out to him was that his testimony under oath, admitting to running books and extortion, was as solid a piece of evidence as the prosecutor could ask for. As guilty as I felt for Igor, I concluded that sacrificing an extorting bookie to win freedom for my innocent client was a fair exchange.

The jury was noticeably upset by Igor's testimony. The jaws on a few of the women dropped; the men were grimacing. These gestures could have been directed toward Igor, I realized. I didn't expect the jury to like him; all I wanted was to shake up their image of our hero victim. Now he was not just a football star, but a convicted killer, a liar, and a traitor to his team. As I changed subjects to the day of the fire, I raised my voice. "Mr. Rubenstein," I shouted, "did Brian McHugh visit your apartment at Cheshire Village in late October of last year?"

"Ya," he said, nodding several times. "He want to talk, so I tell him to come over. I give him a little vodka, we relax, we talk."

"Did anything unusual happen at the apartment building that day?"

Igor frowned. He had a distressed look. "While he was with me?"

"No, no. After he left." I wanted to stay away from the details of their meeting. If the jury learned that Brian wanted to back out of the deal, they might be more sympathetic to him.

"Ya, unusual. The building burns, myself I say that was unusual."

"When did you first notice any smoke or flames from that fire?"

"After Brian left, it was a few minutes. I don't know, four, three, could be five minutes." As I started asking a new question, he held up his hand. "Wait, that is wrong. I smell—smell—smoke. I no see it then. Later, ya. But not then."

"You smelled smoke within five minutes after he left?"

"Ya, is true."

"What did you do after you smelled smoke?"

"I gather some things, then I hear many people out front. I want to put my things in the car so I go out back where my car parked. Brian, he might be in front, I don't know. I not see him again. Then I read in paper that he is dead. That's all."

I had no more questions for Igor and turned to take my seat at counsel table. The courtroom door opened and Hedges stuck his head in, leaning against the half-opened door. Oblivious to the curious eyes of the jury, he gave me the thumbs-up sign. I knew he had found Jack Gibbs and breathed a sigh of relief, silently praising Hedges for his effective—if somewhat unorthodox—investigative techniques. As I sat down, Laflamme began his cross-examination of Igor.

Laflamme laid into him with everything he had. He added a few extra doses of sarcasm to his voice as he castigated Igor for being a bookie and extortionist. When Igor corrected Laflamme and said he was a luck facilitator, Laflamme stopped dead in his tracks. He stared at the ceiling as the courtroom went silent.

"Pardon me, sir?"

"No bookie," Igor explained. "I am Luck Facilitator."

"Luck Facilitator?"

"That is right, ya."

"And what do you call extorting point-shaving from Brian McHugh? An advanced persuasion technique?"

Laflamme spent half an hour leading Igor around, bringing him up one path and down another at will. Igor came across as not particularly bright, but not evil either. He was not the dark, brooding bookie of Mafia fame. He liked his work and truly believed he was helping people. Although his sense of ethics was twisted, he had an engaging personality. All in all, I thought, Igor had a strange appeal. At the very least, even if the jury didn't care for him, their image of Brian McHugh was definitely tainted. And I had achieved my main goal: placing McHugh at the Cheshire Village apartments the day of the fire.

After Laflamme's cross-examination, Judge Taylor announced our morning break. I had fifteen minutes to get ready for Jack Gibbs. At least as ready as I could be.

JACK Gibbs glared at me as he sauntered down the aisle and took a seat in the front row of the audience section. From the back of the courtroom came Glenn Hedges. He walked right to the counsel table.

"You got to be careful with this guy," he whispered in my ear, shaking his head toward Gibbs. "Yesterday I tried again to get a statement from him but he just gave me the same old bullshit: 'I don' have to talk to you, dude.'" Hedges squinted his eyes. "Felt like smacking him upside the head," he said, grimacing.

As I feared, this was going to be a "wing-it" direct examination. "But you might want to know that Mick Ryan's more cooperative than his buddy," Hedges continued, trying to sound upbeat, show me he hadn't failed completely. "He talked to me and confirms your version of what Gibbs said. Don't know if that'll help you any."

"Not much," I said, frowning. "Mick didn't see Evan arguing with McHugh so he's useless. It's Gibbs I need."

"Yeah, well, just thought you'd want to know," Hedges said defensively before taking a seat two rows behind Gibbs.

While I was chatting with Hedges, Raymond had turned around to check out Gibbs. "That's our star witness," he said, disappointed. He studied Gibbs for ten seconds, then shook his head. "Looks like a loser."

Gibbs sat at the end of the bench as far away from me and Raymond as he could get. He pulled at the end of his mustache, scanning the jury as if he were in a singles bar scouting the talent. He was wearing a black silk shirt, the top three buttons open, with black and white patent leather loafers. Disco king hits the links. He was a fashion nightmare, a definite *Glamour* magazine "Don't . . . ABSOLUTELY DO NOT!"

While we awaited Judge Taylor's grand entrance, Laflamme walked over, leaned down to whisper in my ear. "Is that your key witness?" he asked in a low, mocking voice. He pointed to Gibbs sitting with his feet stretched out on the bench. I nodded. Then he gave me the smirk, the same smirk I had seen earlier, which had disappeared for the last five days. The sight of Jack Gibbs had improved Laflamme's spirits considerably, giving him confidence he could undo the damage to the prosecution's case caused by Larry and Evan's testimonies.

"Better hope our dear bailiff, Mr. Lerner, doesn't catch him," Laflamme added. "He'll slap those feet right off the bench. Toss him in a cell for a night for showing disrespect to the court. Wouldn't look so good to the jury."

"Thanks for the warning. Nice to know you have my interests at heart."

"Hey, I do what I can. Sure you don't want to accept my offer?"

"Forget it," I said, sounding bored, but wishing I had more confidence in Gibbs.

Goddamn Hedges, I thought.

Our chit-chat was interrupted by Judge Taylor bursting out of chambers and plopping into his seat. "Call your next witness, Mr. Francis," he ordered.

After taking the oath, Gibbs sat in the witness stand and took advantage of the better view of the jury to pause for five seconds to stare at Amanda Sharpe, the young loosely dressed juror who had caught Laflamme's eye earlier. I hurried the first question before Gibbs could drool on his black silk shirt.

"Mr. Gibbs, are you here today pursuant to subpoena?"

"Sorry? I don't understand." Gibbs turned to me as though he'd never expected me to ask anything. This was not going to be easy.

"I asked if you were here by subpoena or did you appear voluntarily."

He shook his head. "I'm not here because I like the neighborhood, I tell you that. Only reason I'm here is because your investigator gave me this piece of paper; he said I'd be thrown in jail if I didn't show up."

"That piece of paper was the subpoena?"

"I guess. I never did get to read it. You wanna know why?"

"That's okay," I said, not wanting the jury to hear how Hedges had fed the subpoena to Gibbs. "Let's move on." I asked him about his background, shooting out the questions by rote—Where did you go to school? Did you graduate? What kind of work do you do? Jack Gibbs was a terrible witness, droning on in a monotone, his boredom evident. Worrying about the poor impression he was making, I barely listened to the answers. I vaguely heard him say he was a high school dropout and worked odd jobs the last five years, finally getting a regular position last spring as maintenance man and groundskeeper at Portsmouth's historical Strawberry Banke.

My mind wandered. I felt sorry for myself. Bust my butt to defend Raymond, expertly question the prosecution witnesses, turn the whole case around. Now I get shafted by a witness totally out of my control, a witness who didn't want to be here, didn't give a shit about me or Raymond. He only cared about who he was going to screw next.

And to think I had tossed away my whole practice for this case. Five of my civil clients had left me, frustrated when I didn't return their calls. There were seven or eight DWI's I had strung along, continuing each trial so I could work on

Raymond's case. Those clients complained about having criminal charges hanging over their heads. Two of them decided to plead guilty, ruin their driving records, and pay enormous insurance premiums, just to get on with their lives.

I would be the laughing stock of the county . . . no, probably the state. Hot shot Boston lawyer comes north, thinks he can pull one over on the hicks from New Hampshire, gets his head handed to him on a plate. The newspapers will love it, I suspected, especially the *Union Leader*, which had already convicted Raymond.

Wallowing in this self-pity, I asked, "In October of last year, did you visit the Cheshire Village apartments here in Manchester?"

"Say what?" He squinted as if I were speaking a foreign language.

"Cheshire Village," I repeated loudly. "Where a bookie named Igor Rubenstein lives."

He scratched his head, looked at the ceiling. "I remember that name."

My eyes fixated on Gibbs' shirt, the top three buttons unbuttoned. The dark hair from his chest spilled out, blending with the black silk as if it were part of the pattern. Why couldn't my star witness be someone else dressed in black? A priest maybe.

"Did you visit Mr. Rubenstein's apartment in October?"

"If I remember right, I never did get in to see him."

"Did you ever see the victim Brian McHugh at the Cheshire Village apartments?" I pulled from the evidence box an 8 x 10 photo of McHugh courtesy of the St. Andrew publicity department.

When he hesitated, I knew I had to gain control of the situation. I showed him the photo. "Did you see this person outside Rubenstein's apartment building?"

He studied the McHugh photo uncertainly, as if he were reading the financial pages. "I believe I did see this guy."

"Is that the young man you later learned was a football player at St. Andrew College and was murdered?"

"I think that's right, sure."

"Did you see Mr. McHugh talking to another young man?"

"Well . . . I, um . . ."

Gibbs stammered, hesitating; I became worried. My first thought was that he was going to go south on me, pretend he never saw Evan.

"Withdraw the question," I said. "I want to explore a different area."

I walked to the clerk's desk and searched through the evidence box. I located the Christmas card I had received from the Conways, a family portrait in front of the fireplace. I handed the card to Gibbs.

"Do you recognize anyone shown in this photo?"

He turned the photo sideways, looking at it from all angles. "I'm not sure," he answered. Murmuring rose from the jury box, a low rumbling sound.

I was stunned at Gibbs' answer. How could he not recognize Evan? He had clearly seen him arguing with McHugh. My heart was pounding but I pretended his answer was perfectly understandable. I picked up the photo and looked at it again. Evan was dressed in a jacket and tie and perhaps, I thought, the clothes had thrown off Gibbs. So I handed Gibbs another photo of Evan, one I took during my dinner at the Conways' house. He was wearing a V-neck sweater with a cotton, collared shirt underneath. Probably closer to what he was wearing the day of the fire, I thought, at least closer than a jacket and tie.

"How about this one?" I asked. "Do you recognize this person?"

Gibbs picked up the photo with both hands and held it a few inches from his eyes. He studied the photo closely, then put it down. "That's the same guy as in the other photo, isn't it?" Gibbs said. "Same answer: I'm not sure."

My world exploded around me; my worst fears had come true. I froze, stunned.

Judge Taylor leaned over. "Mr. Francis, do you have any more questions?"

As the judge was speaking, I watched Gibbs. He squeezed his lips, flattening them out, as if he were sucking on his tongue. I walked toward him. Five feet away I stopped, my hands together, palm to palm, in front of me. In my desperation I was unaware I had assumed a posture ingrained in my childhood. I was praying, praying fervently that there had been some mistake. My prayers were not answered. Suddenly I was treading water, thrashing around for something to keep me afloat. I felt myself sinking. The water swirled above my head; drowning was imminent. I did the only thing that came to mind. I called timeout.

"Your honor, request a recess. This is obviously a complete surprise."

Judge Taylor looked down at me, his expression a mixture of pity and amusement, as if he were thinking, "Well, sucker, what are you gonna do now?" After what seemed an interminable length of time, he granted my request. I motioned for Hedges to meet me outside and hurried out of the courtroom, careful not to make eye contact with the jurors who probably were looking at me with disgust.

Hedges followed me into the men's room. I turned on the cold water and filled my cupped hands. I bent over the sink, splashed my face, rubbed some water on the back of my neck. Must return to reality. Behind me, Hedges tried to explain.

"Listen, I had no idea. I told you the kid was a strange one. Not surprising he pulled a stunt like this."

Some private eye I hired. Finds my witness, sure enough, but not the same Jack Gibbs I sent for.

"You got anything on him I can use? Something big, not a stolen car, small time burglary, shit like that. I mean something will blow him out of the water." Funny how things change. Here I was trying to impeach my key witness, a suicidal approach. What a brilliant strategy. Ol' Rodger Dodds, my former partner, would be chuckling in his scotch and soda if he heard about this one.

Luckily Hedges could not accommodate my suicide attempt. "Nothing. The kid's a punk, record a mile long, but small time stuff. Breaking into video games, smoking pot, nothing that'll help. I'd say your best bet is to get him to back down, change his testimony a bit."

"Thanks for the advice. Now I can save that thousand dollar consultation fee I was going to pay Flea Bailey. Sure, I'll just get Gibbs to take it back, now he recognizes Evan Conway. Easy."

"Hey, I'm just trying to help here. I'm not the one screwed you over. I tried to prepare this punk, you know that. He didn't want to be prepared." He looked at his watch. "You got ten minutes, fifteen at the most, to put together a plan. Taylor's going to be looking for you."

"Maybe I'll just hide in the stall, tell 'em I'm sick to my stomach. Not far from the truth."

"Hey, why don't you do that. Give me a little time. I think I can come up with something." He opened the door.

"You bailing out on me? Leaving me to drown on my own. Thanks a bunch."

As the door swung shut, I could hear him shouting, "Just stall 'em."

Funny guy, that Hedges.

"ARE we ready to proceed, Mr. Francis?"

"Yes, your honor," I lied. Fifteen minutes in the john, scanning the walls for inspiration, brought nothing. If Hank Lerner hadn't come calling, slapping his baton on the stall door, I probably would have stayed there all afternoon. And Hedges had left me stranded. Not a word. I was on my own.

As I explained all this to Raymond, in a low whisper so the jurors staring at us would not overhear my brilliant strategy, his expression never changed. He had taken Gibbs' testimony quietly, though his knee slapped against the table again. Even though I nearly gasped when Gibbs claimed not to recognize Evan, Raymond just stared straight ahead as if he were studying the witness. It was his life at stake and I was the one losing my cool. Quite a change from the time he took a swing at me in his cell.

Mr. "Glamour-Don't" looked no better. During recess he had stayed in the witness chair, apparently afraid of what I would do to him if we happened to meet in the hall. Near as I could tell, Laflamme didn't even talk to him.

Still with no plan in mind, I took Hedges' advice. I stalled. "Ever have a problem with your memory?"

"Not that I can remember," he deadpanned. The jury giggled. Gibbs looked over as if he couldn't figure out what was so funny.

"Sir, do you recall being in a bar called O'Dowd's Pub in Concord? After a rugby party between Concord and Portsmouth. Do you remember that?"

Time was running out. I had to get to it.

"I been there, so?"

"Isn't it a fact that you were there during a rugby party?" He nodded. "Yeah, that's true."

"Did you tell me then that you had witnessed an argument between Brian McHugh and the young man who had been mowing the lawn at the Cheshire Village apartments?"

"Hey, look, I don't . . ."

Gibbs stopped in mid-sentence. There was a loud thud on the courtroom door. I turned to see Hedges walk in, making another of his dramatic entrances. Only this time he wasn't alone. Beside him was Gibbs' good friend, Mick Ryan, the very same Mick who had heard Gibbs tell me about Evan.

"I remind you you're under oath, Mr. Gibbs," I said. "Do you know the punishment for perjury in this state?"

As I said this, I swept my arm back toward Mick so Gibbs would get the point. If he lied now, Mick would take the stand right behind him, show up Gibbs for the perjurer he was. Gibbs' eyes followed my lead. He squinted, set his jaw tight, scratched his head.

"Ah, well . . ." He hesitated. I had him.

"Do you remember the question, Mr. Gibbs?"

"Sorry, could you say that again?"

"Did you or did you not, on a Saturday afternoon in November, during a rugby party at O'Dowd's Pub, tell me you had witnessed an argument at the Cheshire Village apartments between Brian McHugh and the young man who had been mowing the lawn?"

I had been watching too many TV shows. Perry Mason couldn't have asked it any better. In the seconds after I spit out the question, with the courtroom as quiet as Sunday Mass during Communion, my thoughts turned to TV, but not Perry Mason. In my high school days, when I would plow through my homework while watching the Bruins games on TV, the announcer, a retired hockey player, would repeat the same cliché whenever the game got close: "The tension's so thick you could cut it with a knife." Perhaps this cliché came to me because the only sound I heard was Mrs. Driscoll's wheezing and the irregular sniffles of the juror in seat number one. Twenty-four eyes stared at Gibbs. My credibility, perhaps Raymond's life, hung in the balance. Gibbs turned from Mick to me, to the jury, back to Mick, then wet his lower lip with his tongue.

"I . . . ah, yeah, I guess I did say something like that."

"And you remembered at that time seeing the victim, Brian McHugh, arguing with the young man who had been mowing the lawn?"

"I guess I did; back then, I guess so."

"Do you know the name of this young man who had been mowing the lawn?"

He shrugged. "I sure don't."

"Can you tell this jury anything about the way he was dressed?"

"I'm sorry," he said, finding humility. "I can't." Then he picked up the Conway family photo which had remained on the witness table. "He sure couldn't have been dressed like this, I'm sure of that." He held up the photo and pointed to Evan in his jacket and tie.

"Are you saying that's the person who had been mowing the lawn?"

"No, I said I can't be sure. But I am sure I never saw no one dressed like that."

I decided to move on. "Did you overhear what either Mr. Gibbs or the young man were arguing about?"

Gibbs shook his head.

"You have to answer out loud," Judge Taylor instructed him.

"No, I didn't."

"Did anything unusual happen after the argument?"

Gibbs hesitated and I got another sinking feeling that he was going to hang me. I withdrew the question. "Mr. Gibbs, did you remain at Cheshire Village after seeing Brian McHugh?"

"No, I did not."

"Why is that?"

I detected a change in Gibbs demeanor, as if he were more willing to answer these questions. "Because right after this argument started, if I remember right, I saw smoke coming from the basement."

"How much smoke?"

"A lot. I can't say how much."

"Did you call the fire department?"

"That's right. I ran down to the corner and pulled the alarm. I figured the firemen would take care of everything so I left."

"Did you see Brian McHugh again?"

"No, sir."

"Did you see the young man again, the one who had been mowing the grass?"

He shook his head again, but apparently remembering the judge's instruction, said quickly, "No, I did not."

I had one last question to tie things together. "So the last time you saw the young man who had been mowing the lawn was right after his argument with Brian McHugh and seconds before you noticed smoke coming from the basement?"

I had hoped Gibbs would answer this question in a loud clear voice with all the confidence that truth and right inspire, that he would leave no doubt in the jury's mind as to what had happened. But of course he disappointed me. He paused, stared at the wall, then looked back at his friend Mick. I was worried what he was going to say so I jumped in.

"Isn't that exactly what you told me at O'Dowd's Pub?"

In a confident and sure voice that I worried may have come a question too late, Gibbs answered, "Yes, it is. Exactly."

I stared at him for five long, quiet seconds, giving the jury a good chance to watch this worm squirm. "No further questions," I said, turning my back on my star witness. Before sitting down, I caught Hedges' eye and winked at him, knowing the little I got out of Gibbs was because Hedges had dragged Mick Ryan into the courtroom.

Helluva investigator, that Hedges.

CHAPTER 35

"A masterful examination," Hedges said, shaking my hand.

"Not at all," I said. "All due to superb investigative work."

Raymond sat on the cot, leaning against the wall with his eyes closed, still tense from Gibbs' testimony. "Whichever, that sure was close," he said. "I was scared shitless in there. I got to admit I was second-guessing you, thinking I was right when I said we didn't need Gibbs."

Hedges turned to me. "The look on Gibbs' face when I walked in with his buddy Mick. It was priceless, like he wanted to bolt the hell out of there." He laughed. "And Laflamme, he was getting all cocky, thinking he had you dead to rights. And then Gibbs puts Evan and McHugh together, arguing just before the fire, for Christ sake. If Monsieur Laflamme had himself a shovel I do believe he'd've dug his grave right there. He kept turning back to Mick Ryan, wondering what the hell's going on. I just sat there pretending I was ignorant as could be. And you've no idea how close it was."

"How'd you find him?" Raymond asked.

"Pure luck. I just figured those two always travel together so I circled the courthouse, searching for Gibbs' car. I checked the parking lot, ran up and down Chestnut Street, then Merrimack with no luck. Then I remembered some witnesses parked at the old Zayre's lot a block away so I gave it a try. And there he was, stretched out in the back seat, sound asleep."

"Doesn't sound like luck to me," I said. "That's good thinking, Hedges."

"Well, the rest was easy. I explained to Mick what had happened and he said, 'I was afraid he'd do something like that.' I told him we had no choice but to call him to the stand and since he'd been subpoenaed, he had to go now. He didn't want to screw his buddy, but at least he's an honest guy."

"You took a big chance, you know. Mick was a potential witness so he wasn't supposed to be in the courtroom. If Gibbs hadn't come around, I would've been out of luck. No way Taylor would've let me call Mick after he watched Gibbs' testimony."

"Yeah, but it was worth it, wasn't it?" Hedges said. "Now the jury's got some direct evidence of Evan's motive to kill McHugh. There's your reasonable doubt."

"Maybe," I said, not wanting to get Raymond's hopes up. "But Laflamme almost took it away on cross, made Gibbs look like a moron. Which wasn't all that hard to do. I was afraid Gibbs'd take back the little he gave us, but no matter how hard Laflamme hit, he stuck to his story. Not the greatest evidence I ever saw, but not bad in view of the alternative."

Raymond rubbed his eyes. "I can't wait until this is over."

"Won't be long now," I assured him. "You take the stand tomorrow morning, something we have to work on tonight. Then in the afternoon we close. We could have a verdict in two days."

Hedges checked his watch. "Gentlemen, I'll let you two get to work." He stood up and put on his jacket. "I've got to run anyway. Hot date tonight. You should see her," he winked. "Built like a brick shithouse. Just thinking about her sends shivers up me spine." With a devious grin, he shook Raymond's hand, then waited for the deputy to unlock the gate. "Only problem," he added. looking over his shoulder, "is her parents want her home by ten."

IT was eleven o'clock before I got home. I was exhausted. Raymond and I had rehearsed his testimony over and over until he had his story straight, all the angles covered. I spent a lot of time talking about his demeanor. The substance of his testimony was simple: I left Cathy's, drove straight to the Conways and went to sleep. No, I did not go to the theater; no, I did not shoot Brian McHugh. It was how he said these things that would influence the jury. He had to have just the right amount of indignation when he denied killing McHugh. At the same time he had to seem vulnerable, hurt that anyone would accuse him of such a thing. By the time we had finished I was convinced that he could carry it off.

I opened the refrigerator, pulled out a bottle of Molson Golden Ale. I took a long swig then pushed the button on the answering machine. There were four messages. The tape rewound, stopped. The first call came on. Silence, then click. The second call was the same, another hang-up. Finally, on the third call there was a message. It was Larry. "I've put off calling you—I was so pissed off—but I've got to get this off my chest." His voice was slurred, gruff. "You fucked me bad, real bad. I still can't believe it, especially from somebody I thought was a friend. And to do that to my son, push him around like that in court. . . . You must be real proud of yourself, hot shit Harvard lawyer." He paused, then there was a slamming sound like a bottle hitting a table. I sat down on the couch, stared at the answering machine. "You've made a mess of this whole thing. Who knows if I'll ever be able to straighten it out. I'll tell you one thing though: no matter how this trial turns out, I never want to see your hairy face, hear your faded Boston accent again in my life. Adios, amigo. You are history in my book. Gone, a nobody. I hope you can live with yourself after this. I take that back. I hope you never get another peaceful night's sleep in your life. I want you to lie awake night after night thinking about how you screwed me. Sweet dreams, pal!" He slammed the phone down.

I squeezed the Molson bottle with both hands, not moving. There was another click and I heard Yvette's voice. "Dutch, you didn't call after court today so I wanted to see how you're doing. Everyone was talking about Gibbs' testimony. Must've had ten calls from reporters this afternoon. They all think you're a great lawyer and want your life story. I put a list of their names and numbers on your desk." I closed my eyes and pictured Yvette with the phone to her ear, her long black hair curled over her shoulder and covering her breasts. I thought of the other night and the lust returned. I shifted in my seat as I heard her say, "I wanted you to know how proud I was of you, of how you handled this case, with your friend and all. You've done an incredible job. You're the most ethical lawyer I've ever met." She paused, then added, "And a helluva good lay too."

After the machine clicked off, I drained the bottle of Molson. I picked up my briefcase and pulled out the outlines of Raymond's direct examination and my final argument. I sat down at the desk I had purchased at an antique shop shortly after arriving in Manchester. I bought the desk because it was six feet long and made of solid oak, a piece of furniture I thought would last forever. But after a few months of use, little pieces of wood began chipping off the top. At first a thin strip on the edge, then the strips got wider and longer until the top of the desk looked like a fifteen-year-old's sunburned shoulders after eight hours at Hampton Beach, the pink skin peeling away to expose the pale flesh underneath. And I realized I'd been taken. The desk was not solid oak at all; it was a veneer.

CHAPTER 36

THE media crowded the courtroom for closing argument. Channel 9's Virginia Turner brought an entourage—a cameraman, soundman, scores of assistants—all camped by the door, anxious to pounce on the lawyers as soon as Judge Taylor allowed them. Dan Sweeney sat in the front row, eagerly leaning forward as if this were the most exciting murder trial ever reported in the *Boston Globe*. Not to be outdone by the out-of-town press, the *Union Leader* assigned three reporters to the case, covering every aspect of Raymond's life in more detail than nominees to the Supreme Court.

The *Union Leader*'s coverage had become more and more sensationalized as the trial wore on, headlines blaring my accusations against Evan. After Evan's testimony, the front page carried side-by-side photos of Evan and Raymond with the caption, "Which is guilty? How would you vote?"

After Rubenstein's testimony, the media went crazy. A reporter had called Coach Carlucci at Pine Creek High

School and Carlucci had conceded McHugh's conviction. St. Andrew's Coach Walsh was quoted as "denying vehemently" that McHugh had ever shaved points.

After the lunch break, I made a point to arrive before Laflamme so I could position the podium in the center of the courtroom, below the indentation in the ceiling caused by the skylight, an area known to lawyers as "The Spot." The Spot was an area where the unique architecture of the ceiling created an echo. All the pearly gems spewing from the advocate's mouth would be thrown right back at him. The first time I encountered The Spot early in the trial I stopped in mid-sentence, looked toward the ceiling as if God had spoken directly to me. When I realized that it was a much lesser being, I was disappointed. The jurors stared at the ceiling, puzzled, because they had heard no echo. The strange thing about The Spot was that only those standing on The Spot heard the echo.

I wanted the podium near The Spot for two reasons: One, to make sure I stayed away from it. There was nothing more disconcerting than to have your rhythm interrupted by the sound of your own voice. Two, to throw Laflamme off stride if he decided to use the podium, as he had done more and more during the trial. It was an idea that came to me after watching the Celtics humiliate opponents by taking advantage of the dead spots in Boston Garden, where the ball hit an area of parquet floor and then died. The Celtics knew the location of every dead spot so they forced opposing players to dribble on a dead spot, and before the opponent could recover, stole the ball away.

I arranged my notes on the podium as Hank Lerner led Raymond to his seat. Raymond looked terrible. His skin had taken on the sickly grey color of people who spend all their time indoors. His eyes were bloodshot from a sleepless night, worrying about his testimony. But he had held up well under Laflamme's incessant pounding this morning. As expected, Laflamme had been combative, hammering at Raymond's dislike of McHugh, his threats, his inability to establish the time he left Cathy's. Raymond kept his cool, loudly denying he wanted to kill McHugh, that he drove to the Cinema Manchester, that he climbed through the back window, and that he shot and killed Brian McHugh. "No, I did not," he repeated to Laflamme's questions. "I did not kill him."

When Laflamme changed direction and asked about Evan, Raymond lowered his voice. "I have no idea," he responded to Laflamme's question about whether Evan had killed McHugh. "My lawyer sure thinks so." We had rehearsed this answer over and over, trying to find the right way to keep the jury believing Evan was guilty. If Raymond said he believed in Evan's guilt, then Laflamme could attack him for not reporting his suspicions, make him look like a citizen shirking his duty, as I had done with Killian. But if Raymond came to Evan's defense, said he couldn't believe Evan would do such a thing, the result would be even worse. Laflamme could then stand up in front of the jury and say, "Even the defendant himself does not believe in this cockamamie theory. You heard him. Evan Conway is not the kind of person to commit murder." For sure the vote would be guilty.

The middle road seemed best. Avoid having Raymond take a position, so he wouldn't sound like an advocate, just another person trying to figure out what happened. And by throwing it back at me, he would make sure the jury paid extra attention to my closing argument. It was dangerous having the result depend so much on my credibility, but if the jury believed me—and I sure gained some points with Gibbs' switch—they might just accept my version of the facts.

Now was the time to lay out that version. As Raymond walked to his seat, the crowded courtroom silently staring at him, the door burst open. I half expected Hedges to make another of his grand entrances. Instead, it was a scruffy man with bloodshot eyes wearing olive green pants. He shuffled in, moving slowly, as if he knew he didn't belong and was

daring the bailiffs to throw him out. He pushed his way past
the seated reporters, elbowing into a seat. My eyes bulged
when I realized who he was. I glanced at Raymond, motioned with my eyes. He turned around, surveying the crowd
when he suddenly froze, making eye contact with John E.
Walker, his father. He clenched his teeth, quickly turned
back to the front, cursing under his breath.

"All rise," Hank Lerner shouted as Judge Taylor took the
bench. Judge Taylor immediately instructed the jury on the
purpose of closing argument, telling them what the lawyers
say is not evidence but listen carefully anyway. Sure, I
thought, why would they bother listening to us after that introduction. "Mr. Francis, please begin," Judge Taylor ordered
with no pretense of courtesy.

In most states, the prosecution gets to make the first closing argument and often a second rebuttal argument. But in
New Hampshire, the defense went first and the prosecution
last. I planned to take full advantage of going first by un-
dermining the arguments I knew Laflamme would make. I
positioned myself to the side of the jury box, so the jury
would be looking away from Laflamme and focusing entirely on me. The words came easily, reverberating throughout the courtroom.

"On one level, you have a very easy decision. You have
only two choices: guilty or not guilty. That will be the easy
part. It is getting there that will be difficult. We have presented substantial evidence pointing to Evan Conway as the
murderer. Of course, it is not my job to find the guilty party,
only to disprove my client's guilt. But I was so convinced of
my client's innocence, as well as Evan Conway's guilt, that
I felt compelled to present that evidence to you. I realize you
may not be fully convinced that I have proven Evan Conway's guilt. You may believe someone else—the gambler
Igor Rubenstein or the projectionist Nathan Goode, for example—may have killed Brian McHugh. It does not matter
that you disagree with me. What matters is: if you have any

doubt whatsoever who committed this crime, then you must find Raymond Walker not guilty."

Juror number one, a woman in her mid-forties with brunette hair permed into a round ball, still sniffled continuously. Her cold had gotten progressively worse during the trial and now she had her handkerchief in her hand at all times, dabbing at her red nose every few seconds. I tried not to snarl at the distraction and walked over to an easel I had set up earlier that morning. "Let me review for you why I have concluded Evan Conway is guilty. Let's compare the evidence on both sides." With a flourish, I flipped up the cover of the block paper clipped to the easel. On the first page I had made two columns and written Evan Conway at the top of one, Raymond Walker at the top of the other.

"What evidence has the prosecution presented against my client, Raymond Walker? We'll start with the basics: motive and opportunity." Under Raymond's name I wrote, "1. Motive" and below that "2. Opportunity." I continued: "The motive allegedly was revenge because of a personality conflict. There is no question my client and Brian McHugh did not like each other. They had disagreements, nearly came to blows. There is no question McHugh fired Raymond. But does all this add up to a motive for murder? Ask yourself that question over and over again while you're sitting in the deliberation room. These were normal, everyday disagreements. Some people just don't hit it off. But you've heard no evidence to suggest anything other than normal disagreements. And this was a minimum wage job. Sure, Raymond liked working there, but there're many jobs available paying the same amount. Would a person kill for such reasons? I doubt it."

Then, with a red marker, I put an "X" over "Motive." "Now what about opportunity? The evidence indicates that Raymond left his girlfriend Cathy's house after one o'clock. We don't know the exact time, but we do know—because the Sayewich's cuckoo clock sounded—that it was on the hour. As Cathy testified, the news was on the TV, so it could have been one o'clock, could have been two o'clock. If it was two o'clock then there's no question Raymond could not have committed this crime.

"And remember: Dr. McAulley conceded, though somewhat reluctantly, that the time of death could've been as early as one forty-five. So if Raymond had left at one ten, it would've been impossible for him to drive from Dover to Manchester, park his car, climb through the window, confront McHugh and shoot him, all in thirty-five minutes."

I uncapped my red marker and placed a "/", signifying a half "X" over "Opportunity."

"What other evidence was presented against my client? There was the testimony of Frank Killian." I wrote "3. Frank Killian" under "Opportunity." Then I summarized Killian's testimony, emphasizing his bias against Raymond by turning back toward Cathy who was seated right behind Raymond. Another red "X" over "Killian."

I reviewed the rest of the evidence: the gun, the shoe print. I listed them under Raymond's name, but for these I did not place an "X". They stood in stark contrast to the other evidence.

So far so good. Now for the tough part. "Let's turn now to the evidence against Evan Conway. I'll start with the same two: motive and opportunity. What was Evan Conway's motive for killing Brian McHugh? The evidence suggests a very strong motive: Brian McHugh had caught Evan Conway committing arson. Evan had to eliminate the only witness against him so he climbed in the window of the Cinema Manchester and killed Brian. The evidence is uncontradicted that Evan's father, Larry Conway, recently had lost hundreds of thousands of dollars. Either with his father's encouragement or on his own, Evan Conway decided to help his father out in a big way by collecting on the Cheshire Village fire insurance policy. Larry Conway stood to collect over half a million dollars in insurance."

I took a deep breath. I had the jurors' attention. They did not move. "Evan Conway was the perfect man for this job—no prior criminal record, a good student, from a well-established family." Here I faltered; my eyes watered and I had to stop. I stood still, bit my lower lip and squeezed my eyes shut, trying to dispel thoughts of Larry and Paula from my mind.

With some hesitation, I began. "It is indeed difficult for me to say these things to you. You have heard how Larry Conway and I were boyhood friends. We had no contact for over twenty years and then out of the blue he called me, wanting me to defend Raymond Walker. At first I was flattered he wanted to contact me, but as the evidence came in I began to wonder. There had been a fire at PEVCON's apartment building—Larry's building—and he didn't tell me about it. After Brian McHugh's murder, he learned his target pistol was missing and he never told me. Why? Does his explanation make sense to you? That he had only Raymond's interest in mind. Or is the true reason that he knew I would suspect him? And then we have the testimony of Jack Gibbs, my surprise witness. As you could tell, he turned out to be a surprise even to me. But as poor as his memory seemed, his testimony ties the pieces together. We know Evan Conway mowed the lawn at Cheshire Village; we know Brian McHugh visited Igor Rubenstein the day of the fire; and from Gibbs we know that Evan and Brian argued that day, that the fire started around the time of their argument. And so the conclusion, I submit, is clear: Larry Conway was using me, not to get Raymond Walker acquitted, but to ensure that no suspicion would be thrown in his son's direction." I took a deep breath, let the silence fill the courtroom. "As hard as it is for me to accuse Larry Conway, my oldest friend, and his son of these horrible deeds, I cannot deny the evidence. Motive? Yes, there certainly was motive." I returned to the easel and wrote "Motive" under Evan's name.

I then went through each item of evidence against Evan and listed them on the paper: "2. Opportunity," "3. Gun," "4. Footprint." I pointed out that the gun and footprint pointed as much to Evan as to Raymond. Several jurors nodded. Returning to the easel, I wrote, "5. Jack Gibbs" under Evan's name.

I was spent. I stopped talking and turned toward the easel, pretending to read the two lists I had written. The jurors turned with me, all twelve staring at the lists. Any comparison of the two lists would lead to only one conclusion. The only items of evidence under Raymond's name without a full or half "X" were "gun" and "footprint." Under Evan's name, none of the items of evidence had "X's." The evidence against Evan was clear: motive, opportunity, gun, footprint, and Jack Gibbs. I turned back to the jury.

"What does all the evidence add up to? You must decide that. You must evaluate and weigh all this evidence," I said while waiving my hand at the paper. "There may be some of you who are not convinced that Evan Conway is the murderer. That is understandable, for we have not had the benefit of an extensive police investigation. There are many unanswered questions. But the blame for that lies with the police and, yes, with the prosecution. Do not punish my client if you believe I have not fully done the prosecution's job. Even if you have such doubts, one thing is certain. All the evidence, viewed fairly to both sides, leaves much more than a reasonable doubt as to Raymond Walker's guilt. The prosecution has not proved Raymond Walker guilty beyond a reasonable doubt. It is that simple. And because of that, your duty as citizens is to find my client NOT guilty."

When I sat down, Raymond grabbed my hand and squeezed hard. It was difficult to tell who was sweating more. The crowded courtroom was silent for five seconds. The eerie quiet was broken by someone grunting "Hah!" a disgusted, disbelieving sound. I looked toward the crowd, trying to find the culprit. My eyes met the tired, cynical, blood-red eyes of my client's father. Suddenly someone sneezed, a high-pitched honk that seemed to bounce off the walls. It was our sniffling juror, thankfully distracting the jury from my unfriendly critic. The man next to her said,

"God bless" and the reporters laughed while Taylor pounded his gavel.

My job was essentially over. After Laflamme's final argument, Judge Taylor would instruct the jury on the law and they would retire to deliberate. "Mr. Laflamme," Taylor said, raising his eyebrows at the prosecutor, a signal for him to start his opening.

Laflamme stood up, walked to my easel and carried it to the far wall away from the jury. He turned it around so the jury could not see my comparison of Evan and Raymond. He walked back to the podium. Again he had no notes. To my dismay he picked up the podium and moved it three feet to the left, out of range of The Spot. I should have known better than to try to fool a battle-scarred veteran like Laflamme.

"Ladies and gentlemen, you have been exposed to a most creative defense here." Laflamme was not going to pull any punches; he was coming out swinging. "Not the claim that someone else did it. That happens in every case. If the defendant admitted guilt there would be no need for a trial. But rather the extraordinary claim that the defendant's own friend, who by all accounts was sleeping soundly in his parents' home at the time of the murder, actually committed this horrible crime. To accept the defense version you will have to suspend your common sense. There's no way around it. You would have to completely reject the compelling testimony of Frank Killian, the State's very first witness, who told you of the defendant's admission he planned to rob the theater. Despite defense counsel's best efforts to shake Mr. Killian's story, his testimony remained the same. Surely petty jealousies and idle threats did not lead to Mr. Killian's fabricating his entire testimony, committing perjury. And for what? What did he have to gain? Nothing, absolutely nothing. Do you really believe a man would commit perjury like this just for revenge, because the defendant took the girl he wanted? Preposterous. We know better. Yet that is what the defense would have you believe.

"And who was the defense's star witness, the witness who was supposed to reveal the real killer? You remember the promise Mr. Francis made to you in opening statement—how he would present evidence that would conclusively identify the real killer—remember that? Instead of a witness identifying the real killer, we get someone who cannot even identify Evan Conway's photo. Sure he may have told Mr. Francis one time in the past that he had seen Brian McHugh arguing with *someone* at Cheshire Village. We know that Brian and Evan Conway both were there at various times; we also know both were at the theater together. What does that tell us? Nothing, absolutely nothing. For you to believe Evan Conway killed Brian McHugh you have to reject the police department's conclusion that the defendant Raymond Walker was guilty. In considering these questions, you should recall Mr. Gibbs' demeanor on the stand, especially his shifty manner of answering questions. You have to decide how much weight, if any, should be given to give his testimony. I am sure if I, as the State's representative, had brought such a witness before you, you would have laughed me out of the courtroom. You should treat the defense the same way.

"Let me suggest to you what the evidence has shown. Raymond Walker, a poor high school dropout, given up by his father, unable to hold a job—a loser, there's no other way to put it—had finally found a job he liked. Not the tedious, repetitive work of the rug cleaning plant, but an usher in a movie theater, where he could watch the movies between collecting tickets and refilling the popcorn machine. For Raymond Walker this was the big time. He had it made. And then, suddenly, it was gone. He was fired, rightly or wrongly—that is not the issue—by the victim Brian McHugh. His whole world collapsed, and at the worst possible time, while his girlfriend was expecting a baby, his baby, and he would need money to support his child. Now I don't pretend to know for sure what motivated the defendant to commit this crime. No one but the defendant knows that.

But there are several plausible scenarios. It may be that he was motivated primarily by revenge, to get even with Brian McHugh for firing him. And he took the money as an afterthought, perhaps to make it look like a robbery. Another possibility is he was motivated by money and killed Brian McHugh only when McHugh recognized him. You remember the mask the defendant showed to Frank Killian. It is reasonable to conclude that the defendant followed through on his plan to rob the theater but during the robbery McHugh recognized his voice, and the defendant panicked and shot him. That scenario is entirely consistent with Walker's telling Killian about a robbery and not mentioning murder. Either way . . ." Laflamme raised his voice a decibel, increasing the volume higher than he had the whole trial, ". . . the defendant is GUILTY of murder in the first degree." With each word he jabbed his fist in the air, hammering his message home to the jury.

Laflamme paused, bent down to pick up a cup of water he'd stored on the top shelf of the podium. He sipped the water slowly then returned to the jury, looking them over one by one. "Before I finish," he began softly, the contrast with his previous demeanor keeping the jury enthralled, "I have one more subject I want to talk about. Mr. Francis has done a brilliant job of diverting your attention from the relevant issues in this case." As he mentioned my name, Laflamme turned toward me, slowly pointing in my direction, forcing the whole jury to follow along and look at me. I felt like a first grader on stage for the school play, all those strange eyes staring at you and you don't know where to look. Laflamme continued. "All this business about PEVCON, his boyhood friend Larry Conway, Brian McHugh being a witness to a fire. I have to admit Mr. Francis learned a few tricks practicing in Boston." Laflamme smiled and half the jurors smiled with him. All us New Hampshirites are in this together, they seemed to be thinking. How can we let a lawyer from Boston—of all places—pull one over on us? I fidgeted in my seat, debating whether to object. There was too great a risk of antagonizing the jury so I decided to let Laflamme continue.

"Mr. Francis has introduced all these facts that have absolutely nothing to do with the murder of Brian McHugh and tried to piece together a common thread. But what was it that held these pieces together, what was the only evidence that possibly could link Evan Conway with the murder of Brian McHugh? You know the answer: Jack Gibbs. Pretty weak, wouldn't you say? And why has Mr. Francis taken this approach? Quite simply because it was the only way to get around the overwhelming evidence against his client: Raymond Walker's experience with the murder weapon; his bootprint at the murder scene. Only Evan Conway had used the gun and worn these same boots so why not point the finger at him. But what about the other evidence: Raymond Walker's threats to get even with the victim; his admitted intent to rob the theater."

Stepping away from the podium, Laflamme walked to the far wall and picked up the easel with my chart on it. He carried it toward the jury. I couldn't figure out what he was doing. "Mr. Francis wants you to believe the evidence against Evan Conway is clear." He picked up the red marker and turned toward my chart. "We have seen that there is no real evidence of motive and opportunity." He put an "X" through these items under Evan's name. "Evan Conway had everything going for him; he had no reason in the world to kill Brian McHugh. And no opportunity either; he was asleep in his home when Brian McHugh was killed. His father has confirmed that." Then he circled "motive" and "opportunity" under Raymond's name.

"I'm not going to repeat the evidence on these two witnesses," he said, pointing toward Killian and Gibbs' names. "Suffice it to say the evidence showed that Killian's credibility far outweighed Gibbs'." With that, he put an "X" over "Gibbs" and circled "Killian."

"As I said, you cannot ignore the evidence of the defendant's threats to Brian McHugh, his boasting about robbing the theater. Mr. Francis did not even pretend to link this evidence to Evan Conway; he just brushed over these important facts in his closing argument. And you know very well that if there was any basis whatsoever to charge Evan Conway with this crime, we would have done so. Make no mistake about it: if you acquit Raymond Walker you will be letting a murderer go free. For the sake of the people of the great state of New Hampshire and in the interests of justice, I ask you to return a verdict of guilty of murder in the first degree."

As Laflamme slowly walked back to his seat, I noticed the counsel table vibrating. I looked at Raymond who was staring into space, motionless. I glanced under the table and saw the knee jerking spastically, slamming against the bottom of the table. Only this time it was my knee.

CHAPTER 37

I walked briskly down three flights of stairs, across the bare basement corridor, then up the back stairs to the courtroom lobby. This had been my routine for all three days of jury deliberations, and all I could think of was Laflamme's brilliant closing argument. Even while Judge Taylor was instructing the jury on the law, I hardly listened, Laflamme's argument ringing in my ears.

I stared straight ahead as I walked, not noticing the clerks and bailiffs waving at me, avoiding the faces of lawyers passing by. My mind shutting out everything around me, I repeated this route step by step. On my third pass by the clerk's office, the doors swung open.

"Looking for something? You'd think after all these months you'd know your way around here."

"Huh?" Awakened, I looked up. "Oh, Carter, it's you. Sorry. You know how it is. Jury's deliberating. Judge makes us stay in the courthouse in case the jury has any questions. Worst part of the trial. Absolute worst."

"You're just antsy because there's nothing you can do

now. It's out of your hands. Jury's in control now, and Hank Lerner tells me they're going at it tooth and nail."

"Whoa! What're you saying? Hank's been spying on them?" Everyone knows it's improper to eavesdrop on jury deliberations. Any indication of the jury's leanings might make one side push for a plea bargain before the verdict. But bailiffs usually can't resist. They sit outside the deliberation room, making sure no one goes in or out, safeguarding the integrity of the process. But every once in a while a loud shout will emanate from the room, and curiosity getting the better of him, the bailiff will kick out his legs, suddenly decide a walk is just the thing to stretch them out. The walk, of course, will take him right by the door to the deliberation room.

"You know Hank, loves a good fight. And he said it sounded mighty hot. Hey, at least you got them worked up about it. They convict your kid they're going to feel real bad about it."

"Thanks, some consolation. Twelve-zero, but they felt bad about it. With that kind of result I'll be spending all my time representing the drunks." I started walking away.

"Come on, don't you want to know what Hank heard? Might be useful."

I stopped, but kept my mouth shut, not wanting to solicit this ill-gotten information. I raised my eyebrows.

"Okay, I get it," Carter said, nodding. "All Hank heard was something about your star witness, didn't know what to make of it. He couldn't be sure, but sounded like 'that fuckin' Gibbs.'"

I stared at him. "Hey, your guess is as good as mine," he shrugged. I didn't know what to make of this information and really didn't want to think about it. I thanked Carter, waved goodbye and renewed my walk. It was important to keep moving.

On the next trip by the clerk's office, I realized I'd never answered Carter's original question. I was walking in circles, up one stairs, down another. Walking aimlessly, I felt as

lost as when I first arrived in New Hampshire, having es-
caped a dead-end, loveless marriage, in search of fulfill-
ment, a thirst for some meaning to life, a thirst that seems to
haunt men when they reach forty. What was I looking for?

Back in the courtroom, Laflamme's briefcase was balanced on the edge of the table, beside a stack of files with
papers sticking out of them. No one was there. Other than
the muffled sound of voices from behind the chambers door,
the courtroom was completely silent. I looked around the
room, turning my body as if studying the architectural wonder of a great cathedral. I was struck by the emptiness. Judge
Taylor's high-backed brown leather chair, the fourteen jury
chairs, each with torn cushions on the bottom, counsels'
chairs, the gallery, all empty.

I sat down in the jury box, the seat belonging to juror
number one, the sniffler. Often before a trial I would sneak
into the courtroom, sit in the jury box, and visualize the witnesses on the stand. With my eyes closed I would see myself
standing at the podium or behind counsel table, putting
questions to the witness, using just the right tone and em-
phasis. Then I would listen to the witness's answer, ponder
my follow-up question, anticipate objections, and rephrase
my question. I would picture how the witness appeared to
the jury. Put advocacy aside for a moment, take an objective
viewpoint. On a few occasions I didn't like what I saw, and
after revealing my newfound insights to my client, convinced him to work out a settlement.

This time, though, I had been too caught up in trial prep,
in finding Jack Gibbs, dealing with Larry, that I completely
forgot to sit in the box. But now after the trial, in this silent
and empty courtroom where I had spent much of the past
three weeks, I had time to reflect on the trial. I sat back and
watched Larry on the stand, being cross-examined by his old
friend. He winced noticeably, as if each question inflicted a
new pain. There was a sadness in his voice, the kind of sadness that goes deep into the psyche, clutches at the heart. I
recognized that sadness, because I too felt it.

After Larry came Evan, his clean-shaven face, youthful good looks giving him an innocent, almost angelic, aura. He seemed scared, blinking his eyes, pushing his hair off his forehead. As he picked up the murder weapon, I flashed on him standing stiffly, the gun clasped firmly in his outstretched right arm. Using his left hand to steady his aim, he pointed the gun and squeezed the trigger. The bang was sharp, deafening. Pop, pop, pop. I tried to see what he hit, and it came to me in a blur. It was the shooting range, which I had seen only from the road while driving by at forty-five miles per hour.

Next was Jack Gibbs, looking slick and cocky in his open-necked shirt. "That fuckin' Gibbs," as one of the jurors had said. His testimony obviously distressed me, I could see. With each answer my facial expressions gave me away. Gone was the poker face trial lawyers strive for. My shock was obvious from the jury box. As I sat there, I found myself despising Gibbs all over again, and silently cheering for the defense attorney, me, to tear him apart.

I must have sat like that for a full hour, reliving each witness's testimony, before a hand shook my shoulder. "Wake up, counselor," Hank Lerner commanded, "the time of reckoning has arrived."

THE look on the jurors' faces told me nothing. Some trial lawyers say they can predict the verdict by studying the jurors' eyes, note whom they look at as they file to their seats. If the jurors look at the prosecutor, they say, the verdict will be guilty. I never subscribed to that rule, since I found over the years that the only consistent thing about juries is their inconsistency. And these jurors gave neither of us any help. Their eyes were downcast, staring at their shuffling feet. Like a condemned man walking toward the gallows, I thought grimly.

"Ladies and gentlemen of the jury, have you reached a verdict?" At these words from the judge, Raymond shuddered beside me. I put my arm on his shoulder to steady him.

I could feel his torso shiver, as if he had stepped out of the shower into sub-zero temperature. I squeezed tightly and he looked at me, nodded his head as if to say he was all right.

"Yes, your honor," said the foreman, Mr. Giminsky, the FBI agent. Oh, oh, I thought, the worst choice possible. He handed the verdict form to the clerk, who completed the hand-off to the judge. Judge Taylor raised an eyebrow as he read, turned the paper over, then re-read the whole thing, as if he didn't believe what he was reading. The clerk read the verdict out loud: "We the jury in the above-entitled cause, on the count of murder in the first degree find the defendant Raymond Walker . . ." Now it was his turn to pause, and he looked up from the paper directly at Raymond then glanced at Laflamme standing at my other side. ". . . NOT guilty!"

"Yes!" Raymond jumped in the air, pumping his right fist up and down. At the same time I punched the air in front of me, whispered a rare prayer: "Thank you, Lord." Tears streamed down Raymond's cheeks. He hugged me, rested his head on my shoulder, his tears soaking my jacket. "You were fantastic, unbelievable. I don't know how to thank you."

The jury had just given me all the thanks I needed. "You deserved it, Raymond," I told him while patting his back.

"Don't you worry," he said stepping back, "you're gonna get paid. Soon as I can, I'm bringing some money over, pay your fee."

A noble promise, but not one I expected him to keep. A few months in jail, out of work several weeks before that, he was in no position to pay my fee. I had spent so much time on this case I had been afraid to add up the fee. No, I wouldn't count on Raymond paying me anything. Chalk this one up to experience, an experience I hoped never to repeat.

The press swarmed around us, shoving microphones in Raymond's face. I waved them away. "On my advice, my client does not wish to make a statement at this time. We will be looking into the possibility of a malicious prosecution suit." This was bullshit, of course, but I said it only for Laflamme's benefit. Never too late for a little ribbing.

Another group of reporters surrounded him. When one mentioned malicious prosecution, Laflamme yelled, "That's ridiculous and Mr. Francis knows it. Malicious prosecution—gimme a break." Another reporter asked if the state would now be charging Evan Conway for the murder of Brian McHugh.

"No, we are not. The evidence is insufficient." He turned to me. "Perhaps Mr. Francis can be hired as a special prosecutor, if he thinks he can get a conviction."

I smiled and watched as Laflamme packed files into his briefcase. By now reporters had collared the jurors, making it impossible for me to talk to them, get their insights. Raymond was locked in an embrace with Cathy, who had run to him as soon as the verdict was read. They said nothing to each other except "I love you." I couldn't tell who shed the most tears.

Someone slammed open the courtroom door. I looked up to see the back of John E. Walker, slapping the door open with his palm, shaking his head from side to side. He left without saying a word to his son.

Before Laflamme finished packing, I tore a sheet of paper from my legal pad and scribbled a note. I carefully folded it into a small square and approached him.

"Well, I got to hand it to you, Francis," he said, "you did a helluva job. I never thought you'd pull this one off. Somehow you managed to snowball the jury, just like your client's been snowballing you."

"You're not going to start that again, are you? The jury has spoken. Let's put it to rest. Who are we to question their collective wisdom?"

"Hah, hah," he laughed, shook his head. As he picked up his briefcase, he said, "Punk like that didn't deserve you. You ask me, I think you'll be paying a heavy price for getting him off."

There was no point in arguing. "Here, take this." I slipped

the folded-up paper into the front pocket of his jacket. "Read it later on, when you get home."

He stuck out his hand and I shook it. Looking him in the eye, I realized how much I had come to admire his ability. He had been thoroughly prepared, never lost his cool, and presented a compelling case. Only through a mixture of good fortune, and a fair bit of skill on my part (I had to admit) did I come out victorious.

As Laflamme walked out of the courtroom, reporters sniping at his heels, I had a fleeting feeling of regret for giving him that note. It was childish, sure, and a bit tacky, but what the hell. Anybody with a scoreboard in his office deserves to be brought down a notch. I couldn't help smiling as I pictured Laflamme's face when he unfolded the note and read "61–*3!*"

OUTSIDE the air was crisp and cold, at thirty-five degrees a mild January day. Raymond and Cathy draped their arms around each other, clinging together tightly, afraid something might swoop down and separate them again. Four months pregnant and showing through her wide denim dress, Cathy glowed with happiness. At the bottom of the stairs, she hugged me goodbye, pulling me against her protruding belly. "Thank you so much," she said. "We'll never be able to repay you."

Raymond squeezed my hand, a strong sincere shake, and shook his head. "Oh, yes we will," he insisted. "Just you wait."

As I watched my client and his girlfriend turn the corner around the courthouse, their feet leaving faint prints in the snow dusting the walk, I thought of how much had changed since this case had started. On that fall day in early November when I had met Larry at the Chimes Café, the foliage was at its most brilliant hue and the brisk air carried a feeling of hope, of renewal. Now the trees were bare, the beautiful leaves long since turned brown and brittle. Amidst the barrenness behind the courthouse, surrounded by trees bare and naked, I felt empty, as if I had suffered a great loss.

My introspection was interrupted by a loud voice behind me. "How about a little smile, counselor? You did win, you know." It was Carter, grinning as he descended the stairs two at a time.

"The jury really didn't like Gibbs," I said.

"What're you talking about?"

"What Hank told you they were saying about Gibbs. They must've really hated him."

"What Hank told me?" He shook his head. "I'm sure Hank would never listen in on jury deliberations. No, not Hank Lerner. You must've heard me wrong."

I stared at him, puzzled.

Carter winked, then threw his head back, roaring loudly. "What do you say we go celebrate your great victory?"

I smiled, the tension easing out of my shoulders and neck, and said, "The Green Radish?"

"Where else?"

As soon as we got to the bar I found a pay phone and called Yvette to invite her to join us. When she arrived five minutes later, Carter and I were just starting our second bottle of Molson Golden Ale. "Careful with those," Yvette said. "Remember what happened the last time you drank that particular beer." I laughed and stood up to hug her. "Congratulations," she said. I held her tightly to my chest, feeling her softness. Somehow in the middle of winter she smelled of roses and spring. If Carter weren't there, I might never have let her go.

"Carter Butterworth, this is Yvette Arsenault, my assistant," I said after finally releasing my grip. "You two have talked on the phone."

Carter put out his hand. "Indeed, though I must say it's a pleasure to meet you in person." He gave Yvette a long look. "I was going to say you were fortunate to be working for such a talented lawyer. Now I think he's the one who's fortunate."

"Well, I'm not so sure about that," Yvette said as she glanced at me. "I didn't even want him to take this case."

"But I never would've made it through this trial without you," I said, staring into her eyes, momentarily shutting out Carter.

"Speaking of the trial," Carter interrupted. "I'd like to propose a toast." Carter lifted his bottle.

"Wait, I need a drink," Yvette protested.

Carter waited for the waitress to bring Yvette a glass of Chablis, then said, "To the best criminal defense lawyer in New Hampshire."

As they sipped their drinks I shook my head. "No way. I am but a novice in criminal defense; from now on I think I'll stick with the civil side."

"What're you talking about?" Carter shouted. "You should've heard Judge Taylor this afternoon."

"I'll bet he was pissed. He was ready to hold me in contempt half a dozen times."

Carted nodded. "You know what he does? Right after the verdict he barges into chambers, throws his robe on the couch, slams his fist on the desk. I was just in there to pick up a file but he wants to talk to me. 'That goddamn Francis,' he says. 'Sonovabitch is lucky I wasn't deciding this case. Would've been a lot different, I'll tell you that.' I've never seen him so mad. It was great."

I laughed at the image of Judge Taylor throwing a fit. Hard for him to admit his early impression of the case had been wrong. "Then he says," Carter continued, "'I have to admit, that Francis did a damn fine job. A damn fine job, especially for a paper-pushing civil lawyer.'" Carter laughed.

Yvette put her hand over mine, looked me in the eyes, just as she had a few nights ago. "That judge'll think twice before he doubts Dutch's ability again," she said. Then she added, "And so will I."

I ordered another round of drinks and we carried on, laughing, reliving the trial, swapping war stories until closing time. Carter had a perfect sense of timing and stood up to take his leave before anyone could feel awkward. "Got to be sharp for the morning," he said, shaking our hands. "Keep the wheels of justice spinning, you know."

After he left, I asked Yvette if I could drive her home.

"Sure," she said, "but with one condition."

"Oh, what's that?"

"Only if you stay."

"Stay? What about Russell?"

She put her arm in mine as we walked toward the door. "Russell has a new apartment," she said, smiling. "We thought that was best." She paused. "In view of the circumstances."

My heart raced. "Yes, of course," I said, trying to sound dignified as I breathed in the cold January air. "In view of the circumstances."

CHAPTER 38

I took two days off and spent them almost entirely in bed with Yvette, making love until we passed out from exhaustion. On the first night we called out for Thai food, and sat up in bed eating chicken satay. The next night Yvette said she wanted a Greek salad. I called Nick's Diner but the cashier said they didn't deliver. No problem, I said. I ordered moussaka, a large Green salad with extra feta cheese, and two stuffed grape leaves. Then I called a cab and the driver came by for the money before picking up the food. It felt decadent.

On the third day, Yvette announced that she had to get some exercise. "I'm going to the YWCA and work off all this food," she said.

I sat up. "What about work?"

She smiled and flipped her hair behind her back. "Work?" she said, opening the door. "I think I've earned another day off."

With Yvette gone, my mind wandered, reliving scenes from the trial. I was unable to think of anything else. That happens after a trial. You live with one case day and night for weeks, and when it's over, you still can't let it go. It stays on your mind as you replay the key testimony, the questions you wished you never asked, new questions you wished you had thought of before, and especially the clerk announcing the verdict. Those words get played over and over.

Fragments of testimony popped into my head. "We found the gun in Lake Masabesic," one of the cops had said. "The defendant had obviously thrown it there." Raymond had said Evan asked to go fishing. Evan claimed it was Raymond. Is that when Evan threw the gun in the lake? If so, he must've had the money with him too. What had happened to the money? Then I remembered Raymond said he went fishing for catfish near the big rock. Evan had stayed on the south side of the lake fishing for perch. After the verdict Raymond said something else that troubled me: "Don't worry, I'll take care of you." The more I thought the more troubled I became. Quickly I showered, dressed, and walked to my car.

LAKE Masabesic was covered by a thin layer of ice. The temperature was in the upper 20's. A few days ago, shortly after the verdict, a light snow had fallen and still blanketed the paths around the lake. I parked parallel to the guardrail on the highway and made my way along the northern path. The cold had turned the snow to ice, making the paths slippery. There were already several sets of icy footprints on the path, going in both directions. I walked the path along the lake for quarter of a mile toward the big rock, where Raymond said he'd been fishing. The rock was at a bend in the river where I noticed a single set of icy footprints go off toward the woods. They were faint, obviously made after the recent snowfall. I followed those prints through a strand of pine trees, up a hill, then back down again toward the lake. The prints joined the path again. I put my size ten foot into the prints; my foot protruded slightly at the top.

With the wind whistling off the lake, freezing the moisture on my mustache and beard, I followed the path again for about a hundred yards. Across the lake I could see some kids throwing snowballs but on my side the lake was deserted. The same set of footprints again turned toward the woods. I followed them along a similar pattern as before but this time they stopped at an oak tree a couple of dozen yards from the path and within sight of the big rock.

The snow at the base of the tree had been swept away, exposing the frozen ground underneath. Someone had recently dug a hole a couple of feet deep. From the looks of the frozen chunks of earth, the person must have worked at it for hours. I got on my knees and with my gloved hand pushed aside the loose chunks of dirt, trying to get to the bottom. I found nothing but icy, loose dirt. Looking up, I noticed the footprints returned to the path, then went in a southerly direction back toward the highway.

WHEN I arrived at the office, I felt drained, physically and emotionally spent. I sat at my desk, pondering what I had found at the lake. Unable to concentrate, I stared at the pile of mail that had accumulated in the past few weeks. In my obsession with the trial, I had ignored my other cases, including the daily mail. On each piece was a yellow post-it with Yvette's scribbling. "Sent him a copy," or "calendared," or "continued." She took care of everything. It was true: without her my practice would have fallen apart.

Reluctantly I flipped open a file and began scanning a set of interrogatories when the phone rang. It must be Larry, I thought suddenly. He's calling to chew me out, berate me again for betraying our friendship. I put my hand on the receiver, hesitating for two more rings before lifting the receiver to my ear. I noticed my hand shaking.

"Dutch Francis here."

"Well, well, well, if it's not Mr. Big Shot himself." It was definitely not Larry. "Getting murderers off scot free. Bet you're real proud of yourself. Oh, by the way, a real nice photo in the *Globe*. That clean New Hampshire air must be doing you some good."

"Nice to hear from you, Sherry. It's been a few months now."

"And whose fault is that? Here I was sitting in our town-house all alone, calling you week after week, with nary a return call. Why should a girl put out all the effort?"

"Sherry, you're hardly a girl anymore."

"Just like you, Dutch Francis, to be so negative. Just because I'm a teeny bit over forty doesn't mean I'm ready for the pasture. You know, Daddy says I've never looked better since I kicked you out."

"You kicked me out? Is that what you told him?"

"Can you blame me? He would just hate you forever if he knew you really walked out on me."

"I see. And I suppose you called just to remind me what a mistake I made."

"There you go, always assuming an ulterior motive. Lawyers! How did my life get so full of lawyers?"

"Well . . ."

"Well, alright. There was one other thing. Daddy read all about your little murder trial and thought it was just grand. His ex-son-in-law the hired gun. Made him feel all warm inside, know what I mean? Anyway, he's got this case he wants to talk to you about, very sensitive."

"Surely you're not going to refer me business. That would be too much."

"Now just a minute there. I called you only because Daddy asked me to, as a favor, because he's out of town. A bar association convention on a tropical island somewhere."

"Okay, Sherry, so what's the scoop on this case?"

"One of those sexual harassment things. You know, like with Anita Hill and Paula Jones, only this is a lot worse. And it's up in your part of the world. Daddy thinks because you're such a Big Shot up there in Vermont, Maine, or wherever you are, that you can straighten things out."

"I don't think so, Sherry." I had no desire to renew

acquaintance with my ex-father-in-law. "And it's New Hampshire. Manchester, New Hampshire. The godforsaken place. Remember?"

"How foolish of me. Yes, of course. New Hampshire. Lots of trees and mountains, aren't there? Sounds lovely, dear. But really, Dutchie, why don't you talk to Daddy? You may actually enjoy talking to him, learning what's been happening at the firm."

"Uh, uh. I doubt that." I scribbled down an answer to interrogatory number one. Might as well accomplish something while I'm forced to listen to Sherry.

"Pleazzze." She was going to say it; I just knew it. "Pretty pleazzze." She said it. Chalk scraping on the blackboard. The agony.

"Okay, enough. You know I hate that. All I'll agree to do is talk to Rodger. That's it."

"Oh, wonderful. Daddy will be so thrilled. I just know it. Let's see. Why don't we drive up there and take you to lunch. They do have restaurants in—what's that you call it—oh, yeah, Manchester?"

"Lunch would be fine, Sherry."

"Then Daddy could give you the whole story. It's a date then. I'll make the arrangements, call you when Daddy gets back."

"I'm sure I won't sleep 'til then; the anticipation will just kill me."

"Now, Dutchie, that's enough. Oh, I almost forgot to say congratulations. For getting that murderer off."

"'Accused' murderer, Sherry. He was acquitted, remember?"

"Whatever. All's I know is that it used to be me that you got off. Hah, hah. Cheerio!" *Click.*

IF I had a hard time concentrating before, it was nearly impossible now. Just what I needed. Sherry and Rodger back in my life. Not a pleasant thought.

I was spared the daunting task of tackling the interrogatories by a loud knock on the door. On the way past Yvette's desk, I picked up her calendar to see if she had scheduled any appointments. Nothing. She had drawn a line through the whole day.

Curious at who would drop in unannounced, I unbolted the door. "Hiya, counselor. Got something for you." It was Raymond, smiling and looking dapper in a new black leather jacket and stiff blue Levis.

I stared at him for a moment before speaking. "Enjoying your freedom, I see. Come on in."

"Hey, can't stay long. Someone's waiting in the car." He took five steps in, gazed around the office. "So this is what it looks like. Bet I'm the first client who never got to see your office until the case was over. Mighty fancy."

"It's okay, I guess." I walked toward the inner office, beckoning him to follow. "Why don't you sit down, stay a few minutes."

He stopped at the doorway. "Can't do it. Some other time maybe. Anyway, this is why I came by. Wanted to give you this." He handed me a package the size of a shoe box wrapped in Christmas paper, green background with red and white candy canes.

"Paper was left over from Christmas," he said apologetically. "Just wanted to show you how much I appreciate all your work. It was a thing-a beauty, I'm tellin' ya. I hope this squares things between us."

I held the box in my hand, ran my thumb along the edges. "Raymond, tell me one thing," I said, holding the package in front of me.

"Sure, anything."

With a catch in my throat, I asked, "Have you been to Lake Masabesic recently?"

Raymond's mouth opened but he said nothing. He took a step backwards. "N-no, why do you ask?"

My mind was swirling and my head ached. "Raymond?"

He looked at me, silent.

"Raymond, I can't take this," I said, holding out the package.

He held out his hands and backed up. "Uh, uh," he said. "No way, you keep it. You earned it." Quickly he walked to the door. "Listen, I got to go. You take care of yourself." He pointed at me as he opened the door. "And don't punch out any more clients, you might get stuck taking them to trial." He shut the door behind him, his boots making a tap, tap sound on the marble hallway.

I took the letter opener from Yvette's drawer and unwrapped the box. It really was a shoebox with "Dexter" written on top. But inside, as I had guessed, there were no shoes. Under the white tissue paper were stacks of bills, twenties and tens. I lifted up one stack of twenties, flipped through it. Had to be five hundred dollars there. I counted the stacks. There were at least a dozen stacks of twenties, seven or eight tens. This was my fee. He was paying my fee, just as he had promised. There was only one place he could have gotten so much money. Jesus Christ! I thought, remembering that he had said someone was waiting for him in the car.

I ran through the office to the window overlooking Elm Street. Just as I got there, I saw Raymond opening the passenger door of a maroon Subaru station wagon parked across the street. As the car began moving to my left, the driver turned to check out the traffic. I got a glimpse of his face. Oh, my God! The car eased into the line of traffic. I ran to the corner window for a better view. The dark hair, mustache. I put my hand over my chest, suddenly having difficulty breathing. There was no question about it. The driver was Jack Gibbs.

EPILOGUE

WITH both hands on the handle, I lifted the shovel in the air, leaning with all my weight as I slammed it down. It made a sharp crunch as it sliced through a foot of icy snow. I did the same thing three more times, each cut perpendicular to the last one, forming the shape of a box. Then I slid the flat part of the shovel under the snow. Sweat beaded from my forehead; my arms ached from the effort. Bending my legs to avoid pulling out my back, I lifted up the pile of snow and threw it in a bank I had formed in the gutter.

Usually my landlord took care of shoveling, but last night's storm had taken everyone by surprise, blanketing the state with over a foot of snow. An April snowstorm, even in New Hampshire, was unusual. When a light rain fell early this morning, the snow became icy. Due to the treacherous road conditions, the courts were closed, probably not out of fear of lawyers getting hurt commuting to court. No doubt the powers that be were more concerned with the health and well-being of jurors. Since the landlord's handyman couldn't drive to our building, I decided to take matters in my own hands. In thirty minutes I had managed to clear all of ten feet of our thirty-foot long sidewalk. I had at least an hour of shoveling left.

But I welcomed the exercise. It gave me a chance to work out the stress that had overwhelmed me since Raymond had dropped by with his late Christmas gift. It took me a few weeks to figure things out, but with a little help from Hedges the pieces fit together. Raymond had proven to be much smarter than I ever gave him credit for.

Hedges ran a more thorough background check on Jack Gibbs. For the first ten years of his life, he had lived at 43 Seabrook Way, right next door to my client, Raymond Walker. They must have walked to school together every day, kneeled down together at Sunday Mass. And I never even suspected they knew each other.

The kicker came when we got records for the payphone at the Hillsborough County jail, thanks to Hank Lerner. While in jail, Raymond was entitled to make one phone call per day. The payphone was located along the wall, ten or twelve feet from Hank's desk, far enough away for Raymond to have a private conversation if he kept his voice low. Right after I told Raymond of my visit with Rubenstein, about Rubenstein agreeing to ask around for evidence on McHugh's murder, he made the call to Jack Gibbs. Raymond had set me up.

He must've guessed the police would eventually find the gun and he knew there was no way around the gun. To have any chance at acquittal he had to put the murder weapon in someone else's hands, and the only possibility was Evan. He was smart enough to realize I wouldn't take him seriously if he had been the one to suggest Evan. It had to be a total stranger, someone unconnected to him or the case. He gave me the destination; it was my job to find the route.

But something went awry. After planting the seed at the rugby party, Gibbs got cold feet. He must have realized it was one thing to lie to me, quite another to commit perjury and risk having someone else falsely accused of murder. So he chickened out, took off until Hedges tracked him down. And in court, when he said he wasn't sure he recognized Evan, he was telling the truth. That was why the only facts he would confirm were the ones he had told me in the bar. Raymond must have been shocked, thinking his pal would follow through. Yet even after Gibbs had nearly sealed Raymond's conviction, they obviously remained friends. Gibbs' parents told Hedges that he drove down to Florida with Raymond and Cathy. Sounds romantic. Maybe Jack Gibbs would be the godfather of their child.

Because our Constitution contains a prohibition against double jeopardy, there was nothing I could do to bring Raymond to justice. There was no point in going to the police; they would just shake their heads and laugh at me for being suckered. My theory that Evan had gone fishing only to hide the money and throw away the gun was misguided; it was obviously Raymond, I later realized, who buried the money and tossed the gun in the lake. The hole by the oak tree had been dug by Raymond, retrieving his loot. Raymond'll live the rest of his life knowing he got away with murder. For his sake, I hope I don't bump into him in a dark alley.

Mrs. Luhovey received a hefty settlement from the fire department. The investigators decided it wasn't arson. A homeless man had snuck into the basement where he lit a pile of newspapers in a trash can to keep warm. Somehow he had knocked the trash can over onto some paint cans and the fire spread. Although Evan had mowed the grass that day, he had nothing to do with the fire. No one knew whether McHugh and Evan had seen each other at Cheshire Village, but if they had I was sure they hadn't argued. That much, it seemed, was a figment of Gibbs' and perhaps Raymond's vivid imagination. Larry had not been involved in the fire at all; he was completely exonerated.

I gave the stolen money to St. Andrew College: $11,890. Raymond had kept only a few thousand for himself. I was touched by his generosity. My gift was anonymous but required that the money be used to fund a scholarship for a walk-

on football player from California. It was called the Bruiser
McHugh Scholarship. With the help of free publicity from the
Union Leader, the fund had doubled in a few months.

I called Larry dozens of times since learning the truth. No
one ever answered. Each time I ignored the answering machine, hanging up without leaving a message. Then two
weeks ago I drove by his house. It was a weeknight around
dinner time. I parked at the end of the driveway, cut the lights
but kept the motor on so I could run the heater. The night was
clear and the moon full. It hovered just over Larry's roof. The
lights in their kitchen were on but the curtains were drawn. I
sat there for an hour, watching silhouettes of Larry, Paula and
Evan moving about the kitchen, standing at the sink, washing dishes, sweeping. I debated whether to ring the bell.
What could I say? How do you apologize for betraying a
friendship, accusing your best friend of soliciting arson and
murder, his son of committing them? How do you explain
wiping out a childhood of memories?

My decision was made for me. After an hour had passed,
Paula was standing at the sink when Larry walked up behind
her. He wrapped his arms around her waist, rested his head
on her shoulder. When Evan walked in, Larry stepped back,
put his arm out. Evan came to his parents, and all three
formed a circle, embracing in the middle of their kitchen.

The next day I called again. This time I left a message:
"Larry, I'm truly sorry. I don't expect you to ever forgive you,
but I wanted you to know I really am sorry for what I've
done to you and your family, to our memories of each other."

I lifted the last shovelful of snow and thought of Yvette.
She had been my savior since I had learned the truth, reassuring me when my confidence had reached the lowest point
in my life. How could I have been so stupid? How could I
have betrayed Larry like that? Looking back, I wondered if
I could ever try another case. I doubted myself, the law, the
jury system, everything. The only good to come out of the
case, I concluded, was Yvette.

Yvette and I essentially lived together, alternating from her place to mine, until her uncle called from Quebec City saying her ninety-seven-year-old grandmother was in the hospital. He asked Yvette to fly up and help him care for her. On the drive to Logan Airport, Yvette promised she'd be back in a week. That was three weeks ago. Her grandmother had taken a turn for the worse and had formed a blood clot in her brain. The doctors were waiting to see if it would resolve on its own. If not, she would need surgery and Yvette would have to stay there indefinitely. Last night she invited me to visit her and I agreed to fly up there tomorrow, once flights resumed out of Logan Airport. I just had to be with her, and my practice could survive my absence for another week or so. The longer Yvette was away, the more I realized I loved her more than anything, more than my practice, more even than the law itself.

I returned the shovel to the toolshed and decided to hike through the snow to the Chimes Café. A He-Man's Special was just what I needed to lift my spirits. During Raymond's trial I had been too busy to stop by the Chimes, preferring to spend my mornings preparing witness outlines or getting the day's evidence together. As I trudged through the snow along Elm Street, already tasting Marty's crisp bacon and slightly burnt toast, I was totally unprepared for what I saw.

The Chimes Café had been completely changed. The carved wood sign hanging over the doorway told me the name was the same. But the painted sign on the window had been scraped off. When I looked closer, though, I could make out a faint outline of some letters, a hint of what had been there before. The scattered, disheveled decor had been replaced by ferns, the Naugahyde booths by steel-framed yuppie chairs with wicker seats and glass tables. Where the bar had once been there now was a glass display case and counter. Behind the counter was the menu, dark plastic letters—not even chalkboards—advertising caffe latte, cappuccino, espresso. The only beers were imports. Not a Budweiser in sight.

I pushed my way through the crowd at the counter, all dressed in suits and skirts, and yelled to the college-age girl preparing the drinks. She was thin, in tight designer jeans, her hair neatly tied in a ponytail.

"Where's Marty Loughlin?" I asked.

"Check the back office," she said waving her hand. "He's probably counting the money again."

I made my way to the back and pushed open the office door. Marty sat with his feet on the desk, the newspaper spread out in front of him. He was wearing a tie and a sport jacket that was at least two sizes too small. The sleeves ended inches from his wrists.

"Marty, what the hell's going on here?"

"Well, well, well. Look who's here, stranger. You been away a long time. Things have changed around here."

"You're not kidding. Where's Charlotte? She still working?" I sat on the edge of the desk, looked around at the closet Marty was using for an office.

"No need. I sold this place to a Boston corporation. They have a chain of these places all over New England. The latest thing. I talked them into letting me stay on as a consultant, but they couldn't see fit to keep Charlotte on. She's home watching the soaps, planning next month's trip to the Bahamas."

Marty Loughlin sold out. I never thought I'd see the day. "Glad things worked out for you," I said. "Guess we all have to change with the times."

"Yeah, what the hell, it was time. Me and the wife worked hard all our lives. Nice to relax a little. Hey, why don't you stick around, have some breakfast on the house."

"Only if you can whip up a He-Man's Special."

He shook his head. "Uh, uh. Too bad. Don't even have a stove anymore. Only thing we cook is these little egg things, quiche something or other; we just throw them in the microwave. Or you could have one of those french crescent rolls. Our biggest sellers."

It felt like a punch to the solar plexus. I had to get out of there. "No thanks, Marty, I'll pass. I've got to go. Give my best to Charlotte."

"Will do, and hey, don't be a stranger no more."

On the way out, I noticed only one item left over from the old Chimes. In the corner, near where the wood stove used to be, was one of the paintings that was on the wall when I had met Larry here. It was the one showing the winter scene, ice, snow everywhere but desolate, all the people gone. Its companion painting, the colorful fall scene with all the sportsmen enjoying themselves, was gone. Depressed, I hurried out and dragged my feet through the snow back to my apartment.

MY criminal practice was booming after all the publicity over Raymond's acquittal. Even though I declined all interviews, the *Union Leader* and the *Globe* both wrote features on me, tracing my history and quoting both Sherry and her father. The lunch with Sherry and Rodger had gone better than expected, and I was looking forward to taking on a sexual harassment case. Anything but a murder case, I figured. To my surprise, Sherry and I acted civilly, bickering only when she complained how skinny I was. I couldn't resist chiding her on her complete lack of culinary skills. But there was definitely nothing left between us. At least we had reached the stage where we could be friends, not close friends for sure, but at least acquaintances.

I reflected on all the changes in my life since moving to New Hampshire. I came here to represent the poor, the ignorant, people who normally couldn't get legal help. People like Raymond. But Raymond had used me, taken advantage of my idealism. All I had wanted was justice. I thought I had done the right thing by putting truth before friendship, but it had all gone haywire. To follow my ideals I had paid a terrible price, as Laflamme had warned. I had picked up the tab for Raymond. He was free with no worry of being punished. And I had lost something irreplaceable. Sometimes life is not Dutch treat: not everyone pays his own way.

ACKNOWLEDGMENTS

Writing a novel is a long and solitary endeavor. I was fortunate to meet two talented writers who made the solitude bearable. They were willing to share their time, their skill, and their wisdom. They read every word of *Alibi* and generously offered suggestions that vastly improved the book. To my writers' group members Tom Beaty and Jeff Westmont, I offer my heartfelt thanks. They made me a better writer and *Alibi* a better novel. I have no doubt I will be seeing their own books on bestseller lists in the near future.

Thanks also to Tom for introducing me to his terrific agent, Susan Kelly of the William Pell Agency. Her energy, persistence, and good humor made the submission process almost bearable.

I have been blessed to have Natalee Rosenstein as an editor a second time. She improves everything she touches. I will be forever grateful for her confidence in my writing skills and willingness to take a risk on a first-time novelist.

While writing *Alibi*, I also spent time interviewing other lawyer authors, a project that resulted in an anthology, *Their Word Is Law*. I am grateful to these authors for sharing their insights on the art of writing legal fiction. They were always generous and helpful, particularly Jeremiah Healy, Sheldon Siegel, and the late Barry Reed, who read the manuscript of *Alibi* at various stages. Their kind comments and encouragement inspired me to keep writing.

I couldn't have written *Alibi* without a comfortable writing space. To the friendly staff at Simple Pleasures Café in San Francisco's Richmond District, I offer my gratitude. They provided not only a comfortable writing space but also strong coffee and engaging music that made the many hours at the laptop pleasurable.

Finally, I could never have written a novel while practicing law full-time, and raising four children, if I weren't married to a talented and understanding wife and mother. To Patty I offer my eternal love and gratitude. You're the best! My thanks pale in comparison to your gifts to me: Conor, Brandon, Tess, and Jake, a foursome for the ages.

BIOGRAPHY

A Boston native, Stephen M. Murphy has practiced plaintiffs employment law for over twenty years in San Francisco. In his spare time (Thursday nights between 8 and 11), he writes novels and is finishing another Dutch Francis novel.